Praise f...
"engaging historica...

"Readers will fall in love . . . from ...
—*Publishers Weekly*, starred review, on *The Lost English Girl*

"Enthralling."
—*Woman's World* on *The Lost English Girl*

"Exquisitely researched and beautifully written."
—Madeline Martin, *New York Times* bestselling author of
The Librarian Spy, on *The Last Dance of the Debutante*

"Captivating . . . as immersive as it is enchanting . . . Historical fiction at its
very best."
—Patti Callahan, *New York Times* bestselling author of
Surviving Savannah, on *The Last Garden in England*

"Kelly's novel encompasses everything I love in historical fiction . . . a delight."
—Fiona Davis, *New York Times* bestselling author of
The Magnolia Palace, on *The Last Garden in England*

"A beautiful tale of love, heartbreak, and reinvention . . . Gorgeously written
and rooted in meticulous period detail . . . as vibrant as it is stirring."
—Roxanne Veletzos, bestselling author of *When the Summer Was Ours*,
on *The Last Garden in England*

"A beautifully told story . . . Julia Kelly writes gripping, moving historical
fiction that's not to be missed."
—Kelly Rimmer, *USA Today* bestselling author of
The German Wife, on *The Whispers of War*

"Sweeping, stirring, and heartrending in all the best ways, this tale . . . will
take your breath away."
—Kristin Harmel, *New York Times* bestselling author of
The Forest of Vanishing Stars, on *The Light Over London*

ALSO BY JULIA KELLY

The Light Over London

The Whispers of War

The Last Garden in England

The Last Dance of the Debutante

The Lost English Girl

The Dressmakers of London

Julia Kelly

GALLERY BOOKS

New York Amsterdam/Antwerp London Toronto Sydney New Delhi

G

Gallery Books
An Imprint of Simon & Schuster, LLC
1230 Avenue of the Americas
New York, NY 10020

First Gallery Books trade paperback edition February 2025

GALLERY BOOKS and colophon are registered trademarks of Simon & Schuster, LLC

For information about special discounts for bulk purchases, please contact Simon & Schuster Special Sales at 1-866-506-1949 or business@simonandschuster.com.

The Simon & Schuster Speakers Bureau can bring authors to your live event. For more information or to book an event, contact the Simon & Schuster Speakers Bureau at 1-866-248-3049 or visit our website at www.simonspeakers.com.

Interior design by Erika R. Genova

Manufactured in the United States of America

1 3 5 7 9 10 8 6 4 2

Library of Congress Control Number: 2024942676

ISBN 978-1-6680-3272-5
ISBN 978-1-6680-3274-9 (ebook)

For my wonderful sister, Justine

Part I

Chapter One

At the age of twenty-eight, Izzie Shelton should have been able to twist her damp hair into pin curls in the dark while hanging upside down and singing "God Save the King." However, she and her hair had never seen eye to eye. For years, she'd hardly cared to battle it morning and night and simply wore it pulled back into a low ponytail tied off with whatever scrap of fabric or ribbon happened to be lying around. However, six months ago, she'd resolved to make more of an effort with her appearance. This change had prompted Miss Reid, her mother's longest-serving employee, to raise her eyebrows and make a pointed comment about silly women primping for all the soldiers, sailors, and pilots passing through London. If the truth had been something as simple as seeking male attention, Izzie might have blushed and packed up her pins, resolving not to bother. However, there was far more at stake than that, and so the pins remained in a little dish on the tiny wooden vanity in the corner of her bedroom, taunting her.

That morning, her pin curls had actually come out, but it was the imitation tortoiseshell combs that were giving her all manner of problems. She ripped out the one that was already beginning to slip from her left temple and jammed it back into place, the plastic scraping against her scalp. She winced but soldiered on, twisting her chin from side to side to check that her left and right combs matched. Deciding that they were approximately in the same place and likely to stay for at least as long as it would take for her to ensure the shop was ready to open, she rose from her vanity and glanced at her watch. It was already half past eight.

She was late.

She pulled on a chocolate-brown cardigan and straightened the edges so they lay neatly underneath her white cotton shirt. Then she crossed her bedroom, opened the door, and paused to listen for sounds from the flat's kitchen. Nothing.

She frowned as she peered down the short corridor to Mum's room. The door was closed, and there was no light visible underneath. There had been a time when, if she couldn't hear the tea-kettle whistling or Mum humming while generously buttering thick slices of toast, Izzie would have guessed that her mother had gone down to the shop floor early. However, these days, butter and tea were on the ration and Maggie Shelton was not her old self.

Izzie did up the mother-of-pearl buttons on her cardigan as she walked toward the kitchen. Sure enough, it was empty and neat, as it had been when she'd done the washing up the previous night.

Mum wasn't awake.

Izzie filled the heavy kettle and put it on the hob to heat. Then she carefully measured out one mug's worth of tea leaves into the blue-and-white-striped teapot with the chipped spout. There had been a time where the idea of brewing anything other than a full pot of tea would have been unthinkable in the Shelton household, but that had been before the war. Now, waste was akin to a sin, so if Izzie was only making for herself, she would use just enough precious tea leaves for a brew, leaving the dregs for Mum to pour fresh hot water over if she wanted a cup when she rose.

After waiting for the tea to steep, Izzie poured out her cup and grimaced as she added a bit of powdered milk. Then she made her way out of the flat she'd called home since she was seven years old, clattered down the stairs, and opened the bottom door that separated the flat from the shop downstairs. She took a right down the narrow corridor that ran the length of the shop, and emerged into the world of Mrs. Shelton's Fashions.

To some, the reception of the dressmaker's shop might have seemed rather unremarkable. It was a wide, open room with a big window looking out onto Glengall Road. For as long as Izzie could remember, a dress form had displayed whatever Maggie Shelton thought would entice passing women, and on that morning it was a blind-hemmed coat in black wool with a low closure near the left hip. The workmanship was undeniably fine, but the moment Mum had put it on the dress form, Izzie had known it was wrong.

"What do you think?" Mum had asked, standing back to admire the coat.

"It's beautiful, Mum," she'd started cautiously, "but I worry it's a little old-fashioned."

"What do you mean?" Mum asked sharply.

"Oh, nothing really."

"No, let's hear it. You said it, so you obviously believe it."

Izzie's heart pounded as she struggled for the most diplomatic way to tell her mother the truth, because these were the decisions she wanted to be entrusted to make. To prove herself.

"I think it's the cut," she finally said, deciding that the unvarnished honesty was the best policy if she really wanted her mother to take her seriously as the shop's future proprietress. "It's a bit boxy for the modern silhouette, and *Vogue* hasn't featured dropped waistlines for some time."

Mum's lips twisted. "It is a good coat for a woman who wants to invest in clothes that will last. The women who shop here want quality, not fashion, and they will see quality the moment they lay eyes on this coat."

"I just think we might try something a little different," said Izzie, reaching under the shop counter for one of her sketchbooks that were never far from hand. She flicked through the pages to a coat she'd sketched just the week before. "Something like this."

She watched her mother scrutinize the design, taking in the princess seams that would fit snugly to a woman's body before giving way to a slightly flared skirt. There were no embellishments, just clean lines making for an undeniably chic look. For a moment, hope flickered in her that *this* would be the garment Mum would finally agree to let her add to the shop's offerings, but then Mum shook her head.

"It's not right for Mrs. Shelton's Fashions, Izzie," said Mum.

And, just like that, Izzie's heart plummeted back down to earth.

Now, as Izzie walked around, sipping her tea, she tried not to resent the coat Mum had chosen over hers. Instead, she checked for smudges on the window and door. She tidied up a few papers on the shop counter, which discreetly hid the till, and then brushed the nap on the pair of velvet chairs where customers sat to view Mum's drawings, discuss color and fabric, or wait for their fittings.

Satisfied that the shop floor would stand up to even her mother's discerning eye, Izzie let herself through the white-painted door on the back wall that led to the fitting room. Three of herself reflected back at her from the room's huge triptych mirror. In the center of the room was a circular platform with tufted velvet sides that customers stood on while Izzie and Mum performed the real magic of a dressmaker: the fitting.

Growing up, Izzie had loved watching Mum tuck, pin, and transform a garment until it fit each customer's unique shape. After having caught her peering through the door one too many times, Mum had told Izzie that she could join her so long as she was helpful. That meant fetching fabric samples and bits of trim, pouring cups of tea, or retrieving pins and bits of chalk as Mum kept up a steady stream of questions and conversation with a client. Finally, Mum would step back and declare the fit was "perfection," and Izzie would watch the woman on the platform turn to the mirror, her expression melting into one of satisfied pleasure at the sight of her beautiful garment.

When she'd left school at fourteen, she'd become Mum's assistant. Her older sister, Sylvia, should have had that role, but Sylvia had no real talent for sewing and was relegated to doing the bookkeeping, deliveries, and odd jobs.

Izzie had secretly relished the responsibility of her new position and her mother's attention that went along with it. It had started with jotting down customer measurements and then taking the measurements herself, handing her mother pins and then pinning hems, cuffs, and shoulders on her own. Then, once a customer left, Mum would teach her how to translate those measurements to a pattern that would achieve a perfect fit. Mum then helped Izzie learn the various techniques to create those garments, demanding she redo any work that was not satisfactory before she moved on to anything new until, when Izzie turned eighteen, Mum decided she was skilled enough to call herself a seamstress in her own right.

For years, Mum treated her just like Miss Reid or any of the other seamstresses employed in the workroom. However, gradually over the past two years, Izzie had begun to take over the running of other aspects of the shop. Mum spent more and more of her time holed up in her office, poring over paperwork as the war furrowed everyone's brows a little deeper, and Izzie began to conduct fittings alone, only bothering her mother when issues arose. Then Izzie found herself sitting across from customers on the shop floor, Mum's heavy sketchbooks full of the garments the shop offered on her lap as they flipped through to try to find something that would suit each woman's needs. Once they chose a design, fabric, and color and Izzie had taken measurements, she would fetch her mother for a final look.

It had all been thrilling, this new responsibility, but as the months had stretched on, Izzie had found herself wanting more.

Standing in the fitting room that morning, her fingers itched for her pencil and her sketchbook, but she knew that if Mum came downstairs and found her drawing rather than opening the shop, she'd be swiftly told off for wasting time. No. She would sketch later when Mum was safely behind her closed office door and Miss Reid's Singer was whirring away.

A knock at the shop door pulled Izzie out of her thoughts. She looked up and drew in a bracing breath at the sight of Miss Reid frowning on the other side of the rain-spattered glass.

Izzie unlocked the door and stepped back to let the seamstress in. "Good morning, Miss Reid."

"I don't see what's so good about it. It's been pouring since I left Paddington," Miss Reid said as she shucked off her soaking mac, spraying the shop's wooden floor with rain. "It will be a wonder if anyone comes in today."

Izzie stifled a sigh at the likely truth of that as she followed the older woman through to the passageway.

"Where is Mrs. Shelton?" Miss Reid asked over her shoulder as she passed into the workroom.

"I haven't seen her yet this morning."

She suspected that Miss Reid, who had an opinion about everything related to Mrs. Shelton's Fashions—and the world, really—would certainly have an opinion about *that*, but the older woman simply sniffed.

Irascible as she could be, Miss Reid was a fixture of Mrs. Shelton's, having the distinction of having been Maggie Shelton's first employee. Now, almost twenty years later, the seamstress was still firmly ensconced at the sewing machine closest to the back wall of the workroom. Even after the Allies' retreat from Dunkirk last spring when Miss Bell and Miss Parker had both left to be WAAFs in the Royal Air Force's women's auxiliary branch, Miss Reid had continued to sew on. Izzie begrudgingly couldn't imagine what they would do without her.

"Who is coming in today?" asked Miss Reid as she hung up her coat on a peg stuck in the wall by her machine.

"I'll have to check the book," Izzie said.

In the old days, Mum's appointment book lived in the tiny office off the workroom. Only Mum touched it, because, along with the order book, it was vital to the shop's running—a bible of sorts. However, as a concession to the fact that Izzie was opening the shop more often these days, Mum had begun to leave the book out on the edge of the huge wood-topped cutting table that sat at a perpendicular angle to the four sewing machines that dominated the room.

Izzie opened the clothbound book, flipped to a page marked with a ribbon, and sighed.

"Is it that bad?" asked Miss Reid as she took a seat at her machine.

"Mrs. Wilson is due in first thing, and then Mrs. Cowles has her second fitting at two o'clock."

"And after that?" asked Miss Reid.

"Nothing except for a delivery."

"Really?" asked Miss Reid, incredulous. "That's all?"

She nodded.

Miss Reid sniffed. "I'd wager a guinea that Mrs. Cowles will leave without settling her account. I thought your mother was going to have to call the bailiff on her last time. An entire summer wardrobe cut, sewn, and finished, and six weeks later Mrs. Shelton still hadn't seen a single shilling of it. And where is Mrs. Cowles going to wear it anyway? There's a war on," tutted Miss Reid.

"Mrs. Cowles did pay in the end," Izzie said, remembering the number of thin excuses that the woman had fed Mum until finally she'd shown up to settle her account in August. "And she's already given over her clothing coupons this time."

"That's because the government says she has to. Your mother is too soft on that woman," said Miss Reid.

"Mum believes that everyone deserves a little bit of understanding from time to time," she said.

"That's all well and good, but it isn't as though Mrs. Shelton's suppliers let her have any cloth on credit," said Miss Reid.

"Miss Reid!" Izzie cut across the other woman's complaining. "Shouldn't you be starting your day?"

"There's no need to hurry me, young lady," Miss Reid huffed. But still, the seamstress busied herself peeling the cover off her machine, giving Izzie a blessed moment of peace.

Chapter Two

If this meeting went any longer, there was a distinct possibility that Sylvia Pearsall would scream.

She shut her eyes, praying to be delivered from the ten-minute discussion currently raging about whether the tablecloths at the next War Widows' Fund tea should be white or ivory. Surely what mattered was that the charity raised as much money as possible to supplement fallen soldiers' pensions and help their grieving families.

She opened her eyes again, willing herself to focus. She'd almost skipped this committee meeting, but charity work was the anchor upon which her entire social calendar was built, and she couldn't let go of it. Not when she felt so very adrift.

"Thank you for that fascinating insight into linens, Mrs. Harwell," said Lady Nolan, their chairwoman, finally cutting the speaker off with her usual air of authority. "I'm sorry to say that we have gone past our time."

All around Sylvia, ladies with perfectly coiffed hair and patriotic red lips nodded.

"We shall pick up the matter of the tablecloths at our meeting in two weeks' time. Until then, ladies," Lady Nolan dismissed them.

Dread soured Sylvia's stomach. Much as she'd wanted the meeting to end, now that it was over, she would have to go home. Home to an empty flat and *them*.

Slowly she closed her notebook and capped her Parker pen,

slipping them both into her crocodile handbag. Then she pushed her chair back from the table and rose to her full height, enhanced by leather heels, avoiding everyone's eyes.

If only she could slip out and—

"Shall we walk out together?"

Sylvia managed to arrange her features into a soft smile before turning to Claire.

Married to Sylvia's husband Hugo's school friend Rupert Monroe, Claire had been the first of Hugo's set to welcome Sylvia into their circle. Claire too had been the first to share a knowing look with her when the gentlemen said something a little risqué at supper, the first to compliment one of her gowns at a ball, and the first to congratulate her on her engagement. It had been natural, then, that when Hugo's mother had urged her to consider asking Claire to be a bridesmaid, Sylvia had said yes without hesitation, asking Claire before anyone else.

It was because of this shared history that Sylvia heard herself say, "I'd like that very much."

As soon as they had collected their coats, Claire leaned in and asked in a low voice, "Did you see Lady Winman's hat? It was positively bizarre."

"It was rather avant garde for a charity committee meeting on a Wednesday afternoon," Sylvia admitted, thinking back to the geometric configuration that had bobbed on the head of the slightly aloof Lady Winman, the newest member of the committee.

"It was positively bizarre, that's what it was. Someone really should take her aside and remind her that we're at war." Claire sniffed. "I'm shocked the dowager hasn't done it herself, but—even now—they don't like one another."

"At least the hat was black," Sylvia said because she simply didn't have it in her to rise to the bait of asking why the Dowager Countess of Winman and the current Lady Winman did not see eye to eye.

Claire nodded to the housekeeper holding open the front door of Lady Nolan's Mayfair home and, as soon as they were out of earshot, said, "It wouldn't have mattered if it was bright red and covered in spots. It looked as though she had a deranged stork perched on her head. I suppose that's what happens when you marry up."

Sylvia felt heat creep up the back of her neck, even as she silently scolded herself. Claire was her friend and would never say those sorts of things about her. Besides, as far as anyone knew, Sylvia's father had been a barrister, making the Sheltons unremarkably middle class. It was a truth, just not the entire truth.

"Are you walking home?" asked Sylvia as they reached the corner of South Audley and Tilley Streets.

"Yes. It's doing simply awful things to my shoes, and it's so difficult to find a decent cobbler these days. Every time my maid thinks she's discovered a new one, he's called up to serve. It's incredibly inconvenient," said Claire.

"Then I'll have to leave you here, I'm afraid."

"I'll see you in a fortnight, unless some thrilling invitation comes along sooner. Ta-ta, darling!" Claire trilled with a wave.

Sylvia returned the gesture and then doubled back on herself past Lady Nolan's house and north on South Audley Street.

There had been a time when she would have balked at the idea of walking the nearly twenty-five minutes from Lady Nolan's home to her flat in Marylebone. If she hadn't been able to borrow Hugo's driver, Phillip, for the day, she would have taken a cab. However, Phillip had been called up along with seemingly every cabdriver in London. Women were climbing behind the wheel now, but with the petrol ration firmly in place it hardly made sense to take the short, thoughtless jaunts she used to indulge in. After all, they were all meant to be doing their part for the war effort.

Her feet were beginning to ache when she finally turned onto Beaumont Street. The quiet grandeur of Nottingham Court rose above her, and if it hadn't been for the silent silhouette of a barrage balloon floating in the distance she might have been able to forget about the war for a moment.

Ever since she first walked inside on her wedding night, she'd loved the comfort of returning to the block of mansion flats where she and Hugo lived. She knew exactly how heavy the entryway door was and how the lift gave a little shudder when it reached the third floor, where she would alight and take the short walk down the corridor to her front door.

However, as she performed the familiar ritual that day, she couldn't fight the wave of exhaustion that overwhelmed her. She let herself in, the warm scent of beeswax and lemon furniture polish wrapping around her. The soft step of Mrs. Atkinson announced the cook-general's arrival before Sylvia spotted the hem of the woman's black dress.

"Mrs. Atkinson, hello."

"Good afternoon, Mrs. Pearsall. May I take your coat?" asked Mrs. Atkinson.

"Thank you."

Sylvia slipped off her mink and then set about unpinning her hat. She checked her appearance in the entryway mirror, touching first her dark fringe and then the neat roll of hair at the base of her neck to ensure they were still in place. There was no one there to see her save for Mrs. Atkinson, but she'd learned long ago how much appearance mattered.

She remembered the day, age sixteen, when she caught her mother studying her from head to toe. When she'd tilted her head in question, her mother had said, "You're not clever or talented, Sylvia, so it's a good thing you're beautiful."

She could still recall the way her breath had escaped her lips, almost as though her mother had slapped her, but rather than making her shrink from the mirror, Sylvia had clung to her looks as her one asset. From that day on, Sylvia studied every woman's magazine she could lay her hands on. She knew her hair, thick and a deep chocolate brown, was good, so she took to styling it in long waves swept off her face to highlight her clear complexion. She saved her shillings and purchased powder, rouge, mascara, and lipstick, darkening her lashes and painting her lips a deep red that stood out against her pale skin. She chose her clothes with care, making sure to show off her neat waist and long legs.

Her mother had tsked, calling her vain whenever she caught Sylvia checking her appearance in the dress shop's triptych mirror, but it was her looks that had captured the attention of Hugo Pearsall. When he'd proposed a few months later, she'd believed she had every tool she needed to hone herself into the sort of wife a genteel Harley Street doctor might expect.

So how had she lost him?

"Mrs. Atkinson, I shall take tea in the drawing room please," she said.

The housekeeper nodded and made her quiet retreat to the kitchen. Sylvia waited until she heard the soft sounds of water running to fill the kettle. Mrs. Atkinson would be busy for a least a quarter of an hour.

With a strange mixture of dread and anticipation, she made straight for Hugo's study.

The polished door handle twisted without a sound, and she let herself in. Closing the door behind her, she turned to survey her husband's domain. Everything about the room was masculine, from the heavy club chairs to the paintings of hunting dogs hung on the walls that she was secretly glad were confined to his study. Even the air smelled faintly of man, the remnants of cigar smoke, ink, and coal lingering long after Hugo's last visit home.

Sylvia forced one foot in front of the other until she had rounded the huge desk that had once sat in the study of Hugo's grandfather's country home. Her husband had insisted that it come with them to their flat, even though the men who moved their furniture in had looked at it with great skepticism and more than a little dread. In the end, it hadn't been able to make the turn through the front door and had had to be hauled in through the study window by pulley, creating a great spectacle as the neighbors gathered to watch it rise from Nottingham Court's sweeping drive.

Sylvia's hand shook slightly as she reached for the desk's right-hand drawer. It opened without protest, revealing the contents nestled in red flocked lining. Two bottles of ink, a spare pen, some blotting paper, a letter opener, and a stack of letters.

She counted out one, two, three, four, five of them until she reached the sixth. She set the first five leaning against the blotting paper in the drawer and drew out the sixth letter, opened the envelope, and freed the paper inside.

She unfolded the letter. It was typed—clearly the sender was concerned that a casual observer might recognize their penmanship—and the paper crinkled as she handled it.

My darling Hugo,

Whenever I write you one of these letters it reminds me how little we are together. I want more of your time, your body, everything. Instead, I must content myself with writing to you in hopes that this letter might stir up in you even a fraction of the feeling that I hold for you.

I love you, my darling. I know you will think me rather vulgar for confessing that only in a letter, but I cannot pretend any longer. I cannot sign off with "All my love" and not let you know that that love is not a mere platitude. It is as real as the air we both breathe.

I know you say that we must wait until after this bloody war has ended, but I do not <u>want</u> to wait. Each time my husband comes home on leave, I find it harder to hide my revulsion. I do not know if I could stand the inevitable day when we all cross paths—you with Sylvia and me with him. It is difficult enough knowing that whenever we are in public I cannot even look at you for fear that someone might suspect.

Write to me soon and let me know when it is that I can see you again. You have me forever . . .

All my love,

X

Sylvia set down the letter and closed her eyes, letting the pain wash over her.

Once, when she'd been a new bride, she'd been caught in the rain going from one shop to another in Knightsbridge and ducked into a restaurant to shelter. She'd been speaking to the maître d' when she'd spotted Gerald, a friend of Hugo and hers, tucked into a cozy table in the far corner of the restaurant. The woman he was sitting with and whose hand he was holding was not his wife but rather Margot Weaving, who was married to one of Hugo's fellow club members.

Shocked, Sylvia had backed out of the restaurant and into the rain, walking as fast as decorum would allow her until she reached the welcoming doors of Harrods. Only then, while gasping for her breath, had she allowed herself to think about what she'd just seen. An affair being conducted in public.

When Hugo had returned from his surgery that evening, she'd barely been able to contain herself. It had all come out in a rush, but when she finished her story she realized that her husband didn't look horrified at all. He appeared to be amused.

"Well, what did you expect, darling?" he asked.

"What do you mean what did I expect? Gerald's married to Caroline. We had them for cocktails before the theater in March!"

"Yes," he said slowly, as though explaining to a child, "but he and Caroline already have two boys and that girl of theirs."

She blinked, stunned. "So because they already have children, it's acceptable for him to have an *affair*?"

She whispered the last word, eliciting a laugh from her husband.

"Well, I wouldn't say that Gerald should go walking around announcing it to every Peter and Paul, but I'm hardly surprised. She spends all her time in the country, and he practically lives at his club, not to mention that he's always looking for an excuse to race that new Aston Martin of his. They must hardly see one another.

"I will say, it's poor form of him to go about it in public like that. It's almost as though he wants to be caught. Of course, if Caroline has been having her own fun on the side, that is another matter. I shouldn't be surprised if the daughter's not Gerald's at all, although we'll likely never know. Caroline's intelligent enough not to conduct her affairs in public." He paused. "Are you all right, darling? You look pale. I haven't shocked you, have I?"

He laughed again, which made her feel silly, so she shook her head.

"No, no. I was simply surprised to see them, that's all," she said.

Hugo's eyes softened and he grabbed her hand. "These things happen, darling. As you see a little more of the world, you'll become used to it soon enough."

"But you wouldn't, would you, darling? I don't think I could bear it."

He gathered her close to him. "Silly duck, of course I wouldn't, because no one could be quite like you. You're so refreshing. It's good for me."

Now, sitting at her husband's desk reading the evidence of his infidelity, she felt like a fool for how smug his reassurances had made her. How blind.

She'd discovered the letters when she'd been trying to find, of all things, a stamp. She'd finished her weekly letter to Hugo and discovered that she'd run out of postage in her writing desk. Without thinking, she'd gone into his study, opened the desk drawer, and seen the letters sitting there plain as day. She'd peeked at one out of curiosity and realized immediately what they were. A compulsion had come over her, driving her to read more and more intimate details of her husband's relationship with another woman. When she'd finished the final letter, she'd stared into space. She hadn't cried. She hadn't raged. She'd sat with a sickness in her stomach and wondered.

Now she was forcing herself to go back every day and read one letter at a time, hunting for answers.

Who was this other woman?

When had it started?

Was it still going on?

How had she lost him?

After fourteen years of marriage, that was the question that frightened her the most.

With a sniff, she carefully replaced the letter in its envelope and slid it into its place in the drawer. Then she stood, smoothed down her skirt, and let herself out of Hugo's study.

By the time Mrs. Atkinson appeared with the tea tray, Sylvia had wiped any trace of distress from her perfectly powdered face.

Chapter Three

Tuesdays were always a nightmare, but this one really was the limit.

The telephone had rung at half past eight in the morning, and Izzie had only just managed to race down the stairs half-dressed in time to catch it. A chipper man on the other end had told her that not only would the cloth Mum had ordered the previous week be delayed that morning because of an issue with the lorry delivering it, it would be short ten yards of tweed and five of cotton lawn.

"I do have orders I'm meant to be fulfilling," she'd snapped down the telephone in an uncharacteristic show of spirit.

"Don't we all, miss?" asked the man with a laugh.

"Well, when can I expect the driver this morning?" she asked, fumbling with the buttons on her brown cardigan.

"He'll show up when he shows up, won't he?" the man replied.

The whole thing had thrown her morning off because instead of heading back upstairs to pull on her shoes and finish pinning up her hair, she'd gone straight to the appointment book and tried to figure out what fittings they might need to move around due to the missing materials.

Through all of it, she couldn't help but feel the situation spiraling out of control. *This* was a far cry from what she wanted to be doing—sketching designs and making beautiful clothes for women who could appreciate a touch of modernity in their wardrobes—but, as Mum liked to remind her, it was a part of running a dress shop so Izzie bit her lip, put her head down, and carried on because to show reluctance or resentment might undo all of her good work to prove to Mum that she was capable of managing Mrs. Shelton's Fashions.

When she'd finally wrestled her morning under control again, the fabric delivery showed up just before the ten o'clock opening—a blessing—but it was all wrong—a curse. There was no tweed at all, but boiled wool and all in the wrong colors. Instead of cotton lawn, there was yards of the kind of heavy canvas commonly used for kit bags. It had taken the driver half an hour and two calls to his depot on the shop's telephone to work out that they'd assigned the wrong order to their address. When finally he realized that Mrs. Shelton's order was mislabeled in the very back of the lorry, it was nearly eleven and Izzie was already exhausted.

She was just thinking how very much she would like to lie down and have a nap when a tap came on her shoulder. She turned to see Miss Reid, concern clear on her face.

"Have you seen your mother this morning?" Miss Reid asked.

Izzie looked around as though Mum would somehow materialize in front of them. "Not yet." She paused. "That's unlike her."

"Why don't you look in on her?" asked Miss Reid in an unusual display of consideration.

"That's very kind of you, thank you," said Izzie gratefully.

She left the delivery driver with Miss Reid, said a silent prayer that the man would survive his encounter with the scowling seamstress, and mounted the stairs to the flat.

As soon as she was through the front door, she paused to listen for the sounds of Mum moving around.

All was silent.

She really did have to speak to Mum about this. This was the fourth time in two weeks that Izzie had had to wake her mother to start the working day. If Mum really was so run down, perhaps it was time to ask Dr. Morton to call in on them. Maybe he could suggest something that would help bring Mum's energy back again. Not that she looked forward to revisiting the old argument with Mum about whether it was worth paying the doctor's fee for a house call only to be told that Mum needed rest and good meat for dinner at least once a week.

Izzie knocked on her mother's door and waited for a response. She knocked again. Still nothing.

"Mum?" she called out. "It's past opening time. It's time to start the day."

When there still was no response, she tried again. "I could use some help taming Miss Reid. She's in a mood this morning."

Still nothing.

Izzie twisted the knob and pushed open the bedroom door.

It was still and cool in the room, with the only light coming from the open door and a tiny crack in the blackout curtains that Mum drew every night. She could see dust particles dancing in the sunlight that lanced across the room and fell across Mum's chest.

"Mummy?" A tiny flame of dread flickered to life in her stomach. "Mummy, it's time to wake up."

Forcing herself to creep into the room, she reached the side of her mother's bed. Mum looked peaceful—young, even, without the lines of stress that too often etched her brow.

Slowly, she extended a hand until her fingers grazed the shoulder of Mum's white flannel nightdress. Her mother didn't move.

Izzie backed away a step, her eyes fixed on her mother's face. She could see now the faint blue tinge of her mother's lips, the waxy quality of her skin.

Dumbly, she backed out of the room and retreated down the

stairs to the shop. A part of her mind registered the sound of the deliveryman moving about in the inventory closet and Miss Reid berating him for bumping into the wall, but it felt as though someone had thrown a length of gossamer chiffon over everything, dulling it. She reached for the telephone and asked to be connected to Dr. Morton's surgery.

When he finally picked up the telephone, she said, "Dr. Morton, this is Isabelle Shelton."

"Miss Shelton, what can I do for you today?" asked the avuncular man.

"It's my mother."

"I'm very sorry to hear that. Is she ill? Several of my patients have this flu that is going around," he said.

"She's dead, Dr. Morton," she said numbly.

There was a moment's silence on the line, and then the man cleared his throat. "I'm so very sorry, Miss Shelton. I'll be there at once."

It wasn't until the tinny sound of the operator coming back and asking if she still wanted to keep the line open that Izzie remembered to hang up the telephone.

———

"Good evening, Mrs. Atkinson," said Sylvia as she closed the flat door behind her.

"Good evening, madam. May I take those books for you?" asked the housekeeper.

Sylvia handed the two books to Mrs. Atkinson to allow herself the chance to unbutton her coat.

She'd spent the afternoon at the London Library, happy in one of the Reading Room's deep armchairs. Hugo used to tease her that, despite the furs and jewels he'd given her, it was the subscription to the members' library that she treasured the most, and he wasn't wrong. She read voraciously—a habit she'd acquired after coming across an article in a magazine that said a woman could never be truly accomplished unless she was also well-read—and she loved nothing more than to wander the stacks, never knowing who she might run into. Once before the war she'd been carrying *A Handful of Dust* and had walked straight into the book's author, Evelyn Waugh, as he browsed the books on religion. It had been a thrilling brush with literary notoriety, although when she'd told Hugo about it he'd laughed and told her she was adorable for caring, because everyone knew that Waugh was a sharp-tongued snob.

"Are there any messages?" she asked Mrs. Atkinson, trading her books for her coat.

"No, but the afternoon post came," said the housekeeper. "I thought you might like to read it in the sitting room."

"Thank you," she said, mortified at how grateful she was because answering letters would give her something to do once Mrs. Atkinson left for the evening other than wander around the empty flat like the married alter ego of Miss Havisham, despairing of her husband's affair.

"Supper will be ready in an hour. Would you care for a cocktail before?" asked Mrs. Atkinson.

"A gimlet, please."

In the sitting room, she set the books down on the walnut coffee table and picked up the stack of post that Mrs. Atkinson had gathered on the ridiculous silver tray Hugo insisted they use. There were several invitations to tea—two personal and one to raise funds for evacuated orphans—as well as a letter from her friend Helen, who had decamped to America with her Bostonian husband when the war started. She immediately recognized a thick buff-colored envelope addressed to her as being from Hugo's mother, no doubt wondering if Sylvia had any news of her son.

When she saw the last envelope at the bottom of the pile, her hand froze. It had been years since she'd seen it, but she would know Izzie's handwriting anywhere.

Keeping her eyes fixed on the address, she set down the rest of the post on the sofa next to her and then reached for her gold letter opener. Her heart pounded as she slid the sharp point underneath the envelope's flap and, in one precise move, slit open the top.

18 November 1941

Dear Sylvia,

Mum died suddenly early this morning. Dr. Morton says that it was likely a heart condition, and there was nothing that could have been done.

She will be buried on Friday, 21 November.

Sincerely,
Isabelle Shelton

"Oh, poor Izzie," Sylvia murmured. "Poor, poor Izzie."

She rose and went to the cream-and-gold telephone sitting on top of a small round table in the corner of the drawing room. She lifted the receiver and gave the operator the exchange for the shop.

She could practically feel the obligation oozing off of the page of Izzie's note, almost as though her sister hadn't wanted to tell her but some wisp of familial feeling had forced her to sit down and write. It was the same instinct that sent Sylvia's heart skipping with hope and dread in equal measure as the telephone rang.

Finally, the line connected and she heard her sister say, "Mrs. Shelton's Fashions. This is Miss Shelton speaking."

Izzie sounded wrung out.

"Izzie, it's Sylvia."

"Sylvia." Izzie's voice was flat.

"What happened?"

"It's all there."

"Were you . . . were you the one to find her?" she asked.

There was a sharp breath on the other end. "Yes."

"Oh, Izzie. I'm so sorry."

"She had been rising later and later. I thought it was just because she was exhausted—she was always staying up late to finish orders because it was only Miss Reid and myself helping her and, well, you know how particular she could be about finishing. When she didn't come down yesterday morning, I went to wake her, and"—Izzie's voice cracked—"she was gone."

"Izzie, I'm so sorry," she whispered.

"She had been so pale recently, but we all are with the weather being what it is. But then she was out of breath sometimes too. I just—"

"Didn't Dr. Morton say that nothing could have been done?" she asked.

"But I lived with her. I worked with her. We were around each other practically every second of the day. I *knew* something wasn't right. I wanted her to see the doctor, but she wouldn't hear of it," Izzie said, her voice rising.

"Our mother could have a stubborn streak," she said gently.

"I should have insisted," Izzie continued, as though she hadn't heard Sylvia. "If I had, maybe she would still be alive."

"You can't blame yourself," said Sylvia.

"What would you know about it?" Izzie snapped. "You haven't seen Mum in years."

Sylvia pursed her lips tightly, fighting the instinct to hurl back a barb. Her sister didn't need that right now, and heaven knew it wouldn't help matters.

"Why did you write to me rather than telephone?" she asked. "I would have come straightaway."

"I thought it was best," said Izzie. "Besides, I wasn't certain of your exchange."

"It's the same as it has been since Hugo and I were married," she said.

"I'd forgotten." A lie, she was certain of it, but now was not the time to press her sister.

"Well, I telephoned you because I would like the details of the funeral arrangements," she said, taking up the silver pencil that lay next to the book she used for messages.

"Why?" Izzie asked.

"Because, Isabelle"—her voice hardened—"although you might find it hard to believe, I would like to attend my mother's funeral."

There was a long pause on the line before finally Izzie said, "You made your choice, Sylvia. You aren't regretting it now, are you?"

She closed her eyes. No, she didn't regret her choice. It was just that . . . if she didn't attend her mother's funeral, she was certain she would one day come to hate herself for it.

"The details, please," she said.

She could hear the reluctance in Izzie's voice as she related the funeral arrangements. There would be a service at St. Anne's, their old parish church, on Friday morning. The burial would take place just across Salisbury Road in the Paddington Old Cemetery.

"Thank you," she said when her sister finished.

"You don't have to do this, you know," said Izzie.

"What do you mean?"

"You hadn't even seen her in—what has it been?—three years?"

It was more likely four. In a moment of guilt, Sylvia had decided her annual Christmas card was not enough. Knowing that, in a rare turn of events, she and Hugo would not be spending the Christmas season in Tunbridge Wells at his parents' home, she'd taken it upon herself to suggest her mother and Izzie come for Boxing Day lunch. She'd written the invitation and posted it before she could second-guess her actions, risking Hugo's annoyance when she told him that, much to her surprise, her mother had accepted, making it clear her mother would be coming alone.

The day had been a disaster from the start. Her mother had sat on the very edge of the drawing room sofa, handbag held on her lap like a shield. Sylvia's hopes for a pleasant afternoon dipped ever further as she watched her mother peer about at the flat with a mixture of judgment and resentment. At the lunch she'd taken pains to cook herself, no one spoke. When at last Sylvia had risen to clear the dishes of the final course away, Hugo had retreated to his study, leaving her mother alone. It had fallen to Sylvia to see her mother into a cab, and she'd breathed a sigh of relief as it drove away. That day, she'd resolved never to expose either of them to the discomfort of another holiday spent together again.

Now she stared at the details of the funeral arrangements, wondering what wretched daughter would ever think that about her own mother.

"I will be at the service and the burial," she said, drawing back her shoulders.

"Not Hugo?" asked her sister, the sarcasm coming clearly across the crackling line.

"He's a surgeon lieutenant-commander in the Royal Navy Medical Service," she said shortly. "He has been serving on ships since leaving basic training, Izzie, so he is indisposed."

Her sister sniffed, but apparently even Izzie couldn't find fault with Hugo's service. "Fine."

The line went dead, Izzie's unvarnished disapproval reverberating through Sylvia's chest.

Chapter Four

On Friday morning, Izzie clutched at the lapels of her coat as she walked into St. Anne's with Miss Reid by her side. She would never admit it to anyone, but she'd been terrified waking up and knowing that in a few short hours she would need to put on a black dress, coat, gloves, and hat and say goodbye to Mum.

She'd dressed deliberately, making sure every seam was straight and every hair in place. However, she'd been unable to force herself to put on her hat, the last thing she needed to do before leaving, until the flat's doorbell rang. She'd hurried down the narrow stairs that led to the street and found Miss Reid standing on the front step, sheltering under an umbrella against the swiftly falling rain.

"Put your hat on, Miss Shelton. We'll walk over together," the seamstress had said shortly, and Izzie had done as she was told.

Now, walking into St. Anne's, Izzie was even more grateful for the irascible woman by her side. Izzie was painfully aware of how people turned to stare and then quickly look away. She knew what the modest collection of neighbors, suppliers, and customers must be thinking: *Poor little Izzie. The girl who never left is now all alone.*

She kept her eyes ahead of her until they reached the front pew. It was empty, just as she'd expected it would be. Mum had lost touch with her family, the O'Sullivans, years ago, and Izzie hadn't even known how to tell them about the funeral. And her father's side—the Sheltons—never would have deigned to attend even if Izzie wanted to tell them about it.

Sylvia, she noticed, was nowhere to be seen.

"Will you be all right here, Miss Shelton?" asked Miss Reid.

Izzie wanted to pull her coat a little closer around her neck, but she forced herself to loosen her grasp on her lapels and lower her gloved hands. "Yes, I'll be fine."

"Good. Then I'll just go find a seat."

"Wait!" Izzie's hand shot out to stop her. "Sit with me."

Miss Reid looked horrified. "But the front pew is for family."

"You worked for Mum for nearly two decades. She would want you to be seated in the front," she said.

Izzie was shocked to see Miss Reid's eyes start to shine. "Are you certain, miss?"

She touched the older woman's forearm. "Please."

With a sniff and a nod, the seamstress sank down into the seat next to Izzie. She could sense Miss Reid twisting to peer around, but Izzie kept her eyes forward, willing the day to be over.

"It looks as though it's about to begin," said Miss Reid. "The priest has come to the door."

Izzie squeezed her eyes shut. She wasn't ready to say goodbye. Not yet.

Miss Reid leaned over. "Do you expect Mrs. Pearsall to attend?"

"No," said Izzie quietly. "I told her what had happened, but I'm certain she won't come."

"Well, a woman who looks awfully like her just walked in and took a seat in the last row," whispered Miss Reid.

Izzie whipped around just in time to catch a glimpse of her sister, dressed all in black with a small smart hat complete with a net veil that hid her eyes, sit in the last pew.

The church doors opened once again and the priest led in the pallbearers—all neighbors—who carried Mum's coffin balanced on their shoulders. However, try as she might, Izzie couldn't stop staring at her sister.

Sylvia had come.

Why?

Izzie squinted to try to read Sylvia's face, but the distance and the veil hid her sister's expression, leaving only the thin line of Sylvia's carmine lips.

It wasn't until the priest began the prayer that Izzie tore her gaze from her sister and faced forward again.

———

Sylvia grasped a bit of dirt and threw it onto her mother's coffin. She winced as the earth landed with a hollow thud.

She edged back, her eyes fixed on the dirt-scattered coffin until the grassy edge swallowed it whole. Then she turned, tilting her umbrella a little to better shield her from the rain.

It was all surreal. Maggie Shelton was only fifty-two—far too young to die. That disastrous Boxing Day, her mother hadn't exactly looked hale and hearty, but Sylvia recalled thinking that at least her mother hadn't appeared as bone-tired as she had in those first years of Mrs. Shelton's Fashions when the newly widowed Maggie Shelton had taken on the world with an angry determination.

Mourners were beginning to disperse, but Sylvia stopped at the end of the row of plots. She watched her sister touch a handkerchief to her eyes, Miss Reid placing a comforting hand on Izzie's back. Then the seamstress turned. Sylvia didn't miss the way that Miss Reid's eyes cut to her, nor the lift of Miss Reid's chin as she approached.

"Mrs. Pearsall," said Miss Reid with a curt nod.

"Good morning, Miss Reid," she said, grasping her umbrella a little tighter.

"Well, I can't say that I'm happy to see you given the circumstances, but I thought the priest gave a very good sermon. Speaking of Mrs. Shelton's service to others and her selflessness. It was all very fitting."

"Yes. I think my mother would have approved," she said, catching a flash of black out of the corner of her eye.

Miss Reid followed her gaze to where Izzie was turning from the grave.

"Miss Shelton has been a great help to your mother," said Miss Reid. "It's terrible what happened and far too early for it, but Mrs. Shelton will be happy knowing that the shop is in safe hands with Miss Shelton."

"I'm certain it is," she agreed quietly as Izzie came to a stop in front of them.

"Sylvia," said her sister.

"Hello, Izzie," she replied.

Miss Reid's eyes slid from sister to sister. "I'll give you both a moment, shall I?"

"Thank you," said Izzie.

As soon as Miss Reid was out of earshot, Izzie said, "I see you decided to come."

"I said that I would," she said, studying her younger sister. It had been so long since she'd laid eyes on Izzie, it shouldn't have surprised her that Izzie was a little taller, her hair a little shorter, and her cheeks a little more hollow thanks to age and the ration. Still, she was taken aback at how Izzie had gone from a girl with open enthusiasm to a prim young woman buttoned into a high-necked black coat and modest heels.

"I'm surprised that you were able to tear yourself away from your busy social schedule. Or has Horrible Hugo given you the day off from playing the perfect wife?" Izzie asked.

"I told you on the telephone that Hugo is serving," she said, the old instinct to defend her husband rising up in her despite everything. "Tell me, how are things at the shop?"

"Why?" Izzie's question was sharp as a knife's edge.

She sighed. "Because I'm curious."

"You've never shown an interest in it before."

"Izzie, that's not fair."

"Isn't it? You could hardly wait to leave the shop when you were younger. The moment Hugo came along you were gone," said Izzie.

"You're being ridiculous," she started, but Izzie cut her off with a shake of the head.

"You haven't visited once in fourteen years. You hardly write."

"I write," she said, stung.

"A card at Christmas? That hardly counts."

There had been a time, just after her wedding, when Sylvia had dutifully written every month, just as she did to Hugo's family. However, when her letters had gone unanswered, she assumed that they hadn't been welcomed. Besides there had been so many things to do as a new wife, from decorating their home to answering the onslaught of correspondence and invitations that seemed to come in the post every day.

"You never telephone," Izzie pressed.

"Izzie, the shop only had a telephone installed seven years ago," she said, recalling her mother's boast at Boxing Day. "Before that you used to have to use the box down the road."

When Izzie didn't return her smile, she tried again. "I can imagine that rationing has made things challenging."

"Miss Reid and I are managing just fine, thank you very much," said Izzie.

The sound of someone clearing his throat saved Sylvia from a reply, and she glanced over her shoulder to see a man in a double-breasted black suit with sandy hair standing close. There was something familiar about him.

"Mrs. Pearsall, Izzie, please accept my deepest condolences. Your mother was always very kind to me, and I cannot imagine how much you must miss her," he said.

"Thank you, Willie," said Izzie.

That was William Gray, their neighbor from a few doors down in Glengall Road? It hardly seemed possible that this could be the same reedy boy in striped jumpers who had tagged along behind Sylvia and her sister on their way to school every morning.

"William, it's been so long I hardly recognized you," she said, stretching out a hand to shake his, being sure to speak in the direction of his good ear.

He pressed his hand in hers, his grip firm and reassuring.

"I imagine I look a little different, but I do still have the spectacles," he said, touching the gold-rimmed glasses that perched on his nose.

She smiled at his polite demeanor. He'd always been that way as a child, the boy who thought things through and gave a considered answer to each question he was asked. He'd been quiet but ever-present, one of the few good things about moving from their family home and into the flat above the shop after Papa's death.

"Thank you for coming," she said, slipping into the role of hostess that she wore so easily those days. "We appreciate it."

Izzie huffed, no doubt taking objection to Sylvia referring to them as "we."

"Of course," said William before Izzie could reply, "although I will confess, I'm in the awkward position of being here in both a personal and professional capacity."

"Professional?" she asked.

"Willie was Mum's solicitor," Izzie explained, as though this should have been obvious to her.

Sylvia's cheeks flushed.

"I'm actually glad to have caught both of you together," he went on, having the good manners to overlook Sylvia's embarrassment. "I'm sorry to have to speak of practicalities on such a day, but there is the matter of your mother's will. I realize that it is a difficult time, but could I please ask that you join me at my office on Monday morning?"

"You would like both of us to attend?" Sylvia asked at the same moment Izzie asked, "Why does she need to be there?"

William cleared his throat. "It was your mother's wish that you should both be present for the reading of the will."

It was incredible that, even from the grave, Maggie Shelton thought she knew best. What did it matter if Sylvia attended anyway? Everything would go to Izzie, as it should, because Izzie had stayed and Sylvia had chosen a different life.

"Mrs. Shelton's instructions were very clear on the matter," William prompted.

Sylvia exhaled slowly and pulled out the small notebook she kept in her handbag. "Where is your office?"

She jotted down the address he gave her, and when she looked up, she caught her sister studying her, no doubt taking in her hat, shoes, and handbag. She stood a little taller, knowing that the cut of her Hartnell suit would stand up to even her sister's very keen scrutiny.

"That is a beautiful brooch," said Izzie in a way that told Sylvia she didn't really approve of the diamonds and pearls pinned to her lapel.

"Thank you. It was a tenth wedding anniversary present from

Hugo," she said before turning her attention back to William. "I will see you on Monday."

"Thank you," said William with a neat bow of his head. "I apologize again for discussing business at such a time."

"I must go thank the priest," said Izzie. "Excuse me."

Sylvia watched her walk off, head down, through the cemetery.

She hardly noticed that William had come to stand next to her until he said, "Will your sister be all right?"

She glanced at him and saw the very real concern etching his features. "I wouldn't know. Izzie hasn't confided her thoughts or feelings to me in a very long time."

"Funerals are difficult," said William.

"I've always found them cruel," she said.

"Why is that?" he asked.

"People say they're meant to be about the person who has passed, but I always think people are far more interested in those who are left behind. Who is showing an appropriate display of grief—tearful but not hysterical, devoted but not desperate. We're meant to be stiff upper-lipped but not cold. Perfect in our grief."

Out of the corner of her eye, she could see him turn to her. After a moment, she twisted and met his eye.

"I sincerely hope that you don't actually believe that anyone wants anything from you other than whatever your own true feeling of grief is, Mrs. Pearsall."

"Why is that?" she asked, a little taken aback.

"Because that would mean that someone has convinced you that you have to be perfect at every moment." He touched the brim of his dark gray hat. "Good day."

She watched his retreating back until she could no longer see him around the edge of the cemetery's wall.

Chapter Five

Late Monday morning, Izzie stepped out into the road but then jumped back again when a dispatch rider roared around the corner, narrowly missing her. She cried out, clapping a hand to her chest to slow her heart. She was already late. The last thing she needed was to be flattened by a motorcycle on the way to Willie's office.

The days since Mum's funeral had been some of the hardest of her life. She'd kept the shop closed, unable to bring herself to face the pity of Mrs. Shelton's customers. Instead, she'd pulled the quilt off the sofa and wrapped herself up in the large yellow armchair Mum used to sit in to mend at the end of the night. She hardly ate, she hardly drank. Instead, she grieved and slept.

She was an orphan now, all alone in the world. All she had was the shop.

The shop.

That was what had forced her out of the chair that morning. It was what compelled her to bathe and fix her hair. To dot on a precious bit of her last bottle of scent. To pull on one of her last pairs of nylons and her best shoes, don her coat and hat and gloves, and walk to Willie's office.

Izzie shook her head, double-checked the road in either direction, and hurried across to the door of his building. When she opened it, she found Sylvia sitting primly on the edge of a chair in the entryway. Slowly, she closed the door, examining her estranged sister, whom circumstances had forced her in front of twice in less than a week after so many years apart.

She remembered a time when she'd been proud of Sylvia's beauty. People always commented on how well the Shelton girls dressed—a proper advertisement for the shop, Mum would say with a satisfied smile—but Sylvia always managed to make whatever she wore look somehow more elegant than it did on the dressmaker's form. Now, Sylvia might be beautifully turned out, in her burgundy skirt and jacket with a fur coat on her shoulders and the black hat and veil she'd worn to the funeral perched on fashionably curled hair, but Izzie couldn't muster the pride she'd once had in her older sister.

"Hello," said Sylvia.

"You're early," said Izzie, unable to keep the accusation from her tone.

Sylvia sighed. "How could you possibly disapprove of me being early?"

Izzie lifted her chin. "You were nearly late to Mum's funeral, but you're early to her will reading?"

Sylvia rose to her feet, both hands braced on the handle of her handbag. "What are you implying?"

Izzie knew she wasn't really being fair, but she couldn't help herself. There were too many years of anger and frustration built up inside of her, and while she could keep it from erupting when she didn't have to see her sister, with Sylvia standing in front of her now—

Willie's office door opened, and he stepped into the entryway to greet them. "Good morning, Mrs. Pearsall, Miss Shelton."

Hearing her oldest friend call her "Miss Shelton" immediately sobered her. She squeezed her eyes shut, recalling all too clearly why they were at Willie's office. Mum was dead, and they were there to hear the reading of her will.

"Miss Shelton?" asked Willie.

She opened her eyes and found Willie and her sister staring at her.

"Are you all right?" asked Sylvia.

"Perfectly," she said. And in a way she was, because no matter Sylvia's diamonds and furs or her Marylebone telephone exchange, Izzie had something more valuable: years of memories with Mum.

"If you would both like to join me," said Willie, gesturing to the room that served as his office. It obviously had once been the front sitting room of a house, and it still had a plain but solid fireplace surround framing the coal fire that had just begun to glow with heat.

"I apologize that there was no one to greet you both this morning. Miss Hubert, my secretary, decided to join the Women's Royal Navy Service and received her orders two weeks ago and I haven't been able to find a suitable replacement. Not that anyone ever could replace Miss Hubert," he said. "She is the soul of discretion and has a mind like a steel trap."

"Did she wait long for her call-up? I know that the WRNS is one of the more desirable auxiliary services," said Sylvia, in a way Izzie was certain was meant to show of her superior knowledge of the women's auxiliary services, even though everyone knew that posh girls went into the WRNS, in part because their uniforms were designed by Edward Molyneux and were far more attractive than the other women's auxiliaries' uniforms.

"Not at all," Willie said. "There are rumors going around that there aren't nearly enough female recruits to free up the men needed for the front."

"Well, every little bit helps," said Sylvia.

Before she could think better of it, Izzie gave a faint snort. When she looked up, she found Willie and Sylvia both staring at her.

"Excuse me," she said.

"No, I'd actually be curious to hear how you can possibly find fault with such a simple statement," said Sylvia.

"Perhaps we should move on to—"

"'Every little bit helps'?" she cut across Willie. "What are you doing for the war effort from your mansion flat in Marylebone, then?"

Sylvia held her gaze for a long moment before turning back to Willie. "Perhaps we *should* move on."

He cleared his throat and began to shuffle the papers on his desk. When he was ready, he said, "As I mentioned on Friday, your mother was very clear in some of the instructions she left me, although I regret to say that she offered little insight into why she expressed her wishes in the way she did. That remains a mystery."

"What do you mean 'a mystery'?" asked Izzie.

She thought she saw a flash of sympathy in his eyes, but he looked down again before she could be certain.

"Why don't I begin to read the will and things will become clearer?" he asked. The paper crinkled in his hands as he lifted the edge of the page. "'I hereby declare that this is the last will and testament of Margaret Mary Shelton . . .'"

A long string of anachronistic legal sentences followed attesting to the fact that Mum had been of sound mind when she made the will. Then Mum named Willie as her executor.

Izzie let the words wash over her, worry creeping in. She wished that Mum had trusted her with more of the business side of things at Mrs. Shelton's. She didn't know the first thing about the accounts or where to find anything in Mum's messy office.

No. She might not know the ins and outs of the business when it came to money, but she knew the order and appointment books, and that was a start. She could learn how the suppliers were paid and how to do the accounting and—

"'I leave my estate, including my business, Mrs. Shelton's Fashions; the building at number four Glengall Road; the flat; and the building's contents to my daughters, Mrs. Hugo Pearsall and Miss Isabelle Shelton.'"

"What?" Izzie blurted out.

Sylvia leaned forward, grasping the arms of her chair. "That cannot be right."

"You've read that wrong, Willie. Read it again," Izzie demanded.

"I have only read what your mother wrote here. Her last wishes," said Willie, his tone sharper than it usually was.

This could not be happening. Mum wouldn't have done this to her.

"There must be a misunderstanding," said Sylvia. "Our mother wouldn't have left the shop to me. Surely it must be Izzie's."

"There is more, if you will permit me," said Willie, clearing his throat.

"Please do go on, William," said Sylvia, like she was the lady of the manor.

"Mrs. Shelton continues, 'I hope that, as it has for me, the shop will take care of them when they need it most.'" Willie looked up. "That is all."

"What could Sylvia possibly need the shop for?" Izzie demanded.

Willie looked up at her, the sympathy so clear in his eyes that it made her miserable all over again. "I'm very sorry, Miss Shelton."

"But it's not *fair*." She'd been the one to work for years at Mrs. Shelton's, not Sylvia. She'd steeled herself to harangue delivery drivers and cope with Miss Reid's moods. She'd sewn until her eyes had felt like sand to make sure orders were delivered on time. She'd swept and cleaned and done *everything* to keep the doors open every day. And what had Sylvia done except hitch herself to Horrible Hugo's tailored coattails as soon as she'd seen a chance to escape.

"That's an old will," she said. "It must be. Mum would have changed it after Sylvia left home."

"It's the most recent will," Willie said.

"But that can't be right. Maybe Mum left Sylvia an interest in the building because of the flat, but she never would have left her the business," she insisted.

It was supposed to be hers and hers alone.

"I'm very sorry, Miss Shelton," said Willie, retreating behind his professionalism. "I know that this is the most recently witnessed and executed will because I was the one who drew it up for her. Miss Hubert was one of the witnesses."

"And you never said?" she snapped.

"I had an obligation to my client," he said. "These are your mother's last wishes."

"When was the will made out?" Sylvia asked.

"Your mother spoke to me after she purchased the building in January of 1939. She wanted to be sure that everything was legally sound in case something were to happen to her," Willie said.

But—1939? That meant that for years Izzie had been working every day at Mrs. Shelton's assuming she was helping Mum build the business that she would one day take over and none of it was true. Mum had *lied* to her.

She slumped back in her chair, the rosy tint dissipating from her memories. It had taken her ages to convince Mum that she was capable of accepting inventory or managing the appointment book, and it wasn't until Mum had become overwhelmed by the bookkeeping that she had even allowed Izzie to properly see customers on her own.

How often had Izzie suggested taking out an advertisement in one of the better society magazines in order to attract a new type of clientele with deeper pockets and a need for a more varied wardrobe than their normal customers? How many times had Mum dismissed her sketches as too modern or not practical for the women they served, even taking away her sketchbook from time to time with the excuse that it was distracting her from her real work?

Mum hadn't believed that Izzie could do this on her own. Not one bit. All Izzie had ever been was a helper—not a businesswoman or the designer she so desperately wanted to be—and now she'd lost the very thing that mattered to her most to the one woman in London she couldn't stand.

Her sister.

Chapter Six

Sylvia stared dumbly at the spot on William's desk where her mother's will lay open.

This couldn't be happening. There must be a mistake, because there was no reason that her mother would ever feel compelled to leave any part of Mrs. Shelton's Fashions to her.

In the first months after opening the shop, her mother had tried to teach her to sew, sitting eleven-year-old Sylvia in a corner with a bit of fabric and instructions for a running stitch, whip stitch, back stitch. No matter how often she tried, Sylvia could never make her stitches look like the perfect examples her mother made for her, and her mother had grown increasingly frustrated until finally declaring Sylvia a disappointment. Clearly, someone who could hardly sew a basic stitch could not be trusted to learn how to measure, cut, pin, baste, seam, press, fit, and finish a garment. That meant that Sylvia's only use was to help with the running of the shop: accounting, administration, deliveries, and cleaning. The things anyone could do.

Izzie, however, had shown real talent from an early age, the fabric molding to her will in a way that it never had for Sylvia. The more her sister learned, the more acutely Sylvia felt her failure, until it became clear that there was no room for her to squeeze into the little unit that was Izzie and their mother.

And then Hugo had come along. Hugo, who had *wanted* her to join him in his world of dances and dinners, theater and opera. The drudgery of her childhood became the beginning of a fairy tale, and her husband became the handsome prince sweeping Cinderella away.

So why would her mother ever have thought that Sylvia would want to come back to the shop, let alone need to?

"Well." She breathed out.

"Well?" Izzie barked out a laugh. "That's all you can say?"

"What else is there to say?" she asked.

Izzie shot to her feet, her chair teetering dangerously on its two back legs before landing with a dull thud on the carpet of William's office. "Unbelievable!"

"Izzie—" she started to say, but a sharp shake of her sister's head killed the words in her throat.

"I have nothing to say to you. Nothing," Izzie hissed before storming out.

Sylvia's gaze flicked to William, who sat quietly shuffling the paperwork on his desk.

"I do apologize for my sister's outburst."

He gave her a sympathetic look and said, "The loss of a loved one is always an emotional time."

She dropped her gaze to her gloved hands still clenched in her lap. Everything about what was happening felt wrong. She had to make this right. If only she could figure out . . .

Her head snapped up. "William, if you will please excuse me for a moment."

She hurried out of the office and back through the waiting area. Pulling open William's front door, she looked up and down the road. No Izzie. She darted out to the edge of the pavement, pausing while a lorry passed, then hurried across the road.

Halfway around the corner she spotted her sister's retreating back clad in her beautifully tailored navy coat.

"Izzie!"

The hitch in her sister's step told her that Izzie had heard her.

"Izzie!" Cursing her heels, she picked up her pace until she was half running, a hand clamped down on her hat to keep it from blowing off. "Izzie, wait!"

Izzie rounded on her, the skirt of her coat swinging out. "What do you want from me?"

Sylvia stopped abruptly, hands held wide and low. "I know that you're angry, but we need to talk about this."

"Why? So that you can lord it over me that, even after years of hardly speaking, Mum *still* gave you part of the shop? Or do you want to remind me, yet again, how much better you are than me?"

Sylvia jerked back. "I don't think I'm better than you."

Izzie snorted. "Yes, you do."

"That isn't true," she insisted.

"Oh, stop it, Sylvia. The moment you met Hugo, you decided that you were too good to have anything to do with your mother and your sister. You dropped us and never looked back."

Sylvia opened her mouth to protest but something stopped her. Wasn't what Izzie said at least partially true? Meeting Hugo had opened up her world in ways she'd never imagined possible, but life with him came with expectations. Successful Harley Street doctors who could trace their family tree back to the Norman Conquest on both sides did not marry dress-shop girls. That was why his love for her had been so extraordinary. He'd reached down and pulled her up to him, and she was so grateful she'd set about transforming herself into the sort of wife he would always be proud of.

She'd worked hard burnishing herself with some of the same polish that came so naturally to him. At every dinner and dance

Hugo took her to, she watched the other ladies and absorbed silent lessons from them. She devoured every ladies' magazine she could find and pored over every etiquette book she could lay her hands on. Soon everything from her voice and vocabulary to her carriage and comportment took on a degree of refinement. Although the early years of their marriage had been tinged with the disappointment of trying and failing to have children, Hugo had given her the kind of life even her mother couldn't have dreamed of, and the discipline and sacrifice had all been worth it.

Until she'd found the love letters from another woman in his desk.

"What do you want, Sylvia?" Izzie prompted. "Because if you don't have anything to say, I have things to do at the business that we apparently now own."

"You can have it," Sylvia said quickly. "You can have Mrs. Shelton's Fashions."

Izzie's eyes narrowed as she crossed her arms over her chest. "Why?"

"You've worked there for so long, we both know that it should be yours. Besides, our mother always said that I was a terrible seamstress," she said, trying a smile.

"*Mum*," Izzie said, emphasizing the term of endearment Sylvia hadn't used in years, "would have been happy to teach you if you hadn't thought yourself too good to learn."

Sylvia clamped her lips shut. Izzie had been too young to remember what it had been like in those early years, and Sylvia was not going to take the happy memories of their mother away from her sister. Besides, anything Sylvia said would only fall on deaf ears.

"I want you to have the business," she said firmly. "It should be yours."

"You can't just give me half of a business, Sylvia. Besides, what would Horrible Hugo say?"

He'd be horrified to learn that she now owned a dress shop, because he'd made very clear when he'd proposed that she would never have to work again. He wanted her at home, and her time would be far better used on the philanthropic work that ladies like Claire did.

"Hugo has other things to occupy his thoughts. Izzie, think about it. What am I going to do with a stake in a dressmaker's shop?"

She knew the moment the words were out of her mouth that it was the wrong thing to say, because Izzie lifted her chin the way she'd always done when she was squaring off for a fight.

"I don't need your charity," Izzie said.

"I'll sell it to you then," she said quickly. "At a fair market price. We can even have it valued if you like. There must be people who do that sort of thing." Claire was always telling her about the discreet little men who slipped into the homes of the well-to-do to value jewelry and furs, fine art and furniture, and save families from the indignity of walking into an auction house or—worse yet—a pawnbroker. Surely someone must do the same for businesses.

"Fine," said Izzie. "I'll telephone you with my offer, and I'll have Willie draw up the paperwork. The sooner we can have this done the better, so I can go back to the way things were."

Izzie turned on her heel and strode away, the tails of her coat billowing out behind her. As Sylvia watched her sister go, she wondered why there was a nagging tug at her heart, asking her if she really wanted things to be just as they were.

Chapter Seven

Izzie pressed hard on the bridge of her nose, willing the numbers in front of her to change. It had been a week since Mum's funeral and four days since she'd learned that the shop she'd poured herself into for years was not hers, and now she was facing the reality that it might never be.

"There has to be a way," she muttered, staring at her post office savings book, order and appointment books, and the scraps of paper she and Willie had spread in front of them. For the past few hours, they'd pored over everything and come to one conclusion: it didn't amount to much.

"I'm sorry, Izzie," said Willie, sighing as he leaned back in one of the wooden chairs they'd pulled up to a corner of the cutting table. "Short of asking Sylvia to create some sort of loan agreement between the two of you—"

"No," she said sharply.

"Then you either need ready money or something you can sell that would equate half of the value of the business."

It was simple arithmetic. She did not have anywhere near enough in her personal savings to buy Sylvia out. The money would have to come from somewhere else.

"Do you know the value of Mrs. Shelton's?" asked Willie. "Maybe there is enough money in the accounts that you could use half to buy Sylvia out."

"I don't know how much money is in the shop's accounts," she muttered.

"It shouldn't be too difficult to figure out. If you'll show me the account books, I could take a look for you."

Her cheeks burned as she looked down at her hands. "I don't know where Mum kept them."

"How have you been conducting business since you reopened?" asked Willie.

Izzie looked up at the ceiling, too mortified to meet her friend's eye. "There is a box with a small amount of money in it under the counter. Mum would clear it out each week and put it in an envelope to take to the bank." At least that's what Izzie assumed Mum had done.

"Do you know which bank she used?" asked Willie.

Izzie shook her head miserably. "Sylvia made the arrangements years ago."

Willie let out a long breath. "Well, the account books must be around here somewhere. Didn't Mrs. Shelton do all of her business in the office?"

"She did, it's just . . ."

It had taken her three days to work up the courage to open Mum's office door, and the moment she did, she'd pulled the door shut again, overwhelmed by the disarray.

Mum had never tolerated anything but pin-straight perfection in the front rooms of Mrs. Shelton's, and the workshop was a study in controlled chaos, with different orders in different states of production neatly set out for Mum, Miss Reid, or Izzie to work on. For as long as Izzie could remember, the employees of Mrs. Shelton's had always been responsible for the upkeep of those rooms. However, since Sylvia left home, the office had reverted to being solely Mum's domain.

Izzie wasn't entirely certain how long it had been since Mum had done a proper clear-out of the office—certainly since before the war—and it showed. Outside of a small square of cracked leather blotter, it was impossible to see the surface of the modest wooden desk that sat close to the one blank wall of the office. Bookshelves lined two other walls, and those were packed with sample books, files, loose papers, catalogues, and folio-style notebooks. A small table and two chairs were piled with shoe boxes and cardboard boxes of the same artifacts, and yet another pile prevented the door from fully opening.

And somewhere in there were the account books Izzie had never been allowed to touch.

"Izzie," said Willie, "you and Sylvia are equal owners in this business. The value, including any profit, is half yours. Once you find those account books and figure out how much is in the business, you'll have a better idea of where you stand. And if there is still a difference between the price Sylvia will accept and what you have, you could work out an agreement that would pay her a portion of your half of the profits."

"I will not take charity from my sister," she said firmly.

"It isn't charity," said Willie.

"It is when I need this business and she doesn't. Besides, she doesn't want anything to do with it."

It galled her that she would have to *share* Mrs. Shelton's Fashions with her sister, who had hated the shop from the moment Mum had opened it. Her sister, who was ashamed of Mum's years of hard work because Sylvia thought working an honest job was somehow beneath her.

"I hope that, as it has for me, the shop will take care of them when they need it most."

The words from Mum's will only made her angrier, because why would Sylvia ever need the shop when she had Horrible Hugo?

"I could try to ask a bank for a loan," she said, grasping for a sliver of hope.

"The chances that they will lend to you as an unmarried woman are slim unless a man will guarantee the loan for you."

The injustice of it stung even though she knew he was right.

Tears pricked her eyes. Before last week, she had been champing at the bit to prove to Mum that she was more than capable of taking over more of Mrs. Shelton's, but now that she had, she felt as though she were already underwater.

How on God's green earth had she ever thought she could do this?

"What about selling the building?" Willie asked. "It's the most valuable asset you have, especially with the housing crisis that the Blitz landed all of us in. My guess is that if you put it on the market, someone would snatch it up and probably convert the ground floor into flats. You and Sylvia could walk away with a tidy sum each—enough for you to buy her out and take the stock, the customers, and the name to another, cheaper location."

"No!" The word burst from Izzie's lips before she could stop herself. "I'm sorry, Willie, but no. Mum worked too hard to buy the building from our landlord. Besides, Mrs. Shelton's wouldn't be Mrs. Shelton's if it wasn't here in Glengall Road."

"Then what about considering Sylvia's offer?"

"That's what we're trying to work out, isn't it?" she asked.

He held her gaze. "I mean her original offer. You told me that she was willing to give you everything."

Izzie stared at him. "Do you really think I would believe a thing she said?"

"What incentive would she have to lie?"

"If she gave me the shop, she'd hold it over me for years," she said.

"But what would she have to gain—?"

"Sylvia only does what's good for Sylvia," she said fiercely. "You'd be able to see that if you hadn't spent the last two decades in love with her."

The words fell like an anvil in the middle of the room, and Izzie watched with growing horror as her friend's lips twisted as though he didn't trust himself with the words trapped behind them.

"Willie, I am sorry," she tried. "You know me and my stupid mouth, always saying the wrong thing and making a hash of it."

Instead of replying, he rose to his feet and resettled his glasses on his nose once again. "I think I'll go put the kettle on."

He walked out of the workroom without a backward glance, leaving Izzie feeling about six inches small. And that was what she deserved, wasn't it? Willie was one of the constants in her life, a neighborhood boy who had somehow grown up into a friend and confidant. She had precious few of those these days, yet she was pushing him away because she was angry about her sister.

She slipped out into the passageway. Wille, who stood at the tiny galley kitchen, was just putting the kettle on the gas ring to heat.

"I'm sorry," she said.

He pulled down the everyday teapot she and Mrs. Reid used when having a cup of tea in the workroom. Then he lifted the tea towel where she'd left the leaves from her afternoon brew drying and did his best to shake them into the pot.

Uncertain whether he'd heard her or whether he was ignoring her, she angled herself closer to his good ear and said again, "I'm sorry."

He braced his hands on either side of the counter he stood at, his gaze resolutely on the cabinet door ahead of him.

"I am prepared to pretend that you didn't just insult me as both a solicitor and your friend by implying that my judgment isn't sound when it comes to your sister," he said.

"I'm sorry," she whispered again, shame staining her already red cheeks a deeper shade.

"You'll notice it isn't Sylvia who I am speaking to at half past nine at night when I could be in bed with a book." He finally spared her a glance. "I know you are grieving. I also understand that, as your friend, I should afford you a certain degree of grace. However, I will not allow you to take your anger out on me."

"Please forgive me," she whispered.

He waited an excruciatingly long moment before nodding. "You are forgiven. I understand that things between you and your sister are tense and have been for some time, although I hate to see it. You two used to be thick as thieves."

No, Izzie's entire world had revolved around her older sister. The two of them had done everything together, especially after Dad died and Mum had been run off her feet opening the shop. Sylvia had been the one to make sure Izzie was dressed and at school on time, and even after Sylvia left school to work at the shop full-time, Sylvia had always had time to listen to her struggles and help her with her schoolwork. Izzie had adored her sister, and that had made Sylvia's rejection all the more painful.

"I'm tired, and I need to figure out how to buy the shop," she said, her voice cracking.

Willie scrunched up his brow, and she thought for a moment that he might argue with her. Instead, he said, "I know that you live and breathe this shop, and I want to see you at the helm of Mrs. Shelton's Fashions as much as you do. However, you might need to accept that you don't have the means to buy it outright. Not yet."

Izzie shook her head. "There has to be a way. Let's make the tea and go over everything again."

Chapter Eight

It turned out that selling a business was not straightforward. At least it wasn't when Izzie was involved.

Sylvia had walked away from the will reading at William's office assuming that it would be a simple matter of gathering the funds together. Given that the shop's fortunes were now half her sister's, Sylvia had no doubt that Izzie would be able to come up with the money. After the first lean years of the business, their mother had been proud that Mrs. Shelton's Fashions had always turned a modest but tidy profit.

However, when nearly a week had gone by with no word from Izzie, Sylvia found herself on the sitting room telephone, asking the switchboard to connect her to the shop.

"Things have been busy here," said Izzie by way of explanation as soon as Sylvia began to inquire about the shop. "I haven't had a chance to even think about your offer."

"Is everything all right?" she'd asked.

"Miss Reid and I have been run off our feet. We were closed for a few days after Mum . . ." Izzie cleared her throat. "We were closed, and we lost some time."

"But it's Saturday." It was the reason that she'd waited until that afternoon to telephone. Their mother had kept half-day trading hours on Saturdays, only taking morning appointments.

"Yes, it is," Izzie replied slowly, as though speaking to a child, "and if you remember, Mum always used Saturday afternoons to catch up on orders. That is what Miss Reid and I were both doing before you rang."

Sylvia bit the inside of her cheek. She had forgotten about that.

"Once those orders are delivered," Izzie continued, "I'll be able to sort through Mum's office and find the account books."

"You don't know where the account books are?" she asked, sitting up a little straighter. "I thought you said you were practically running the business."

Izzie hesitated, and Sylvia could picture her sister twisting the telephone cord around her index finger as she did when she was grasping for an answer. Finally, Izzie said, "They're in the office. I'm sure they are."

Sylvia frowned. Their mother had been a talented seamstress but not a natural businesswoman, habitually neglecting tasks she cared about less than sketching and sewing garments. Sylvia remembered the state of things when she'd left school and started doing the accounts at fourteen. It had taken weeks to sort out the mess of her mother's office, and more to implement a system to account for all of the orders, expenses, and income flowing in and out of the business. Sylvia had been the one to take a reluctant Maggie Shelton to the bank and practically hold her mother's hand as her mother opened an account for the business. Before her wedding, she'd walked her mother through everything to make sure she understood and could maintain the system, but that had been years ago.

"Do you need help?" she asked. "I could come around and—"

"No," Izzie said quickly. "I have things in hand. Don't worry."

Except worry was what Sylvia did. It was one of the things that made her so effective as a member of the War Widows' Fund committee. She worried about how much money they would raise, who would sit next to whom at which ball or tea, how they could secure the support of important members of high society whose mere presence at an event could put it under the spotlight. All of it would consume her until she felt as though she couldn't ignore it any longer. Then she would channel that energy into the sort of focus that allowed her to tick items off to-do lists with ruthless abandon, all while blocking the uglier parts of the world out. It helped her ignore the war and—lately—Hugo.

It was worry that occupied Sylvia's mind two days after her telephone call to her sister. Her bus pulled up to her stop, and she tucked her white silk scarf a little more firmly into her mink against the wind of the chilly early-December night before she stepped off onto the pavement. The buildings were hardly visible thanks to the inky dim of the blackout, and it took her a moment to orient herself. Sure of her direction, she made her way carefully home to Nottingham Court, her heels clicking against the icy concrete.

Izzie, she knew, would never believe her if she confessed that there was rarely a day when she didn't think about her old life. It happened whenever Sylvia took out her sewing basket to do some half-hearted mending, her mother's criticism of her stitching still echoing in her mind. Walking past a butcher's displaying liver or kidneys brought back the visceral memory of all the inexpensive meals they'd eaten after Papa had died. And whenever the doorbell of the flat rang unexpectedly, a little flicker of fear still flashed in her chest, too close a reminder to those first lean days of Mrs. Shelton's when their mother would tell them to hide and keep quiet in case it was Papa's creditors looking to collect on the debts he'd left behind.

Why, even the dinner party she'd just come from that Monday evening was full of reminders of the way she'd used to be. She'd once called a napkin a serviette because she hadn't known better, and the

first time Hugo took her to supper in a restaurant, the soldier-like
rows of seemingly endless silverware that made up the formal dinner service had intimidated her so much she'd nearly knocked over
a glass of claret. But she'd learned and nodded wordlessly as he
gently corrected her with a light touch on the elbow during their
first months together.

Yet the veneer of polish she now wore as Mrs. Hugo Pearsall
could never completely hide the fact that she had once been Miss
Sylvia Shelton.

Sylvia welcomed the warm light from her building's lobby as
she pushed open the door, nodding to Mrs. Bellington-Norton
from the second floor as she went.

"Mrs. Pearsall," said the venerable barrister's wife, who wore a
calf-length sable and held the lead of her little puffball of a dog,
which yapped at everyone it saw.

"Good evening, Mrs. Bellington-Norton," she said over the little dog's barks.

"I have been meaning to ask you to tea. The refugee society I sit
on the committee of is planning a ball, and I would appreciate any
advice you could lend me," said her neighbor.

A surge of pride swelled up in Sylvia's chest, and she lifted her
head a little higher. Miss Sylvia Shelton would never be invited to
help with a committee ball, but Mrs. Hugo Pearsall was.

"I would be happy to help in any way I can, Mrs. Bellington-
Norton."

"Come around Thursday afternoon, if you would," said Mrs.
Bellington-Norton over her dog's increasingly loud yaps.

With a nod of assent, Sylvia stepped onto the lift, feeling frac-
tionally brighter.

She hardly noticed the ding as the doors opened, her legs

automatically carrying her to the front door. She let herself in, frowning as she realized she'd left the entryway light on. Usually she was so careful about checking that every switch was off before leaving the flat, but she'd been tired that evening and she must have missed it. She would, she decided, write Mrs. Atkinson a note asking the housekeeper not to wake her with breakfast as usual.

She closed the door and put her beaded evening bag down on the side table before unclasping her mink. However, as she was about to slide the coat off, her eyes fixed on the reflection of a naval officer's hat hanging on the entryway hatstand.

Moving very slowly, she smoothed her hands over the front of her midnight-blue silk Molyneux gown and straightened the halter-neck straps. Then she walked to the sitting room door and opened it.

In the armchair farthest from the door sat Hugo, reading an evening newspaper with one leg crossed ankle to knee. He looked up, said, "Hello, darling," with the same dispassionate tone that one might use to greet the milkman, and returned to his paper.

Sylvia gripped the doorframe with one hand, willing herself to stay upright. They'd been married nearly fifteen years, but he was still as handsome as he'd been the day he trotted up to the door of his friend's house as she stood on the doorstep, a boxed-up dress she'd been delivering balanced in her arms. He'd helped her ring the bell because it had turned out his friend's mother and Mrs. Shelton's most well-heeled customer were one and the same. He'd looked her over from top to tail and then smiled as though he couldn't think of anything more delightful than meeting her. It had been that smile that had slain her, and the absence of it now sent a pang through her chest.

When had he stopped lighting up when she walked into a room? She wanted to ask, but instead she said, "You're home."

He glanced up and then inclined his head. "Clearly."

"I wasn't aware that you had leave."

"I don't," he said, his gaze settling back on his newspaper. "I have been called to London for meetings at the Admiralty. We are discussing how the Royal Navy coordinates its medical corps. Where have you been?"

"The Alexanders had a dinner party," she said.

He sniffed, but she knew that he approved. After all, there were rumors that Mr. Alexander was being considered for a knighthood.

"Who was there?" asked Hugo.

Before she could answer, she heard the rustle of fabric and turned to find Mrs. Atkinson bearing the glass and silver soda bottle that normally lived on the bar cart in the sitting room.

"Oh, Mrs. Pearsall," said the housekeeper, "isn't it wonderful having the surgeon lieutenant-commander home?"

Sylvia shot Hugo a look, but he was watching Mrs. Atkinson set down the soda water.

"Mrs. Atkinson, I thought you were leaving early tonight," she said.

"Oh," said the housekeeper, busying herself as she poured out a measure of scotch and then added soda to it just as Hugo liked it. "I was all set to go after you left, but then Lieutenant-Commander Pearsall arrived."

"Mrs. Atkinson was kind enough to give me supper," said Hugo.

Sylvia couldn't help the annoyance rising in her. He made it sound as though it had been Sylvia's negligence that there hadn't been anything for him to eat when he came home, rather than his failure to inform her that he would be in London.

"Would you like a drink as well, Mrs. Pearsall?" Mrs. Atkinson asked.

"No, thank you," she said.

"You might as well enjoy it while it still isn't rationed," said Hugo.

"I'm fine," she said to Mrs. Atkinson. "You may go now."

"Good evening, madam," said the housekeeper before adding, "It's good to have you home safe and sound, Lieutenant-Commander Pearsall."

"Thank you, Mrs. Atkinson," said Hugo, his gaze hardly rising from that damned newspaper.

The housekeeper shut the sitting room door, leaving husband and wife alone together for the first time in months.

"If you had let me know that you were coming home, I wouldn't have gone out," Sylvia started. "I would have made sure that we had something decent in for supper rather than whatever Mrs. Atkinson had to put together on short notice."

"She didn't mind," said Hugo, turning the broadsheet's page.

"How long will you be at home?" she asked.

"Does it matter? It is my home."

It was *their* home. The shop above the flat had never felt really like home, so it had meant a great deal to her to have a beautiful place that was at least partially her own. Hugo had indulged her from the first day, allowing her free rein to decorate every room save his study. She'd chosen things she thought he would like, understated and not too feminine. She'd shown an elegance and restraint she'd quietly applauded herself for, congratulating herself on being clever enough to find a man who would wrap her in the cotton wool of his class and affluence.

"I'm asking a simple question, Hugo," she said, not bothering to keep the annoyance out of her tone. "You could do me the courtesy of answering it."

He gave a huff of frustration, the pages of the newspaper

crinkling violently as he shook it out in front of him again as he always did when he wished she would stop speaking.

"I'll be in town for a few days before returning to base," he said.

"You see? That wasn't so very difficult," she said.

"I have rather a lot on my mind, Sylvia. I can't be expected to apprise you of every small matter," he said.

"Then I take it you haven't read my last letter?" she asked.

His eyes stayed resolutely on the page. "I'm not certain that it was delivered when I left."

"I wrote to tell you that my mother died."

At least that merited a glance up and a furrowed brow. "Died? But she was hardly fifty."

"She was fifty-two. The doctor said it was a condition of the heart. He thought that the stress of the war and trying to keep the shop open during rationing might have also contributed."

"No doubt it did," said Hugo, his eyes drifting back to the page.

She stared at him. He'd just learned that his mother-in-law had died, and he had nothing more to say? It wasn't as though he knew her mother particularly well, but surely he should offer her some comfort.

"I went to the funeral."

"Oh yes?" he muttered.

"I saw my sister."

He sighed. "Sylvia, would you please come to your point? I have very little time that is my own these days. All I wish is to read my paper and drink my—"

"My mother left me half of the business, the building, and its contents."

That, she was satisfied to see, had shocked him. "She left you the shop?"

"Yes," she said. "Well, half of it. Izzie has the other half."

"What could she have been thinking?" He scoffed. "As though you would want half of a shop."

"Why wouldn't I?" she asked.

"Come now, Sylvia," said Hugo in that infuriating tone he used when he thought she was being ridiculous. "No one we know works in trade."

She gave a little laugh. "'No one we know works in trade'? Half the members of your club are in business of some sort or another. The Hargreaves are in cosmetics, and they have a string of shops. Or what about Mr. Yarley? He sells automobiles."

His eyes narrowed. "Mr. Hargreaves is the president of his family's company, and Mr. Yarley wouldn't know the first thing about selling an automobile if his life depended on it. He owns factories that *make* automobiles. They are in business; they are not in trade."

"That is a ridiculously thing to say, Hugo, and snobbish to boot. You sound as though you were a disapproving father in a nineteenth-century novel."

"Disapproving fathers in nineteenth-century novels knew a thing or two. I took you out of that shop, Sylvia, and don't pretend that you weren't grateful for it," he said.

He was right, and yet his words hurt all the same. The shop was the world she'd come from, and she expected her husband to have some sympathy, understanding, compassion—something.

"Well, it really doesn't matter anyway," she said. "I'm selling my share to Izzie."

She waited for him to ask her what she would do with the funds, but instead, he cocked his head. "That should keep you in Hartnell for some time. If it turns out to be worth anything. Right." Hugo set his newspaper aside and rose. "I'm going to my club."

"But you just came home," she began to protest, her anger beginning to dissolve into desperation. "It's half past midnight."

He shot her a look. "I only have so long in London, Sylvia. There are people I must see."

Are you going to see her? The question choked her, but she forced what she hoped was a smile. "Who could be more important than the wife you haven't seen in six months?"

"Don't be sentimental, Sylvia. It doesn't suit you," he said.

"Is it sentimental to want to spend time with one's husband?" she asked.

"You know what I mean," he said.

"I'm not sure I do."

He sighed, and disappointment crashed down on her. No matter what he'd done, he was still her husband, still the man she had fallen in love with and given up so much for. He might have drifted from her, but this was his home. He should want to be here. With her.

"I could ring Claire and a few other friends and see if they would like to join us at the club tomorrow," she offered, fighting to keep the naked hope from her voice. "I'm afraid Rupert's still in Scotland, but it would still be jolly."

He tapped the folded newspaper against his palm once, twice, three times. She thought for a moment she had convinced him, but then he shook his head.

"I must change into my dress uniform," he said.

Then he walked out of the room, leaving Sylvia staring at the empty doorway.

Chapter Nine

Izzie awoke on Wednesday morning with a start. It took her a moment to realize that it hadn't been the harsh ringing of her alarm clock that had woken her but rather a vehicle in the road.

"The newspaper," she muttered, falling back onto her pillow.

She considered for a moment pulling the covers over her head and retreating to the land of nod, but she knew it was unlikely she'd get any more sleep. Already she was thinking about the day ahead. Two women were coming into the shop for fittings and—with any luck—Mrs. Evesham would finally come by and pay her bill and collect her winter coat, as she'd been promising for the past week and a half.

With a groan, Izzie swung her legs out of bed and slid on her slippers and quilted navy dressing gown. It was cold in the flat even for the third of December, but she was loath to light the fire in her bedroom. A reliable source of coal was hard to come by, and she needed whatever she could find for the dressing room downstairs, because it wouldn't do for customers to shiver.

She yawned as she shuffled to the door of the flat and let herself out onto the landing. Half awake, she tried to remember what was in the larder for breakfast.

At the bottom of the stairs, she walked past the door to the shop and to the flat's front door. She opened it and stooped to pick up the morning's edition of the *Daily Telegraph*. Dad had subscribed to the newspaper, and Mum had kept the subscription long after his death, although she'd rarely had time to read it. Izzie glanced at the headline as she often did, clucking her tongue as she read:

BRITISH REINFORCING LIBYAN ARMIES
NAZIS BREAK THROUGH TOBRUK CORRIDOR

It seemed that every bit of good news these days was accompanied by something negative.

She stepped back inside, but just as she was reaching to close the flat's door, a headline on the far-right column of the front page stole her breath. Underneath an advertisement for Gordon's gin, it read:

UNMARRIED WOMEN TO BE CONSCRIPTED
20 TO 30 AGE GROUP

"No," she murmured as her eyes quickly scanned the text.

All unmarried women between 20 and 30 are to be conscripted. Married women will not be compelled to join the Services, though the power to direct them into industry will continue, the article read.

Izzie read it twice, desperate to find some loophole. There was the possibility of exemptions, the article said, but only in the case of extreme hardship, if a woman was caring for children or dependents, or in the case of conscientious objectors. Apparently there were special penalties for women who refused to comply with the new rules.

In the road behind her, someone honked their horn, reminding her she was standing in her dressing gown and slippers for all the world to see. With a shaking hand, she shut the door behind her and sagged against it.

"What am I going to do?"

She was twenty-eight years old, unmarried, and with no children or elderly relatives to care for. She was healthy and physically capable of serving in one of the military's women's auxiliary services or doing farm work for the Women's Land Army. She would have to go.

Panic began to climb up her chest. What would happen to Mrs. Shelton's Fashions if she was conscripted? Miss Reid had never expressed an ounce of interest in the business of the shop, refusing to see clients unless it was for a fitting. Maybe she could apply to a committee, arguing a hardship case because she was the sole proprietor of her family's shop.

Except she wasn't.

Sylvia owned half of Mrs. Shelton's Fashions.

Izzie groaned. If Sylvia owned half of the shop, she would never be able to convince a committee that keeping a dress shop open was more important than serving.

Sylvia owns half the shop.

An unwanted thought began to form in her mind, but she didn't know what else she could do. She was desperate. She couldn't lose Mum's shop, not after all the years she'd put into it. Not after finally having the chance to prove to everyone that she could run it.

Izzie forced herself to walk to the shop's telephone. She steeled herself and then picked up the receiver. After giving the operator the exchange, she waited for the call to be connected.

There were three rings on the line and then she heard her sister say, "Pearsall residence."

"Sylvia."

"Izzie?"

She swallowed and forced herself to say, "I need your help."

Sylvia looked up at the front of the two-story building that contained her family's dress shop and flat for the first time since she'd left fourteen years ago.

"I need your help."

They were four words she never thought she'd hear her sister say, and the shock of them that morning had compelled her to respond "Tell me what I can do" before she'd even stopped to consider what it all might mean.

She glanced down, checking that her outfit still looked as pristine as when she'd left the flat. She'd put on a navy wool crepe dress, and on top of her carefully brushed pageboy she'd placed a cream hat held in place with a pearl-topped hatpin. Her coat was of inky black boiled wool, and she hesitated for a moment before pinning to it the sapphire brooch Hugo had given her for their fifth wedding anniversary. Since the weather looked cold but not particularly wet, she'd risked a pair of black suede heels that matched her structured black leather handbag, which opened with a gold clasp, and her black leather gloves.

She hoped that the clothes would hide the deep smudges of purple under her eyes. She hadn't slept much since Hugo had returned home, instead lying as still as she could because she didn't dare touch him. In the mornings, she'd wait until he rose and left the flat before leaving bed. When he would come home to change for his club, she would stay in the sitting room, exchanging only the simplest of pleasantries with him. She didn't try to convince him to stay home for supper or bring her along on a night out for fear that he would reject her once again. She hated not knowing where he was or who he was with.

Every afternoon he was away, she would check his desk and count the love letters. Perhaps some women might have taken comfort in the fact that their number never changed, but she resented that they were still there, a keepsake from his affair.

Their own courtship had been too swift and all-consuming to necessitate letters back and forth. Instead, their first months had been full of flowers and treats and time spent together. Hugo would pick her up in his Frazer Nash Fast Tourer, whisking her away from the back roads of Maida Vale to the theater in the West End, supper at the Ritz, or dancing at The 43 on Gerrard Street—sometimes all three in one evening. Then there were the parties hosted by his school friends that featured lashings of champagne and caviar, wild dancing, and cavorting of all kinds. On Hugo's arm, she'd been drunk on a kind of glamour she'd only dreamed of.

He'd carried her along with him on a wave of love and excitement that hadn't stopped when they'd married. If anything, he'd been even more perfect, pulling her deeper into his world until, one day, she began to notice he sent her fewer bouquets. Their holidays were no longer spent mostly in bed, drinking one another in, but rather with a gathering of Hugo's friends, who played tennis, swam, and drank with equal fervor. It was the natural way of things, she told herself, this sinking into the comfortable routine of a married couple. He was busy at his surgery, and she had plenty of things to occupy her time. They still were invited everywhere. They still made a handsome couple.

It had been enough, until she'd learned of his infidelity.

She shook her head. There was no time for that sort of thinking now. She had an appointment to keep.

Sylvia opened the door of Mrs. Shelton's Fashions, the familiar bell jangling to announce her arrival. No one was in the front of the shop. Uncertain whether or not she should allow herself through to the back rooms, she lingered, taking in the dressmaker's form on display. It was clothed in the same solid, dependable type of dress her mother had been turning out for years. It was the sort of thing that sold well to an older, conservative clientele, if memory served, neither highlighting nor hiding the body too much. She cocked her head to one side and decided that it was . . . fine. Unexciting, uninteresting, and perfectly fine.

"You're here."

Sylvia turned to find her sister watching her from the door to the back.

"You've oiled the hinges," she said, nodding to the door. "It always used to squeak when it opened."

"We have put some work into the place since you left," said Izzie.

Sylvia's heart broke a little at her sister's sharpness. She hated how stilted every conversation between them seemed, full of weight and meaning. She felt like a general with a battlefield map, trying to figure out what each sentence might mean, how it would be interpreted and twisted to deepen her sister's disdain for her.

She cleared her throat. "Perhaps you'd like to tell me what you need my help with."

Izzie rolled her shoulders as though preparing to do something odious. "Why don't you come back? We can sit in Mum's office."

She followed her sister down the narrow passageway to the back of the shop and through the door to the workshop. The whir of the sewing machine stopped as Miss Reid looked up.

"Hello," she said with a nod to the seamstress before glancing around with a frown. All of the other machines were empty. It was strange. She remembered the workroom as a vibrant space, filled with work and chatter punctuated by the hum of sewing machines and the snip, snip, snip of dressmaker's shears.

Without a word, Miss Reid lifted her nose and went back to her sewing, the thrum of the machine filling the lonely space once again.

When Izzie opened the door to Mum's office halfway, Sylvia's stomach sank. Every surface was covered with paper. There were shoe boxes spilling over with receipts, books crammed so full that their pages no longer closed properly, and what looked like order sheets everywhere. The bookcases that had once housed neat rows of box files she'd worked so hard to order were stuffed to the brim with all manner of things.

"Watch the door," said Izzie as she entered sideways.

"Doesn't it open any farther?" she asked.

"No."

Sylvia angled her body to slip in, staring at the mess around her in despair.

"I haven't had a chance to properly tidy since the funeral," said Izzie quickly.

"It looks just like it did when I started doing the accounts. Do you know how long it took me to put everything in order and set up a system that our mother could follow?" she asked.

"It's just a little messy," said Izzie, immediately defensive. "Mum had a lot of things to do, and so do I."

Sylvia picked up what looked like an invoice. It was for fourteen yards of patterned cotton lawn ordered from Liberty of London and dated nearly five years ago. There were none of the marks on the top that Sylvia had used to keep track of when an invoice had been received, whether the goods were acceptable, and when it had been paid. Looking at it, she couldn't tell whether her mother had seen it let alone settled it.

"I left our mother with clear instructions—"

"Fourteen years ago," Izzie cut her off. "You can't expect everything to be the same after all that time."

Sylvia pursed her lips, not wanting to admit that it felt strange that Mrs. Shelton's Fashions hadn't remained frozen in amber just as she'd left it.

"And why do you keep calling her 'our mother'?" Izzie continued. "You used to call her Mum."

"You can't expect everything to remain the same. Didn't you just say so yourself?"

Izzie sniffed before shutting the office door and scooping up a pile of papers off one of the two wooden chairs squeezed into the small space in front of their mother's desk.

"You're not going to take her chair?" Sylvia asked, nodding to the worn leather chair behind the desk.

"No," said Izzie.

A petty part of Sylvia thought for a moment about taking the chair for herself, but then she remembered all of the times she'd seen her mother in it, hunched over the books or counting out notes and coins to make a deposit at the bank. Instead, she sat facing her sister, primly crossing her ankles and folding her hands one over the other.

They sat for a moment in silence, the only sound the ticking of old pipes in the building's walls. Finally, Sylvia asked, "What did you want to see me about?"

Izzie seemed to brace herself. "Have you read the newspaper this morning?"

"I haven't had the time," she lied. The truth was that until Izzie's telephone call she hadn't even emerged from her bedroom because she'd been waiting for Hugo to leave. Mrs. Atkinson had only just brought her first cup of tea when the telephone rang. The paper, which was usually laid next to her place at the table when Hugo was not at home, had been untouched.

"Then you don't know?"

"I don't know what?" she asked.

"I'm being conscripted."

Her brows shot up. "What?"

"All women between twenty and thirty are being conscripted. I need to register by mid-month. You do too, actually—you're under forty—but you won't be required to serve. At least not yet."

They couldn't call Izzie up. They just couldn't. Her sister was meant to be here at Mrs. Shelton's Fashions, the one place in the world Izzie loved.

But instead of saying all that, Sylvia asked, "What about the shop?"

Izzie started to speak but then stopped herself.

"Perhaps Miss Reid could take it on?" Sylvia asked.

Izzie shook her head. "Not Miss Reid. She's already working flat out as it is. If we want to have any hope of staying open, it's vital that she remain focused on sewing."

The way Izzie said "we" didn't pass Sylvia by, but she pressed on. "Then you'll need someone from the outside. Perhaps I could help you hire someone."

"I can't hire someone. There isn't time, and besides"—Izzie cleared her throat—"I don't know if we could afford to pay another member of staff."

"Is the shop not doing well?" she asked with surprise.

Izzie shifted in her seat. "I don't know."

"Haven't you had the chance to look at the account books yet?" she asked, looking around.

"I haven't found them." Izzie opened the top drawer of the desk, drew out a ledger, and dropped it on the desktop. "Until then, you're welcome to work through the orders and try to make sense of it."

Sylvia's stomach soured. "What do you mean, 'make sense of it.'"

"It looks as though Mum kept a good record of orders, but I have no idea what expenses have been paid. To find out what the business actually has by way of funds will require going through orders placed, inventory, invoices, and wages and reverse engineering the lot," said Izzie.

"But she must have been keeping records. How else would she know how much she has to pay in tax?" she asked, panic rising in her voice.

"Sylvia, I can't even find Mum's post office savings book to see what she had in her personal account."

Sylvia stared at her sister, aghast. "What happened?"

Izzie sighed. "The war. We were doing well enough, I think, then war broke out and two of our girls left to join up. They said they wanted their choice of service. Clever of them, really.

"Then rationing started and everything became harder. Orders began to slow when people started to have to use coupons."

"Can the business even survive?" Sylvia asked.

"Yes, of course it can," Izzie snapped. "We still have orders from our loyal customers. Maybe not as many as before, I'll grant you, but business will pick up again once rationing ends."

"And when will that be?" she asked.

Izzie's expression hardened. "We just have to weather things for a little bit longer."

Sylvia sat back heavily in her chair. "Did you know?"

"What?" Izzie asked.

"Did you know before Mum died how dire things had become?"

"Things are not dire, Sylvia." Izzie sniffed. "And this line of questioning does not solve the problem of me having to go off to serve."

"No. No, of course not," she said, backing away from the topic. "Could you do it?"

"Do what?"

"Run Mrs. Shelton's," said Izzie.

She stared at her sister. "Are you serious?"

"You said yourself that you practically used to run the business for Mum."

She held a hand up. "I did not say that. I said that I did the accounts. There were a number of things that Mum never let me do. I wouldn't know the first thing about running a dress shop."

"Miss Reid can take care of the customers," Izzie insisted. "She might not like it, but she'll become accustomed to it. You would only need to pay the bills as they come in."

Sylvia began to shake her head. "You know that's not true, Izzie. Making sure that a business stays on its feet, especially when we have no idea what the state of it really is? That's a huge job. I'm not the right person for it."

"But Sylvia, there isn't anyone else."

For the first time since Sylvia had spoken to Izzie by their mother's grave, Izzie sounded defeated.

"Is there really no one else?" Sylvia asked.

"No one."

She sighed. "Tell me how you think it would work." When Izzie straightened, she added, "I'm not saying that I will do it. Just explain it to me."

"Right," said Izzie, taking a deep breath. "I have to register and then wait to be called up. I don't know when that will happen. I can work up until that moment and leave you notes or, if you really think that it would help, you could come in a few times and I could show you where things are.

"Then, while I'm serving, we can write each other. You can send me questions about anything I haven't explained, and I can tell you what to do. You don't have to do much," Izzie promised.

A plan that simple would never be foolproof. There would be problems at the shop that needed sorting, or Miss Reid would need guidance, and Sylvia would inevitably find herself back where she had been at eighteen.

But then she thought about Hugo, who had been so dismissive

when she told him about her inheritance. Hugo, who had turned up his nose at anyone in "trade," managing to insult Izzie, their mother, and Sylvia in the process. Hugo, who hadn't even had the decency to offer her his condolences when she'd told him that her mother had died.

She looked up and found Izzie watching her with an expression that was at once guarded yet desperate.

"I suppose that all of this means that the sale is off," Sylvia said.

"Only until the war ends," said Izzie.

"Fine," she said.

"Fine?" Izzie asked, her eyes widening.

"I'll do it. I'll run the shop. We can correspond via letter, and whenever you can take leave, you can come and check up on me, since I know you'll be itching to do that."

Izzie gave a little laugh of disbelief. "You really mean it?"

"Don't you?"

"Trust me, if I had any other options, I would have exercised them. You're certain Hugo won't object?"

Oh, she had no doubt that her husband would have all manner of objections, but she had no intention of telling him. His assignment in London was temporary, and soon he would be off on whichever base or ship the Royal Navy decided needed him.

"Leave Hugo to me," she said.

There was a pause as they simply stared at one another.

"I feel as though we should shake hands or something," she said.

"I don't think that will be necessary, do you?" asked Izzie.

"No." Sylvia sighed. "No, I don't suppose it will be."

Instructions for Running Mrs. Shelton's Fashions

1. The shop is open from ten o'clock to five o'clock Monday, Tuesday, Thursday, and Friday, and from ten o'clock to two o'clock on Wednesday and Saturday. On days you are expecting deliveries, it is best to arrive by no later than eight o'clock in the morning. Please be certain that all deliveries are cleared from the shop floor and the dressing room before any customers arrive.

2. There are two books that are vital to running the shop. One is the appointment book and one is the order book. All appointments go into the appointment book and then are confirmed the day before by telephone. If a lady wishes to place an order, either by coming into the shop or by telephone, her order is noted down in the order book. You can also, at this time, schedule her first fitting. Please be sure to speak to Miss Reid before agreeing to any expected timeline for the completion of an order so that she may be certain that the work can be done in a timely manner.

3. There is a box in the workroom in which we keep cards that detail all customers' measurements. Miss Reid will no doubt do most of the work measuring the ladies, but please do be discreet and never suggest that what a lady tells you her measurements are may not be accurate based on the information on her card. It is always best to insist that remeasuring is our policy for each new garment.

4. You will, of course, be familiar with the coupon system for clothing rationing as a customer; however, it is a little more involved as a business. All coupons must be noted down and then cross-checked against the Board of Trade's records. This is vital. Any error could bring an investigation into the shop's business practices. The last thing we need is to be accused of working with the black market.

Chapter Ten

I zzie closed the latches on her case and straightened. She looked around her bedroom. This flat had been home for as long as she could remember, and it felt wrong to leave it.

She picked up her orders from off of the bed. She was to report to Innsworth in Gloucestershire, where she would join her fellow new members of the Women's Auxiliary Air Force. The orders had come faster than she'd imagined when she'd stood in the queue at the recruitment office and declared her preference to join the WAAF because that was the service that Miss Bell and Miss Parker had left Mrs. Shelton's Fashions for, and a secret part of her liked how exotic anything to do with airplanes felt.

Then, shortly after she'd registered, Japan had attacked Pearl Harbor and the United States had entered the war. On the same day that she received her orders, the Americans joined the war against Germany. Everywhere she went, it seemed that people were abuzz with the news that the Yanks would join the fight. The war was again inescapable.

Izzie folded her orders and tucked them into the pocket of her jacket. She'd worn her best suit even though she knew it wouldn't really matter. Once she arrived on base, she would no doubt be issued the uniform that she would wear for who knew how long. Still, it felt right to leave the shop dressed in her best, a tribute to Mum's insistence that the Shelton women always be well turned out no matter where they went.

She lifted her case and let herself out of the flat, locking the door behind her. The last time they'd met, she'd given Sylvia a set of

THE DRESSMAKERS OF LONDON • 81

keys along with those for the shop in case something went wrong, but she doubted her sister would ever venture upstairs. Although Sylvia had seemed intent on listening to what Izzie had had to say during those awkward afternoons of training, Izzie couldn't let herself believe that her sister really cared what happened to Mrs. Shelton's. Still, what other option did she have?

She made her way down the stairs and stopped. The interior door leading to the shop was ajar. She was certain she hadn't left it like that the previous night, because she hadn't wanted to give herself an excuse to go back inside, certain that if she did, it would be impossible to leave.

She was about to close the door when it swung wide and Sylvia appeared, still wearing her hat, gloves, and that enviable mink.

"What are you doing here?" Izzie asked.

"I'm going with you to the train station," said Sylvia, as though it were the most obvious thing in the world.

Izzie bristled. "I'm perfectly capable of taking myself."

Sylvia sighed. "No one is saying you aren't, but I woke up this morning with the strange feeling that if the last time I saw my sister during this war was over an old ledger, I'd regret it. Strange, I know, but it's the truth."

"So you broke into the shop?" she asked.

Sylvia held up her copy of the key. "I let myself in. Apparently that's something I'm meant to do now, no later than ten o'clock in the morning."

"Nine o'clock," she corrected. "Earlier if you need to be here for deliveries and—"

"I know. I know. You've already told me all of this *and* left me extensive instructions so I don't manage to run our mother's shop into the ground within the first few days," said Sylvia. "I did work here too, you know. I remember our mother's rules."

"It's been so long, I thought you would have forgotten," she said.

"I've tried to, trust me," said Sylvia with a weary smile. "Now, come along or you'll never catch your train."

"You really don't have to come," she said.

Sylvia reached out to grasp her hand. Izzie started at the shock of it, but Sylvia didn't let go.

"I'm going with you, Izzie. The matter's settled, and there's no use in trying to change my mind," said Sylvia.

"Fine. We'll take the bus."

She waited to see if her sister balked at the suggestion of taking something so humble as the bus, but Sylvia simply nodded in the direction of the door and said, "Lead on."

The sisters didn't speak much on the bus ride from Maida Vale to Paddington Station, but that didn't bother Sylvia. She was there, and that was the most important thing.

Izzie didn't want her company—that much was clear—but Sylvia had kept imagining her little sister surrounded by dozens of other girls heading for Innsworth as friends and family embraced them and tearily told them to stay safe while Izzie stood alone.

The bus pulled up to a curb and Izzie began to gather up her things. "This is us."

She followed Izzie as they squeezed down the aisle and stepped off onto the pavement in front of the station. The day was cold, a wind whipping around Paddington and creeping between the seams of her coat. She pulled the collar of her mink a little closer.

"Where do you suppose I'm meant to go?" asked Izzie, looking around as though the train station was completely foreign to her.

Sylvia realized that she didn't know whether Izzie had ever left

London outside of their summer day trips to the seaside when they'd been children. She herself had certainly never stayed in a hotel before she'd met Hugo, because there had hardly been anywhere to go and little money to spare. Maggie Shelton had had no family to speak of, and Papa's family had made it clear that they were not interested in seeing their son's widow and daughters.

"Which is your train?" Sylvia asked.

"The 10:04," said Izzie.

"Let's go in and check the boards."

This time Sylvia forged ahead, weaving through people at the station entrance and into the station hall. It felt as though the entire world was at Paddington. Fresh-faced young soldiers with nary a crease in their uniform mixed with those who had the haunted look of men who had seen too far much over the past two and a half years. Mothers clung to children's hands, a reminder of the mass evacuations that had taken place right as the war started and then again after the Blitz, and older men wore the uniform of the Home Guard with pride.

Sylvia stopped in front of the board and scanned until she saw it. The 10:04 train.

"Platform ten," she said, trying to push down the panic tightening her chest.

What was she doing? She was supposed to be answering correspondence before bathing and dressing ahead of taking tea at her neighbor Mrs. Bellington-Norton's flat, not standing in the middle of a train station, waiting to put her little sister on a train.

Every worry she had pushed aside while Izzie had trained her rose in her throat at once, choking her. Parliament might have put a ban on women serving in any role that resembled combat, but that didn't mean that WAAFs and other women weren't in danger all the time. Bombs and bullets and shrapnel didn't discriminate.

Clearing her throat, Sylvia did her best to smile. "Right, I'm sure we can find platform ten somewhere—"

"Sylvia."

She gestured over Izzie's shoulder. "I think, if memory serves, it's just over there beyond—"

"Sylvia, stop! Why are you doing this?" Izzie demanded.

She took a step back. "Why am I doing what?"

"This!" Izzie cried, sweeping her hand back and forth between them. "Taking me to the station. Playing at happy families."

"But we *are* family. You're my sister."

Her little sister, the girl who had toddled after her when they were children, who had always wanted to do whatever Sylvia was doing. Four years the elder, it had been Sylvia who had comforted Izzie after Papa's death when their mother had been too distracted with worry about how they could possibly live without his salary, let alone with the crippling interest on his debts. Sylvia had found Izzie shaking with fear when her sister had had her first monthly courses and had shown her how to wear a belt and what to do with her cloths. She'd been there for Izzie's first date with a spotty boy from two roads over whose mother had her clothes made at the shop, and it had been Sylvia whom a tearful Izzie had come to after spotting that same boy kissing another girl a week later after he hadn't even tried to kiss Izzie.

That that little girl was now going off to war petrified Sylvia.

"I appreciate you taking care of the shop while I'm gone, but I do not need you to escort me any farther," said Izzie.

Sylvia scrambled for a way to explain but found herself falling short. She didn't know how to speak to her sister with the frankness she once had without plunging them into the middle of an argument.

Finally, she said, "I thought you might want the company."

"No. You thought that because Mum died and I need you, you

get to be my sister again," said Izzie, her voice icy enough to freeze the entire ticket hall.

"I've always been your sister," she protested weakly.

"You chose to stop a long time ago," said Izzie.

Sylvia's natural defensiveness rose up in her. She'd done what she'd had to do, hadn't she? She hadn't had Izzie's and her mother's talent. All she'd had was youth and beauty and the good luck to meet a man who had loved her enough to overlook her background.

If the roles had been reversed, she was certain Izzie would have done the same.

Still, looking at her little sister with her case in her hand, waiting to board a train to join the WAAFs, she couldn't bring herself to start that fight.

"I know you don't believe me, but I'm trying to do the right thing," she said.

Izzie closed her eyes for a moment as though finding strength. "I appreciate you coming to the train station with me. However, I think we should say goodbye here."

Sylvia swallowed back the emotion rising in her throat. "Whatever you think is best."

Izzie stuck out her free hand. "Goodbye."

She took her sister's hand. Leather gloves brushed each other, a brief squeeze, and then it was done.

"Good luck," she said, stepping back. "I'll write to you."

"Thank you."

Sylvia watched her sister walk away, people swallowing Izzie up.

She stood there, staring after her sister until well after the 10:04 train had blown its whistle and pulled out of Paddington on its way west.

Part II

19 December 1941

Dear Sylvia,

I have thought of a few vital things that I neglected to put in my notes before I left.

Mrs. Thomas is meant to come in for the final fitting on Tuesday, but it is noted down in the book as Monday because she was confused when she telephoned and rang back while I was fitting a customer. Please ensure that Miss Reid is aware so she can be prepared.

Miss Keynes might come in soon to pick up a skirt. Mum was rather lenient on when she settled her account due to Miss Keynes being on her own, and you can expect Miss Keynes to make good when she can. (There could be more, but that is what I have gathered from the order book.)

Do not forget to telephone Harbour & Farrow Mills to inquire whether they will have any fawn tweed this season. We are running rather low and it's far more appealing than the dark stuff that they saddled us with last time we ordered from them. I know there's only so much selection on offer at the moment, but really, they can do better than that.

Please write me back soon and with news of how things are going at the shop.

Sincerely,
Isabelle Shelton

---

22 December 1941

Dear Izzie,

Happy Christmas if this letter reaches you in time!

How are you? How are you settling in to your training? Is it simply dreadful or are the other girls nice? I imagine that joining the WAAF would be something like going back to school but with rather more war involved. And airplanes, of course.

I wonder if you'll meet a nice man in blue. The Royal Air Force really does have the best uniforms . . .

Since it has only been three days since you left, there is not a great deal to report. I do appreciate your note about Miss Keynes. I shall use a firm but polite hand with her because really she must pay. And you did note down the fact that Mrs. Thomas's appointment was now on Tuesday, never fear. I imagine that you forgot amid all the excitement of leaving for your training.

Miss Reid continues to be a source of great jocularity and general good spirit in the workshop. Just yesterday she deigned to speak to me in order to ask me to pass her a seam ripper she had left on the cutting table as I was passing through the workroom. Of course, she did first ask me if I knew what a seam ripper was, as though I don't have one in my own mending basket at home . . .

Don't fret too much about the shop. I know that you will no matter what I say, but I want you to know that it is in safe hands with me.

Yours,
Sylvia

————————

Happy Christmas from us to you

Dear Izzie,

I hope this card finds you well. I am wishing you all of the best this Christmas and into the New Year.

Yours,
Sylvia

————————

27 December 1941

Dear Sylvia,

Happy Christmas. As you can imagine, it was not the cheeriest of holidays, being in a training camp, but some of the other girls in my Nissen hut made the best of it by stringing up paper chains and singing carols as we coaxed as much heat as we could from our little stove. We also had something approximating a Christmas meal in the mess, although I cannot say that Christmas pudding improves when it is cooked by WAAFs on a training ground.

Please be kind to Miss Keynes. She really is a dear old thing, and she's been a customer for so long. I know that Mum would have wanted her to be treated with some leniency.

Did you telephone Harbour & Farrow before Christmas? Keeping in close contact with our suppliers really is vital—even more so than it is in peacetime!

Sincerely,
Isabelle Shelton

————————

30 December 1941

Dear Izzie,

Yes, I managed to speak to Mr. Farrow from Harbour & Farrow just before they closed for the Christmas season. Once we cleared up an initial bit of confusion that I am, in fact, your sister, we got on a treat. He is going to send us fifty yards of dark gray tweed that I'm sure you will approve of, and he won't charge us a shilling for it.

(This is a joke. He has ten yards of fawn that he thinks he can hold for us, which Miss Reid tells me should be enough for Mrs. Chapman's skirt, and Mrs. Webb's suit, should she decide to finally have it made up.)

I've been spending a great deal of time at the shop because I have quite the challenge ahead of me sorting through the paperwork in the office and trying to bring some order to it. I'm particularly interested in finding the bankbook or a checkbook—anything, really, that would give me an inkling as to how our mother was running the financial side of the business before she passed.

As you might imagine, organizing the office alone is a monumental task, but I have no doubt that I am up to the challenge, especially with Hugo away again. (He was home earlier in December for meetings, but the Royal Navy was rather Scrooge-like and forced him to return before Christmas, which is why he did not sign our Christmas card to you.)

I forgot to write and tell you that before we closed for Christmas, Miss Reid asked if there was any news from you about your training. It went something like this:

Miss Reid, at her machine: Have you had a letter from Miss Shelton?

Me, crossing the workshop to go to our mother's office: Why yes! She wrote me just yesterday.

Miss Reid: How is she getting on then?

Me: I don't know. I shall ask her for you.

It was—I would have you know—the most pleasant exchange we have had since you left. So you see, Izzie, it would be a great help to me if you would send some news so that I can continue to encourage Miss Reid to speak to me. Whatever the censor will allow through will suffice. We are waiting with bated breath.

Wishing you a happy New Year,
Sylvia

Chapter Eleven

With a harrumph, Izzie let her hand holding her sister's letter fall into her lap. Sylvia had written hardly anything about the shop, spending most of her time on jokes that weren't particularly funny, criticism of Mum's organization of the office, and demands that Izzie write to her news from camp.

She scanned the letter again.

So you see, Izzie, it would be a great help to me if you would send some news so that I can continue to encourage Miss Reid to speak to me.

"Your glare could burn a hole through that letter."

Izzie's head jerked up. She'd come to the base's NAAFI, a canteen of sorts where servicemen and women could pay a few shillings for some comforts like a cup of tea and the luxury of a moment's peace that could not be found in a cramped hut she shared with three dozen other girls. She'd intentionally chosen an empty table away from everyone else, but apparently her efforts had been for naught, because now a tall, grinning woman in an ill-fitting uniform stood in front of her, one hand on her hip and the other holding a cup of tea.

When she realized that the woman was looking at her expectantly, she cleared her throat. "It's just a letter from home."

"Ah, I understand those. I swear that if I receive another note from Mamma about the horrors of having the house taken over by the army, I'll scream," said the woman cheerfully. "Not that she should complain, when the army has allowed Daddy and her to stay on in the old dower house."

The army? A dower house? Where on earth did this woman live?

The woman stuck out her hand. "Aircraft Woman Second Class Alexandra Sumner. How do you do?"

Izzie cautiously extended her own. "Aircraft Woman Second Class Isabelle Shelton."

Alexandra gave a nod to the letter Izzie still held, sending her tight blond curls dancing merrily around her face. "Is it very bad?"

Izzie looked down at the letter and sighed. "No, it's not that. It's just . . . it's from my sister."

"You have a sister?" Alexandra brightened. "I've always wanted a sister."

"I'd be happy to give you mine," Izzie muttered under her breath.

Alexandra laughed. "Is she a nightmare?"

"Yes," she said bluntly.

"What has she done?" asked Alexandra, dropping into the chair opposite Izzie, clearly settling in for a story.

"I wouldn't even know where to start."

"Why don't you begin with that letter?" suggested Alexandra before taking a sip of her tea.

"I own a dressmaker's shop. Or technically, *we* do. My mother died and left it to both of us, but I'm trying to buy Sylvia's half from her," she said.

"A difficult inheritance. It's a tale as old as time," said Alexandra with a serious nod.

Despite her initial shock at Alexandra's attention, Izzie couldn't help but smile. "I don't know if I would call it that; it's just that Sylvia hasn't really been interested in the shop at all since she left at eighteen."

"Did she run away to join the circus?" Alexandra asked, clearly hoping Izzie would say yes.

This time Izzie laughed. "Does that ever happen outside of books and films?"

"I don't know. I hope so. It would be frightfully exciting," said Alexandra.

"Well, Sylvia didn't do anything nearly that daring. She married a man I can't stand."

"The plot thickens. Is he an utter beast?" asked Alexandra.

"I call him 'Horrible Hugo,'" she admitted.

"The villain. Tell me, why do we detest him?" asked Alexandra.

Izzie leaned in. "He's a snob. He always looked down on Mum and me."

Her companion made a sound of disgust. "Why did he marry your sister if he's such a snob?"

"She's always been the beautiful one," Izzie started. "She still is."

"So are you," said Alexandra.

"I have mousy hair that refuses to hold a set most days, a nose that's too big for my face, and thin lips. I am not beautiful," said Izzie, shaking her head to emphasize the point.

"No, you look like Joan Fontaine in *Rebecca*. I can very easily imagine you transforming from cardigans to that chic black dress that beast Maxim tells her to change out of because he doesn't understand the first thing about glamour," said Alexandra before adding, "But I can tell that no amount of arguing will convince you, so why don't we return to the matter at hand: the letter?"

Izzie sighed. "When I had to register, I realized that there would be no one to mind the shop if I was called up. I couldn't see any alternative but to ask Sylvia. She's old enough that she didn't have to join up, you see. Only I think it might have been a terrible mistake."

"Why is that?" asked Alexandra.

Izzie made a face. "I thought I could help her run the shop by writing back and forth, but she's never going to be able to do it. There are so many little things to know, like how Mrs. Beecham likes a good ten minutes of chat before you go about the business of her fitting, and if you hurry her she will be insulted. Or what about Mrs. Lang? Her bills are paid by a Mr. Talworth and not her husband, so it is vital that we send the delivery to the Lang household but *never* with the bill. Oh, and if Miss Birch 'pops in' one afternoon and orders an entire new wardrobe while smelling of gin, it's worth double-checking any order by telephone the next morning to confirm that she does, in fact, want the clothes."

"That does sound like a great number of things, but why can't you simply answer her questions when she writes to ask them?" asked Alexandra.

"Sylvia thinks she knows everything, and she's far too proud to ask when she needs help. Instead, she's insisting that I write about my news from Innsworth."

"That is generally how letters work," said Alexandra.

"But that isn't what we agreed upon at *all*," said Izzie, her frustration growing. "Sylvia made it clear as day that she wanted nothing to do with Mum and me after she was married."

"Was that her decision or this Horrible Hugo fellow's?"

"I'm certain Hugo didn't help," Izzie conceded, "but ultimately the decision was Sylvia's."

It had started the moment Sylvia told Izzie she was engaged. Izzie had been thrilled—what fourteen-year-old wouldn't be delighted that their beloved, beautiful sister was to be married to a man who had swept into their lives like a fairy-tale prince?—but then Sylvia had begun having tea with Hugo's mother, who had a great number of thoughts about how the wedding should proceed. Suddenly every conversation was about what people would *think* and how Hugo's family friends would expect this or that from the ceremony. Izzie had listened to it all, slightly in awe of the family her sister was marrying into, until it came to the dress and the bridesmaids. Then Izzie understood that Sylvia had changed—and not for the better.

"Sylvia wants to pretend that the last fourteen years didn't happen," Izzie said.

"Do you think she could be a little ashamed of what she did?" asked Alexandra.

"What do you mean?" she asked with a frown.

Alexandra shrugged. "Sometimes people come to regret the decisions they made a long time ago."

"Not Sylvia. She knew exactly what she was doing when she met Hugo."

"I'm sorry, Izzie," said Alexandra. "Families are tricky things."

Izzie sighed. That they were.

"What does your family think about you becoming a WAAF?" she asked.

"Oh, they're all in favor of it. Daddy is mad for flying. He flew in the last war. I think if they would let him, he'd be up in a Spitfire in a flash—not that Mamma would allow it. She says it's bad enough having three sons in the RAF," said Alexandra.

"Three sons?" Izzie asked in surprise.

Alexandra pulled a face. "Yes. I have the misfortune of having three older brothers. Awful, all of them, although I love them all to pieces.

"Having brothers is a real nuisance. They're enough worry when there isn't a war on. I've told all of them that if they manage to get themselves killed, I'll be very cross and will haunt them for the rest of time. They had the audacity to point out that hauntings generally don't work like that. Rascals." Alexandra glanced at her watch. "Do you fancy another cup of tea?"

Izzie opened her mouth to say yes, but something made her hesitate. They might wear the same uniform, but everything about Alexandra, from the cut-glass polish of her accent to her dower house, told her that they were from very different worlds. How would they ever have enough in common to make it through another cup of tea's worth of conversation?

"I should write Sylvia back," she said, stuffing her sister's letter back in its envelope.

"Oh." For a moment, there was real disappointment in Alexandra's face, but then, just as quickly, her sunny smile returned. "Of course you should. You have a shop to manage."

As Izzie walked away she couldn't help the temporary tug of doubt that settled low in her stomach. She glanced over her shoulder back at Alexandra, who remained alone at the table, toying with the handle of her teacup. She recognized that look. It was the same one she'd worn as she watched her fellow seamstresses at Mrs. Shelton's Fashions bundle up in their coats, chattering about which film or dance they would go to that evening. No one ever invited Izzie, because she was Mrs. Shelton's daughter.

She'd told herself that she didn't care. Proving to Mum that she was capable of running the shop was more important. Yet that hadn't stopped the creep of loneliness as she walked by pubs cheerful with full tables or stepped around gaggles of women spilling out of cinema doors after a film.

And now, knowing that Mum hadn't trusted her enough to leave Mrs. Shelton's Fashions to her, she had to ask herself if it had all been worth it.

Next time Alexandra asked, she decided, she would say yes to that cup of tea.

5 January 1942

Dear Sylvia,

You have asked me to write to you about my camp and training. Here it is—or at least what I can tell you without bringing out the censors' black pen.

Everything runs to a routine here. There are about thirty girls to a Nissen hut, and we are woken every morning by a bell. We jump up and into our clothes for physical training. A WAAF NCO named Corporal Murphy runs us through our drills. Sometimes it is things like calisthenics. Other times we are made to run. Then we shower and dress again before going to the mess for breakfast.

You might be surprised to learn how much of the rest of our day is spent in classes. Apparently there is a great deal to learn when becoming a WAAF. We have lectures on how to use our gas masks and what horrible sorts of things will happen to us if we're not fast enough. We've learned about the RAF ranks, how to address an officer, and how to keep our equipment.

I shall stop myself there because I doubt that the censors will thank me for listing too many more of the specifics. Suffice it to say that it feels as though I am back in the schoolroom—which is not what I was expecting when I registered.

Despite all of the routine and the strict rules around when we are meant to do things, we do have some free time. We have a "make do and mend" period in the afternoons when we are meant to care for our uniforms and generally ensure that our bunks and hut are kept clean and tidy.

Now, I hope that you will agree I have written a great deal about my time here on base—enough even to satisfy your curiosity. Will you please do me the favor in return of telling me how things are faring at the shop?

Which customers have been in recently, and what have they ordered? Have you managed to smooth things out with Miss Reid? I know she is a prickly character, but Mum always insisted that she has a heart of gold.

Please send me news. I'm desperate to know what is happening at the shop.

Sincerely,
Isabelle Shelton

Chapter Twelve

ylvia stood in the shop's inventory cupboard, clipboard in hand, surrounded by bolts of material. It was, she knew, a luxury to have so much fabric already on hand given the extreme restriction on rationing. However, thanks to Miss Reid's explanation, she'd learned that all of this fabric posed two problems for Mrs. Shelton's Fashions:

1. The Board of Trade's restrictions precluded them from selling garments made of certain materials like silk, which was meant to be used for parachutes.

2. All of this beautiful fabric represented money that was sitting in the shop's inventory that could have been used elsewhere.

Sylvia hadn't intended to find herself anywhere near the inventory cupboard when she'd agreed to help Izzie mind the shop. It certainly hadn't come up in her sister's training. However, she'd spent most of Christmas all alone in her flat with only her thoughts and the wireless for company. Finally, on the twenty-seventh of December, as London began to emerge from its Boxing Day haze, she'd dressed and boarded a bus for Maida Vale. She'd unlocked the shop, closed the door behind her, and breathed deep, taking in the scent of wool and beeswax polish. Then she'd pushed off the door and returned to her mother's office to continue tackling the monumental task of sorting out the mess of paperwork.

Almost without thinking, Sylvia had come back the next day, and then the next. When Miss Reid had returned to work after the New Year, the seamstress had raised a brow at the sight of Sylvia using the wide cutting table to sort out receipts and invoices from years past. Sylvia had waited for the inevitable comments and criticisms to start, but instead Miss Reid had gone to her machine and begun working on seaming a gray wool dress.

Two days later, Sylvia had found a post office savings book stuffed in the back of her mother's lower desk drawer and, after opening it and seeing the balance of just over £462, a sense of dread had washed over her. Years ago, when she'd taken over doing the books at Mrs. Shelton's Fashions, Sylvia had insisted that her mother stop mingling her business and personal accounts.

"You might think it's easier now, Mum, but just wait until the taxman comes asking to look at the shop's books," she'd argued.

Maggie Shelton had pulled a face, but Sylvia had finally convinced her to go to a bank and open an account just for the business. Then, each week, she'd walked her mother's profits to the bank to make a deposit, earning her mother's grudging thanks when it had come time to work out and pay the shop's taxes that year.

She'd assumed that system must have remained in place, but when she saw such a high balance in the post office savings book, that old fear crept in again. Had Maggie been blending her accounts?

Sylvia continued to search, separating bills for the electricity and water from materials, empty envelopes with totals written on the front of them that she feared had once held notes and coins from scraps of old women's magazines she suspected had been kept for inspiration. A few loose sketches went with a clothbound sketchbook that had been stuffed into a bookshelf.

It was while organizing invoices by year that she quickly realized she had no idea how her mother or Izzie had kept track of what fabric they had in-house and how much had been used on various orders. The shop, she was learning, was like a jumper: pull one loose bit of yarn and the whole thing could unravel.

She checked a tag on a bolt of burgundy bouclé wool and noted down the starting and remaining yardage of the material. She remembered standing on a stool at about twelve years old, reading off the markings to her mother as they performed this task. She'd been desperate then to do anything to please her mother.

"Mrs. Pearsall?" came Miss Reid's voice from outside the closet.

"Yes?" she called back.

Miss Reid stuck her head around the door. "Are you still taking inventory?"

"Yes," she said with a sigh. "I don't know the last time it was done."

Miss Reid looked around her at the disordered cupboard. "Mrs. Shelton used to insist on it being done each month."

"And how long ago did she stop?" she asked.

Miss Reid pursed her lips. No doubt unwilling to criticize the good mother in front of the bad daughter, the seamstress said, "You asked me to let you know if Miss Keynes telephones."

"I did," she said.

"Well, she's standing in the front now, wanting to pick up her order."

"I see." Sylvia set her clipboard down. "Thank you, Miss Reid. I'll take it from here."

"May I ask what exactly you are planning on doing?" Miss Reid asked.

"I'm going to have a discussion with Miss Keynes about her outstanding bill."

She walked around Miss Reid, aware that the seamstress watched her as she went. At the door to the reception, she paused and set her smile.

"Miss Keynes, I believe," she said as she opened the door.

A slender woman in a light tweed suit with dark brown accents at the pockets and lapels turned around. "Yes . . . ?"

"How may I help you?" Sylvia asked.

Miss Keynes tilted her head, not a hair on her elegantly streaked blond-and-gray head shifting with the movement. "I beg your pardon, but I don't know you."

"I'm Mrs. Pearsall, one of the new owners," Sylvia said.

"New owners? But I was expecting Mrs. Shelton or her daughter."

"I'm sorry to have to tell you that my mother died in November," she said, crossing her hands in front of her. "I'm her eldest daughter. My sister, Isabelle Shelton, and I now own the shop together."

At least for the time being.

Miss Keynes's suspicion melted into compassion as she stepped forward, placing a hand on Sylvia's arm. "Oh, my dear. I'm so very sorry for your loss. Your mother had a good soul. She will be dearly missed."

"Thank you," Sylvia said, twisting her body slightly to release herself from Miss Keynes's grasp.

"And your sister. How is she coping?" asked Miss Keynes, craning her neck as though expecting to see Izzie walk through from the back of the shop at any moment.

"She's serving in the WAAF now. I've taken over the management of the shop in her absence," she said.

"How fortunate for your dear sister to have your help. Well, I imagine that you have a great many things to keep you occupied here. I'll just take the skirt I ordered and leave you in peace."

"Of course, Miss Keynes. I'll just ask Miss Reid to box it up for you." She reached to open the door to the back of the shop and found Miss Reid standing right behind it.

"Eavesdropping now, Miss Reid?" she asked in a low voice.

"Well, I never—" Miss Reid began to bluster.

In a voice loud enough for Miss Keynes to hear, she asked, "Would you please box up Miss Keynes's order?"

"But I thought you said . . ." At Sylvia's sharp look, Miss Reid trailed off. "Yes, of course, Mrs. Pearsall."

With Miss Reid dispatched to the back, Sylvia turned once again to her waiting customer. She moved to the front counter, opening up the order book she'd stashed there in anticipation of this moment.

"I can see from our records that you've been a loyal customer of Mrs. Shelton's Fashions for many years," she commented, not hinting at the hours she'd spent poring over her mother's scribbles to decipher the extent of Miss Keynes's orders. While the office might be a mess, Sylvia had been grateful to learn that her mother at least marked down who had paid and whose bill was still outstanding.

"Oh yes, I've been coming here for eight, maybe nine years," said Miss Keynes. "Your mother always appreciated the old ways of doing things. I've had my clothes made since I was a little girl. None of these department store dresses for me."

"I'm very glad to hear it." She ran her finger down the page to the number she'd tallied, checked, and checked again. "I believe you will find that, including today's skirt, your bill stands at forty-three pounds and four shillings."

Miss Keynes gave her an indulgent smile. "Thank you for reminding me. I shall be certain to stop by my bank the next time I come in. I was thinking about a green dress in wool—"

"Miss Keynes, I'm afraid I really must insist that you settle your account today," Sylvia said firmly as Miss Reid came through the door and placed the white box tied with the shop's signature blue ribbon on the counter.

Miss Keynes tittered. "Well, I can't do that, my dear. You see, I don't have the necessary funds on me at the moment."

"The banks are open for another"—she glanced at her watch—"four hours. I'm certain that should give you sufficient time to withdraw the money."

"But I couldn't possibly make it to my bank and back in that time! It's practically across town!" cried Miss Keynes.

"Perhaps Miss Keynes would be able to write a check," said Miss Reid, her expression inscrutable.

"Thank you, Miss Reid, but I think we would much rather settle the bill in bank notes. If it's all the same to you, Miss Keynes," said Sylvia.

Miss Keynes reared back. "Well, I never."

"You are, of course, most welcome to come back tomorrow to pay the account in full." Sylvia placed her hand on the box. "We would be happy to keep your skirt safe until then."

Miss Keynes's gaze fixed on the box. "Your mother was always very understanding . . ."

"I'm afraid that this shop is no longer able to extend lines of credit to our customers. We are asking all our ladies to settle their outstanding accounts. You understand, given the uncertainty of the world we live in now," she said with a smile.

"I supposed I could pay for the skirt now," Miss Keynes muttered, unclasping the gold top of her handbag.

"That would be most appreciated, but I'm afraid that given the size of your debt, I must insist that you settle the bill in full before we can release this skirt to you." An idea dawned on her, so she added, "I should also mention that all future orders will require a deposit equal to half the price of the garment as well as the appropriate number of clothing coupons before any work can begin. The rest of the payment should be made upon collection."

Miss Keynes looked between her and the box and then back to her again. "This is most distressing. I'm certain your mother would not approve."

"Unfortunately for all of us, my mother is no longer with us," she said.

Miss Keynes's hand flew to her chest. "My goodness . . ."

"If you would like me to write an invoice for the full amount with an itemization of the clothing items that have not yet been paid for, I would be happy to do so," Sylvia finished with a sweet smile.

Miss Keynes clutched her handbag to her stomach as though she thought Sylvia would rip the thing from her. "That will not be necessary. You will have your money within the week."

"I'm certain that I will," she said.

Miss Keynes sent Sylvia one last horrified look and then scurried out of the shop.

When the bell at the top of the door fell quiet, Sylvia turned to Miss Reid and said, "Well, we shall see if she's good to her word."

"What if she doesn't bring the money?" asked Miss Reid.

"Then I will speak to her one more time, and if she still will not pay, I will speak to the bailiffs," she said, closing the order book.

"She's been one of your mother's best customers for many years," said Miss Reid.

"What she has been doing is virtually stealing from my mother for many years. We are no longer taking orders from her until her account is paid in full," she said firmly, picking up the box.

She could hear the clatter of Miss Reid's shoes on the wood floor of the passageway behind her.

"Your mother never required deposits," Miss Reid called out.

"That was my mother's business, not mine," she said, pushing open the workroom door with her hip. "Things change."

"Have you written to your sister about this? Requiring a deposit may offend some customers," said Miss Reid.

She walked through the open door of her mother's office and set the skirt box on a free spot on the increasingly neater desk. Then she turned back to Miss Reid, placing her hands on her hips.

"Then that is a fact that our customers will have to accept," she said.

"I really don't think—"

She held up both hands. "Miss Reid, I am going to be frank with you. Mrs. Shelton's Fashions is teetering on the edge. How badly it's teetering is still a mystery to me, but what I've found so far is not good.

"If things do not change, there will be no more orders to make up. There will be no more wages for you. There will be no more shop for my sister to come home to. I can understand why you might not believe me when I say this, but I do not want that to happen. However, to avoid that, we cannot continue to do things the way that we've always done them. We are carrying all of the costs of doing business up front when we have no deposit at the commissioning of a garment outside of clothing coupons. It makes no sense."

Miss Reid crossed her arms. "And what if all our customers leave us for other dressmakers? Business has been hard enough to come by with rationing in place."

"Then we will find new customers. Ones who will pay."

"How?" asked Miss Reid.

Well, that was the question, wasn't it? Still, she might not yet know how to transform the shop's fortunes, but she knew that it would not be helped by allowing the likes of Miss Keynes to take advantage of the Shelton women's kindness.

"Just ready yourself for all of the new orders that will pour through those doors, Miss Reid."

The seamstress sniffed but retreated to her sewing machine without another word.

Once she was alone, Sylvia let out a deep breath. She would figure out a way to make this all work. She had to.

In the meantime, she had every intention of returning to the inventory cupboard and figuring out how to break the news of the Miss Keynes incident to her sister.

Chapter Thirteen

"I should not have to remind you how important it is that you take these aptitude tests seriously, ladies," Corporal Murphy said from her position at the top of the column of women lined up for daily drills. "It is imperative that the WAAF and the RAF know the full extent of your skills so that it can be decided how you will be best deployed."

Over her weeks at Innsworth, Izzie had been told over and over again that the women of the WAAF were vital for freeing up more men to train as pilots, navigators, and bombers. Women would take the places of mechanics, cooks, drivers, and orderlies. There would be WAAFs in charge of armories at various bases across the country, and it would be WAAFs who would work in bomber command as plotters keeping tabs on the many RAF planes that flew operations nightly.

Despite all the talk that a WAAF could be called upon to do anything, she knew that any officer would take one look at her skills and background and assign her to a tailor's shop on a base. She would spend her war sewing on patches and repairing uniforms.

She tried not to think about how uninspiring that all sounded. Mum might have kept a close handle on everything going on at the shop, but each customer coming in had presented something new and different to work on. The designs might not have been Izzie's own yet, but at least it had been real sewing and not a sort of assembly line of mundane tasks.

A quick movement out of the corner of her eye caught her

attention. She glanced over in time to see the blond top of the head of the posh woman who'd spoken to her a few days ago—*Oh, what is her name? Allison? Amelia?*—dip down below the rest of her row. Then, the woman—*Alexandra!*—stuffed something into the patch pocket of her uniform tunic.

Alexandra caught Izzie's eye and shot her a conspiratorial grin before turning back to attention.

When Corporal Murphy finally dismissed them, Izzie wove her way through her fellow recruits to Alexandra, who was clutching at her tunic with her right hand.

"Is everything all right?" she asked.

Alexandra pressed her free hand to her lips, repressing a giggle. "I looked down while Corporal Murphy was speaking and realized that a button had popped off my shirt and was lying at my feet. It must have worked its way down below my tunic belt somehow. It's lucky I saw it, or who knows how long my unmentionables might have been on show once I'd taken off my tunic."

Izzie couldn't help but laugh. "It's a good thing you spotted it."

Alexandra dug into her pocket and held the shirt button up. "The only problem is, now I have to sew it back on, and I'm all thumbs when it comes to a needle and thread."

Whether it was out of the goodness of her own heart or to repent for not having accepted the offer of a cup of tea from Alexandra when they'd spoken in the NAAFI, Izzie didn't know, but she said, "Well, we can't have you running around like that. Come with me, and I'll fix it."

"Oh, would you? I'd be ever so grateful," said Alexandra in a rush.

"Like you said, we can't have your unmentionables on show for the entire base to see."

"I knew this would happen, you know," said Alexandra as she followed Izzie back to Izzie's hut. "I even told the quartermaster when they issued me a uniform that the shirt wasn't the right size, but she told me that every girl loses weight during basic training. I suppose she didn't realize just how prodigious the bosoms of the women in my family are. It's almost a thing of legend.

"On top of that, they gave me a man's tunic because the quartermaster said it was the only thing on hand that would fit me in the shoulders. Naturally, that means that the rest of the tunic is so large I'm practically swimming in it."

"It's ridiculous that we're two years into the war and they're still struggling to make proper uniforms for women," Izzie said.

"They called us up, but they weren't ready for us," Alexandra agreed.

Izzie held open the door to her hut for Alexandra and then hurried over to her bunk, where she'd stored a basic kit of sewing supplies in a tin that was small enough to fit in her kit bag.

"Right, let's see what the damage is," she said.

Alexandra peeled off her jacket, revealing a shirt that gaped to show off a flash of peach silk trimmed with French lace.

"One more button lost and I might as well end up in one of those clubs I'm not supposed to know my brothers sometimes go to in Soho," said Alexandra with a laugh.

Izzie grinned. "I can sew it back on for you in a jiffy, and later I can take a look at altering all of your uniform to fit you better if you like."

It was going above and beyond, but she couldn't let this poor woman run around with a tunic that looked as though it should fit a rugby player. Besides, there was something about Alexandra's warmth and openness that made her want to help.

"You can do that?" Alexandra asked in awe.

Izzie laughed. "I'm a dressmaker, remember? I reworked my own uniform during my very first make do and mend."

"How clever. I was wondering how it was that that your uniform looks like it fits you so much better than any other girl's," said Alexandra.

Moving efficiently, Izzie cut a length of thread and threaded her needle while Alexandra peeled off her shirt. Izzie took it and set to work securing the button, wrapping the shank, and tying off the thread.

"There you are," she said, snipping the thread and handing the shirt back to Alexandra.

"Thank you!" said Alexandra, sounding utterly delighted. "Do you really think there's anything that can be done to make it fit properly?"

As Alexandra buttoned her shirt, Izzie tilted her head to examine the way it stretched over her chest.

"It won't be regulation," Izzie warned.

"I just want something that fits," said Alexandra.

"I can insert some panels through the sides that will give you a bit more room. And maybe some darts for shape." She nodded firmly. "Why don't you come back here in the afternoon and I'll see what I can do?"

Alexandra pulled on her uniform tunic and then clasped Izzie's hands. "Thank you."

"It's nothing."

"It isn't. I appreciate it."

"You go," Izzie said, blushing a little. "I'll tidy these things away."

As Alexandra rushed off and out of the hut, Izzie couldn't help but feel that, for the first time since she'd arrived at Innsworth, she might have made a friend.

"Is someone knocking?" asked Gladys, the girl with the bunk across from Izzie's later that afternoon.

"Hello!" called out Alexandra, sticking her head inside the door of the hut. "Permission to enter?"

Izzie, who had been idly drawing a floor-sweeping gown that would never pass rationing, set aside her pencil and sketchbook and waved. "Over here."

Alexandra, who was holding a spare uniform shirt and her tunic in her hand, hurried along the rows of beds. "Hello. I hope that this is still all right."

"Absolutely. Why don't we start with your shirts first? It seems like they're in the most need of attention," she said.

Alexandra obediently stood, arms held slightly out, while Izzie took up her tailor's chalk and began to mark where she wanted to insert the panels on each side.

"Right, that one is done. Why don't you pop the other one on?" she said.

"Who taught you how to do all of this?" asked Alexandra.

"My mother. She worked for a tailor before she met Dad, but she stopped working after they married. He died when I was seven and left us without any income. She opened the shop because she really didn't have any other choice," said Izzie, standing back to check the fit of the shirt. "That one's done too. Why don't we look at your tunic?"

Alexandra put on the tunic and said, "That must have been difficult for your mother."

"It was," she said, reaching for a box of pins and beginning to lift and pin the shoulders on the tunic to correct the fit. She would have to chip in the shoulders, which would require a bit of work, but it would make a world of difference.

"Mum loved him very much," she continued. "She was devastated when he died. My sister was too. She's a few years older than me, so she remembers him far better than I do."

"Sylvia is your sister?" asked Alexandra.

She smiled. "You have a good memory."

"It can be terrible when someone dies unexpectedly," said Alexandra. When Izzie looked up at her sober tone, Alexandra blushed and said, "My father's older brother died in the last war."

"I'm very sorry to hear that," said Izzie. "Lift your right arm, please."

"On top of losing his brother, my father had to take on an entire set of responsibilities that he never anticipated would be his."

Izzie nodded and placed a couple of pins along the side seam of Alexandra's tunic. When she'd begun helping her mother take customers' measurements, she'd quickly learned that a dressmaker's shop was not just a place where dresses were made. It was where many women revealed their deepest secrets and insecurities. It was also vital that, no matter how intense her curiosity, a seamstress never push a customer to divulge anything that woman didn't wish to say.

"If you could lift your left arm now," she said.

Alexandra did as she was told, and Izzie set about pinning to match the right side. Then she stood back to check everything. "Lift your arms to shoulder height and cross them in front of you. I want to be sure that you have enough room in the shoulders."

Alexandra followed her instructions. "It feels good."

"How is the length?" she asked.

Alexandra peered down. "A little long, I think."

"I agree," she said, folding the hem. "About here?"

"Yes," said Alexandra.

After she'd pinned the hem, Izzie stepped back again. "It needs a little shape. If you're willing to risk Corporal Murphy's wrath, I can add a couple of darts at the bust."

"Would you?" breathed Alexandra. "It would be wonderful to feel more like a woman and less like a sack of potatoes."

Izzie laughed and traced out where the darts should go.

"There. You're all done," she announced after a final check.

"Thank you. When do you think you'll start?" Alexandra asked.

"I can start on the shirts tonight, if you like. That seems to be the most pressing need after this morning," she said.

"That would be wonderful. What will I owe you?"

All at once, something in Izzie deflated. She wasn't at the shop, and she hadn't thought once about charging this charming, guileless woman. She'd only offered to help because she'd wanted to.

Immediately, Alexandra seemed to sense something was wrong. "I've offended you. I'm very sorry. Sometimes I just put my foot straight in it."

"You didn't offend me," said Izzie quickly.

"I did, and I'm very sorry," said Alexandra putting a hand on her forearm. "I really am."

There was such genuine feeling in the other woman's apology that Izzie gave her a small smile. "Why don't you buy me our next cup of tea at the NAAFI, and we'll call it even."

"That's far too little for the work you're doing," argued Alexandra.

"Two cups of tea then."

"Three cups of tea and chocolate to go with each. You choose the time and the place," said Alexandra, sticking out her hand.

Izzie laughed and shook her hand. "You drive a hard bargain."

"I really should go. I must tidy my bunk for the next inspection, or I'll be sent to the brig."

"Do they do that to WAAFs?" Izzie asked.

There was an amused sparkle in Alexandra's eye. "I shouldn't like to find out."

As soon as Alexandra was gone, Izzie began to tidy her sewing things away into their tin.

"Well, isn't that a turn-up for the books."

She looked up as Gladys rolled over, wide-eyed, and said, "You've been so quiet, Izzie, I didn't know that you knew Lady Alexandra."

"*Lady* Alexandra?" she asked.

"You don't know?" asked Gladys.

"Evidently not."

"She's the daughter of some earl or another. You'd think that they would have put her in some sort of officer role, but maybe they're waiting until she's out of training," said Gladys.

"Are you talking about Lady Alexandra?" asked Valerie, whose bunk was two down the row. "I heard she was here, but I thought she would be more elegant than *that*."

"She's perfectly elegant, and not only that, she's my friend. I won't hear another word against her," said Izzie fiercely.

Valerie raised her hands. "I never meant any offense."

When Valerie turned her back, Gladys leaned over the gap between Izzie's bed and her own and said, "That serves Valerie right. She's the most frightful gossip. You should hear some of the things she says about the girls."

Izzie simply stared at her, hardly able to believe that Gladys was passing judgment on another woman's tendency to gossip.

"I heard you talking about altering Lady Alexandra's uniform," Gladys continued. "Could you do the same for me?"

Izzie opened her mouth to say no but then she stopped herself. Gladys wanted her uniform altered, and why shouldn't she?

"Yes. I can do that."

Gladys grinned. "Thank you! I hate how the skirt bags around my waist. I keep having to haul it up on parade."

"I'll need to finish Lady Alexandra's things first, but then I can take in your skirt. It will probably come to a few shillings, but I'll give you a proper price when I take a look at it."

"Oh, thank you!" Gladys chirped again.

Izzie turned back to her bunk, a slow smile spreading across her face as she realized she'd just figured out a way to earn a bit of money toward the purchase of the shop while she was a WAAF. As her mother had always said, every little bit helped.

7 January 1942

Dear Izzie,

I was beginning to worry that you hadn't gone off to training to be a WAAF but instead were conducting a wild love affair with a devastatingly handsome man who had convinced you to run off with him. (Perhaps an American. I imagine we'll begin to see some of their kind on our shores soon, given that they're now in this wretched war.)

I am both disappointed and heartened to find out that you have, in fact, been diligently working to become a WAAF! I can't decide if all the drills and classes you've been put through sound like fun or hard work. Either way, I imagine that you are doing just fine for yourself.

As an acknowledgment of the great sacrifice you have made in writing to me about something other than the shop, here is my report.

Miss Reid continues to be a great source of joy and optimism in this dark time. Just the other day she said "Good morning" and "Good evening" unprompted. By the end of the month, she may voluntarily inquire after my health and comment on the weather. What she does not know is that I fully intend to stack the proverbial deck in my favor by plying her with cups of tea made with leaves that have only been steeped once before. I am also considering paying her outrageous compliments about her sewing to see if that will spark any hint of a smile.

Aside from my impressive progress with Miss Reid, I think you will be pleased to hear that I have dealt with the Miss Keynes situation. There were a few tense moments when she came into the shop on Tuesday to pick up her skirt. However, I boldly held it hostage and told her that she would not be having it until she had paid the balance of her account. She was almost as horrified as when I told her that moving forward she would also be required to pay a deposit of half at the commissioning of any future garments and pay the balance when she picked up the garment. (This is a policy I have decided to put into place for all customers, not just Miss Keynes.)

As you can imagine, the lady was not pleased that I had taken a stand against her bad behavior and she went away in a huff. However, by the end of the working day she had returned with forty-three pounds and four shillings, which you will be happy to know clears her debt entirely. She made some noise about never being treated so poorly in her life, but she left with her skirt, so I imagine she is happy enough.

After the roaring success of dealing with Miss Keynes, I have begun to ring round to the ladies holding our other delinquent accounts—or at least the ones I could find in the shop's records. (Did you know that Mrs. Lang's account is not paid by her husband but by a Mr. Talworth? What a scandal if that ever made its way out among the housewives of Maida Vale!) There has been some grumbling and some complaints about the war making things so much more difficult, but I am happy to say that most of the ladies have seen sense and agreed to settle their accounts.

By my calculations, we should be up nearly five hundred pounds in uncollected payments by the end of the fortnight. It is not a sustainable business strategy, naturally, but every little bit helps.

As I have been sorting things out, I've been thinking about what you said about customers not coming in as much as they once did because of needing to hoard one's coupons. While we certainly face a challenge with how many garments our customers can purchase each season or even each year, surely there is no reason we can't increase the number of customers to the shop. To that end, I must ask if you have ever considered taking out advertisements? Miss Reid deigned to speak to me enough to tell me that she doesn't remember our mother ever trying advertising. I thought perhaps we could place a notice in _The Lady_ or the _Tatler and Bystander_—or both? I suppose _Vogue_ might be a bit ambitious right now, but I don't see any issue with dreaming of one day.

I should also mention, I found some old correspondence from a Mr. Manon, the man at the bank who helped me open the shop's account before I left home. Did you ever hear our mother mention Mr. Manon from Whitmore's or the account more recently? The letter I found was two years old . . .

Yours,
Sylvia

10 January 1942

Dear Sylvia,

Oh, I wish you hadn't done those things! Miss Keynes has been a customer of Mrs. Shelton's Fashions for so long that we should show her some grace. Mum trusted that she would eventually clear her account because she always has. Now she might very well take her business somewhere else and we will have lost a customer who has been with us for so many years!

I hope you are joking about ringing around to the women who have unsettled accounts. There are reasons that none of those bills have been paid. Money is tighter than it ever has been for everyone, and we can't know what the ladies who patronize the shop may be going through.

Mum always believed that a woman should be well dressed no matter what her situation. She would never have approved of the idea of holding our customers up for money like we are highway robbers in a penny novel. She would have wanted us to extend understanding and grace to these women rather than bully them.

Also, I should not have to say this, but it is vital that you not speak to <u>anyone</u> about who pays Mrs. Lang's bills. She is a well-respected member of the Women's Institute and she does the flowers for her church. If the scandal were to get out it would be awful. You must promise me that you will not tell a soul!

Sincerely,
Isabelle Shelton

P.S. I don't recall Mum ever mentioning Mr. Manon. Bookkeeping and designing were the two things she never relinquished control of, even in her final months.

13 January 1942

Dear Izzie,

Calm yourself. I promise that I did not bully a single one of our customers. (Well, perhaps Miss Keynes, a little bit, but that was only because she was so bold-faced about what she was doing.) All I did was ask for payment that was past due—sometimes nearly a year past due—for work that had already been done. It is what any other business owner might have done if they had found themselves in the same unfortunate position.

I understand that our mother was grateful to the ladies who have been customers for years. However, you cannot deny that these same women have been taking advantage of that generosity. Payment whenever suits the client is no way to run a business. A shop cannot continue to be a shop if there is no income. Plain and simple.

With the new rules I have put into place regarding deposits and payment, we should no longer have this issue, and I can refocus my thinking on other aspects of the shop.

I have decided that I am going to take out advertisements promoting the shop in several of the local papers. I am hoping that will drive new business from ladies who are interested in using their coupons on something a little more interesting and unique than what they can find in the department stores. My only concern is that Mum's patterns are a little tired; however, I'm certain that Miss Reid can work some of her magic to refresh them.

Don't worry about where the money for the advertising will come from. I've decided to use some of my pin money toward it. There's little else that one's allowed to buy these days.

Yours,
Sylvia

P.S. Did you know that there is a Mrs. Talworth on our books as a customer as well? I wonder if that is the same Mrs. Talworth as Mr. Talworth, Mrs. Lang's clothing-purchasing paramour . . .

Chapter Fourteen

Sylvia snuck a glimpse at her watch as she hustled as quickly down South Audley Street as she dared in her heels. She'd had every intention of making it to Lady Nolan's meeting in good time, having planned to arrive ten minutes early to join the other ladies of the committee as they mingled and sipped cups of tea. However, when she'd opened the shop that morning, there had been no electricity. Given that she and Miss Reid were expecting Mrs. Chapman for a fitting, followed swiftly by the arrival of a Mrs. Karber, who wanted a new winter dress, Sylvia had marched to the telephone box down the road to ring both women to reschedule their appointments. Then she'd made a long, expensive telephone call to the electricity company to explain in a decidedly stern tone that she had, in fact, paid the shop's bill as Izzie had instructed and that the power should be restored immediately. Many coins later, she'd received the reassurances of a harried clerk that the lights would be back on in no time.

She'd shot out of the telephone booth and into the shop to scoop up her handbag. An agitated Miss Reid had tried to stop her to speak, but Sylvia had called over her shoulder that whatever it was would have to wait until she returned.

Now, after sitting on a slow-moving bus for what felt like hours, she skipped up the three steps to the front door and cranked the old-fashioned bell key. Lady Nolan's housekeeper answered almost immediately.

"Good afternoon," she said breathlessly, daring to hope that the meeting might not have started.

"Mrs. Pearsall, I believe the other ladies began at two o'clock," the housekeeper said as she took Sylvia's coat.

Sylvia's heart sank. She would have to walk through the drawing room, find a seat, and sit down while everyone scrutinized her.

Bracing herself, she followed the housekeeper to the drawing room and waited for the woman to open the door for her. With a deep breath, she pulled her chin back and walked into the belly of the beast.

From her Louis XIV chair at the top of the room, Lady Nolan observed her entrance with a raised brow. "Mrs. Pearsall. So good of you to join us."

Sylvia forced herself to smile even as she felt every other woman's gaze settle on her as she began to round the circle of chairs. "I do apologize for being late."

There was a long pause before Lady Nolan inclined her head. "If you will take your seat, we can begin again."

Naturally, the only chair that was free was all the way on the other side of the room from the door. Sylvia finished her promenade around the backs of the other ladies' chairs and primly took her seat.

Claire shot her a querying look, and Sylvia shook her head, trying to convey to her friend that everything was fine even if she couldn't help feeling rising embarrassment at having drawn the wrong sort of attention to herself.

"As I was saying," Lady Nolan began, "the food bank proved to be a great success, especially in the East End, where people are still struggling after the bombings. Additionally, the Christmas coat drive showed promise, although—understandably, perhaps—the number of coats donated was far fewer given the clothing ration. People appear to be hoarding their clothing. Quite selfish of them really."

There was a murmur of agreement from the other ladies that Sylvia thought was rather rich given how many women had recently shown up to these committee meetings wearing an array of coats from their extensive prewar wardrobes.

"Now, I have spoken to several organizations that we have previously worked with," continued Lady Nolan, "and they all agree that, while the distribution of food and clothing is important, what war widows really need is monetary donations. To that end, I would ask that all of you turn your thoughts to how we might go about raising money for relief aid this spring."

There was another murmur of agreement, and Sylvia unclipped her handbag to retrieve her notebook and pen. She'd found that these days, if she didn't write things down, they slipped from her memory as soon as they entered it. However, far from being annoyed at the development, she embraced it. The shop and its many tangled problems provided a welcome distraction from Hugo.

As soon as he'd left London just before Christmas, she'd started her dutiful weekly letters once again, telling him that Izzie had been caught up in the recent conscription orders but leaving out any mention of the shop or its sale. She'd written him again on the twenty-second that she wished him a happy Christmas and saying that she'd sent his mother and father a card, forging his signature so that it would look as though he'd signed it when he'd been in town during early December. It was such a farce—she suspected that the card she received from the senior Pearsalls also contained a forged signature from Mr. Pearsall—but it seemed like the thing to do. To keep up appearances and pretend that everything was normal.

Normal . . . Her mind skipped over the word, like the needle of a gramophone over a deep scratch. What was normal about a husband who failed to write and let his wife know he'd be coming home—even if only for a short while? Who could conduct an affair with such brazenness and arrogance that he kept letters in such an easily discoverable place? Who at the worst of times made her feel as though she should be grateful that he had ever condescended to pay her any attention at all.

Once, she'd thought his love would be enough to sustain her through anything. Now she wasn't so sure.

———————

The rest of the meeting passed without incident, and when Lady Nolan finally dismissed the ladies of the committee, Sylvia began to gather up her things, her mind already turning to the shop. She was just shutting her handbag when Claire approached.

"Is everything all right?" her friend asked, eyes wide with concern.

"Yes, of course. Why wouldn't it be?" she asked.

"Well, the way you rushed in . . ."

"Time ran away from me," she said, edging around the truth. Claire might be her friend, but Sylvia had never dared divulge the entire truth of her background to her. It wasn't that she was ashamed of Mrs. Shelton's Fashions exactly—why would she have put so much work into the shop recently if she was?—but she had a certain reputation to uphold as Hugo's wife.

"You should be careful," her friend said, glancing around to make sure no one could hear them. "Apparently, in the summer before the war started, Lady Nolan had a stern word with Mrs. Miller after she was late three meetings in a row. She threatened to expel Mrs. Miller even though Mrs. Miller claimed her tardiness was due to her obligations volunteering to help refugees."

Sylvia flushed remembering the way that the harried Mrs. Miller had burst into Lady Nolan's drawing room on a stream of apologies. At the time, she'd sat there with great superiority, thinking that the woman should give more care to managing her diary.

Now Sylvia wished she'd done something—anything—to show the other woman that she understood, because Mrs. Miller had quietly dropped the committee shortly after the war broke out, and Sylvia hadn't seen her since.

"There's no need to fret. I don't intend to make a habit of being late," she said.

"Good." Claire glanced at her watch as they left the drawing room. "If we go to Claridge's now, we can have tea and then stay for champagne."

"I'm sorry, I can't this afternoon," she said, as Lady Nolan's housekeeper settled her coat onto her shoulders. She needed to go back to the shop to make sure the chaos of the morning had abated, the lights were back on, and nothing else had gone wrong in her absence. Miss Reid was there, but the seamstress had made it very clear what she thought of Sylvia taking an afternoon off when the entire point of the shop closing early on Wednesdays was to package orders and take care of all manner of business.

Claire laughed. "Oh, don't be ridiculous. Where could you possibly need to go at four o'clock on a Wednesday?"

She set her lips in a thin line. "I'm sorry, I really can't. We'll have tea soon."

She gave her friend a little wave as she hurried back down the road to the bus stop that would return her to Maida Vale.

16 January 1942

Dear Sylvia,

I don't know if you are intentionally trying to be provocative, but you are doing a very good job at it. Mrs. Shelton's Fashions only exists because of Mum, and it will only remain a shop that she would be proud of so long as we maintain her very high standards of service and quality. They might seem strange to you, given how long you have been away from the business, but things are the way they are for a reason.

I know you think you are being generous and perhaps a little clever in considering advertisements for the shop, but it won't work. Last year, right after the ration came in, I convinced Mum to let me place an advertisement in the local newspaper because I thought that perhaps we could bring new customers in and make up for the restrictions on what women could buy. Nothing came of it. Not a single new customer said that she'd seen the advertisement.

I know that you will likely hate hearing that Mum might have been right, but in this she was. Women go to their neighborhood dressmaker. (Or worse, a department store.) They won't travel across London for a service that they can find closer to home.

Trust me on this, Sylvia, and save the money.

Sincerely,
Isabelle Shelton

P.S. Yes, Mrs. Talworth is a customer of the shop, but she hasn't been in for a number of months because she has been with child. I shouldn't have to mention this, but if she does ring for an appointment, please make sure there is no possibility of Mrs. Lang also coming in on the same day.

_____

19 January 1942

Dear Izzie,

I might not know a great deal about running a dressmaker's shop, but I do know that a business cannot survive if it does not have paying customers. I am still sorting through the accounts—it is a more monumental task than I imagined it could be—but everything that Miss Reid tells me confirms that we have lost many of those customers who supposedly were so loyal to Mrs. Shelton's. We need new women coming through the door and spending their money and their precious coupons with us. There is nothing else to it.

Advertising <u>will</u> work. I appreciate that you may not have had the success you hoped for when you placed your advertisement last year, but I want to try. I will use my own funds, if necessary.

Please believe me when I say that. I really do want to try to help this shop and hand it back to you in a better state than you left it. It feels as though it's the least I can do.

Yours,
Sylvia

P.S. I would not dream of allowing Mrs. Lang and Mrs. Talworth to meet, you have my word. However, could you imagine the dramatics that would ensue if I did?

------

21 January 1942

Dear Sylvia,

You cannot simply waltz in and change everything about Mrs. Shelton's Fashions because it suits your whim. Mum did things the way she did for the simple reason that they worked. How else would she have built the business from nothing?

Mum had far more experience than I have, and miles more than you do. You <u>must</u> see that.

I appreciate that you are taking the time to straighten out the shop's accounts. However, that is all you need to do.

Sincerely,
Isabelle Shelton

Chapter Fifteen

Izzie pushed her letter into the postbox and prayed that it would arrive at Sylvia's flat before her sister did anything rash. It was quite possible, she was beginning to realize, that asking Sylvia to take over while she was away had been a terrible idea, but what other recourse did she have at the time?

She turned and nearly walked straight into someone. Her hand shot out to steady the other woman, and that was when she realized the woman had a familiar face.

"Oh! Lady Alexandra, I didn't see you there."

Immediately the other woman's expression fell. "So you know then?"

"Know what?" she asked, a little confused before she realized what she'd called the other woman. "Oh, one of the other girls told me. I think I'm meant to call you Lady Alexandra. Is that not right?" It wasn't as though a dressmaker from Maida Vale had frequent enough brushes with the aristocracy that she was completely up on her honorifics and forms of address.

"No, no, it's right," said Alexandra gloomily.

Izzie frowned. "What's the matter?"

Alexandra chewed on her lip. "It's silly, really. I just . . . All of the girls in my hut found out about Daddy, and they started acting a bit, well, funny. I just thought . . ."

"No one was mean to you, were they?" Izzie asked sharply.

"No, nothing like that," said Alexandra.

"Then what?" she asked.

Alexandra heaved a sigh. "It's little things. They stop talking when I walk into the hut. If I queue up for a shower, everyone will step out of the way."

"They're treating you differently."

Alexandra nodded. "It's silly, really, but I was educated at home, and there aren't many girls my age nearby. I thought I might meet other women during the Season, but then, of course, court presentations were suspended when the war began."

"You're lonely," said Izzie, understanding more than her new friend could probably know.

"I suppose it sounds ridiculous. Daughter of an earl, lonely. Why should anyone want to spend any pity on me?"

"It doesn't matter who your father is, you can still be lonely. I should know."

Alexandra looked up. "Really?"

"Yes." It surprised Izzie a little bit that she really believed it to be true. Her circumstances might be different, but what friends did she have outside of the dress shop other than Willie? When she'd been in school, it hadn't really mattered, because she'd had Sylvia at home. But when Sylvia left, Izzie's world had shrunk down to the shop.

"I thought that by joining the WAAF I would fall into friendship with all sorts of girls," said Alexandra. "Didn't you?"

"I was mostly preoccupied with what would happen to the shop," Izzie admitted.

"Oh," said Alexandra.

She hated to see this young woman who seemed to have boundless enthusiasm and a forward sort of kindness to match so down, so she drew back her shoulders and stuck out her hand.

"Aircraft Woman Second Class Sumner? It's a pleasure to meet you. I'm Aircraft Woman Second Class Shelton, and I was just going to NAAFI. Would you like to join me for a little friendly chat?"

Alexandra brightened. "Really?"

"Really. Besides, you owe me a cup of tea, remember?"

Alexandra laughed. "Three cups of tea. I am a woman who always pays my debts."

As they started to walk together toward the NAAFI's entrance, Alexandra asked, "Has the word from home improved at all?"

"Sylvia is making changes."

"What sort of changes?" asked Alexandra.

She told Alexandra about the deposits and payments upon collection. The advertisements and Sylvia acting as a debt collector.

"She's on such a tear, I worry she's going to drive our customers away," Izzie finished.

"What is wrong with asking customers to pay, or with advertising?" asked Alexandra.

"Mum thought it made the shop seem common, as though we were begging for business," Izzie said.

Alexandra cocked her head to one side. "Then how are you supposed to find new customers?"

Izzie shifted uncomfortably. It was exactly what Sylvia had written to her and, if she was being truly honest, what she had wondered when she'd fought so hard to place that advertisement in the paper the previous year.

"Mum believed in the power of our reputation. One woman tells her sister who tells her neighbor that she really must go to Mrs. Shelton's Fashions for her clothes," she said.

"Well, I'm certain that it's a system that works very well, especially if you have such a loyal set of customers," said Alexandra before approaching the counter to order them two cups of tea and two chocolate bars.

As they waited, Izzie chewed the inside of her cheek. Mrs. Shelton's Fashions *had* had loyal customers—and they still did—but it was obvious that far fewer of them were coming in to the shop these days. And the way that Sylvia had written with such relief about retrieving £500 in the unpaid accounts made her wonder just how badly Mrs. Shelton's Fashions had been impacted by the war.

When they were settled at a table, Izzie said, "Perhaps I'm being a bit too harsh on my sister."

"She might have some good ideas, if you're willing to listen," said Alexandra.

"I just don't trust Sylvia. She hasn't had any interest in the shop since she got married—"

"To Horrible Hugo, the man we can't stand?" Alexandra asked, quoting Izzie back to herself. "What it is that makes him so awful?"

"He's always thought that Mum and I were below him."

"Then why did he marry your sister?" asked Alexandra.

She sighed. "She was beautiful, and she was completely caught up in him."

"How so?" asked Alexandra before taking a sip of her tea.

"As soon as Hugo took Sylvia out for the first time, she started to change. She'd always paid close attention to her appearance, but she began to alter how she behaved, how she spoke. Suddenly she had no time for us at home. It was all dancing at nightclubs and going to the theater and spending time with his friends who were far more sophisticated than anyone we associated with—even Mum's customers. It was almost as though she started to believe she was too good for all of us on Glengall Road, but she seemed happy, so I was happy for her.

"Then Hugo asked Sylvia to marry him." Izzie cradled her cup as she stared into it. "I'm her only sister, so you would think that it would be obvious I would be asked to be a bridesmaid in the wedding, wouldn't you?"

Alexandra nodded.

"Well, when she first told me she was engaged she was so overjoyed she started talking about what kind of dress Mum should design me," she said. "A week passes, and Sylvia sits me down. She says that she's had a think and wouldn't it be best if Hugo's friend's wife Claire stood up for her? Sylvia claimed that Mrs. Pearsall, her future mother-in-law, thought it would make more sense for a grown woman to stand up with her. Besides, Sylvia didn't want to burden me with the job."

"But you didn't think being your sister's bridesmaid would be a burden at all, did you?" asked Alexandra gently.

"No. I think Sylvia let Mrs. Pearsall convince her that if I wasn't up there at the altar with her it would be easier to keep Mum and me and the dress shop quiet."

"But you're family," said Alexandra.

"That didn't matter. Sylvia told us that we weren't to talk about the shop at the wedding, and she refused to let Mum make her wedding dress. Mrs. Pearsall took her to Worth instead to find something 'more suitable.' As though Mum wasn't just as skilled as the seamstresses at Worth.

"The entire wedding was terrible. Hardly anyone spoke to Mum and me at the church, and no one seemed to know who we were. But the wedding breakfast was the worst. Mum and I were stuck in a corner of the room, and Sylvia didn't once look our way. We left early."

"I can understand why," said Alexandra.

"Sylvia has always hated the shop. She used to talk all the time about what things were like when Dad was alive. He came from a good family, went to the right sort of schools, knew the right sort of people. He was in his pupilage, training to become a barrister, when he met Mum. She was working as a seamstress at his tailor's, and they met when he came in for a fitting. Mum said that once his suit was finished, he came in the following week for a pair of trousers. Then it was a shirt, a jacket." She smiled. "Finally, when he had nearly an entire new wardrobe, he plucked up the courage when her employer was called to the telephone to ask her to dine with him.

"Mum said that they fell in love so fast she hardly gave a thought to the fact that she hadn't met his family before they became engaged. When she did, she realized that marrying a seamstress was not what the Sheltons had in mind for their only son."

"Oh no," murmured Alexandra.

"Mum and Dad married, and they had Sylvia and me. They were happy until one day Dad was struck down by a lorry on his way home from work," she said.

"How tragic," whispered Alexandra.

It was more tragic than Izzie would admit to Alexandra. She'd only been seven when it happened, but over the years, Mum had given her little snatches of the story until she'd finally been able to piece it all together. The sudden shut-off of income that had sent the family teetering on the line of poverty.

"Mum had no family of her own, so she opened the dress shop out of necessity," she explained. "Without it, I don't know what she would have done."

It was one of the things about her mother she was most proud of. Even in dire straits Mum had managed not only to survive but to build something successful. How Sylvia could turn her nose up at that, Izzie didn't understand.

Alexandra gave an embarrassed little laugh. "And here I was feeling sorry for myself because I sometimes feel awkward speaking to other women because I'm an honorable."

Izzie smiled, appreciating Alexandra's self-deprecation.

"It sounds as though your mother was an extraordinary woman," said Alexandra.

"She was. She taught me everything I know about sewing."

And yet . . .

How often had she shown Mum a sketch of a potential design for a customer only to be turned down? How often had Mum told Izzie she wasn't ready to run the business? How little had Mum really trusted her with that in the end she'd left half the shop to Sylvia?

As though sensing that she needed a change of topic, Alexandra said, "And now you're here."

In a NAAFI, on a training ground, dressed in a WAAF's blues.

"Where do you think they'll send you?" asked Alexandra.

"I assume a tailor's shop," Izzie said. "What about you?"

"I just hope they assign me to anything but cooking, if not for my sake then for that of those who would have to eat my food," said Alexandra.

"It can't be that bad," Izzie said with a laugh.

"Our cook tried to teach me because my mother thought it's a valuable skill every woman should know a bit of. She didn't think she would one day become a countess when she married Daddy, you see. The only problem was, it turns out that even the family dogs wouldn't eat my cooking, and they'll eat anything."

Izzie laughed. "Well, wherever you go, at least you'll have a uniform that fits you."

Alexandra struck a little pose. "I've been asked so many times how I managed to alter it so well, I've been singing your praises."

"That might explain all of the girls coming to ask me to take in and let out skirts," Izzie said. "I should probably give you a cut."

Alexandra shook her head. "I wouldn't dream of taking a shilling. Besides, maybe you can make enough to buy your sister out of the other half of your shop."

Izzie smiled and took a sip of tea. "Maybe I will."

Wouldn't that be something?

21 January 1942

Dear Izzie,

You will be very pleased to hear that our first advertisements touting the excellent work of Mrs. Shelton's Fashions have been placed! I have selected the Tatler, The Lady, Sketch, The Times, and several of the smaller newspapers here in London to begin with. If they are successful, I will consider expanding to Country Life to see if we can attract the horsey set. We certainly have enough tweed for it . . .

Now we wait!

Yours,
Sylvia

———————

22 January 1942

Dear Mr. Manon,

My mother, Mrs. Peter Shelton, was the owner of Mrs. Shelton's Fashions, a dress shop in Glengall Road, and was a long-standing customer of your institution. I regret to inform you that she passed away quite unexpectedly late last year, and I am currently helping my sister, Isabelle, put the shop's affairs in order.

A number of years ago, you assisted my mother and me in opening an account at Whitmore's. Unfortunately, due to some delinquency in the shop's bookkeeping, I am unable to discern whether my mother continued to bank with you at the time of her death. I have not been able to recover any records related to any recent transactions and would appreciate any information you can give me.

Thank you for your assistance on this matter.

Sincerely,
Mrs. Hugo Pearsall

_____

26 January 1942

Dear Izzie,

Since you haven't written back to me, I considered leaving you be. But then I thought, "No. You need to help your sister understand what you're doing and why."

I remember when I was seventeen and eighteen, it felt as though the shop bell never stopped ringing. While I didn't have as much to do as you and the other seamstresses, I was always running round with endless deliveries and helping our mother with inventory and invoices. Mrs. Shelton's Fashions was always wonderfully busy.

You cannot honestly tell me that the shop feels that way now. I don't know if it is the war or our mother's health or simply changing fashions, but it has the feeling of a place that's at risk of being left behind.

I know that it won't mean much to you, but it mattered to me that you asked me to look after things while you are away. I won't let you down.

Yours,
Sylvia

_____

26 January 1942

Dear Mrs. Pearsall,

I am very sorry to learn of the passing of your mother. Please accept the most sincere condolences of myself and everyone at Whitmore's.

Despite the unfortunate circumstances that prompted your letter, I am glad that you have written. I recall you and your mother very well, and for some time I had been attempting to establish a correspondence with Mrs.

Shelton. As you are currently handling the shop's affairs, might I suggest it would be best to discuss matters in person? I will ask my secretary to ring the shop to arrange an appointment.

Your faithful servant,
Geoffrey Manon

---

28 January 1942

Dear Izzie,

Please do not ignore my letters. I understand that you're angry with me, but you cannot not write to me.

Yours,
Sylvia

---

28 January 1942

Dear Sylvia,

I haven't written to you in some time because my orders came in, necessitating a very quick scramble around my hut to pack and bundle myself on a train. I imagine that any post you have sent me in the past few days may take some time to catch up to me, but I will be able to answer any specific questions you may have about the shop as soon as I receive them.

I am not, as I predicted, being sent to work in one of the tailor's shops at an RAF base. Instead, I have been assigned to go on for further training in handling barrage balloons.

The good news for me is that a new friend of mine will be joining me in my training unit. Her full title is the Honorable Lady Alexandra Sumner, daughter of Lord Menby, although she insists that I call her Alexandra.

I imagine that you think it will be a great coup that I have managed to secure a friend with so lofty a rank. However, I can reassure you that Alexandra is nothing like you would expect an earl's daughter to be. She is friendly and open—in fact, it was she who approached me first to chat.

I'm certain that you've met far more distinguished women in the circles that you and Hugo move in, so perhaps you won't be so impressed. However, I hope that you will be happy to hear that I've made a friend.

Sincerely,
Isabelle Shelton

---

30 January 1942

Dear Izzie,

I will admit, I was surprised when I opened your last letter and saw nothing about the advertisements or the shop. I was certain that you would be furious with me for what I've done, but then I kept reading and realized that you probably have no idea what has happened because my letters hadn't reached you yet. I don't know whether to prepare to feel foolish or to brace myself for your anger. I hope that it is neither.

I'm so pleased to hear you've managed to befriend such a lovely woman in the short weeks that you've been away from Maida Vale—never mind the title she holds. Lady Alexandra sounds like a delight, and I'm very glad you've met her.

You mentioned that I might not be impressed that you are mixing with an honorable because Hugo and I must brush elbows with people like Lady Alexandra's family often. The truth of the matter is far more mundane than you think. While it is true that, before the war, Hugo had a great number of distinguished patients, our circle has fewer lords and ladies in it than you might expect.

I sit on the committee of a charitable organization run by a woman named Lady Nolan, who is the wife of a baronet and is at great pains to remind everyone of that fact on a regular basis. There was quite the set of ruffled feathers last year when another member of the committee suggested in a meeting that we invite the Countess of Winman to join us because her husband owns all of those newspapers and her presence might be good for our fundraising efforts. Lady Nolan turned a particularly revolting shade of puce at the idea of no longer being the first lady in the order of precedence, but there was nothing she could do, because the suggestion had been made out in the open, and to turn it down would look vain and uncharitable. So now Lady Winman quietly sits in our committee meetings, and I hardly know what she makes of all of it.

I suspect that if Hugo had his way, we would have every lord and lady he knew to supper.

I must run, but before I do I should mention that I have an appointment with Mr. Manon from Whitmore's in a week's time. I have great hopes that he will be able to shine new light on the mystery of Mrs. Shelton's accounts!

Yours,
Sylvia

[Unsent]

31 January 1942

Dear Sylvia,

I will be the first to admit that my introduction to RAF Titchfield has been a soggy one. It has rained the last ten days straight, and it feels as though we must slog through six inches of mud every time we line up for parade. A few of the bolder WAAFs tried to complain, but our corporal quickly reminded them that the conditions could be far worse wherever they are stationed. How, I don't know, because other bases surely must have snugger accommodation than our Nissen huts, but I didn't dare actually ask.

Miss Reid will be pleased to hear that I have a steady little business here of altering uniforms for my fellow cadets. It started with altering the uniform of my friend Alexandra, and word soon spread to the rest of the camp—

———

31 January 1942

Dear Sylvia,

All of your letters sent to Innsworth arrived at once with the afternoon post as I had just sat down to write to you.

Since you seem intent on ignoring all my advice, all I will say is that if the advertisements fail to bring in any new business, you will have no one to blame but yourself.

Sincerely,
Isabelle Shelton

Chapter Sixteen

A woman in a gray department store suit that didn't quite fit her around the shoulders stopped in front of an office door, knocked gently, and then opened it to announce, "Mrs. Pearsall to see you, Mr. Manon."

Sylvia stepped around the banker's secretary as Mr. Manon rose from his desk and greeted her with an appropriately solemn look.

"Mrs. Pearsall, my deepest condolences," he said.

"Thank you," she said, taking the banker's warm, dry hand.

"How are you and your sister?" he asked. She remembered his kind, gentle manner. He'd handled her stubborn mother, who hadn't really seen the purpose of their visits to the bank, beautifully, and now she realized that just seeing him made her feel as though a weight were lifting off her chest.

"As well as can be. Izzie has been called up to the WAAF, so I am doing my best to manage while she is away," she said.

"We must all do what we can in times like these," he said with a nod. "If you would care to sit."

She sank down into the chair he gestured to, placing her handbag at her feet and folding her hands in her lap.

"I will be frank with you, Mrs. Pearsall," said Mr. Manon, smoothing a hand over the front of his suit before sitting, "I have been concerned for some time about your mother's affairs. It has been nearly five years since she and I have spoken in any significant way, and the last record I have of her making a deposit was . . ." He consulted a paper in front of him. "It looks as though it was November of 1938."

Sylvia's lips parted. Nearly three and a half years was an eternity when it came to a business.

"I tried to contact her several times, both by letter and telephone, but I'm afraid that when I was able to converse with Mrs. Shelton she made it clear that she did not see speaking to me as a matter of great urgency," said Mr. Manon.

"Well," said Sylvia, "I cannot pretend I'm happy to hear that. However, I'm also not entirely surprised. Do you know where she has been banking? The shop has continued running in that time. She must have been doing *something* with the money in all those years."

"I'm afraid that is something I cannot help you with," said Mr. Manon, setting the paper back down.

Sylvia sighed. It had been enough of a struggle to make her mother see sense about the need for a proper account for the business with a proper bank. It was unlikely that her mother had gone to yet another institution to go through the entire rigmarole again years later.

No, if Sylvia had to guess, her mother had been overwhelmed by the bookkeeping and had neglected all of the procedures Sylvia had put into place, instead reverting to her old habits. That meant slapdash accounting, lost receipts, and a mixing of personal and business income in her mother's post office savings account.

After all of her work sorting out her mother's office, Sylvia was facing yet another mess. It felt never-ending.

"I know you said the last deposit was in 1938. Have there been any withdrawals against the account since then?" she asked, holding on to one last shred of hope that her mother might have been sensible and done some basic things like pay her taxes.

Mr. Manon shook his head. "There have been no deposits or

withdrawals from that date. Would you like to close the account? I could have the funds withdrawn for you today."

She huffed a laugh. "It's a wonder there is anything still in there to withdraw."

"A little," he said, that same small smile playing on his lips. "I know what a great help you were to her when you were younger, Mrs. Pearsall."

She could sense the bank manager's sympathy, but she didn't want it. What she actually wanted was to set things to rights, to fix all of the straining seams at Mrs. Shelton's Fashions, because she was not going to be the sister who let it fall to pieces.

She rolled back her shoulders. "Please keep the account open, Mr. Manon. I can promise you that you will begin seeing deposits once again."

"I'm very glad to hear it, Mrs. Pearsall," he said. "Is there anything else I can help you with this morning?"

There were so many things she needed help with, from attracting new customers to finding out why Hugo had strayed, but this man couldn't help her with any of that. Instead, she would have to rely on the one person she'd always been able to turn to. Herself.

"No, thank you," she said, rising to her feet, "but I expect we shall be seeing a great deal more of one another in the near future."

———

After leaving the bank, Sylvia made her way to Glengall Road via a stop at Mrs. Reynolds, Glengall Road's finest—and only—grocer, which was located two doors down from Mrs. Shelton's Fashions. Miss Reid had told her that Mrs. Reynolds had started selling sandwiches five years ago, becoming something of a lunchtime staple in the neighborhood. Sylvia had intended to go in earlier, but between the shop and her committee work, she'd been too busy.

However, going to the bank had been a difficult thing, and Sylvia had always thought difficult things deserved to be rewarded.

She waited patiently until the woman ahead of her in the queue collected her sandwiches and stepped aside. Then she fixed a smile on her face and said, "Hello, Mrs. Reynolds. I don't suppose you remember me."

The grocer peered at her over the edge of her glasses and then said, "Mrs. Pearsall."

The woman's tone wasn't exactly warm, but Sylvia soldiered on. "You do remember."

"How could I forget? You were always stealing oranges off of my stand," said Mrs. Reynolds.

Sylvia shifted from foot to foot. This was not the reception she'd expected. There had been a time just after the Shelton women had moved into the flat above the shop when the widowed grocer had doted on Sylvia and Izzie. She could remember Mrs. Reynolds giving them bits of fruit in the summer and occasionally stopping them on a cold winter's day for a cup of cocoa brewed on the old gas ring in her storeroom.

"I do apologize for the oranges," she said, realizing too late that she was fiddling with the leather strap of her handbag. She forced her fingers to still. "It has been a very long time."

Mrs. Reynolds huffed. "When Miss Shelton said you'd be minding the shop, I couldn't believe it. We all thought you believed you were a bit too good for Glengall Road now."

"'We'?" Sylvia asked.

Mrs. Reynolds crossed her arms over her aproned chest. "Everyone on the road."

"Well, I'm back, so clearly *everyone* was misinformed," she said.

"What do you want then?" asked the grocer.

"Two sandwiches, please."

"What kind?" asked Mrs. Reynolds pointing to a chalkboard. "Everything's written there, except chicken and cress is off."

"Whatever you think looks best." Mrs. Reynolds looked about to protest, so Sylvia added, "I thought I would bring Miss Reid lunch, as she's been working so hard."

The grocer's eyes narrowed, no doubt annoyed at being robbed of the prospect of fobbing off her least appealing sandwiches on Sylvia if one might be for Miss Reid. "That woman must be a saint. She's doing all of the sewing and carrying on the business for your sister as well. I would say that's going above and beyond, wouldn't you?" asked Mrs. Reynolds as she put the paper-wrapped sandwiches on the counter.

"You're right, Mrs. Reynolds. Miss Reid is a saint for everything she does for Mrs. Shelton's Fashions. However, make no mistake that I am the one running the business," she said firmly as she put down her shillings.

"You?" asked Mrs. Reynolds.

"You said so yourself that I'm back to mind the business, and that's precisely what I am doing."

Sylvia dropped her coin purse back into her handbag, scooped up her sandwiches, and left.

When she stepped outside, she found it had started misting with rain. She put her head down and hurried along the pavement to Mrs. Shelton's front door, hoping her hair would hold up for the short trip. She pushed inside, the bell jangling merrily, and let her eyes sweep over the front of the shop. It was neat as a pin, just as her mother had always insisted it be. Satisfied, she let herself through to the back of the shop.

"I'm here!" Sylvia called out as she entered the workroom. "I brought lunch."

However, she stopped short when she saw the expression on Miss Reid's face.

"We have a problem," said Miss Reid, rising from her sewing machine.

Her shoulders slumped. "Another?"

Surely she should be allowed a little time to recover before the next issue reared its head.

Miss Reid picked up a letter that sat open on the worktable and thrust it at Sylvia.

"Normally I wouldn't open the post, but Mrs. Moss, who has a shop in Ladbroke Grove, telephoned while you were out asking whether we'd seen the Board of Trade's new letter. I told her no, and she said we'd want to open it as soon as the post arrived," said Miss Reid.

Sylvia's stomach dropped. One of her mother's fellow dress-makers—and rivals for customers—wouldn't be ringing about a communication from the Board of Trade unless the news was very grave indeed.

She took the letter from Miss Reid and began to read.

It was a notice from the Board of Trade describing new austerity measures called the Making-Up of Civilian Clothing (Restrictions) Orders that were being put in place as part of the utility clothing scheme. The scheme, which had begun the previous year, dictated everything from the kind of wool that could be produced to the prohibition of leather trimmings. However, this went further. The Board of Trade was now telling the women of Britain how many pleats there could be in a skirt and how many buttons on a jacket or coat. Visible trimmings, pockets, and embellishments were out. The number of seams on a garment, the size of lapels, whether buttons could be covered—all of it was subject to restrictions.

Sylvia looked up with alarm. "Surely this can't be real."

"It is. Apparently it's all to save cloth, as though we weren't already doing enough of that," said Miss Reid.

Sylvia kept reading down the page, as Miss Reid muttered, "It's a travesty. What business does the Board of Trade have telling me whether I can have nine pleats or eight in a skirt?"

She sighed. "It looks as though it's two inverted or boxed pleats or four knife pleats according to this."

"It's like they want to strip away every bit of style we have left and run shops like this one into the ground. It isn't right," Miss Reid huffed.

It might have been unpatriotic, but Sylvia couldn't help but agree. It was one thing to restrict the amount of clothing—and therefore cloth—that a person could buy over the course of a year, but dictating how that clothing was designed felt particularly mean in a time when beauty and pleasure seemed in short supply.

"At least the men haven't gotten off completely scot-free," she said with a thin smile. "It looks as though turned-up cuffs on trousers are to be a thing of the past. And the rule about buttons applies to them as well."

"And what of the things we already have in production?" asked Miss Reid. "It doesn't make any sense to scrap everything that's already cut."

"There must be something about that." She shuffled through the papers. "Ah, yes. Here it is. Apparently a general license has been released to allow drapers and tailors to continue to produce garments that are ordered before the first of April or cut before the first of May. That should buy us some time to finish what's already commissioned and underway."

"But it still doesn't account for what we'll do after that," said Miss Reid.

"What do you mean?" she asked.

"None of your mother's designs take the new rules into account. It means that after the first of April we won't be able to make and sell the very clothes this shop was built on," said Miss Reid.

Sylvia's heart began to beat a little faster. "But surely they can be adapted."

The seamstress tilted her head in acknowledgment. "Some of them, but not all. Possibly not even many."

"Why not?"

"It's pure logic, really. Take an accordion-pleat wool skirt. If the government says new skirts can only have four knife pleats, you can't make accordion-pleat skirts any longer. Any pattern calling for that would be useless, and something entirely new will have to be dreamed up in its place. Or what about an eight-button suit jacket that now must be two buttons? The entire front would have to be reconstructed, otherwise it won't close, let alone sit properly on the body. You might as well start again with a new design," explained Miss Reid.

"But you alter clothing all of the time," she said.

Miss Reid crossed her arms. "Alterations work with the existing structure of a garment."

"Can't you create designs from scratch using a pattern block?" Sylvia asked, growing desperate.

"Blocks are really just stencils meant to show how much fabric is needed to cover the body. You still need someone to come up with the concept of a garment, because there is no design to a block." Miss Reid held up her hand. "And even if I wanted to start designing patterns—which I do not—all of that takes time. If I'm occupied with that, who will actually make the clothes?"

Sylvia hated to admit it, but she could see the seamstress's point. Her advertisements had brought a few new orders into the shop, and they needed Miss Reid working on fulfilling those orders to stay afloat.

Calm. It would do no one any good if she did not stay calm.

"What options do we have?" she asked.

"I'll go through your mother's pattern book and adapt what I can, but I suspect it won't be enough. That means you either find someone who can design or we begin to steer customers to the *Vogue Pattern Book*," said Miss Reid.

Sylvia shook her head at the mention of the commercial pattern book. She could still hear her mother saying, "Any fool with a needle can make a dress from a commercial pattern. Women come to Mrs. Shelton's Fashions for good dresses that they won't find anywhere else."

Sylvia might not favor the style of frumpy, old-fashioned cloth-ing her mother produced, but there was no denying that one of the shop's greatest selling points was that the ladies who had their clothes made there wouldn't walk into a room and find another woman wearing the same garment.

If the shop lost that distinction, what would prevent a lady from going to a rival dressmaker? Why wouldn't she take her clothing coupons and money to a department store, where a dress might cost that little bit less?

"We have some time," Sylvia said. "I'll figure it out. I just need a moment to think."

Miss Reid raised a thin brow. "I hope you think quickly, because May will be here before we know it."

7 February 1942

Dear Izzie,

I realize that you may still be angry with me about the advertisements. However, I have some important news that I suspect you will agree is worth putting aside our disagreement for.

Yesterday, Miss Reid and I learned that the Board of Trade has decided to change the clothing utility scheme. It is now regulating the design of new clothing. Everything from pleats to hem length to buttons are affected.

I have copied out the Board of Trade's letter so that you may see precisely what the changes involve. However, the brief summary is this: any excess must go. The new rules are all meant to save cloth, which we are told will mean a great deal to the war effort. Apparently the Board of Trade believes that this war will be won one shrunken lapel at a time . . .

The changes do not go into place until May, and if customers place orders for bespoke clothing before March, they can still be made up in the old way. However, as you can imagine, when the changes do go into effect, many of the designs Miss Reid currently works from will no longer be viable.

Miss Reid assures me (after a great deal of complaining) that she can probably alter some of our mother's more basic patterns and any very simple garments that a client brings in to copy. However, she doubts she will be able to offer anything close to the level of service that our customers have become used to. It will become impossible, she tells me, to give our ladies the full range of the shop's design book to choose from.

I must admit that I don't yet know what we are going to do about this, but I will think of something.

Yours,
Sylvia

_____

10 February 1942

Dear Sylvia,

I had not yet heard about the Board of Trade's changes. Thank you for letting me know.

Are you certain that Miss Reid cannot be persuaded to make up some sketches that will satisfy both our customers' tastes and the Board of Trade's directive? It really doesn't seem like too much of a stretch for a woman of her talents.

Sincerely,
Isabelle Shelton

———————

14 February 1942

Dear Izzie,

If you can persuade Miss Reid to do something that she does not wish to do, you have my admiration. The woman is as stubborn as an ox, but, as you have pointed out before, she is vital to keeping the shop open, so I shall have to do my best to keep her happy.

I will come up with a solution. Just give me a little more time.

I should also let you know that I have done some further investigation into the state of the shop's accounts. The same day that the Board of Trade's new instructions arrived, I went to see Mr. Manon at Whitmore's. He confirmed my worst fears that our mother had not touched the business's bank account in years.

I imagine that you can understand for yourself why that is a very dire thing indeed, and why I felt the need to figure out what our mother had been doing with the money. I believe, after a great deal of sorting out and organizing, that I may have something of an understanding. I found old copies of our mother's post office savings book and, looking through it with the order book side by side, I believe I can point to deposits she made that match up to the income from orders completed every month or so.

I will be honest with you, Izzie, when I realized what our mother had been doing, I nearly began to cry out of frustration. However, crying never did anyone any good, and so I turned my mind to the most pressing matter at hand. The taxman. I have asked William to make inquires on our behalf with the Inland Revenue to find out whether our mother was delinquent on her taxes and whether we will be faced with paying any penalty. It is beyond William's usual role as a solicitor, but I didn't know whom else to turn to.

I know that you won't like to hear that our mother might not have been the best with business matters, but I hope you will look past the fact that I am the one saying this and see that if these things are not addressed, it could be very bad for Mrs. Shelton's Fashions indeed. However, that is what I am determined to do—address them—because you must have so many things on your mind. Leave everything with me.

I hope things are still going swimmingly at that training camp of yours. Whenever I see a barrage balloon flying over London, I think of you.

Yours,
Sylvia

———————

14 February 1942

Dear Mr. Manon,

I realized that I neglected to ask you a rather important question upon our last visit. Would it be possible to ensure that my sister, Miss Isabelle Shelton, has full access to the account we spoke about? I should like her to be able to have all privileges of deposit and withdrawal.

Thank you again for your assistance.

Sincerely,
Mrs. Hugo Pearsall

Chapter Seventeen

I zzie checked her cable for a final time and then stood back from the barrage balloon.

"All right?" asked Alexandra from her station a few feet away.

"I think so," she said, staring at the balloon. Mere days ago, she wouldn't have been certain, but now . . .

"Start up winch!" came the call from Molly, a young Londoner who couldn't have been more than twenty but who was now in charge, sitting inside the cab of the huge mechanical winch that controlled their balloon from the back of their lorry.

Izzie, Alexandra, and a third woman from their new unit named Grace snapped into action. Grace and Alexandra grabbed the lines tethering the huge balloon to the ground so Izzie could slip the metal hook off the net that spanned the width of the balloon. Their team of three raced to the other two sets of lines on their side of the balloon while, opposite them, Amelia, Nancy, and Lottie, who made up the rest of their unit, did the same. With the last hook released, Izzie could feel the balloon's steel anchoring wires begin to tighten as it rose skyward.

Izzie, Alexandra, and Grace ducked and scurried off to a safe distance, and Amelia, Nancy, and Lottie came into sight as they rounded the balloon too.

"Engine ready!" shouted Molly.

The engines kicked into gear and began to churn, letting the balloon float out.

After a moment, Molly called, "Balloon flying thirty feet!"

"Stop winch!" shouted Corporal Tennyson, their instructor.

"Stop winch!" Molly repeated.

The balloon hovered in the air, safely anchored on all sides, and she and the other women of her unit all tracked the movement of the balloon in the wind.

Izzie felt triumph fizz up in her. They were supposed to wait for their assessment from Corporal Tennyson, but she knew they'd done a good job. After weeks of lectures on engineering, mechanics, safety, and meteorology not to mention practical classes on ropes, knots, and splicing, it was rewarding to finally have an ascent that had gone without incident.

She'd been shocked when she'd received her orders that she was to join a barrage balloon unit at RAF Titchfield for a ten-week training course. However, there was no arguing with a direct order. Not in the WAAF.

With her kit bag in her hand and Alexandra by her side, she'd boarded an open-backed vehicle driven by a fellow WAAF who had ferried them from Innsworth to the Hampshire base that was to be their temporary home during their additional training. As soon as they'd arrived, they'd been assigned to a modest hut with the rest of the girls in their unit, and then training had begun in earnest.

Izzie had seen barrage balloons dotting strategic places across the London skyline to try to deter Luftwaffe efforts to dive-bomb the city. However, she hadn't really thought about what went into making one of them fly. The work was physical, done at all hours and in all weather except high wind, and she swiftly learned that the balloons themselves weren't necessarily a deterrent the way anti-aircraft guns were. Instead, their job was to haul up and down the unmanned balloons to try to make it harder for German bombers to hit their targets accurately. A well-flying balloon could mean the difference between a direct hit and minimal damage.

"Tension four hundred weight. No slack on drum!" Molly called.

"Start winch!" shouted Corporal Tennyson.

"Start winch!" replied Molly. "Haul in winch!"

The winch groaned as it pulled in the balloon's steel cable.

"All right, ladies. Take her to bed!" shouted Corporal Tennyson.

The girls on the ground lined up to catch the winch cable and wrestle it steady until Grace could secure it to the tether at the back of their balloon vehicle. Then Molly climbed into the lorry's driver's seat while the rest of them ran around to the back and caught up the tail rope.

Slowly, Molly steered them into the base's balloon hangar while the rest of them followed, keeping the balloon from swinging around. As soon as they were in their designated place, they anchored the balloon and began the breakdown process.

When, finally, the balloon was deflated and everything in its place, Corporal Tennyson clapped his hands in front of him.

"Excellent work, ladies. A much smoother ascent and descent than yesterday, and your time has decreased as well. You've all earned your cup of tea in the mess today," he said.

The little group cheered.

Corporal Tennyson allowed them the tiniest of smiles before dismissing them.

As soon as they were released, the merry chatter and laughter that Izzie had come to associate with their unit started up. The seven of them moved in a pack, spilling out of the hangar and onto the tarmac of the airbase. Since arriving, they'd been encouraged to bond as a unit, living together, working together, eating together, and Izzie, much to her surprise, had come to like the other girls. She even managed to get on with Nancy, who probably had the warmest of hearts once you peeled back all of her nettles. However, she would forever be thankful to whichever officer had assigned Alexandra and her to the same unit. In a new group of seven, it felt good to have one friend she'd known from before.

Amelia, as always, forged a path for them at the head of the group, while Alexandra fell into step with Izzie as they walked back together.

"We're getting better," said Alexandra.

"That we are," she agreed, rolling her shoulder.

"Is something the matter?" asked Alexandra with concern.

"It's nothing," she said. "I nearly slipped when I was doing my first checks and I had to brace myself on the rope. I feel as though I've nearly wrenched my shoulder out of its socket."

"Nothing a rest and a good cup of tea can't fix," said Alexandra.

"It's funny to think that not long ago the worst injury I could do to myself was run the sewing machine over my finger or cut myself with a pair of shears."

"Run a sewing machine over your finger? Please don't tell me you've actually done that," said Alexandra, looking a little green at the thought.

Izzie laughed. "When I was thirteen. The needle went clear through the pad of my index finger. It was my own fault. I wasn't paying attention."

"That sounds horrible," said Alexandra.

She shrugged. "Mum bandaged me up and told me that it was a rite of passage for every seamstress and that I'd never do it again if I had any sense."

"And did you?" asked Alexandra.

"I always make sure I know where my fingers are these days."

Ahead of them, Lottie gave a cheery wave to one of the members of the RAF ground crew working on a plane near the entrance to one of the hangars, earning Lottie a gentle smack on the arm from Nancy.

"He didn't even bother to show up for your date at the NAAFI last week," Izzie heard Nancy say.

"That was all a misunderstanding. He said that he was made to scrub his barracks floor because he'd failed inspections that morning," said Lottie.

Nancy spun around, walking backward as she appealed to Izzie and Alexandra. "Can you talk some sense into her?"

Izzie laughed. "We all tried that last week, remember?"

They'd all gathered around a sobbing Lottie who, after being stood up at the NAAFI, had announced to their entire hut that she was never dating another RAF man again. Ever.

"Oh, I was just being silly," said Lottie.

"I don't understand why you let those fliers jerk you around," said Nancy.

"Have you seen Sergeant Johnson?" asked Lottie, her eyes going wide. "He's so handsome."

"He's just like all the rest of those Brylcreem boys. He thinks that just because the RAF lets him wear his hair a little longer than the rest of the services, he's God's gift to women. He's not even a pilot, Lottie!" Nancy cried in frustration as they entered the mess.

"Oh, let her have her fun," said Alexandra. "At least someone is."

"I have fun," said Nancy.

"What are we arguing about now?" Grace asked, looking back as they queued up at the tea urns.

"Nancy's trying to protect Lottie's heart from Lottie again," said Izzie.

"And Nancy insists that she's capable of having fun, so that must mean she'll be at the dance this evening to prove it," said Molly with a grin.

Nancy groaned when the other women gave another cheer.

"Fine. I'll stay for an hour," Nancy said.

"And dance at least a half dozen times?" Molly teased.

"Once," said Nancy.

"Four times," said Lottie, egging Molly on.

"I'll dance as many as Izzie does," said Nancy.

"Why me?" she asked.

"Because you're the only sensible one around here," said Nancy.

"Sensible?" She wasn't entirely certain she liked the idea of that being her reputation. It sounded . . . well, it sounded boring.

"We're *all* going," said Alexandra, putting a hand on Izzie's arm. "Isn't that what we agreed on? 'One for all and all for one'?"

Amelia scrunched up her nose. "I thought that was *The Three Musketeers.*"

"Do you want Nancy to go or not?" asked Alexandra as they settled down to a table with their cups of tea.

"'One for all and all for one'!" Amelia, Grace, Lottie, and Molly cried in unison.

"I cannot wait to take these boots off," said Alexandra, stretching her long legs out under the table.

"Corporal Tennyson almost looked proud of us today," Amelia said.

"Where do you think they'll send us when we're done?" asked Grace.

"We still have a lot to learn," said Nancy, ever practical. But then she added, "I think we'll become part of the Number Twelve Balloon Squadron. We're already here for training, why wouldn't they roll us into one of the Titchfield units?"

"I hope we end up stationed in London," said Molly. "Then I could see my mum whenever I have an afternoon's leave."

Izzie couldn't have agreed with Molly more. If she was stationed in London—or really anywhere along the Thames estuary—she stood a decent chance at being able to make it back to the shop from time to time. Even staying at RAF Titchfield as Nancy suggested would be fine. It wasn't exactly close, but she'd still be able to brave the trains and make her way back to base on twenty-four or forty-eight hours' leave.

"Well, I for one hope that we're far, far away from London," announced Alexandra. "It seems a shame not to go somewhere completely different."

"I heard they're thinking about sending balloon units to Egypt," said Grace.

"So far away?" Izzie immediately balked at that idea.

"WAAF balloon units in Egypt?" asked Nancy. "Whoever heard of such a thing?"

"Why not?" asked Amelia.

If they were sent to Egypt, how would she even begin to help Sylvia manage the shop and—

"I'd go," said Grace.

"Well, it isn't as though we have much of a choice," said Nancy.

No, it wasn't.

"My question is whether the Americans will need balloon girls now that they've started arriving," said Amelia.

"I would have thought they'd have their own balloon units," said Nancy.

"I've never met an American before," mused Grace. "I wonder what they're like."

"Rather like us, I should think," said Nancy.

164 • JULIA KELLY

"Except with funny accents," said Molly with a laugh.

"Right," said Lottie, setting down her empty cup and pushing back from the table. "As fascinating as this conversation is, I'm going to see what I can do about my hair before the dance tonight. Is anyone coming with me?"

"I'll go with you if you'll help me put my hair up," said Amelia.

"Me too," said Grace.

"Oh, come on. We might as well all go," said Nancy.

"I still have a bit of tea left," said Izzie lifting her cup.

"I'll stay with you," said Alexandra.

She shook her head. "No, don't worry about me. I'm just going to finish here and then stop in to see if I have any post."

"Are you certain?" asked Amelia.

"Positive," she said.

"Could you see if any letters have come in for me?" asked Grace.

"And me," said Lottie.

"If you don't mind, Izzie," said Molly.

"Why don't I play postwoman for everyone?" she asked with a smile.

She watched her fellow WAAFs shuffle off, the stream of conversation continuing until she could no longer hear them. Their chatter reminded her of the good days of the shop, when Mum had employed Miss Reid and at least two other seamstresses, with other women coming in to help when times were particularly busy. After feeling rather alone at Innsworth, it had taken coming to RAF Titchfield and being embraced by her unit to make her realize that she'd missed the chatter of women punctuated by whirring sewing machines and the sharp snip of scissors cutting out fabric that she'd grown up with.

However, despite that, she cherished her snatched moments of solitude as well, and living with six other women in a hut didn't give her many of those.

When she was certain that the other girls were gone, she stood, cleared her cup and saucer, and made for the base's post office. Unlike at Innsworth, this was a proper post office with two WAAFs sitting behind the counter and no doubt more sorting the post in the back. She had to wait for a few moments behind a couple of men before she could step up to the counter.

"Post for Shelton, Sumner, Reece, Dixon, Harlow, March, and Calpert," she said.

"You want seven people's post?" asked the WAAF.

"They're the other girls in my unit," she explained.

The WAAF gave her a weary look and handed her a scrap of paper and a pencil. "Could you write those down?"

Izzie dutifully scribbled the names down and then handed over the piece of paper. After a few minutes, the WAAF returned with a bundle of envelopes.

"Thank you," she said.

She walked away, sorting through the letters until she came to one with her service number and name on it. She paused in the doorway of the post office, her eyes fixed on her sister's familiar handwriting. After nearly two months of exchanging letters, it still felt strange every single time Sylvia wrote to her, even more so that the letters were filled with news from the shop. Who had come in. Which customer had brought her own fabric to have made up, and who was looking ahead to the next batch of clothing coupons, which would be issued in June, with obvious anticipation.

But it wasn't just news that came between the crisp sheets of Sylvia's writing paper. There were worries too. The Board of Trade's changes were one thing, but Izzie was even more concerned about the bank accounts, the paperwork, the uncollected debts. She would never admit this to Sylvia, but she couldn't understand how Mum had allowed things to become so lax.

Heat flushed her cheeks as she remembered her swift anger over Sylvia's letter about forcing Miss Keynes's hand and making her pay for all of the beautiful things Mum had made for the woman. There was no denying that Sylvia had managed to collect all of the balances owed to them on more accounts than Izzie wished to admit. However, it still felt all wrong. Mum had been so adamant that they not do anything to drive away potential future business—a fact that Sylvia *must* have remembered from when they were children—and Sylvia had simply walked in and done away with all of that.

Sylvia was meant to be minding the shop, not changing every single thing about it.

A cough and an "Excuse me, Miss" prompted her to look up and realize that she was blocking the way for a senior officer. She saluted him and scrambled to step out of his way while apologizing.

Outside of the post office in the rapidly falling dark, she decided that she didn't want to open her sister's letter that evening for fear that it would only make her angry once again. Instead, she would get ready for the dance, enjoy an evening with her friends, and read it first thing in the morning.

26 February 1942

Dear Izzie,

I am happy to report that Mrs. Shelton's Fashions has gone into the home furnishing business.

I realize that it is far less glamorous than designing clothes, but the other day a woman came in all in a rush asking if we could run up some blackout curtains for her. Apparently her house was bombed and she and her daughter have had to move into her sister's spare room. She was a little embarrassed because she said she's handy with a needle and blackout curtains are well within her reach, but she's also working on the line at a factory as part of her war work so she simply doesn't have the time.

I told her that we all need a little help from time to time, and there is no shame in coming to a dressmaker's to have curtains made. Our new customer happily handed over her blackout fabric and paid her deposit. She should be picking up her new blackout curtains next Monday, and—perhaps even better—she promised that she would be telling all the ladies on her shift at the factory about the excellent service she received at Mrs. Shelton's!

I know you might object to the idea of making up curtain orders because it isn't the sort of thing that our mother would have taken on. Miss Reid certainly raised her eyebrows when I told her, and I feared that I might be in for an argument. However, she simply took the measurements and told me she would start on them right away.

The only other news I have for you is that Miss Reid is hard at work trying her best to adapt our mother's patterns for the Board of Trade. A few of the skirts seem to be salvageable, but I'm afraid she isn't happy with a single jacket toile she's made. She's taken to using me as a live model, poking and prodding me in all sorts of ways. I shall have to be careful not to offend her, otherwise I might find myself on the wrong end of a stray pin!

Yours,
Sylvia

4 March 1942

Dear Sylvia,

I know that you have probably been expecting a disapproving sort of letter from me, but quite the contrary: I fully approve of the idea of taking in curtains, cushions, and the like. There should be very little to those kinds of orders for a seamstress of Miss Reid's abilities, and they are another way to bring money in. I would hate to think of the entire business going over to soft furnishings, but as a supplement I have no objections.

I must also thank you for sorting out the matter of the shop's accounts. You say that you know I will disapprove of you telling me that Mum did not have a head for business. Quite the contrary, one of my great regrets is that I could not convince her to relinquish more of the responsibility for the running of Mrs. Shelton's to me in her final months.

~~I wonder sometimes if she knew that she did not have much longer on this earth, but then I find myself asking why, if she did believe that, she did not do more to make sure that I knew how to run~~

I have been doing a little bit of business myself here at RAF Titchfield, although it initially started at training camp. As you can imagine, it's quite the thing to outfit all of the thousands of girls who have been called up, and the RAF is doing its best. However, I don't think anyone really accounted for how many WAAFs would need uniforms, and we're all a little thrown together.

Naturally, I made a few tweaks and changes to my own uniform for fit, and others noticed. I did some alterations for Alexandra, who was in quite the bind thanks to having broad shoulders and a larger bust, and some of the other girls in my hut caught on. I thought that perhaps my services would no longer be needed in RAF Titchfield, but that has not been the case at all. Instead, I find myself with a steady stream of customers and a tidy sum of pocket money that I will be able to add to my wages.

I have also found, much to my surprise, that there is a great deal of sewing needed in the maintenance of a barrage balloon, as each unit is in charge of keeping the balloon's silks in good working order. This might be why I was singled out for a balloon unit rather than tailoring, as I had expected. There is one other girl in my unit, Grace, who is a dab hand with a needle, and we often find ourselves happily sitting with our boots off, chatting and stitching away inside a huge deflated balloon that's propped up so we can see.

It is a strange war.

Sincerely,
Isabelle Shelton

———————

8 March 1942

Dear Izzie,

It is obvious that you inherited our mother's entrepreneurial side! I am not at all surprised that you have become the de facto seamstress for the girls in your unit and across the base. If the uniforms I've seen are any indication, they are very lucky to have you.

What do you think of the idea of Mrs. Shelton's Fashions going into the uniform tailoring business? There must be officers from the women's auxiliaries in London who are in need of Miss Reid's skills, and at least we wouldn't have to worry about the Board of Trade's restrictions.

I hope that you've also managed to find some time for fun amid all your training and sewing. Perhaps you might even meet a handsome pilot at a dance on base.

I envy you in some ways. I used to love dancing.

Yours,
Sylvia

P.S. Why do you take your shoes off when you sit inside the balloon?

---

12 March 1942

Dear Sylvia,

You have it all wrong. I'm not entrepreneurial at all. All I wanted to do was help out a friend and word spread. That's all.

The money a customer would pay for a uniform is the same as the money she would pay for a dress, as far as I'm concerned.

Sincerely,
Isabelle Shelton

P.S. We take our shoes off because our boots could damage the silk of the balloon.

Chapter Eighteen

And I should like a blouse made as well," said Mrs. Sutton, resting her hand on a brown wrapped package that she'd held on her lap since she'd entered Mrs. Shelton's Fashions.

"Of course. May I ask what the material is?" asked Sylvia, leaning forward in her seat in the shop's front room.

"A cotton lawn," said Mrs. Sutton, opening up the paper as carefully as she might have if it had contained precious treasure. "My daughter sent it to me from America."

Sylvia eyed Miss Reid, who stood at the counter behind Mrs. Sutton, pretending that she was doing something with a bit of paperwork. The seamstress raised a brow, and Sylvia instantly knew why. While it was entirely possible that Mrs. Sutton's daughter had sent her the fabric—anyone who could get their hands on cloth these days was doing it by any means possible—the Board of Trade had only just warned them about steep penalties for businesses and customers who supported the black market.

"May I see the fabric?" Sylvia asked.

Mrs. Sutton gently lifted a length of blue-and-white-striped cotton lawn free.

Sylvia took the cloth with due respect, discreetly looking at the name on the selvage edge as she admired it. "Smythe" was printed in black. She let out a little breath of relief. It was an American producer after all.

"It's lovely," she said, even as Miss Reid craned her neck to see the fabric.

"Perhaps something with a chevron," said Mrs. Sutton. "I think that would be just the thing with my linen skirt."

"Yes," Sylvia said hesitantly as Miss Reid began to adamantly shake her head from side to side. "Although if you wish for something that can stretch between the seasons, might I suggest a simple blouse?"

Mrs. Sutton's face fell a little. "Yes, I suppose that would be more practical. It really is a bother having to think of these things. I wish we could go back to the days when you could have something new every season."

Behind Mrs. Sutton's back, Miss Reid gave Sylvia a nod of approval.

"We all hope those days will return soon," said Sylvia, handing the cloth back to Mrs. Sutton. "So that will be one suit in a lightweight wool crepe and one blouse, off coupon. Miss Reid, perhaps you could show Mrs. Sutton the selection of sketches that would suit her?"

"Yes, Mrs. Pearsall," said Miss Reid, stepping out from behind the desk. "I'll just fetch our book."

When, finally, Mrs. Sutton had selected her items, paid her deposit, and handed over her coupons to be cross-checked against the Board of Trade's records, Sylvia bid the woman goodbye and shut the shop door. She waited a beat or two and then turned around to Miss Reid.

"We need more sketches," said Miss Reid.

She let out a weary sigh. "I know. I was certain for a moment that Mrs. Sutton was going to insist on a chevron top. What's wrong with that anyway?" she asked.

"If she hadn't wanted sleeves, lapels, or a button band, nothing. However, none of our patterns will suit," said Miss Reid.

"Surely it can't be that difficult to cut a dolman top or something like it," she said.

Miss Reid folded her arms over her chest, and Sylvia put her hands up.

"I know, I know. You sew, you don't design. You've told me," she said, rubbing her forehead just above the hairline so that she didn't take the powder she wore every day off of her skin. Cosmetics were becoming increasingly difficult to find, and wasting any felt like a shame.

"It's ridiculous that we can only offer our customers three suits," she muttered, exhaustion settling over her.

She'd thought that running the shop wouldn't require too much from her, but over the past two and a half months she'd realized just how naive that had been. She was there every day. She and Miss Reid had settled into a routine, with Sylvia greeting customers and managing the business, and Miss Reid sewing away. Each night, she found herself going home later. She couldn't even recall the last time she'd accepted an evening invitation.

She sighed. "I'll think of something."

Sylvia felt a light pressure on her forearm and jerked back a little before realizing that Miss Reid had touched her.

"*We* will think of something," Miss Reid corrected her.

Sylvia stared at the seamstress, stunned at the show of reassurance from the usually ornery woman.

Swiftly, Miss Reid withdrew her hand and straightened her shoulders. "Now, no more dillydallying. I have fabric to cut."

She dipped her head, allowing them both a graceful exit from an unusual display of compassion neither of them were completely comfortable with.

———

Sylvia waved goodbye to Miss Reid that evening at six o'clock. Then she shut and locked the shop door, pulling the blackout curtain over its glass pane.

The next part of Sylvia's day was only just beginning.

Back in her mother's office, she opened the desk drawer and extracted a bottle of whiskey she had borrowed from the bar at home. She was in the shop so many evenings these days that it made sense to bring refreshments in.

It wasn't as though she was trying to avoid going home. There was simply so much to do every day. Orders, invoices, coupon checks, bookkeeping—all of it fell to her by simple virtue of the fact that there was no one else to do it. However, she didn't mind. She'd forgotten that there could be comfort in the black-and-white surety of numbers.

That evening, however, she had grand plans of turning her attention to the last frontier in the office: a bookshelf stuffed with old notebooks and sketchbooks, the odd piece of loose paper sticking out.

Sylvia poured herself a whiskey, took a sip, and began.

She grabbed as many books as she could with one hand and hauled them over to the now-clear surface of her mother's desk. Opening the cover of the top one, she found herself looking at drop-waist dresses and coats with long lapels and low single buttons. Opera coats with exaggerated collars and simple boxy-cut suits. Notes in her mother's familiar handwriting about fabric and finishing accompanied each drawing. She ran her fingers along the lines of a long cocoon coat. These must have been some of her mother's sketches from her first years of running the shop. While Mrs. Shelton's Fashions never would have catered to flappers and jazz girls, the silhouettes of the era had penetrated every level of fashion.

The next book contained more separates, mostly skirts and

blouses. Maggie had clearly been focusing on the everyday wear that most of her clients had come to her for.

The third book had a few evening gowns dotted throughout the pages, and even a tennis outfit.

Sylvia set it aside and shuffled through a few loose sheets of paper that had been stuffed between books, groaning when she realized they were invoices from five years ago. She would have to file them away with the rest of the paperwork she had organized and check them against the system she'd re-implemented.

She reached for the fourth book. There was no question of throwing out the sketchbooks. They were the legacy of Mrs. Shelton's Fashions, a way of tracking the history of the shop and her mother's many ideas. She had to admit it was impressive that the dress shop her mother had set up in 1920 was still operating.

Without thinking, she opened the cover of the sketchbook in front of her and immediately stilled. While the other books had been filled with her mother's intricately detailed sketches full of technical details written in the margins, this was something different. The lines were sketchier, giving an impression of the body rather than fashion plate–like accuracy. But it was the suit on the first page that really gave her pause.

The outfit was far more pared down than most of her mother's designs. The skirt was simple and slim, ending just below the knee. The jacket was single-breasted, with deep, thin lapels more reminiscent of a man's suit but with more shaping through the waist than the usual boxier designs that her mother favored.

There were no notes written next to the suit, but she knew without a doubt that this was not her mother's work.

Sylvia flipped to the next page, her lips parting. The suit was just the beginning. She began to page through the book faster and faster. There were blouses, skirts, coats, and even ladies' trousers, which Sylvia was certain Mum would never have approved of. Some of the clothing was fanciful—bias-cut ballgowns with plunging necklines and sweeping trains and none of the loose drop waists that her mother had always insisted ladies of a certain age felt most comfortable in. There was a level of restrained glamour in this book that Mrs. Shelton's Fashions had never seen before.

This. This was the sort of clothing that Mrs. Shelton's should be offering its customers.

The shop's doorbell rang, pulling her attention away from the sketchbook.

She pushed away from the desk and hurried to the front. She edged the blackout curtain back and found herself staring at William. He gave her a little wave.

Quickly, she unlocked the door. "Hello."

"Hello, Mrs. Pearsall."

Sylvia laughed. "Oh, come now, William. I've known you since I was eleven. It sounds ridiculous, you calling me Mrs. Pearsall."

"Well, in that case, hello, Sylvia," he said with a half smile. "May I come in? I don't want to be the reason that you're scolded by the air raid warden for breaking the blackout."

She opened the door, letting light spill out into the twilight, and shut it swiftly behind him.

"How are you?" he asked, removing his hat.

"I'm well," she said.

A silence settled between the two of them until he said, "I wasn't sure whether you would still be here."

"I was just going through some things in the office," she said, not wanting to let on how late she had intended to stay.

"I thought maybe you would be off to some dinner or the theater," he said with a smile.

"Oh, I thought I'd take the night off from the Dorchester and The 43," she said, although she hadn't set foot in either in what felt like ages. "Are you on your way home?"

"I have my fire-spotting shift tonight." He looked down at his hat, seemed to notice that he was playing with the brim, and stilled. "I thought I would stop by. To see how you're doing."

Something warmed in her at his awkwardness. "That's incredibly kind of you. Won't you come back? I could put the kettle on."

He swayed forward a fraction, almost as though he wanted to cross the threshold of the door to the back of the shop, but then he smiled apologetically. "No. No, thank you. Not tonight. I did want you to know that I received this from the Inland Revenue."

He dipped a hand into the pocket of his jacket and pulled out an envelope. Sylvia's heart leaped into her throat when he held it out.

"I'm not certain I want to open it," she confessed.

"The news won't be any better or worse for leaving it unread," he said softly.

She swallowed. "You're right—I know you're right—and yet . . ."

"Would you like me to open it?"

She felt a little ridiculous, but nodded nonetheless.

He slipped a finger under the flap and tore the envelope open. She watched his face, cool with professionalism, as he skimmed the contents, his eyes flicking efficiently over the page.

When he looked up, she held her breath, but then he grinned. "It appears that the tax liability for Mrs. Shelton's Fashions is all in order."

Sylvia sagged against the shop's counter. All of that worry—all of that time wondering if she was going to receive a dreaded letter in the post saying that Mrs. Shelton's owed far more in back tax than she knew the shop's meager accounts could pay—was gone.

"Sylvia, are you all right?" asked William.

"Never better," she said, giving a little laugh.

"You're crying," he said.

She lifted a hand to her cheek and found it wet. "So I am."

William produced a handkerchief, crisp and clean, just as she'd known it would be, from his pocket.

"I suppose I'm relieved, really. I was worried that something terrible would happen, and Izzie would be so disappointed in me," she confessed, the words she'd never spoken aloud before tumbling out to this man who had once been her childhood companion as swiftly as her tears. "I don't think I could stand it if I lost Izzie her shop."

"It's your shop too," said William.

"Only for as long as it takes for this wretched war to finish and for her to come home."

Feeling suddenly awkward herself, she dabbed at her tears and then handed him back his handkerchief. "Thank you, William. Are you certain you won't stay for a cup of tea? It's the least I can do after crying all over your linen."

He took the handkerchief and tucked it back into his pocket. "Thank you, but I really should be going."

"Of course," she said.

He nodded and stepped back to settle his hat. "Good night, Sylvia."

"Good night." She moved to open the door but then, with her hand on the knob, stopped herself. "It was good to see you, William."

He smiled, and then tugged on the brim of his hat. "It was good to see you too."

She opened the door and he brushed by, leaving her alone in the shop once again.

The following day, when Miss Reid came in Sylvia was ready and waiting, seated in a chair she'd pulled up to the cutting table. She had the sketchbook she'd found open in front of her, a cup of tea half-drunk next to her hand.

"Good morning," said Miss Reid, shrugging off her black wool coat.

"Miss Reid, will you come look at this?" Sylvia asked.

With a frown, the seamstress put her coat on her usual peg, deposited her handbag next to her machine, and walked over. As soon as Miss Reid's eyes landed on the sketchbook, she let out an "Oh . . ."

"Do you know where this sketchbook came from?" Sylvia asked.

Miss Reid glanced at Sylvia, then at the sketchbook, then back again. Finally, she said, "It's one of your sister's."

Sylvia traced her fingers over a sleek black evening coat.

"I knew she liked to draw, but I didn't realize she could do this," she murmured.

Miss Reid lifted her chin and nodded. "Not long after you left, your sister began to carry a sketchbook around with her everywhere. I used to ask her what was in it, but it was a full year before she showed me anything. They were good. A bit too romantic for my taste, but good.

"However, as she became older, she became more interested in what the couture houses in Paris were making. She stripped back all of the fabric flowers and bows. She became very good," said Miss Reid, as close to beaming with pride as Sylvia had ever seen her.

"She must have showed them to our mother," Sylvia said, turning a page and looking at the designs with new eyes. "I found this on the bookshelf in my mother's office."

"Miss Shelton did show her sketches to your mother from time to time," said Miss Reid carefully.

"But," she prompted.

"I believe Mrs. Shelton thought that they weren't suitable for the shop's clientele," said Miss Reid.

"Then why was this stuffed onto the bookshelf with all of my mother's drawings?" Sylvia asked.

Miss Reid's lips tightened. "On occasion, Mrs. Shelton would become frustrated with Miss Shelton spending her time drawing and confiscate a book."

"She took Izzie's sketchbooks away from her?" Sylvia asked in shock.

"Only when they were interfering with your sister's work," said Miss Reid, rising to the defense of her old employer.

Sylvia stared down at a bias-cut dress with a low, sweeping back and immediately she understood. Her mother would have hated this style, showing off and celebrating a woman's figure rather than hiding it. It would have felt modern, even radical, to Maggie Shelton. Too French. Too Hollywood. To begin dressing this woman would have been a risk because it would have meant evolving, growing, changing. It would have ruffled the feathers of the shop's old-guard customers.

"Many of these designs are perfect for the Board of Trade's utility scheme," she said. "They are simpler than my mother's designs, and they'll require less fabric."

She thought for a moment that Miss Reid might protest, but instead the seamstress gave a sharp nod. "They are."

"I doubt we'll have much call for evening dresses, but the everyday separates would work well with only a few modifications." She glanced at Miss Reid. "Do you think you could create patterns based on some of these designs?"

"I can try," said Miss Reid.

Sylvia closed the book. "Then, Miss Reid, I think we may have found a solution to our problem."

Chapter Nineteen

Izzie and Grace were standing inside of a deflated balloon, checking seams to make sure there were no tears or weaknesses that would affect its flight, when Alexandra stuck her head into the balloon's opening.

"Sergeant Delafield is here. She wants to speak to all of us," said Alexandra, excitement making her beam.

Izzie and Grace exchanged glances at the mention of their commanding officer's name.

"Is it our orders?" Izzie asked, lowering her voice.

"I think so," said Alexandra before disappearing.

Izzie picked her way to the entrance, making sure not to catch any fabric. When she stuck her head out, she saw the other girls of their unit standing to attention, Corporal Tennyson and Sergeant Delafield facing them.

"Airwoman Second Class Shelton and Airwoman Second Class March, please put on your boots and join the rest of your unit," said Corporal Tennyson before nodding to Sergeant Delafield. "Your commanding officer has news for you."

Izzie and Grace both scrambled to wiggle on their boots. As she laced up, Izzie realized that her heart was in her throat. She and the girls had spent so much time speculating about where they might be dispatched that for it now to be real felt almost strange. Romantic as Egypt might feel to a girl from London, she hoped—prayed even—that the unit would be sent to her hometown or anywhere in the South East. If she was within easy distance, she would be able to pop into the shop and make sure that Sylvia wasn't running the place into the ground.

That, she realized as she tied off the second knot on her boot and stood, wasn't really fair. Although they'd clashed about the advertisements, Sylvia had been right to start taking in blackout curtains and uniforms, and Izzie wasn't too proud to admit that *something* needed to be done about the shop's books and that she was glad she hadn't been the one to do it.

Now properly shod, Izzie fell into line with the rest of her unit.

"I know that you've been waiting for your orders," Sergeant Delafield began. "I wanted to let you know personally that this unit has been selected to help defend north Norfolk at RAF Horsham Saint Faith."

Norfolk? The bubble of hope that had been forming in Izzie's stomach burst. Fareham, where RAF Titchfield was, might have been on the edge of Portsmouth Harbor, but at least there were easy trains back to London. Being stationed in East Anglia would send her into an area of the country completely foreign to her.

"Norwich and its surrounding area as well as the Norfolk coast remain of great strategic importance to the RAF," said Sergeant Delafield. "The Americans have also expressed an interest in setting up air bases there, making it even more of a target for the Luftwaffe."

A giggle rose up from Lottie at the mention of American GIs. Sergeant Delafield's eyes narrowed at the interruption, but their commanding officer continued on.

"Remember your training. It will stand you in good stead in the heat of the moment when everything around you seems to be chaos. I suggest that you pack your kit bags carefully, because you have been granted forty-eight hours' leave," the sergeant finished.

This time all of the women of the balloon unit broke out into murmurs, and their commanding officer's cool demeanor cracked into a smile.

"I thought that might be a popular decision," said Sergeant Delafield. "You will be expected at RAF Horsham Saint Faith on Saturday the fourth of April at eleven o'clock. There you will receive further instructions. Now, if there are no further questions . . ." Sergeant Delafield's gaze swept over them. "Good luck."

"Ladies, there will be time for chatting later," Corporal Tennyson said, cutting through their excitement. "You have a balloon to check and store. Back to it."

All of the WAAFs scattered. Izzie and Grace unlaced and pulled off their boots as quickly as they could and climbed back into the balloon to finish their work. As soon as they gave the all-clear, the rest of the unit worked to pack and store the balloon. The feeling of anticipation was palpable as Corporal Tennyson checked their work.

Finally, he said, "All right then. Since Aircraft Woman Second Class Reece looks as though she'll explode if I don't let you go."

"I will, sir," Lottie reassured him.

"You're all dismissed," he said.

Everyone, including Izzie, let up a cheer, and Corporal Tennyson walked off, smiling as he shook his head.

The balloon girls scattered. Lottie went off to say goodbye to her various boyfriends on base with the express intention of extracting promises that the men would come visit her at RAF Horsham St Faith if they ever were in Norfolk. Molly went to collect everyone's post one last time. The rest of the women, including Izzie, hurried back to their hut.

Izzie didn't want to waste any time. She had permission for leave, and she intended to use every bit of it.

"Where are you going to go, Nancy?" asked Amelia as they hauled out kit bags onto their beds and began to pack.

"I don't really know," said Nancy. "I doubt I'll be able to make it to York and back in time to make base."

"Then you'll come home to Southampton with me. You too, Grace, if you think Northumberland is too far," said Amelia firmly. "Mum will be delighted to meet you after all of my letters."

Izzie, who was folding a shirt, saw the faint hint of a smile cross Nancy's usually stern features.

"What about you, Izzie?" asked Grace. "Are you going home to London?"

"Wild horses couldn't keep Izzie away," said Alexandra with a laugh.

"Alexandra's right. I want to go to the shop," she said.

"And check in on that sister of yours, no doubt," said Alexandra.

"Letters!" called out Molly as she walked in with the post and began distributing.

"Nothing for me?" asked Nancy.

"Just Amelia, Grace, and me," said Molly with an apologetic smile. "The girls at the post office said that they'd forward along anything that comes while we're gone."

"What are the rest of you London girls going to do with your leave?" asked Amelia.

"I promised my little sister I would visit the first chance I got," said Molly.

"My parents wrote to tell me they've given up the dower house because the army wanted to house some Polish officers there, so they've decamped to London," said Alexandra.

There was a chorus of teasing "ooos," but Alexandra just laughed. Izzie knew that her friend had been nervous about talking about her family when they'd arrived at RAF Titchfield, so she'd immediately made it clear that Alexandra was her friend and that neither of them cared that one was an earl's daughter and the other made clothes for a living. It had worked a treat.

"You'll stay with them then?" asked Nancy.

"One of my brothers, George, is on leave, so I will see him too. I'm almost as excited to clap eyes on him as I am to see this famous dress shop of Izzie's."

Izzie paused, the shirt she'd been folding suspended in air. "We only have forty-eight hours. Do you really want to take time away from George and your parents to see my shop?"

"Of course I do. Besides, I thought you could use some moral support going back for the first time."

She blinked in surprise. "Really?"

"Izzie," said Alexandra indulgently, "that's what friends do for one another?"

Emotion rose in Izzie's throat.

"All right," she said, swallowing hard. "We'll go."

Chapter Twenty

No, that will not be acceptable," said Sylvia down the office telephone she'd had installed three weeks ago after growing tired of taking all her calls in the corridor.

"I'm sorry, madam, but that's the best I can do," said Mr. Harding on the other end of the line.

Mr. Harding was, Sylvia had decided, her archnemesis. He was in charge of all deliveries for Fuller & Crosgrove, which was one of the suppliers her mother had apparently used for years, if the receipts she'd found were anything to go by. Considering that she had never once in her time at the shop seen an order from Fuller & Crosgrove show up on time and in full, she wondered why.

Every telephone call to Mr. Harding to fix an order cost her precious time she didn't have. It was, she had to admit to herself, becoming more and more difficult to keep all of the plates in her life spinning. The shop was like a needy child, tugging at her skirt. It might have been fine if that was all she had to contend with, but there was also the matter of being Mrs. Hugo Pearsall. She ran their household, directing Mrs. Atkinson in what needed to be done around the flat, doing the accounts, and paying all of the bills in her husband's absence. Then there was the social aspect of her life. She couldn't exactly stop answering letters or turn down every single invitation from friends because of the shop, because no one was supposed to know about it. Nights out had been easy to beg off of because of the blackout and the cold winter they'd had, but that still left luncheons, committee meetings, and teas to try to juggle around the shop's needs.

Sylvia straightened in her mother's desk chair and prepared to fight the familiar battle. "Mr. Harding, I will not be paying your invoice until you bring the correct order to the shop."

"You took delivery of it, Mrs. Pearsall. There's nothing I can do," said Mr. Harding.

"Half of the order was missing, and the other half was wet through. What did you do? Leave it out in the rain because you knew it was coming to me?" she asked, her voice sarcastically sweet.

"Now, Mrs. Pearsall, there's no need to make accusations. If you'll pay for the order, I'll see to it that the missing items are sent to you," said Mr. Harding.

"No, you will see that the entire order is sent to me as soon as possible in full, and I expect a discount of twenty-five percent," she said.

The man scoffed. "Mrs. Pearsall, I understand that you may not be familiar with how this business works—"

"Mr. Harding, I have been in the garment trade since I was eleven years old, so I suggest that you take another tack, because you will not find any success trying to cow me into agreeing with you," she said sharply.

"Now, now, I didn't mean any offense."

"I'm certain you would never do anything so unwise," she said, knowing she sounded utterly unconvinced.

The man sighed. "I can send you the missing items, but only after you've paid."

Outside of the closed office door, she heard Miss Reid's sewing machine stop its whirring. There were no appointments scheduled for at least two hours, but walk-in business had begun to pick up a little in the past month. Sylvia tried her best to greet any woman who entered with a smile and the sort of gentle attention she received when she had her clothes made at Hartnell or Worth, but she was at a critical juncture with Mr. Harding. This time she let Miss Reid handle whoever had come through their door.

She leaned forward, elbows on the desk as she cradled the telephone receiver closer to her ear. "Mr. Harding, I find myself growing tired of our little discussions, so I will explain what will happen. You will send the complete order again—dry and undamaged—as soon as humanly possible. You will also send a new invoice less the amount of twenty-five percent of the total of the order. If you do no not do this, I will make it my personal mission to telephone every dressmaker, tailor, and designer in London and explain to them that it would be in their best interest not to trade with Fuller and Crosgrove because of your unjust business practices."

The man was so quiet, Sylvia thought that they might have become disconnected until a deep sigh filled her ear.

"Ten percent," said the man.

She smiled. "Twenty."

"Fifteen," he said.

"Twenty."

"Fifteen is more than I give anyone."

"You'll give us twenty, and you personally will ensure that any future orders for Mrs. Shelton's Fashions are received full and on time," she said firmly.

Mr. Harding made an exasperated noise and then said, "Fine. You'll have it within the next three days."

Sylvia sat back in her chair with a grin just as there was a knock on the door.

"I look forward to receiving the order then, Mr. Harding." She settled the telephone back on its cradle and then called out, "Come in!"

Miss Reid opened the door, and Sylvia knew from one look at the woman that something was wrong.

"What is it?" she asked, sitting up abruptly.

"Mrs. Pearsall, you're going to want to come now," said Miss Reid in a loud whisper.

"Why? What's the matter?" she asked standing. "And why are you whispering?"

Miss Reid glanced over her shoulder. "It's— Well, you'd better just see for yourself."

Sylvia rounded the desk and was almost to the threshold of the office when Miss Reid pushed the door open to its full width, revealing Izzie in uniform with a tall, blond WAAF at her side. Sylvia was about to greet her sister when Izzie looked up with righteous fury in her eyes, and Sylvia knew instantly that this would be no happy family reunion.

Izzie couldn't believe what she was seeing. She was standing in the middle of the workroom, Alexandra at her side, staring at a spread of her own sketches covering half the table. It looked as though they had been cut out of one of her sketchbooks with a penknife, which would explain why the clothbound cover sitting on the edge of the table was starting to collapse in on itself a bit. And if that wasn't enough, the other half of the table was taken up by pattern pieces cut from draft paper and what looked like part of a muslin toile.

Miss Reid, who had clapped her hand over her mouth at the sight of her the moment she'd walked through the shop's front room, now stood with her back plastered against the wall next to Mum's office while Sylvia looked stunned in the doorway.

"What is this?" Izzie asked, snatching up a sketch of two women wearing skirts that hit just below the knee topped by short jackets, each with a narrow lapel.

"Izzie, I was going to write to you—"

"What is this?" she demanded, shaking the paper at Sylvia.

It only made her angrier when Sylvia lifted her chin as though she were preparing herself to speak to one of those bloody women's committees she served on.

"I found them on the bookshelf in the office," said Sylvia. "Miss Reid tells me they're yours."

Izzie rounded on Miss Reid.

"They're very good, Miss Shelton," Miss Reid started, her eyes downcast.

"When I realized that many of them suit the new Board of Trade utility scheme, I asked Miss Reid to do what she could to try to translate them to patterns," Sylvia continued.

"You're *making* them?" Izzie hissed.

"I don't understand, I thought you would be pleased to see your sketches become real clothing we sell," said Sylvia.

It *was* what she had wanted for so long, but not like this. Not with her sister digging up sketches that Mum had already rejected. She was not going to put work that would make her mother ashamed out into the world. She wouldn't do it.

"Izzie, what's the matter?" asked Alexandra in a low voice.

Her friend's question barely registered. "You have no right, Sylvia. No right!"

"I was only trying to help," said Sylvia.

"You were supposed to mind the shop. Perhaps take an order or two. That is all," said Izzie fiercely. She knew she was being unreasonable. From her letters, it sounded as though Sylvia had done a great deal to sort out the shop's books and draw in new business, but using her sketches without Izzie's permission was beyond the pale.

"Miss Shelton," Miss Reid cut in, "your sister has worked hard these last months. She is here every day to open up the shop, and I know that she stays on well beyond when I leave for the evening. She's delivered parcels and sorted out lost orders. She takes consultations, and she even had a new telephone installed."

"You would defend her after everything you know she did?" asked Izzie.

Miss Reid drew herself up to her full height. "Your sister is no longer an eighteen-year-old girl. She grew up."

"Miss Reid," Sylvia whispered.

"I cannot believe you are taking her side," Izzie said in disgust. "You were here for all of it. You saw how fast she was out that door as soon as that husband of hers came along. She couldn't wait to turn her back on Mum because she never had one bit of respect for Mum or this shop." Izzie's gaze cut over to Sylvia, who was standing pale and pinch-lipped. "Because that's what it was, wasn't it? You hated Mum. You hated this shop. You hated all of us."

The truth hung heavy as fog in the middle of the room, and for a moment no one dared to breathe.

"There are no sides here," Miss Reid finally said. "All that matters is that your mother's shop stays open."

"It is supposed to be *my* shop now." Tears began to prick behind Izzie's eyes, but she wouldn't cry. She wouldn't let her anger and her frustration win. "I am supposed to know everything that happens here. That was the agreement, Sylvia."

"I'm sorry I didn't write to you first," said her sister. "Miss Reid and I didn't want to get your hopes up before—"

"My hopes up? These are private," she said, her voice cracking. "I never meant for anyone to see them."

It was a lie but she couldn't stop herself. Seeing her sketches spread out in front of her and patterns made from them didn't give her the joy she'd once dreamed of. Instead, she felt violated. Exposed.

"Izzie, the sketches really are perfect," Sylvia tried to reason.

"They are, Miss Shelton," said Miss Reid with a weak smile.

"Izzie, what is really the matter?" Alexandra asked in a low voice, touching Izzie's arm.

It was the calm kindness in her friend's tone that brought all of those held-back tears spilling down her face.

"They aren't good enough," said Izzie, a sob escaping her lips.

"That's not true," said Sylvia.

Izzie shook her head emphatically. "Mum said they were not good enough for our customers, and they aren't. They were just a silly thing I did."

"I'm telling you that they are just what we need. It was a godsend finding them," said Sylvia.

Izzie wanted to curl up under the cutting table and hide from everyone. Instead, she wrapped her arms around herself. "No," she said firmly. "No one wants to buy clothes like that."

"*I* want to buy clothes like this," said Sylvia.

"What good does that do us when we all know that you would never deign to have your clothes made at a place like Mrs. Shelton's?" Izzie lashed out.

It gratified her to see Sylvia rear back. "That's not true."

"What are you wearing right now? What is that?" she demanded. "Hartnell? Hardy Amies? Or perhaps it's Jacqmar? When was the last time that you went to a place like Mrs. Shelton's to have your clothes made? You didn't even let Mum make your wedding dress. Your own mother, who was a dressmaker." When her sister didn't answer, Izzie continued, "Don't tell me what is best for this business when you wouldn't even condescend to spend your money and your clothing coupons here."

Her breath came fast as she braced herself for Sylvia's response. A part of her wanted her sister to rise to the bait and finally tell her what she really thought of Mrs. Shelton's Fashions. At least then it would all be out in the open.

Instead, Sylvia simply said, "I'm sorry, Izzie."

She scoffed and dashed away the last of her tears. "That's all you have to say?"

"I'm sorry for many things. I've made so many mistakes in my life—more than you can ever guess," Sylvia said. "I would be happy to explain anything to you that you like, and I will offer up every apology that I have."

Izzie shook her head. "You're years too late."

Sylvia folded her hands in front of her and looked down. "I understand."

Izzie looked around, taking in the familiar sewing machines, the fabric, pins, shears. She saw the wan look on Miss Reid's face, Alexandra's clear worry, and Sylvia's reticence.

"As soon as I'm demobbed, I want you out of this building," said Izzie. "We will make whatever arrangement necessary to complete the sale. Willie will handle all of the paperwork. In the meantime, I would ask you to keep your letters to me focused on the business of the shop.

"Alexandra and my balloon unit will be stationed at RAF Horsham Saint Faith in Norfolk. I will come up to London as often as I am granted leave. You do not need to be here when I arrive. Miss Reid can give me any updates in person that are necessary."

She leaned over the table to begin gathering up her loose sketches and tucked them into the cover of their book. Then she marched into Mum's now-clean office and stuffed the sketchbook back on the bookshelf where it belonged.

"Isabelle Shelton, you are acting like a child," said Miss Reid as Izzie emerged into the workroom again.

"You wouldn't have dared speak to my mother that way, Miss Reid," Izzie warned.

"Perhaps I should have," fired back the seamstress.

"Don't test my patience, Miss Reid. You will not like it."

Miss Reid planted her hands on her hips. "Then fire me."

Izzie hesitated. She couldn't fire Miss Reid. Not if she wanted the shop to survive the war.

"I held my tongue for too long with your mother because she took me in and gave me a job when no one else would, but I won't make that same mistake with you," said Miss Reid. "If you really want to be the owner of this shop, you must see that the changes Mrs. Pearsall has made are necessary. If you could put aside your own bloody-mindedness, you would realize that she's trying to save this place, not run it into the ground."

"You are welcome, from here on out, to keep your opinions to yourself, Miss Reid," Izzie said. "Come along, Alexandra. We're leaving."

"Izzie, maybe we should talk about this," said Alexandra quietly as Izzie led her down the corridor to the front of the shop.

"There is nothing to talk about," she said.

"But why don't you want your designs to be used?" Alexandra asked as Izzie stepped out into the street. "Your sister and Miss Reid said that your sketches are perfect."

"They were wrong. Mum knew best, and she said they weren't right. 'Frocks for film stars' she used to call them."

"What woman doesn't want to feel a little chic right now?" asked

Alexandra with a cautious smile. "Besides, your sister wouldn't have chosen those sketches if she didn't think they were right for your clientele."

A part of her deep down in a secret corner of her heart wanted to believe that her friend was right, but she couldn't escape the echo of her mother's words. Izzie wasn't ready. She wasn't experienced enough. She didn't know the first thing about designing for real women. The sketches were just a fantasy. They would never sell. Mrs. Shelton's was founded on the backs of good, practical garments.

"My mother built this business from nothing. She was right," she said firmly.

Alexandra chewed her lip, but then nodded. "If you say so."

Izzie gave a sharp nod. "I do."

Part III

17 DESIGNERS SHOW UTILITY
SCHEME COLLECTION TO FASHION TRADES

Seventeen of London's top designers showed their latest designs Friday in a fashion show meant to celebrate the simplicity of the Board of Trade's recent austerity regulations.

"We are determined to show that the Civilian Clothing Order, known as CC41, is a challenge that we are more than ready to embrace," said Mr. Maxwell Shepperton of the House of Shepperton, Mayfair. "Rationing need not mean a dreary wardrobe."

The recent adoption of these new rationing rules as part of the Making-Up of Civilian Clothing (Restrictions) Order means that everyone from the humble neighborhood dressmaker to the most well-known of fashion houses must follow a series of restrictions meant to save valuable cloth. The Board of Trade believes that this could conserve millions of yards of cotton and wool for the war effort.

A-line skirts, blouses with simple darts, and military-inspired jackets proved to be the most popular silhouettes, with each designer showing one ensemble. Several designers set themselves the extra challenge of proving the versatility and ingenuity of their designs such as reversible jackets to create two outfits for the coupons of one.

Designers also showed that utility cloth need not be bland, with the new simplicity of silhouettes perfectly highlighting patterns such as stripes, spots, and other bold patterns.

"We have no doubt that the ladies of Britain will embrace these designs, feeling well-dressed while saving their coupons," said Mr. Shepperton. "We are all trying to do our bit."

—*The London Lady*, 6 April 1942

6 April 1942

Dear Izzie,

I am more sorry than I can say that I did not write to you to ask your permission before using your sketches. I truly did think that it would be more of a disappointment if I'd told you that I found them and Miss Reid had not been able to work from them. I can see now that I was wrong.

Please believe me when I tell you I was only thinking about the success of the shop.

Yours,
Sylvia

—————————

10 April 1942

Dear Izzie,

I imagine that you have now settled into your new assignment at RAF Horsham St Faith. I hope that you and the rest of the women in your unit are able to stay safe. I think of you every time I hear an air raid siren and worry that your work as a WAAF leaves you more vulnerable than most.

Things are as they ever were at Mrs. Shelton's Fashions. William rang the other day to find out how you are and ask after the shop, and Mrs. Reynolds continues to glare at me every time she sees me in the road. I've decided that both of these events are reassuring in their consistency.

The only real change is Miss Reid. Without me needing to ask, she has offered to take on the responsibility of opening the shop each morning, and she no longer complains as loudly if I need to run out for an appointment in the afternoon. She has stopped telling me that every new order I take will be impossible. (Before making the impossible happen, of course.) Instead, she asks when more work will come, and she even has ideas. I believe she took the Board of Trade's restrictions personally and is determined that they won't get the better of us.

I do have some good news to share. We had our first commission for an officer's uniform the other day. We are making the newly promoted Subaltern Vera Garson from the Auxiliary Territorial Service her first properly tailored dress uniform. She could not have been more delighted when she came in to have Miss Reid take her measurements.

Yours,
Sylvia

———————

15 April 1942

Dear Izzie,

I am sorry. I can tell from my unanswered letters that you don't trust me. That is my fault, and I will continue to apologize for as long as I have to for you to believe me that I am sincere. You are my sister, and I have always loved you. You must believe that.

I have been thinking a great deal about what you said in the shop that day. Your designs are beautiful. Anyone with an eye would be able to tell you that, and I do not know why our mother tried to convince you they wouldn't sell. They will. I am certain of it.

Our mother was stubborn, Izzie. I think that is one of the things that allowed her to build a business when no one would help her. However, it also made her shortsighted. She believed so much in what had worked in the past that she couldn't see what possibilities might be in front of her.

Trust me when I tell you that I move in circles where your designs would be sought-after. There are women who want to dress in the things you've dreamed up, even in a time of war. I promise you that.

You have talent, and it is a shame not to show that talent off to the world.

Please reconsider and allow me to use the sketches moving forward. I know that you have your doubts, but I promise you that between your designs and Miss Reid's construction, Mrs. Shelton's could produce beautiful things.

Yours,
Sylvia

P.S. Miss Reid tells me to pass along the message that she thinks you're being stubborn only for stubbornness's sake. I do not know if that will persuade you, but at this point I will use anything I possibly can to plead my case, so I am putting this in here on the off chance it will help.

Chapter Twenty-One

Izzie's hand shook as she finished addressing the envelope and put her pen down on the wooden shelf behind her with a firm click.

For the past two and a half weeks, Sylvia had written to her, trying to apologize and failing miserably with every new letter. However, this last one had been the limit. Not only had her sister invoked their mother, but Sylvia had tried to act as though she knew the first thing about what Mum was like.

"I'm going to post this," Izzie said, sliding off her bunk and landing neatly next to her work boots. "Does anyone have any letters they need taken?"

Amelia and Grace looked up from their card game and murmured a "No, but thank you."

Lottie, who had been playing around with a new way to dress her hair, asked no one in particular, "Do you think my curls will stay if I wear my hair like this for the dance on Friday?"

"No," Nancy muttered as she turned a page.

"You didn't even look up from your book!" Lottie cried.

"I didn't have to," said Nancy tartly.

Alexandra, who had been propped up on her elbow reading on the bunk underneath Izzie's, closed her book and said, "I'll go with you, Izzie. It saves me from listening to Nancy and Lottie bicker again."

"We do not bicker," said Nancy with a sniff.

"You do," said Alexandra.

"Izzie," Nancy appealed to her.

"You do," echoed Izzie.

Nancy opened her book with such force she nearly snapped the spine.

As Izzie and Alexandra stepped out of their barracks and into the early-spring sun, Alexandra said, "I love Nancy, I really do, but that doesn't mean I don't want to throttle her half of the time."

Izzie laughed. "She does go after Lottie more than she should."

"I think she secretly wishes she was as good with men as Lottie is," said Alexandra.

"You're probably right."

"Gosh, it's good to be outside," said Alexandra, throwing back her head as the wind ruffled both of their hair.

It was beginning to feel as though the English summer might actually be on its way. All around them, the air base buzzed with activity like a hive. They had been at RAF Horsham St Faith for just over a fortnight, but already she'd become used to the constant sound of planes and the smell of oil and fuel.

"Did you finally decide to write your sister?" asked Alexandra after they rounded an administrative building.

Izzie held up her letter. "Yes."

"Are you going to accept her apologies?" asked Alexandra.

"No."

Alexandra nodded, and Izzie appreciated that her friend didn't try to push the matter any further.

In the hours after her fight with Sylvia, Izzie had worried what Alexandra must think of her. Her cheeks had flamed hot red when her friend had walked her to Mayfair and the largest house Izzie had ever laid eyes on. Lady Menby, Alexandra's mother, had come out of a drawing room in a neat suit of aubergine wool and greeted Izzie as though she were a long-lost relative. Then came Lord Menby and one of the famous brothers, George, everyone speaking all at once as they kissed Alexandra and shook hands with Izzie and demanded stories of the WAAF. When finally Izzie, slightly overwhelmed by the reception and by what had just happened at the shop, managed to catch her friend's eye, Alexandra announced she wanted to see Izzie settled and led her up to a guest room.

"This is where you'll be staying," said Alexandra, opening the door to one of the most beautiful spaces Izzie had ever been in. It had white wallpaper trimmed in gold, and a plush pale blue carpet underfoot. The moment she stepped inside, shame washed over her. How could she have lost her temper with her sister and argued so crudely in front of *Lady* Alexandra.

Her expression must have changed because Alexandra immediately said, "We'll have none of that. Whatever you're thinking, stop it."

Izzie sank down on the edge of the bed. "What you must think of us Sheltons . . ."

"I think that family can be complicated," said Alexandra, as though it was the most natural thing in the world that Izzie should have lost her temper with her sister like she had. "No one's family is perfect, and I certainly don't expect yours to be."

Her friend's quick understanding that afternoon in that huge house in Mayfair had been a comfort, and she'd spent the rest of her short leave wrapped up in the warmth of Alexandra's family. However, as soon as they had arrived at RAF Horsham St Faith, Sylvia's letters had started arriving, and Izzie knew that she could only put her sister off for so long.

"You know," said Alexandra as they walked, "I've been thinking about something your sister said."

"What's that?" Izzie asked.

Alexandra seemed to hesitate before saying, "It isn't my place really, but what if your mother was wrong?"

"Wrong? About what?"

The questions must have sounded harsher than she'd meant them to, because Alexandra quickly said, "It's only a thought."

The instinct to defend her mother roared up in her, but Izzie shoved it down. Alexandra was a friend and was only trying to help.

"Please tell me more," she forced herself to say.

"Well," Alexandra started, "it sounds like Sylvia is trying to help the business. You said yourself that she sorted out the shop's accounts, and it sounds like her advertisements have brought in some new customers."

Izzie started to protest, but Alexandra shook her head.

"Let me finish, Izzie. I think your sister is doing her best in a difficult situation with rationing and the war, but at least she's trying."

"She took my sketches without permission," Izzie said stubbornly.

"Yes, she should have asked, but I saw your sketches, Izzie. They're beautiful. Why wouldn't you want them to be sold?" Alexandra asked.

The emotion that had been threatening to choke her for weeks welled up in her throat again. "That's kind of you, but this is all just because Sylvia feels guilty."

"What does your sister have to feel guilty about?" asked Alexandra.

"Sylvia and Mum never saw eye to eye. When Dad died, he left Mum with virtually nothing. He was a barrister, so I've never understood why, but Mum never spoke about it. I do know that she went to his family for help. Apparently they never approved of the marriage, so we barely saw them when Dad was alive, but my grandfather gave her enough money to buy the shop to provide us with a living.

"Sylvia hated the shop. She's four years older than I am, so she remembers our old house and what it was like to have a maid to do all of the chores. Mum always said Dad treated Sylvia like a princess, showering her with pretty dresses, books, and singing lessons.

"Apparently Sylvia told Mum that moving into a flat above a dressmaker's shop and being forced to help out whenever she wasn't in school was embarrassing. I think that's why, when she met Horrible Hugo, she didn't want anything to do with Mum any longer. It was as though she washed her hands of us."

Fourteen-year-old Izzie had checked the post every day for months after Sylvia came back from her honeymoon, but the invitation to come stay at the newly married couple's flat had never appeared. Instead, there were only increasingly short responses to Izzie's letters about the shop until, finally, those dried up all together.

Crushed, she'd gone to Mum in tears, but instead of comfort her mother had given her a stern talking-to.

"Your sister's life is different now, Izzie. You need to understand that, or she'll break your heart over and over again," said Mum.

"But I'm her sister," Izzie sobbed.

Mum's lips pinched. "Sylvia is Hugo Pearsall's wife now. She doesn't have time for us any longer. One day you'll understand."

And one day Izzie did. Sylvia had vaulted up the social ladder and entered into the ranks of women the Sheltons aspired to dress but could never be.

"What are you going to do now?" Alexandra asked, breaking into Izzie's thoughts as they reached the post office.

She sighed as she slipped her stamped envelope into the post box on the outside of the squat building. "Use every bit of leave I have to go to London. I just hope the trains aren't too horrible."

As they rounded the corner of the post office building, Izzie collided with a wall of khaki.

"Whoa!" came a man's accented voice, a hand on either of her arms steadying her as a thud sounded near her feet. "Are you okay, miss?"

She looked up and found herself staring up at a man. A tall, blond, tanned man wearing the widest smile she'd ever seen.

"I'm very sorry, sir. I should have been paying more attention," she said, stepping back.

"It's all my fault. I was trying to read and walk at the same time," he said, as he stooped down and scooped up a pad of paper scribbled all over with notes.

"You're American," she said dumbly.

"That I am," he said with a laugh before sticking out his hand. "Staff Sergeant Jack Perry, Iowa born and raised."

"Izzie. I mean, Aircraft Woman Second Class Isabelle Shelton. From London."

There was a small cough to her right, and when she turned, she realized that Alexandra was watching on with open amusement.

"Oh. This is my friend Aircraft Woman Second Class Alexandra Sumner," she said.

"How do you do, staff sergeant?" asked Alexandra, taking his hand.

"You ladies are WAAFs?" asked Jack.

"We are," said Alexandra.

"We're in a barrage balloon unit." Why could she not string together more than a sentence when speaking to this man?

Alexandra shot her a pitying look.

"What's an American doing on an RAF base?" Izzie asked hesitantly, trying again.

"I've been asking myself that same question, but my commanding officer reassures me that we're taking in more than just the

THE DRESSMAKERS OF LONDON • 209

view." He leaned in and gave them both a conspiratorial smile. "You didn't hear this from me, but we're having a look around to see if the United States Army Air Forces might like to move in or at least become your neighbors."

"Goodness, does that mean there are more than just you here?" asked Alexandra.

He laughed. "I'd say you're likely to see a few more air force men in the future. Consider me a member of the advance team," he said.

"Just wait until Lottie hears about this," said Alexandra.

"Who's Lottie?" he asked.

"Oh, you'll find out," said Alexandra.

He tugged on the brim of his cap. "Well, Aircraft Woman Second Class Sumner and Izzie from London. I hope the boys and I will be seeing both of you around."

"There's a dance this Friday at a placed called the Assembly Hall," Izzie blurted out. "There'll be a band and everything. All of the girls from our unit are planning on going."

"Will you be there too?" he asked, his eyes fixed on hers.

"Yes," she breathed.

He nodded. "Good. I'll see you then. Goodbye, ladies."

"Goodbye," said Alexandra cheerfully.

"Goodbye," Izzie echoed quietly as he walked off.

"Well, it looks as though the American invasion has well and truly started."

"Yes," Izzie murmured.

Alexandra spun around, clearly delighted. "Isabelle Shelton, I have never seen you at a loss for words before."

"I wasn't at a loss for words," she protested weakly.

Her friend snorted. "At least you managed to tell him about the dance."

"He's probably far too busy to come," she said, hoping very much that he would prove her wrong.

"Oh, I think he'll make a point of coming after meeting you," said Alexandra.

"Don't be ridiculous," she said with a shake of her head.

"Izzie," said Alexandra, slipping an arm through hers, "I think you'll find that, on this one rare occasion, I am not the ridiculous one."

20 April 1942

Dear Sylvia,

Do not pretend that you know the first thing about what Mum was like.

Sincerely,
Isabelle Shelton

Chapter Twenty-Two

Sylvia lifted her head. Yes, there it was again, a rapping coming from the front of the shop.

She set her pencil down on the notebook she'd been staring at for the past ten minutes and pushed away from her mother's desk. Then she hurried to the front door. Careful, she peeled back a bit of the blackout to peer outside. On the other side of the glass, William held up a brown paper bag.

Quickly, she let him in.

"You have perfect timing," she said as she wrestled the blackout back in place.

"Why is that?" he asked, removing his hat.

"I was just about to force myself to start something I've been putting off for days."

"And now that I'm here you can put it off a little longer?" he asked.

She grinned. "You see? The perfect excuse."

"In that case, you might be even happier to see me." He unrolled the scrunched-up to top of the bag to reveal a pair of parchment-wrapped sandwiches. "I thought that you might be hungry, so I brought some dinner by."

She thought about the dish cooked by Mrs. Atkinson that was no doubt sitting in the oven at home, waiting to be heated up and eaten alone at the flat's dining room table.

"Sandwiches sound like just the thing," she said. "Let me give you some coupons for whatever's in them."

He shook his head. "There's no need. I once did a little work for Mrs. Reynolds's son when he had a problem with the lease on the building for his hardware shop a few roads down. She doesn't mind adding a little extra to an order from time to time."

She put her hand to her chest in mock horror. "Mr. Gray, are you admitting that you are dealing on the black market? And you, a solicitor."

He shot her a smile. "I thought that the girl who used to pinch oranges from the stand outside of Mrs. Reynolds's shop wouldn't mind."

"That is just one of the many grievances Mrs. Reynolds has against me," she said.

"I remember you always used to smell like orange oil afterward," he said.

She blushed. When she'd been younger and just learning how to primp, she used to take the peel of the stolen oranges and rub it behind her ears because she couldn't afford scent. To think that he would have remembered a little thing like that . . .

"Will you come back?" she asked. "I can't promise much in the way of dining facilities, but I can make us some tea."

"Now that is a fair trade for sandwiches," he said.

She led him to the office and cleared a bit of space for him before going to make tea. When she returned, she found him looking around, the unwrapped sandwiches sitting on their paper next to her notebook.

"Here you are," she said, handing him a cup.

"Thank you," he said. "It must have been quite the job tidying this place."

"It was more than a tidy," she said. "My mother's record-keeping system baffles me. It took me until the first week in March to sort through the paperwork, let alone reconcile the account books."

He winced. "Was it really that bad?"

"I found receipts for fabric purchased in 1932 in the same box as a bag of buttons and bits of ribbon, and that chair you're sitting on was held up by an order book from 1929," she said.

"How is the flat?" he asked.

She stilled. "I don't know."

"Sylvia, you have been up to the flat, haven't you?"

She cleared her throat. "No. Not yet. The shop has been keeping me so busy, I've hardly been able to give it a thought."

Working at the shop had been hurdle enough. She wasn't yet ready to climb the steep stairs to the upper floor and immerse herself completely in the life she'd once had.

"Do you know, I tried to help Izzie sort through all of this when you both first inherited," he said.

"And you didn't run away screaming?" she asked with a laugh. "You are a wonder, William."

"I nearly did."

"I can't say I blame you," she said.

He sat back, seeming to study her.

"You're making me nervous, William. What is it?" she asked, half-joking.

"How do you think the shop was doing before your mother's death?" he asked. He must have seen her surprise about such a direct question because he quickly added, "I would ask your sister, but I fear Izzie might have been too close to assess it fairly."

"Honestly," she started slowly, "I think it has been struggling for some time—and not the way Izzie thinks. From what I can tell from the paperwork I've found, rationing did have an impact, but things were beginning to slow well before that."

"How long?" he asked.

"Since before the war. In some ways, it appears my mother made some good decisions. She had no debt to speak of and she did have some money saved, but none of the records I've found show any investment either. There have been no efforts at advertising or expanding Mrs. Shelton's customer base. There has been no expansion into children's clothing, soft furnishings, anything. It's almost as though my mother tried to preserve the shop in aspic."

"Have you told Izzie?" asked William, biting into his sandwich.

"I doubt very much she would listen to me."

"Why not?" he asked.

"Oh, William. I've made such a hash of things," she said.

"What happened?" he asked.

"I found some sketches that Izzie made. They're beautiful—a real cut above what Mum ever designed even in her heyday. Miss Reid and I thought that we use could use them as guidance to try to bring the shop's offering in line with the new Board of Trade restrictions, but I was so excited I didn't think to ask Izzie's permission. She'd drawn them, so I assumed she wanted to see them worn by customers.

"When she came back on leave and saw what we were doing, she was furious." She shook her head. "She doesn't trust me."

"Write to her. Explain why you did it," said William.

"I have. I've written so many letters, and this was all she sent back," she said, reaching into the desk to pull out Izzie's most letter that amounted to one devastating line: *Do not pretend that you know the first thing about what Mum was like.*

She watched as William read it and let out a long breath. "She's angry."

"That's why I tried to apologize."

"No, Sylvia. Your sister is angry. About everything."

"What does Izzie have to be angry with me about? She's hardly spoken to me since I married Hugo," she said.

William's expression hardly changed, yet she couldn't miss the pity in his gaze.

"Well," he finally said, "that is something to think about, isn't it?"

"We lost touch. It happens sometimes in families," she said, but even as she said it she had to fight not to squirm. As the elder of the two sisters, Sylvia's job had been to look out for Izzie, and she'd enjoyed having her little sister running around after her, bright-eyed and curious. But when their mother began to take Izzie under her wing and train her, Sylvia had felt pushed out. Lonely.

But that was not Izzie's fault. That argument had been between Sylvia and her mother.

"Give her time. Your sister is still grieving your mother," he said.

"And the fact that our mother bequeathed the shop to both of us?" she asked with an arched brow.

"And that," said William.

She sighed. "I will never understand why she did that."

"Perhaps Mrs. Shelton thought you would need it one day," he said. "Like she wrote in her will."

I hope that, as it has for me, the shop will take care of them when they need it most.

Sylvia shook her head. Why would she need the shop to take care of her? If anything, the shop needed her and her time and patience sorting it out.

"Give Izzie time," William repeated, "and keep writing to her. She'll eventually listen to reason."

She dipped her head, not knowing what to say to that. This giving and taking advice felt so intimate—something reserved for a husband—but she had known William since she was a child. There was no calmer, more steadfast man than him.

"May I ask you something?" she finally asked.

"Anything," he said.

"That's very unlike a solicitor, agreeing to answer a question without knowing what it is."

"I left the office an hour ago, and I'm determined not to be a solicitor again until nine o'clock tomorrow morning. You are free to ask whatever you like," he said.

"What is it like not going off to fight?"

"Ah, that question."

"I don't mean any offense," she hurriedly added.

His lips tipped up a fraction of an inch. "I know you don't, Sylvia, but not everyone is so generous if I don't take the time to explain about being deaf in my left ear."

Her heart broke a little to hear that, because she couldn't stand the thought of anyone thinking less of the gentle, considerate man she'd grown up with.

"It isn't easy," he admitted. "I know that sounds ridiculous given that I'm here, relatively safe in my solicitor's office while tens of thousands of men are off fighting."

"No, it doesn't," she said.

He gave her a smile. "Thank you. Being told that a chance accident when you were a child means you aren't even fit to drive an ambulance for the medical corps is humbling and humiliating in equal turns."

She shuddered, remembering too well the day it had happened. It was about two years after the Sheltons had moved to Glengall Road. Her mother believed Sylvia, at thirteen, was old enough to sweep the shop floor and do other odd jobs. However, nine-year-old

Izzie was still allowed to run wild with the other neighborhood children so long as she was back for supper when the church bells rang six. That was why, when Izzie had raced into the shop, crying that William was hurt, Sylvia had followed Mum and Miss Reid out of the shop like a shot. William was lying on the ground, clutching the side of his head as blood trickled down from his ear.

Apparently William and the other children had found some sticks from a nearby park and were pretending to be buccaneers. One of the children slipped while thrusting, and a stick had gone straight into William's left ear, puncturing the eardrum.

"Your hearing never came back then?" she asked.

He shook his head. "I haven't heard a thing in it since. What is your husband doing in the war?"

She shifted in her seat, suddenly acutely aware that this was the longest she'd been alone with a man who wasn't Hugo in years. Except that was ridiculous. William would never do anything untoward. For goodness' sake, her mother had trusted him to handle her affairs. If Izzie had any sense and the inclination to marry, she would open her eyes and realize that a good man was waiting right here in front of her.

Only, when Sylvia looked at William, she found she couldn't imagine him as Izzie's husband.

Sylvia cleared her throat and said, "Hugo is a surgeon lieutenant-commander in the Royal Navy Medical Service."

"You must be very proud," he said.

"Yes." The word stuck in her throat, coming out more croak than confirmation. "He is away a great deal."

"That must be difficult."

Not as difficult as she had once found it.

She cleared her throat and then gestured to the notebook she'd set aside. "I should probably finish this."

William sat up a little straighter. "Of course. I didn't mean to keep you so long."

"You didn't!" she rushed to say. "That is, I appreciate you sharing your contraband sandwiches and a little bit of company as well."

"Well, I'll let you finish your supper," he said as he began to fold the parchment into precise lines until all that was left was a neat rectangle, not a crumb to be seen.

She smiled as she showed him to the shop door. Of course William wouldn't leave a crumb behind. He would never be so inconsiderate as that.

———

Several hours later, Sylvia let her handbag slip off her wrist and onto the flat's entryway table, only just catching it as it teetered, threatening to fall onto the polished hardwood floor. Then she lifted her hands to her hat to unpin it and cast it aside. She didn't even bother to check her appearance in the mirror. All she wanted was to pour herself a couple fingers of whiskey, sink into bed, and sleep for twelve hours.

She toed off her shoes, leaving them in the entryway. She would pick them up before Mrs. Atkinson arrived the following morning, but at that moment she couldn't be bothered. Trying to rub the tension out of the back of her neck, she made for the sitting room and its generously stocked bar cart. It had been weeks since she'd entertained anyone at home, but keeping the bottles topped up and waiting seemed like the civilized thing to do even if the recent alcohol shortages meant that it was harder than ever to find certain spirits in London shops.

She pushed open the ajar sitting room door and stopped short when she saw a pair of highly polished black shoes poking out from behind one of wingback chairs in front of the coal fire. The edge of a newspaper dropped into view and she heard the sound of paper crackling and fabric rustling as Hugo twisted to peer around the chair's wing.

"You're home late," he said before twisting back around again.

Sylvia closed her eyes, praying that when she opened them he would be gone—a figment of her imagination.

She was not so lucky.

Doing her best to pull on the composure she'd shed at the front door, she padded across the floor to the bar cart and poured herself a whiskey. Not two fingers. Four.

Drink clutched to her chest as though it were a talisman, she turned on her stockinged feet.

"You didn't write to tell me that you were due leave," she said.

He glanced up at her, closed his paper, and then folded it once again. Finally, he said, "I'm not on leave."

"Another meeting in London then," she said, remembering his unannounced appearance in December.

"The work I did with the admiralty and the navy's medical service was a success. I've been reassigned to London to continue it. I can't say much else, of course. You understand."

Sylvia stared at her husband. He was coming home.

Many years ago, when they'd still been in the first flush of their marriage, she might have thought it would be romantic for him to surprise her like this, but this had no romance about it. There was no kiss, no hug, no hello even. Just a simple statement of fact laced with disapproval—"You're home late"—followed by the bombshell news that he had been reassigned.

She took a long drink of her whiskey and then asked, "Does that mean you will be moving back home?"

"Into my own home? Yes, I should think so," he said.

She nodded shortly.

"I can't imagine that will be a problem for you, will it?" he asked.

"No," she said automatically. "Why should it be?"

"You're back so late. I had thought that perhaps it might inconvenience you to have your husband home."

She burst out laughing at the suspicion on his voice. "Oh, Hugo. You don't have to worry about that. Unlike some, I actually believe in the vows that we exchanged when we were married."

The jab and every unspoken confession it represented hung in the air between them, and for a moment she thought he might acknowledge the letters in his desk drawer. *That* would be a start, her tired brain reasoned. Just the simple admission that he had strayed from their marriage.

He did not, however, say a thing.

"If you must know," she continued, "I'm very busy at the moment. You might find that I am often home late."

"Your charity work keeps you out past the blackout?" he asked.

She tilted her head to one side to study him. "Frequently. Committee work is more involved than you might think."

"I suppose Rupert can sympathize, can he?" he asked.

"I'm certain he can. Claire is also very busy," she lied easily before taking another drink. In truth, she had no idea how her friend managed her social diary when her husband was home from leave. It had been weeks since the pair of them had seen each other outside of a War Widows' Fund meeting.

Hugo held her gaze for a moment longer but then said, "I don't anticipate being at the flat much myself. There is too much to do, and I might find it easier to stay at my club some nights. It's closer to the Admiralty."

Despite all of the resentment and anger she'd stored up over the letters, her heart sank. He wasn't even back one evening, and he was already trying to find ways to wriggle out of being at home. To find ways to spend time without her and with his mistress.

All of a sudden, the strain of holding herself together so tightly these past months for the sake of the shop, her sister, her committee, her marriage, all of it was too much. Exhaustion swept over her.

"I'm off to bed," she announced. "Good night, Hugo."

She could feel his eyes on her as she walked out, but in that moment she couldn't find it in herself to care.

Dear Izzie,

I hope you will forgive me for not writing to you for a few days, but I do not want you to think that it is because I didn't receive your last letter. On the contrary, I wanted to carefully consider what you said.

You are right. I don't pretend to know what our mother was like after I left home and you stayed. I can't pretend that that simple fact alone doesn't make you eminently more qualified to understand more about our mother than I ever could. Yet, in some ways our mother must have been as much a mystery to you as she was to me. Why else would you have been so surprised that she left Mrs. Shelton's Fashions to both of us?

There is one thing that I suspect I know of Maggie Shelton that you do not because you were far too young. Our mother was brave.

You were only seven when Papa died, so you might not remember those terrible days after the police came to our door and told our mother what happened. It's strange that, other than our tears, the thing I remember most about that time is the telephone ringing and ringing. I loved the telephone with its candlestick receiver, but I didn't understand why anyone would want to telephone us when everything was so sad. Years later, I realized that it must have been Papa's banker and his solicitor. Perhaps it was the creditors descending like vultures, trying to collect their piece of him now that he was dead.

This went on until one day, our mother announced we were going out. She dressed both of us up in our very best clothes—she made beautiful frilled dresses for us out of love rather than necessity in those days—and took us on the bus. I remember that she held both of our hands tightly the entire way, and when we climbed off the bus she checked us over, straightening collars and fluffing bows. I didn't understand why she wanted us to be perfect, but I could tell it was important, so I stood up as straight as I could and tried not to undo her good work.

It was only when we were walking up to the front door that I realized we were at Papa's parents' house. I remembered the black door standing out starkly against the white-painted front from our Christmas visits. I do not recall ever crossing the threshold other than during the festive season.

Our grandparents' housekeeper let us into the drawing room and told us to wait. To my eleven-year-old mind it felt like we were there for an age, although I suspect that in reality it was only twenty minutes—just long enough to assure our mother of the reception she was about to receive from the elder Sheltons. When, finally, our grandmother and grandfather entered the room, it was clear that they did not care to see us. But our mother sat there, her back unbending, and explained the situation. Papa had overstretched himself to purchase our house in Ladbroke Grove. There was a mortgage. There were other debts. There was no money, and the creditors were calling to try to collect whatever they could.

"Our son would never be so irresponsible," our grandmother had said, clearly horrified at the news of Papa's debts.

"I can assure you that he was," said our mother, her voice taking on that hardened quality it had when she was no longer willing to tolerate a person's denial.

The longer our mother spoke, the more I could see our grandparents clam up. They wouldn't look at you or me, and I wanted to reach out to tell our mother to stop. Whatever she was doing, stop, because these people did not want us there in their drawing room.

Then she asked for help.

She told the two of us to stand up and she said, "Peter always intended for the girls to receive a good education. Sylvia already has a place at an excellent school, but there is the matter of the fees. Will you please help your grandchildren?"

Our grandfather ordered you and me out of the room then but I already knew. The answer was never going to be yes.

We left and I thought that would be it, but after a fortnight, our mother put on her Sunday best once again and left us with the next-door neighbor. When she came back that afternoon, she said that she had been to see our grandparents and that everything was arranged. She explained that things would be different from now on. We would be moving. There would be no more trips to the seaside, no more cook or maid-of-all-work. We would both go to new schools. Our mother would open a shop and begin to work.

To this day, I don't know how our mother convinced the Sheltons to give her enough money to set herself up in business. Did she humble herself and allow them to berate her for ruining the future of a son for whom they had great ambitions? Did she threaten to expose them for their miserly ways and their willingness to abandon their granddaughters? Whatever she did, I didn't understand at the time the magnitude of her sacrifice for us. However, I've lived enough of life to have come to admire her greatly for doing what she had to in order to provide for us.

However, for all of our mother's bravery and her determination, she was a woman, flawed and complicated. The very thing I admire her for—pulling herself up out of difficulties, first when she married our father and then again after he died—made her terrified of anything that might threaten her place in the world once again. You cannot deny, Izzie, that our mother would not take risks, and that is why Mrs. Shelton's Fashions has been producing the same dresses since the twenties even as fashion has evolved. Our mother found a niche and built a business out of her talent as a seamstress, but she was neither a fashion plate nor a tastemaker.

Perhaps I should have been more straightforward with you weeks ago. Mrs. Shelton's Fashions is in trouble. Our mother never carried debt, and she bought the building that Mrs. Shelton's occupies as soon as she could. Both of those have proven to be incredibly prudent decisions. However, she was deficient and unwilling to accept help in many other ways. Our clientele has begun to dwindle to the point that we need to bring new customers through our doors, and quickly—otherwise we may not have doors to open any longer. We need to adapt to the Board of

Trade's new rules, and that means evolving our business practices and our designs. We cannot stand on outdated principles. Mrs. Shelton's _must_ change.

I ask you to believe me when I tell you that the business will not survive the war in its current state. That means that sometimes we will we need to go against our mother's years of wisdom and experience. Sometimes we will need to openly defy her very fundamental beliefs about what the business could be. We must evolve.

I made a promise to myself when you left on the train for Innsworth that I would protect the shop while you are gone. I apologize again for not thinking to ask to use your sketches, but I hope you will believe me when I say that I was only doing what I thought was best for Mrs. Shelton's Fashions. For you, Izzie.

Yours,
Sylvia

P.S. William stopped by the shop the other night while I was doing some work after closing for the day. I sometimes worry that he is lonely and has to settle for my company. Anyway, he asked after you.

Chapter Twenty-Three

Izzie nearly stumbled as Lottie and Amelia danced up to Alexandra and her in the lane and swept up their hands to tug them along.

"If all of you don't hurry up, we'll be late!" called Amelia over her shoulder.

"All right, all right," said Izzie with a laugh.

"I don't know why there's such a rush," grumbled Nancy behind them, but even she couldn't completely hide her excitement.

The moment they'd arrived at RAF Horsham St Faith, they'd learned that the Assembly Hall dances were the highlight of everyone's month. Apparently every WAAF and RAF man from all over north Norfolk who could manage permission to leave base would pour in and, fueled by a band and pints, would dance and flirt the night away. It was a bit of fun, a break from the business of war.

"Do you think there will be officers there?" asked Grace, who was walking with Nancy.

"I'm counting on it," Lottie sang out as she looped her arm through Amelia's and the pair of them fell back into line with the others.

"I'm hoping for one of those Americans Alexandra and Izzie spotted," said Amelia with a laugh.

"Wouldn't that be a treat?" said Molly dreamily.

Alexandra nudged Izzie. "Do you think we should demand a finder's fee?"

Izzie smiled a little but didn't say anything.

"You aren't nervous about seeing the staff sergeant again, are you?" asked Alexandra in a low voice.

"I'm thinking about Sylvia's letter."

Her sister's latest letter had been a strange blend of apology and explanation, and it had disturbed Izzie. The things her sister wrote about, she couldn't remember. Not a bus ride to her grandparents' house, not meeting them in the drawing room. And try as she might, she couldn't recall Mum telling them about debt or that their life would be different from that day forward.

And yet, while once she might have dismissed the letter outright, there was something in Sylvia's words that made her pause. A balance. An acknowledgment of the good of Mum that Izzie could always cite and the bad that she never would say out loud because it sounded too much like a betrayal.

But it was the lines at the end of the letter that had really taken Izzie's breath away. The business might not survive the war if things didn't change. It was, she realized now, what had caused the low, hollow dread in Izzie's stomach for months before Mum's death. It was all there, from the appointment book that looked more open than ever before to the orders for one dress and one skirt from customers who only two years before might have ordered two dresses, two skirts, two blouses, and a coat in one fell swoop.

But perhaps the most startling realization had been that what Sylvia wrote sounded plausible because she hadn't pointed to any one disastrous decision. Mrs. Shelton's was in a slow decline that you could almost miss if you weren't looking.

"Izzie, can you stop worrying about the shop for a couple of hours and enjoy yourself at a dance?" asked Alexandra gently. "I promise there is nothing you can do from the Assembly Hall."

"You're right," Izzie said.

"Besides," said Alexandra, giving her a nudge, "what could be more fun than walking into a dance with a partner already singled out?"

"Alexandra . . ."

"Don't Alexandra me. I saw how you looked at that American staff sergeant," her friend teased.

"How did she look at him?" asked Grace.

"Like he was the sun and she was a sunflower," said Alexandra.

Izzie laughed and gently whacked her friend on the arm. "Tosh."

"True," Alexandra pushed.

It was true that a certain tall, handsome American staff sergeant whom she'd stumbled into had flitted into her thoughts from time to time over the past four days. There was something about his easy, casual smile that made her want to turn to it, and it didn't hurt that he had the full, rich voice of a film star. Not that she would ever give her balloon girls the satisfaction of knowing that. She would never hear the end of it.

"He probably won't even be here this evening," she said.

"I hope he is and that he has six good-looking friends with him," said Lottie with relish.

"That's the spirit," said Alexandra as the Assembly Hall came into view. The white-painted front glowed in the moonlight, and even from a distance Izzie could make out a steady stream of patrons moving between the dance hall and the pub next door to it. Although the windows and doors were covered in accordance with the blackout rules that were especially crucial in an area that was such a target for air raids, music pulsed from the building, beckoning them closer.

After the balloon girls had all piled through the front door, past the blackout curtain, and paid their admission, they walked into the dance hall to a sea of couples swaying to "The Way You Look Tonight."

"Look!" Lottie pointed to the small stage at the far end of the dance floor upon which stood a WAAF in uniform in front of a microphone. "They have a singer!"

"Where should we sit?" asked Nancy, looking around.

"Sit? We're not going to sit tonight," said Amelia.

"You're going to be too busy dancing," said Lottie with a laugh as she stuck her arm out into the crowd and stopped a man with a flying officer's single stripe on his uniform.

"What are you doing?" asked Nancy, panicking.

"Hello there," said Lottie cheerfully to the man while Amelia gave Nancy a little shove in his direction. "Would you like to dance with my friend Nancy?"

Izzie leaned in to ask Alexandra, "Do you think we should save her?"

"Lottie, I really don't think—" But Nancy broke off when she looked up at the soldier who had caught her around the waist to stop her from falling. "Oh. Hello."

"Hello there. Would you care to dance?" he asked.

"Yes, please," Nancy said, her voice breathless above the band.

"I think she's fine," said Alexandra with a laugh.

"Lucky her," said Molly.

"Good work," said Alexandra as Lottie rejoined them looking more than a little smug. "Or quick work. I can't decide which."

"Necessary work. I like Nancy, I really do, but she needs to loosen up a little," said Lottie.

"It looks as though she's loosening up just fine," said Izzie, watching Nancy and her soldier press a little closer than was entirely necessary to dance the quickstep.

"Right," said Amelia. "It's decided then."

"What is?" asked Grace.

"Tonight, everyone finds a soldier or a sailor or a flier to fall a little bit in love with," said Amelia.

When all of them began to protest except for Lottie, Amelia said, "I didn't say you had to marry the man, but tonight we're all dancing and having a good time."

Alexandra glanced at Izzie. "What do you think?"

Izzie looked around her at the exuberant outpouring of joy captured within those four walls. This was about more than just blowing off a little steam. Next month, some of the men and women dancing and laughing here would be gone, and no one could be certain who that would be.

Tonight was about tonight. Nothing more.

"All right," she said. "Where do we start?"

"I'd be willing to hazard a guess that the usual rules of society balls don't apply," said Alexandra. "Lottie, I think this is your area of expertise."

"All right, debutante." Lottie straightened her shoulders and tossed her platinum curls back as she cast a determined eye over the dance floor. "Find a man you like the look of across the room and catch his eye. Then look away and look back again with a little smile."

There was a beat, and then Amelia asked, "That's it?"

Lottie shrugged. "It always works for me. Sometimes, if I really like the look of him, I'll give him a little wave so I don't leave him guessing."

"It cannot be that easy," Alexandra whispered to Izzie.

Izzie and the other balloon girls watched as Lottie scanned the crowd. After a moment she stopped and locked eyes with a flier leaning against a column, cigarette in hand. She looked away, looked back, smiled, looked away again, and then glanced back to give the man a little wiggle of her fingers. The man straightened, put his cigarette out, and made his way over.

They all watched in amazement as he stopped in front of Lottie.

"Hello," he said, offering her his hand. "Would you care for a dance?"

"I would, thank you," Lottie said, resting her hand in his. As the man led her to the dance floor, Lottie looked over her shoulder at all of them and grinned in triumph.

"She's incredible," said Grace in wonder.

"It's like watching Fred Astaire do the waltz," said Alexandra.

"I want to try it," said Amelia and Molly at the same time.

Alexandra dipped her head. "I don't think you need to try anything, Izzie. Look who just walked in."

Izzie turned around and spotted Staff Sergeant Jack Perry near the door with three other men. He adjusted the cuffs of his jacket as he scanned the room. She held her breath until his eyes fell on her. There was a beat, and then that sunshine smile lit up his face.

He gestured to his friends and then made a beeline straight for her.

When he stopped in front of her, he said, "Aircraft Woman Second Class Shelton, I hoped you'd be here."

A laugh bubbled to her lips. "It sounds so formal when you say it like that."

"What should I call you?" he asked.

"Most people just call me Izzie."

"Well, Izzie, I'd be honored if you would call me Jack," he said.

"Who are your friends, Jack?" she asked, feeling bolder than she had in ages.

"Sergeants Ben Martin, Harry Pitcher, Albert Proctor, and Jeff Browning of the USAAF at your service," he said.

After Izzie made quick introductions of Alexandra, Grace, Molly, and Amelia, Jack leaned over to her. "I'd be delighted if you would say yes to a dance with me."

Without another word, she put her right hand in his. He placed his free hand on the small of her back and led her into the flow of dancers, lifting her right hand in his as they began to fox-trot.

"You had me worried," he said as they settled into the dance.

She looked up quickly. "Worried?"

"I was certain that I would walk in and you'd be dancing with some flight lieutenant or another," he said.

She laughed at that. "I don't think any flight lieutenant would ever condescend to dance with me."

"Why not?" he asked, sounding offended on her behalf.

"First of all, he would outrank me by leaps and bounds."

"All the more reason to impress you with his rank."

"And secondly, that would require a flight lieutenant to have ever given me the time of day."

"I can't imagine a man who wouldn't pay attention to you if he saw you," he said.

She blushed. "Be serious."

"I am serious," he insisted. "You're lovely."

Goodness. She wished for a moment that she could freeze time and pull Lottie aside to ask what on earth she was supposed to do when a man spoke to her like this.

"Where in America did you say you're from?" she blurted out.

"A town called Newton in Iowa," he said. "You said you're from London?"

She nodded. "A neighborhood called Maida Vale."

234 • JULIA KELLY

"And what's in Maida Vale?" he asked.

"My mother's dressmaker's shop," she said. "That is, it was my mother's. She died in November."

"I'm sorry for your loss," he said, his gentle words wrapping around her like a hug.

"Thank you," she said.

"Who is running the shop while you're here?" he asked.

"My sister, Sylvia," she said. "I was posting a letter to her when I ran into you."

"Then I'll have to thank your sister one day, because without that letter, I wouldn't have met you."

"That might be the only thing to thank my sister for," she said.

He frowned. "You two don't get along?"

She paused, wondering at the most gracious way to explain things to him. But when she saw his open, earnest expression, she simply said, "We didn't talk for a number of years, but when my mother died, we both inherited the business."

"You don't sound thrilled about that," he commented.

"No, I'm not," she said honestly. "I worked right by Mum's side until the day she died. Sylvia left home as soon as she married. It's not fair."

The song ended, and she expected him to step back, to put some distance between the two of them. However, he held on to her as he said, "It's funny, but something similar happened in my family."

"Really?" she asked.

The band started back up again, and he led her into the next dance.

"My family has sold farm equipment for the past thirty years. My older brother, Louis, never showed any interest in the store. He went off to Iowa City for college and played football until his knee gave out. He was talking about going to law school out east after graduation. Louis always had the book smarts.

"When Dad died, I'd been working for the business officially for a couple years, but really I'd been selling on the shop floor since I was fourteen. I was pretty mad when I found out that Dad hadn't changed his will, and he still had the business going to both of us."

"What did you do?" she asked.

"I was certain that Louis would sell his half to me and go off to Connecticut for his law degree. Instead, he stayed in Newton. Turns out that the first night he was back for Dad's funeral, he met Muriel."

"Muriel?" she asked.

"My now sister-in-law," said Jack with a smile. "He fell head over heels in love with her at first sight, and from that day on, law school out east was off the table."

"But didn't that bother you?" she asked.

"That Louis found the love of his life? No. That he blew up all my plans in the process? Sure. I did plenty to work up a head of steam while thinking about how I'd put in all of the work and he was going to just swoop in.

"Then Louis came to me with an idea. He told me he wanted me to hire him, just like I would any other employee, to run the business side of things. I told him I didn't need someone to do all of that, that I could handle it, but he finally talked me into it by promising me that it would free me up to do the actual business of making all of the money he would be minding.

"For the first six months, we fought like cats and dogs, but it turns out Louis was right." He laughed and gave a shake of his head as though he couldn't quite believe it. "I had more time to talk to customers and to sell. Louis and Muriel got married, and after they had their first son, the business had its most profitable year."

236 • JULIA KELLY

A little flicker of hope flamed up in her chest. Perhaps she and Sylvia could find a similar sort of peace. Perhaps they could find a way to work together, to save the business—

A brick wall of an obstacle rose in front of her. Louis had wanted to come back to his old life in Iowa. Sylvia would never condescend to do that.

"Who's minding *your* shop while you're both off fighting?" she asked.

"That old football injury kept my brother out of service, no matter how hard he argues with the draft board. He does everything else he can, selling war bonds and things like that, but I know it's killing him to be left behind.

"Now, I don't know your sister from Adam, but I do know that sometimes people can surprise you."

She sighed. "I'm glad things worked out between you and Louis, Jack, but Sylvia isn't like that. She only stepped in because I was conscripted and there was no one else to do it."

He inclined his head. "Let me ask you this. When you asked your sister for help, did she kick up a fuss?"

"No," she said slowly. It had been the opposite. Sylvia had said yes without hesitation or protest, and even though Izzie thought her efforts were misguided, Sylvia had written to her consistently over the past few months. Izzie had to begrudgingly admit it sounded as though her sister had thrown herself back into the business.

"Well, that must count for something," said Jack.

"Maybe." She hesitated. "She offered to sell her share of the shop to me as soon as I can find the money."

"Will you say yes?" he asked.

"I already have."

"Then there's no problem, really. You'll own it soon enough, I'm sure."

"Thank you." But something made her pause. Being away from the shop and reading about Sylvia setting to rights all of the things that were wrong at Mrs. Shelton's Fashions made Izzie feel strangely . . . distant. Certain aspects of the business terrified her, there was no denying it, but before Mum had died, she'd been champing at the bit to prove that she could run the shop. However, the thought of returning after the war and picking up where she'd left off seemed daunting. Sylvia had made so many changes and with such confidence, would Izzie even know where to begin when it came to bookkeeping or managing unpleasant customers?

As though reading the doubt creeping into her thoughts, Jack said, "How about we not talk anymore? Why don't we just dance?"

Izzie swallowed down her hesitation and let him pull her a little closer. "Yes. Let's."

A half hour after the band played its last song, Izzie, Alexandra, Lottie, Amelia, Molly, and Grace all spilled through the door of the barracks, buoyed by beer and jubilation.

"You should have seen the expression on Harry's face when you kissed him on the cheek, Grace," said Amelia, buckling over with laughter.

"It's a wonder the man didn't float away," said Alexandra.

"He's sweet," said Grace with a dreamy smile.

"Do you know who else is sweet?" asked Lottie, rounding on Izzie with a grin. "Staff Sergeant Jack Perry."

"Oh, look at her blush!" said Amelia, pointing at Izzie as she collapsed onto her bed.

"I'm not blushing," said Izzie.

"You are," said Molly.

"She's right," said Alexandra.

"Did you kiss the staff sergeant?" Lottie demanded.

"I did not," she said primly, although by the end of the evening she'd been tying herself up in knots wanting to. But Jack had been a gentleman through and through, walking with her as he and his friends escorted them back to the gate of their base.

"He asked if he could write to me," she said.

There was a loud chorus of "Ooo!" and then the girls fell over themselves giggling.

"Hey, where's Nancy?" asked Amelia looking around.

"She's probably still necking with that flying officer Lottie shoved at her," said Molly.

"Necking?" cried Amelia.

"I saw them around the corner of the pub as we left," said Molly.

"And you didn't say anything?" asked Amelia, incredulous.

"Of course she didn't," said Lottie. "That would have ruined things for Nancy."

"But imagine the expression on her face if she knew we'd caught her," said Amelia with a grin.

As Amelia and Lottie bickered good-naturedly back and forth, Alexandra leaned over to Izzie and asked in a low tone, "If the dreamy Staff Sergeant Jack Perry is good to his word and sends you a letter, will you write back?"

"If I like his letter, I think I will," she said, even though she knew that she would be waiting for the post every day until he did.

April 27, 1942

Dear Izzie,

I hope that you were serious when you said that I might write to you because I've been wanting to since the moment I left you on Friday night. However, I forced myself to wait because I didn't want you to think that I'm the sort of man who rushes into things without considering them carefully.

The truth is, I haven't thought of much besides you since our first dance together. The only thing that's saved me from being made an object of fun by all the rest of the guys is that Harry's feet still haven't touched the floor after your little redheaded friend kissed him.

As you can imagine, the USAAF tries its best to keep our minds off of pretty girls and on the task of surveying for and building bases, but I don't think I'll be able to sleep until I find out whether you want to see me again.

Thinking of nothing but you,
Jack

_____

29 April 1942

Dear Jack,

I will admit, I was beginning to grow very cross with you until, on Tuesday morning before heading out to tend to our balloon, I received your letter. I ripped it open straightaway, and I was so happy to read that you've been thinking about me just as I've been thinking about you.

I must admit, I wasn't certain you would come to the dance on Friday. I very much wanted you to be there, but I assumed that you would have forgotten me as soon as you met me. Alexandra tells me that is ridiculous, but there hasn't been much time for dances and men while working at Mrs. Shelton's Fashions all these years.

I would very much like to see you again.

Yours,
Izzie

Chapter Twenty-Four

*S*ylvia clutched her umbrella, doing her best to steady it in the rain. It was not the usual misty drizzle that often hung over London during the winter, but the sheeting rain of the spring that pounded the pavement so hard that it bounced back up and soaked the tops of her leather shoes as she hurried along.

She was just turning the corner onto Glengall Road when a lorry roared by, driving through a deep puddle. The mucky water splashed up across the pavement, drenching her.

Sylvia screamed in horror as the lorry sped off and left her standing dripping on the side of the road. Everything from the bodice of her dusty-rose dress to her stockings and shoes was now soaked and stained.

"Would you look at that!"

Sylvia turned to see Mrs. Reynolds, broom in hand, looking on from her shop doorway. She braced herself, expecting the grocery owner to click her tongue and say something caustic about how Sylvia had probably done something to deserve the soaking. Instead, Mrs. Reynolds asked, "Are you all right?"

"Yes, I think so, but my dress is ruined," she said with a sigh. She would have to go home to change—when, she didn't know because she had a stack of invoices to pay and a committee meeting looming over her afternoon before she would need to return to the shop to finish her work.

"Inconsiderate man," grumbled Mrs. Reynolds. "He looked hale and hearty and young enough to serve, so I don't know what he was doing behind the wheel of a lorry in London."

"If ever there was an argument for women drivers, it's this," Sylvia said. A woman never would have driven off without a word.

"Is that what your sister's doing?" asked Mrs. Reynolds.

"I beg your pardon?" she asked.

"Those of us around the neighborhood have been wondering about her. We know she joined the WAAF, but no one's had any word from her," said Mrs. Reynolds.

Sylvia hadn't had much word from Izzie either recently. The last letter she'd sent Izzie had been a risk. When she'd sat down to write it, she hadn't meant to detail their mother's humiliation at the hands of the Sheltons. It had simply come out as she grasped for a way to try to make Izzie understand that there might only be four years between them but the sisters might as well have been from different generations.

"She's on a barrage balloon unit in East Anglia," she said.

Mrs. Reynolds nodded her approval. "All of that silk needs someone good with a needle to keep an eye on it."

"I suppose it does," she said.

"Do you know if she has to be out in air raids? I hate the thought that she might be in harm's way?"

"I don't know. I try not to think about it too much," she said.

"I remember when your mother first opened her shop. You two were just children."

"That was a long time ago," she said.

"You were a bit of a terror, truth be told," said Mrs. Reynolds.

"I don't know about that," she said with a laugh. When she saw Mrs. Reynolds's brows raise, she quickly added, "I apologize."

"It's a lovely thing watching children grow up, even if they aren't yours," said Mrs. Reynolds. "We were all so proud of you when you married that man with his beautiful suits and his elegant manners. What was his name?"

"Hugo."

"Mrs. Meed from the tea shop and I used to take tea with your mother every Wednesday afternoon. Mrs. Shelton managed to stretch out the details of your wedding for weeks," said Mrs. Reynolds.

"My mother talked about my wedding?" she asked in surprise.

When she and Hugo had become engaged, she had been deluded enough to think that her mother and Izzie might play a central role in her wedding. That hope had lasted only until Mrs. Pearsall, Hugo's mother, had set her straight. In one afternoon, Mrs. Pearsall had made her see what a burden planning a society wedding would place upon her mother and Izzie. Her fiancé's mother told her how naturally a dress shop owner would be happy to see her daughter clad in the undeniable quality of a Worth gown. And it had been Mrs. Pearsall who had pointed out how awkward a fourteen-year-old would feel when standing up as a bridesmaid among all of those distinguished men and women who would naturally attend Hugo's wedding.

The afternoon had been overwhelming, and Sylvia had walked away conceding everything Mrs. Pearsall had wanted. Yet it wasn't until later that she realized that it would fall to her to deliver the news to her mother and Izzie. There would be no Mrs. Shelton's Fashions bridal gown or trousseau. Izzie would not be a bridesmaid. Even wrapped up as she had been in Hugo and concerned as she was that she do nothing to embarrass him and risk the engagement, she could see the hurt in her mother's and Izzie's eyes as she told them.

Sylvia cringed now at the memory of it even as Mrs. Reynolds said, "We were all so proud. A Glengall Road girl made good. We hoped there might be news about a baby one day."

"Hugo and I were not blessed," she said quietly.

Mrs. Reynolds lifted her chin. "Your mother never said, but I suspected as much. Mr. Reynolds and I found that children were not in God's plan for us either."

There had never been any question of God for Sylvia and Hugo. It had been one of science, and one that, despite all of the years of appointments with specialists and recommended treatments, even a doctor of Hugo's skill could not conquer. They'd never stopped trying for a child—not officially—but it simply had faded away from all of their conversations.

"You have my sympathy, Mrs. Reynolds," she said.

A flicker of understanding seemed to soften the grocer's expression, but then Mrs. Reynolds nodded curtly. "I should go back to my counter. Please pass along my well-wishes to your sister in your next letter."

As Sylvia watched the other woman turn, she could feel where the cold water from the road had seeped into her dress and through her girdle. When she reached the dress shop door, she pushed it open, dropped her umbrella into the nearby stand, and immediately made her way to the back of the shop in search of a towel. She was picking at the fabric of her skirt when she nearly ran into Miss Reid.

"Oh! I didn't see you there," she said by way of apology.

Miss Reid's brow crinkled. "You're all wet. Didn't you bring an umbrella?"

"Yes, but that didn't stop the passing driver from dousing me with water from the road. I can't greet customers like this." She glanced at her watch. "And I'm due at a meeting at two o'clock.

With the buses the way they are right now, I don't know if I'll have enough time to go home and change."

Miss Reid pursed her lips and then turned on her heel and marched back in the direction of the workshop, leaving Sylvia watching her until Miss Reid called over her shoulder, "Are you coming?"

Something about the seamstress's determination set her feet into motion.

In the workshop, she watched Miss Reid lift one of the shop's cardboard delivery boxes and set it on the cutting table. Miss Reid worked the top of the box off and folded back the tissue.

"I can't take one of our customers' dresses," Sylvia protested as Miss Reid drew a black garment free from the tissue.

"This isn't an order," said Miss Reid, shaking the dress out and revealing a simple garment with a slim skirt, gathers under the bust, and three buttons marching up the bodice. A modest shoulder pad gave the dress a slightly military effect.

"Then what is it?" she asked, peering at the dress.

"I didn't see the harm in trying my hand at some patternmaking with your sister's designs, so I fetched the sketchbook from the office bookshelf." Miss Reid glanced her way as though trying to read Sylvia's reaction. "I worked for your mother for nearly twenty years, Mrs. Pearsall, and I won't say a bad word against the woman. However, she was wrong about Miss Shelton. This is a good design, and it's not the only one. There are good pieces in that sketchbook. Ones we can sell. Mrs. Shelton would have been able to see that if she hadn't been so stubborn, and so would your sister."

Sylvia could feel appreciation bloom in her chest as she took a step closer to finger the fine wool. She lifted the hem of the dress to examine the nearly invisible stitches.

"You didn't tell me you were making this up," she said.

"I wanted to see how it turned out before I told you. I . . ." Miss Reid cleared her throat. "I didn't want to disappoint you if it didn't work."

Wasn't that the same excuse she'd given Izzie?

"Where did you find the fabric?" she asked.

"The inventory room. It's too good not to use. And technically, you own it, so it's off coupon," said Miss Reid.

"I suspect that the Board of Trade would find that a rather creative bending of the rules, so perhaps we won't tell them. Just this once." Sylvia smiled at the older woman. "Do you think it will fit me?"

The seamstress's cheeks flushed. "Well, I didn't make it for you, but yes. I should think so."

She thought about thanking Miss Reid, but she suspected it would only cause more embarrassment for them both so instead, she asked, "Well, why don't I go try it on and see?"

She picked up the dress to carry it to the fitting room, but she didn't miss the look of pride on Miss Reid's face as she went.

Chapter Twenty-Five

A few hours later, Sylvia held her breath as Lady Nolan's housekeeper opened the drawing room door for her a full twenty minutes after that day's meeting of the War Widows' Fund committee meeting had started. Once again, every lady in attendance swiveled to look as she strode in, and once again she lifted her chin to brazen her way through their stares.

She knew that she should have left the shop earlier, but she'd lost time trying on the black dress Miss Reid had magicked out of nowhere. When the seamstress had insisted on taking the hem down slightly to account for Sylvia's height, she could hardly have said no. Sylvia knew an olive branch when she saw one.

She'd gone through the week's invoices while waiting for Miss Reid to finish the alterations, and then a new customer had walked in with no appointment but with two daughters, fifteen and seventeen, in tow, sending Miss Reid and her scrambling to serve all three women in what would prove to be the shop's biggest order in a fortnight.

After the customers left, Sylvia had grabbed her handbag and only just made her bus, congratulating herself on managing to do it all. However, the bus had to be rerouted because a work crew had hit a water main while repairing bomb damage, forcing a main road to close and snarling traffic.

And so, yet again, she was late.

"Mrs. Pearsall, I see you have decided to join us after all," said Lady Nolan as Sylvia rounded the back of the circle of chairs and settled into a seat next to the newest member of the committee, Lady Winman.

"My apologies," she said, settling her handbag next to her chair.

"Mrs. Pearsall, I should hate to have to remind you that our work is important and deserves our full attention. Can we be reassured that you intend to be prompt in your attendance to these meetings from now on?" asked Lady Nolan.

The barb was finely honed, and once it might have hit her right in the softest part of her insecurity that *any* misstep might see the door to this world close in her face. However, now she found herself balking at her hostess's words. The War Widows' Fund committee work was important, but there were a dozen ladies on the committee. Mrs. Shelton's Fashions only had Miss Reid and her. The shop had bills that had to be paid, and customers had to be served. If she didn't do those things, no one else would.

"I apologize for my tardiness," she said, fighting to keep her voice level.

"I should hate to think that you are making lateness your new hobby, Mrs. Pearsall," Lady Nolan continued to needle.

"Perhaps I should, as time seems to be the only thing not rationed at the moment," Sylvia snapped.

Soft scoffs of disbelief peppered the room along with one stifled giggle next to her. Sylvia slid her gaze over to Lady Winman, who had raised an index finger to her lips, clearly trying to keep her laughter in.

"Well," said Lady Nolan, shifting in her seat and looking down at her notes, "since you are here, perhaps you would like to start our discussion of ideas for our next fundraising event, Mrs. Pearsall."

Damn. With Hugo's return and the argument with Izzie, Sylvia had hardly given the fundraising event a single thought even though Lady Nolan had prompted all of them to bring ideas at the end of their last meeting.

"Well, I should hate to preempt anyone who wishes to go first," she hedged, glancing around the room at a dozen expectant, judgmental faces. She caught Claire's gaze, and her friend shook her head slightly.

"Please, do go on, Mrs. Pearsall," said Lady Nolan. "We have discussed at great length the fact that we have exhausted the reasonable bounds of our usual efforts. We are in need of new ideas, which I'm certain you have in abundance."

Sylvia smoothed a hand over the skirt of her dress, and suddenly she had it.

"A fashion show."

Lady Nolan frowned. "A fashion show?"

"Yes," she said, the idea forming rapidly as she recalled an article she'd read a few weeks before.

"Wasn't that just done by Digby Morton, Edward Molyneux, and some others? I read about it a few weeks ago in *The London Lady*," said Mrs. Hartwell.

"Yes, but we would do it differently. We would focus on local dressmakers here in London. They don't receive nearly as much attention as designers do."

"Don't dressmakers just copy what more talented designers do?" asked Claire with a scoff.

"Many dressmakers do have the skill and talent to design themselves," Sylvia argued.

"Which, I'm certain, is why so many of your dresses are made by dressmakers no one has ever heard of," said Claire with a conspiratorial wink.

"This dress was designed and made by a London dressmaker,"

she said, waving a hand down the black dress her sister had designed and Miss Reid had sewn.

There was a wave of murmurs, and Claire lifted a brow. "I stand corrected. I thought you lived and died by your Hartnell."

"What exactly is your proposal, Mrs. Pearsall?" asked Lady Nolan.

"We would invite a number of local dressmakers to each create an original ensemble that aligns with the Board of Trade's new austerity measures and uses utility cloth. We can tell them we want them to show that, despite the restrictions, fashion is alive, well, and within reach.

"The show would be a ticketed event, with the proceeds going to the charity," she continued. "We could invite an audience of women and let them know that they can purchase the garments at the end of the show if they choose. If we do that and invite the fashion trade publications, I imagine many dressmakers would be even more inclined to join because it would encourage patronage."

"Since she took over as editor at *Vogue*, Audrey Withers has been keen to show women how they can keep up appearances and maintain morale even with rationing on," said Lady Winman. "We could write to the magazine to invite them to cover the event."

"But does *Vogue* really have any interest in a small group of seamstresses no one's heard of?" asked Claire. "Their pages are filled with Molyneux and Jacqmar, not Mrs. Bloggins's frocks from the shop down the road."

Sylvia's eyes narrowed at her friend's continued criticism even as Lady Winman said, "I should think Miss Withers would be very interested. The magazine seems to have a real interest in covering all aspects of the war. They've been writing about the clothing ration extensively, and they're keen on promoting domestic fashion in all forms. I would be happy to ask Miss Withers. We are both volunteers with the London Fire Brigade."

Disloyal though it was to her friend, Sylvia couldn't help but feel triumphant when Claire sank back into the chair looking mollified.

"What I want to know is who would be the models? Most young ladies are in the auxiliary services now," said Mrs. Neil, a slight woman who wore silver glasses on a chain.

"The ladies of this committee," Sylvia jumped in, causing a stir.

"Not all of us have a model's figure any longer," said Lady Nolan primly.

"This show would be about women of all ages, shapes, and sizes," she explained. "Practical dressing for the practical—but fashionable—woman."

To her great surprise, Lady Nolan turned to the other women and said, "Well, I hope that you have all come with ideas as robust as Mrs. Pearsall's because her fashion show will be very hard to best. Mrs. Neil, you are next."

As Mrs. Neil fumbled with her notebook, Sylvia sank back in her chair with a sigh of relief.

———————

It took time to listen to all the ideas pitched for the committee's next fundraising event, even with Lady Nolan ruthlessly cutting off anyone who seemed unprepared with a curt "I think we've heard enough."

Reassured that the focus of the afternoon's meeting had shifted safely away from her, Sylvia busied herself by making a list down the right side of her notebook of all the things she needed to do when she returned to Mrs. Shelton's, starting with submitting the coupons they'd collected that week to the Board of Trade for cross-checking.

When Lady Nolan finally declared the meeting over, Sylvia shot to her feet. However, a light hand on her forearm stopped her.

"I hope you don't mind me saying, but your dress is lovely," said Lady Winman.

"Oh, thank you," she said, a little taken aback. Before this meeting, the countess had hardly spoken to her. Now, in the space of a single afternoon, Lady Winman had not only offered up Audrey Withers of *Vogue* in support of Sylvia's fashion show but she had a compliment for Sylvia's wardrobe.

"Would you mind passing along the name of your dressmaker?" asked Lady Winman. "I've struggled to find one I like."

"Oh," she said as Claire slid into her field of vision. When she'd mentioned that she was wearing a dressmaker's design, she hadn't thought that anyone might want to know the name of the shop. Now she realized that it had been a risk to open herself up like that. Still, to have a customer like Lady Winman . . . Well, wouldn't that be a coup?

"I would be happy to find the address and send it to you, my lady," she said firmly.

Lady Winman pulled a small gold case out of her handbag, flicked it open with her thumbnail, and handed Sylvia a heavy cream card bearing her name and address. "Please do. The silhouette really is beautiful."

"Thank you," said Sylvia.

Lady Winman nodded a goodbye and then made her way out of the emptying drawing room.

As soon as the countess was gone, Claire asked, "What was all that about?"

Sylvia passed her thumb over the beautiful paper of Lady Winman's card and then looked up at her friend. "Nothing really." She slipped the card into her handbag and snapped it shut harder than necessary. "If you'll excuse me, I have an appointment to keep."

Claire caught up to her as Lady Nolan's housekeeper handed Sylvia her coat.

"Sylvia, don't be like this," said Claire.

"Like what? I have an appointment," she said, slipping her arms into her sleeves.

"You're cross because I challenged your idea just a little bit, aren't you?" Claire asked, her heels clicking as they both descended the three steps from Lady Nolan's front door to the road.

"I'm not."

"Your dress is beautiful, I was only a bit surprised. You always seemed so devoted to your usual fashion houses. And it's black. It's an interesting choice for someone who isn't in mourning."

It was funny that she'd never noticed before how compliments from Claire had to be handled carefully because they so often came surrounded by thorns.

"I was not aware that you were so intimately acquainted with the contents of my wardrobe," Sylvia said, keeping her gaze forward.

Claire grabbed her arm, forcing her to stop or risk toppling both of them onto the pavement. "What is the matter? If you'd like me to apologize, I will, but something is the matter."

"Nothing is the matter," she said.

Claire rolled her eyes. "You're preoccupied. You're always late. Whenever I see you, you're rushing off somewhere. It's almost as though you don't want to spend any time with me." Claire paused. "Or there is someone else in your life you want to see more?"

Was there an accusation wrapped up in that comment, or was Sylvia simply imagining it?

"I'm busy," she said.

"We're all busy these days. My maid just had the audacity to tell me she's been called up as a Land Girl. Can you imagine her digging up potatoes in the countryside? But do you know what I did when I found out? I put on a dress and went out for supper and dancing—much to Rupert's chagrin," said Claire.

"I thought Rupert was stationed in Scotland," she said.

Claire waved a hand. "Oh, he's home on leave. Three weeks, if you can believe it. I suspect that means he'll be sent somewhere terribly far away next."

"Really? Hugo hadn't mentioned Rupert was home," she said.

"Is Hugo back too? My word, it's practically raining husbands in London."

"Yes, well, Hugo's hardly home. His work keeps him busy," she said. That and his insistence on dining at his club most nights.

Claire's eyes lit up and she grabbed Sylvia's arm. "I have an idea. Why don't we go out together—the four of us for dinner and dancing, just like old times."

She should be able to say yes immediately, but the truth was, she had no idea whether Hugo would want to go to a restaurant and on to a nightclub with her. She knew so little about her husband these days.

"I'll think about it," she finally said.

"Excellent," said Claire, already sounding lighter. "Well, that meeting was one for the ages, and all the credit should go to you. Did you see Lady Nolan's face when you defied her and talked back?"

A smile touched Sylvia's lips. "She did look rather shocked, didn't she?"

"Because no one's ever put her in her place before. And what about Lady Winman? For months she's hardly said a word, and now she's offering up the editor of *Vogue* the same way someone might lend out a spare handkerchief."

"I think she wants to be helpful," Sylvia said.

"Personally I'm shocked she's still attending meetings. I didn't think she'd last," said Claire.

"Why is that?"

Claire leaned in. "Well, before she was Lady Winman, apparently she was just plain old Miss Carter, a writer for one of Lord Winman's ladies' magazines.

"The rumor is that Lord Winman took a liking to her. His mother, the Dowager Lady Winman, did her best to break the couple apart, but Lord Winman declared that he wouldn't give Miss Carter up because he loved her too much. In the end, the Dowager Lady Winman had to concede because the count *had to marry* Miss Carter, if you understand my meaning.

"I've also heard that the Dowager Lady Winman nearly refused to hand over the Winman rubies when her son married," Claire continued. "Can you imagine the indignity she must have felt when those jewels that have been in the family for nearly three centuries hung for the first time around the neck of a woman who writes columns? I would have died of embarrassment."

Sylvia watched the smug smile on Claire's face as her friend of years spread gossip about a woman whose only sin, as far as Sylvia could tell, was having had a career. Claire had always liked talking about who was doing what with whom, but Sylvia had never really minded. Her friend had been a fount of information that Sylvia could use as she tried to navigate all the unspoken relationships and rivalries that only people in the know would ever be privy to. But there was an edge to all of this gossip, and all at once Sylvia couldn't be certain how far their friendship would stretch if Claire found out Sylvia's secrets.

The daughter of a widowed seamstress who ran a shop.

A wife who couldn't give her husband a child.

A woman who couldn't keep a husband in her bed.

She could practically hear what Claire would whisper about her if she only knew.

"*No wonder he ran to another woman. We never really knew any-thing about her or her people, but we were all willing to overlook that for Hugo's sake. If you ask me, you always could tell that she's not quite the thing. There've been little hints all along. It's a good thing really that there never was a child.*"

"Do you know," said Sylvia, cutting off her own harsh thoughts, "I think that Lady Winman's story is very romantic."

"Romantic?" Claire laughed. "It's preposterous."

"A man who is in love decides that nothing will stand in the way of being with the woman he wants to be with? That is the sort of thing you see in films or read in novels," she said.

Claire sniffed. "Well, I don't know about that, but I would be care-ful about becoming too close to her. She might be a countess, but she's not the right sort of countess, if you understand my meaning."

"Claire, I think I understand your meaning perfectly."

And she wasn't certain why she'd ever tolerated it.

1 May 1942

Dear Lady Winman,

Thank you for your kind words about the dress that I wore to the recent meeting at Lady Nolan's home. The dress shop is Mrs. Shelton's Fashions at 4 Glengall Road, Maida Vale.

Yours faithfully,
Mrs. Hugo Pearsall

———————

1 May 1942

Dear Mrs. Pearsall,

After much consideration of all of the ideas suggested at Wednesday's committee meeting, I have decided that your suggestion of a fashion show displaying the creativity and talent of London's best dressmakers is the most likely to receive the kind of attention and therefore charitable support that this committee wishes for the sake of our unfortunate war widows.

I will inform the other ladies of my decision at our next meeting on the 13th of May. In the meantime, I would ask you to begin to compile a list of dressmakers to approach as I do not wish for us to lose any time. We will keep the directive simple: they are to design and create an ensemble with the fall/winter season in mind that embraces the constraints of the austerity measures. You will please present this list to me so that I may approve it before you begin to approach any businesses.

I trust that, despite your recent rash of late attendance, you will be able to carry out this task in an efficient manner.

Yours faithfully,
Lady Nolan

May 2, 1942

Dear Izzie,

I am writing to you as soon as I received your letter so that you know how relieved I am that you wrote back. I can only imagine that a girl like you has so many men trying to court her, but I'm honored to have even a little bit of your attention.

Nothing would make me happier than to take you out properly—or as properly as a man can when he is at the beck and call of the USAAF. I know that I have leave on Friday, May 8, if you can manage permission to leave base.

There are so many things that I want to know about you. What is your favorite movie? Do you like the spring or the summer best? Where was your first kiss? If you could go anywhere in the world, where would it be?

They're silly little things, but all parts of you that I want to know better.

Yours,

Jack

4 May 1942

Dear Jack,

I think I'll answer your simple questions first:

My favorite film is <u>The 39 Steps</u>.

My favorite season is autumn because I love the mornings when I wake up and there's a chill in the air that makes me want to wrap my coat a little closer around me.

Before the war, I dreamed of going to Paris and visiting all the beautiful couture houses. They are supposed to be the height of achievement when it comes to design and construction of clothing, and it would be a dream to be able to look inside for even one afternoon.

One of my favorite things about being a dressmaker is taking something as simple as a flat piece of cloth and creating something sculptural out of it. A beautifully cut dress—like a perfectly tailored men's suit—is a thing to behold because it isn't just the garment itself but the way it fits the person it was made for.

I think that is one of the things I most admire my mother for. She understood the power that clothing has to transform a woman. In the right dress, a woman will stand a little taller and perhaps walk into a room a little differently. It can make her feel confident or special in a way that nothing else can.

I suppose, in that way, dressmaking is in my blood.

I have been thinking a great deal about your story of what happened between you and your brother after your father died. I don't know if I have enough good in me to forgive Sylvia, because it wasn't just the business and Mum she left behind. It was me.

I missed my sister. I was fourteen and felt all alone.

I don't know why I'm writing this to you. I hardly know you.

If you still wish to see me on Friday, I will be able to leave base after five o'clock.

Yours,
Izzie

———————

4 May 1942

Dear Lady Nolan,

Thank you for your letter. I am delighted to hear that you believe that my idea for a charity fashion show has enough merit to pursue it.

I understand the desire to compile a list of names for the committee's consideration swiftly. I will do my very best.

Yours faithfully,
Mrs. Hugo Pearsall

4 May 1942

Dear Sylvia,

I've spoken to Rupert, and he insists that we make arrangements to have supper with you and Hugo. Will Saturday suit?

It will be such fun to see our men!

Yours faithfully,
Claire

Chapter Twenty-Six

"ello, may I speak to Mrs. Nickelson please?" Sylvia asked, cradling the telephone receiver against her ear.

"Speaking," said a woman with a soft Scottish accent.

Sylvia straightened. "Mrs. Nickelson, my name is Mrs. Pearsall. I'm one of proprietresses of Mrs. Shelton's Fashions in Maida Vale. I wonder if I might have a moment of your time to discuss a business proposition with you."

"Yes?" the other woman dragged out the word.

"I'm also a member of a committee that does charitable work to support soldiers' widows in need," she said, speaking more rapidly for fear of losing Mrs. Nickelson's attention. "We are holding a fashion show that would feature a number of London's best dressmakers to promote the wonderful, skilled work of local dress shops. Given your considerable reputation when it comes to constructing"—she glanced down at her notes—"coats, I felt that our list of participating dressmakers wouldn't be complete without you."

There was a pause on the other end of the telephone. "What did you say your name was, Mrs. . . . ?"

"Pearsall," she supplied.

"If you are the owner of a dress shop, then I'm certain you are aware that this is a challenging time," said Mrs. Nickelson. "I've started taking in officers' uniforms to mend. Male officers."

"I understand, it's difficult for all of us right now. However, that's precisely what we're trying to address with this fashion show. We wish to make a virtue out of the Board of Trade's austerity measures, show women that it is possible to enjoy fashion in a time of war, and remind them that their neighborhood dressmaker is the best person to help them do that."

There was a pause on the other end of the telephone, and then Mrs. Nickelson said, "All right then. What could it hurt?"

Sylvia waggled her pencil in a silent little cheer. "Very good. I will be in touch with further details by letter, or you can telephone Cunningham 4930."

After they said their goodbyes, Sylvia replaced the receiver and then placed a tick next to Mrs. Nickelson's name. It had not been easy putting together her list of dressmakers to contact, and not everyone had received her invitation as swiftly or as warmly as Mrs. Nickelson. Since she'd begun making her calls, a few had scoffed at the idea that a fashion show of unknown dressmakers would receive any attention, while switchboard operators had been unable to connect to the exchanges of two, leaving Sylvia wondering whether they had fallen victim to the bombs that had rained down on London at intervals for the past year and a half.

However, she kept ringing friends, making discreet inquiries as to where they had their clothes made, and pulling on the surprising fountain of knowledge that was Miss Reid, who seemed to be an encyclopedia of who specialized in what sort of garment. The additional work kept her occupied, for which she was eternally grateful, because it gave her another reason to avoid Hugo.

When Claire's invitation to supper had come in the post, Sylvia had thought at first to quietly decline it and save herself the indignity of dressing up and pretending she didn't know about the letters in Hugo's desk. However, Rupert was Hugo's very good friend from school and a member of the same club, so she couldn't be certain that Rupert wouldn't also extend the invitation in person.

That morning, she'd caught Hugo at home changing into his dress uniform.

"Claire and Rupert have invited us to supper on Saturday," she said from the bedroom doorway.

Hugo glanced at her as he adjusted the collar of his jacket. "Really?"

"Apparently Rupert is home on leave, and Claire thinks it would be fun to go dancing afterward. 'Like old times,' I think she put it."

Hugo's gaze fixed on his reflection in the long bedroom mirror again. "You should say yes."

"Really?" she asked.

"Why wouldn't we?" he replied, as though he hadn't spent a fortnight avoiding her.

That morning, before going into the shop, she wrote Claire a reply saying that she and Hugo would be delighted.

The office telephone rang, and Sylvia answered with her usual greeting, "Mrs. Shelton's Fashions, this is Mrs. Pearsall speaking."

"Hello, I wanted to inquire about having a new dress made. My daughter is to be married, you see," said the woman on the other end.

"How exciting! Many congratulations to your daughter," she said as she opened the shop's appointment book. "It looks as though we have availability on Thursday or next Tuesday in the afternoon if you would like to come in."

"Thursday at eleven o'clock would suit me," said the caller.

The shop's doorbell rang, and as Miss Reid waved a hand at the open office door to silently say that she'd answer it, Sylvia mouthed, "Thank you."

"Very good, may I have your name?" she asked the caller.

"Mrs. Harris."

"Then we shall see you Thursday at eleven o'clock, Mrs. Harris.

And may I ask, how did you learn about Mrs. Shelton's Fashions?" she asked.

"I believe it was an advertisement in *The Lady*," said Mrs. Harris.

Sylvia grinned. Another potential customer from her advertisements.

She said goodbye to Mrs. Harris and replaced the receiver. She could hear the muffled sound of Miss Reid speaking to some customer—likely Mrs. Temple and her daughter, who were both due for fittings at one o'clock.

Closing the appointment book, Sylvia made her way down the corridor to greet the Temple women before leaving them in Miss Reid's capable hands for their fitting. However, when she walked through to the reception, she found it wasn't the Temples examining the dress form displaying a linen suit but Lady Winman.

"My lady," she said, stopping short.

Out of the corner of her eye, Sylvia registered the shocked look on Miss Reid's face at Sylvia's deference. A flash of surprise passed over the countess's face too—no doubt for completely different reasons—but Lady Winman quickly regained her polite composure.

"Mrs. Pearsall, I didn't expect to find you here," said Lady Winman.

Miss Reid took a hesitant step forward. "I was just showing her ladyship this summer suit, madam."

From the way that Miss Reid addressed Sylvia, there could be no denying her position of authority at the shop. A few months ago, she might have stammered some excuse and tried her best to explain away her association with the dressmaker's shop. However, she had worked too hard for that. She might not be able to sew like Izzie or their mother, but she had put her own form of work into Mrs. Shelton's then and now, and she wanted her due credit.

"Miss Reid is our head seamstress," she told Lady Winman, approaching the dress form. "The suit is lovely, but the cut is perhaps a little boxy compared to the sort of jacket I've noticed you normally wear, my lady. If you don't mind me saying so."

Lady Winman smiled. "I don't mind at all. And you are quite right."

"I would recommend something more elevated and tailored. If a linen suit is what you are looking for," Sylvia finished.

Lady Winman's lips tilted up a touch. "I would like that very much."

"Miss Reid, why don't you fetch Miss Shelton's sketchbook?" asked Sylvia.

"Are you certain, madam?" asked Miss Reid, who hadn't lost her slightly stunned expression at the appearance of a countess on the shop floor.

Sylvia knew without having to consult Lady Winman that her mother's sketches wouldn't suit the countess and her streamlined, simple elegance. And while some women like Claire might think that the Countess of Winman wasn't the "right sort of countess," Sylvia knew that any countess wearing a Mrs. Shelton's Fashions design would be good for business.

It would have to be her sister's sketches. She just hoped Izzie would forgive her.

She gave Miss Reid a firm nod. "Please."

Miss Reid retreated to the back of the shop faster than Sylvia had ever seen her move.

Turning back to Lady Winman with a smile, Sylvia pointed to a chair. "If you would like to make yourself comfortable."

"Thank you," said the countess.

"Would you care for a cup of tea?" she asked.

"No, thank you. It is kind of you to offer."

As Sylvia lowered herself into the chair opposite Lady Winman, the countess said, "So you own a dress shop."

She folded her hands across her lap. "Half of one, yes."

Lady Winman smiled and began pulling off her gloves. "Yet it is called Mrs. Shelton's and not Mrs. Pearsall's."

"It is."

There was a pause long enough for Sylvia to begin to question whether she'd been entirely wise in confiding in the countess. However, Lady Winman finally said, "I imagine there is a very good reason for that, and I hope one day you might tell me. However, I understand if you don't wish to do that today, because I know how funny high society can be when it comes to women and business."

Despite all her rationalization, Sylvia's shoulders still inched down a fraction at the countess's words. "Yes. Although apparently it is all well and good for men to be in one of the more gentlemanly professions."

"Including earls," said Lady Winman with a little quirk to her lips.

"You were a writer before you met your husband," Sylvia said cautiously.

"And an editor. That was the job I was most proud of—the one I worked hardest for, for so many years. People so often forget about that when they gossip." Lady Winman sighed. "I know I'm an anomaly. The countess who grew up a professor's daughter with no dream of ever being presented at court."

"May I ask how you cope?"

Lady Winman tilted her head, her dark hair falling over her eye. "With what? The gossip? Or the end of my career as I knew it?"

"Both."

The countess seemed to consider the question. "I worked for one of Alistair's magazines when I met him, and the editor in chief thought it inappropriate that I continue on, no matter how much Alistair railed at him. Of course, none of his competitors would employ me, so I had to make a choice between my career and him. As much as I loved the magazine, I love Alistair more."

"But isn't it difficult?" Sylvia asked almost before she could stop herself.

When Lady Winman laughed, it was genuine, full-throated. "Of course it's difficult. Sometimes it feels impossible, and all I want to do is scream. I know that some people think I trapped my husband, that he had to marry me. But I know that they're wrong. Not only because my daughter came a year after we married but because I know my own heart. He is the only man who could have made me want to give up the life I had for the one I have married into."

Sylvia blushed.

"Now I've gone and shocked you," said Lady Winman, amusement lacing her voice.

"No, you haven't. It's . . . refreshing."

"Then perhaps you'll indulge me a little. How long have you owned half of this shop?" asked Lady Winman.

"Not long at all. My sister and I inherited equal portions when my mother died late last year," she explained. "Izzie is currently serving with the WAAF."

"I'm sorry for your loss," said Lady Winman.

"Thank you." She paused, knowing that she probably shouldn't say more but finding it difficult to turn off the tap of frankness now that it was open. "I actually grew up above the shop. At least after the age of eleven. My mother opened it shortly after my father died."

"Then being a woman of business runs in your family," said Lady Winman.

An unexpected swell of pride filled Sylvia's chest. "I suppose it does," she said, just as Miss Reid returned with Izzie's sketchbook in hand.

"Thank you, Miss Reid," she said, taking the book. "Perhaps you would stay and offer your advice to Lady Winman about cut and fabrics?"

Miss Reid's brows shot up, but then she nodded. "If you wish."

"Now, my lady," Sylvia said, "shall we see if there is something in here that will suit?"

"I've never dressed a countess before," said Miss Reid as soon as Lady Winman had left the shop, having fallen in love with a sketch of a light-green-and-white-striped summer dress that wiped away any thought of a summer suit.

"I would imagine it's a first for the shop," said Sylvia, trying to hide her smile at the thought of what her sister—or even her mother—would say about this.

"How do you think she learned about us?" Miss Reid asked.

"Do you remember the day I was splashed coming in and had to change into the dress you'd made from one of Izzie's sketches? Lady Winman was at the meeting that I had to run off to. She complimented the dress you made, and I gave her the name of the shop," she said.

She could see Miss Reid's eyes slide over to covertly examine her. It hadn't escaped her attention that something had slowly shifted between them since Izzie's deployment. Miss Reid seemed, of late, far more willing to pitch in for the front-of-house work than she had when Sylvia arrived. Gone too were the sly comments about Sylvia's character. She hadn't known whether it had been her new policies around payments, the advertisements, or her enthusiasm about tackling every problem from missing deliveries to the austerity announcements. However, Lady Winman's appearance seemed to be the final confirmation Miss Reid needed to believe that Sylvia really was invested in the shop's future.

"Well, I suppose some good came out of that lorry splashing you then," said Miss Reid.

"I suppose it did."

"Will you tell your sister about Lady Winman?" asked Miss Reid.

"Yes. I owe her a letter about the fashion show. I meant to ask her if she had ideas of whom to approach as well."

"Will you tell her that the countess chose one of her sketches?" asked the seamstress.

Sylvia hesitated. "That I'm not so certain of. She hasn't forgiven me for pulling the sketches in the first place. I can't imagine she'll be delighted with the news that I've sold one of them."

"But you've apologized."

"I've written letter after letter. Nothing seems to make a difference."

She could see now what a mistake her last letter had been. Izzie held her anger with Sylvia too close to her chest for simple apologies and explanations to heal the wounds around her sister's heart.

"Why don't I put the kettle on, and we can go over the week's orders together?" she suggested.

"Yes, madam," said Miss Reid.

Sylvia stopped short. "Miss Reid, you've known me since I was eleven. You really don't need to call me 'madam.'"

Miss Reid lifted her chin. "So long as you're the owner of this shop, that's exactly what I'll call you. I won't hear any argument against it."

Sylvia couldn't entirely hide her grin at the sort of olive branch her old rival appeared to be offering. "Thank you, Miss Reid. That means the world to me."

"Oh"—Miss Reid batted a hand in front of her—"don't turn sentimental on me. Your mother never was the sentimental type."

"No," said Sylvia with a little laugh. "I don't suppose she was."

May 6, 1942

Dear Izzie,

There is nothing in the world that could interest me more than whatever it is that you wish to tell me. If that is about your sister and the shop, I am happy to listen.

I will call for you at the gates at five on Friday. I cannot wait to see you.

Yours,
Jack

P.S. Do not think for one second that I missed the fact that you left out your answer to my question about your first kiss.

Chapter Twenty-Seven

S uch excitement fizzed in Izzie's stomach that she could almost forget about the unopened letter from Sylvia tucked into her tunic pocket. It was five o'clock on Friday, and Jack was waiting for her. Jack, who'd told her that he couldn't stop thinking about her and whose last letter had mentioned first kisses.

She spotted him leaning against a post just outside the gate of her base, and when they locked eyes he pushed off of it with a grin, stooping to pick up the long strap of a khaki bag that was sitting on the ground next to him.

"Hello," she said as she approached.

"Hello to you. Aren't you just the prettiest girl in the world?" he asked.

She blushed. "Don't be ridiculous."

He reached up to touch a lock of her light brown hair and then let his hand drop to his side. "I'm just saying exactly what I see."

"I'm glad you came," she said.

"You weren't worried I wouldn't show up, were you?" he asked with a sweet smile.

The truth was, yes. Despite their evening of dancing and all of his letters telling her how much he wanted to see her, a part of her hadn't quite believed that he was really real.

She'd driven Alexandra and the other girls of her unit crazy asking, "What if he changed his mind?" and, "What if Friday comes and he's forgotten all about me?"

Each time, someone would put their arm around her and reassure her that Jack would be there, just as he'd promised, and now here he was.

He tapped the bag that hung off his shoulder. "I hope you don't mind, but I took the liberty of rustling up some provisions for us. Shall we?"

She took his offered arm and they set off together, a breeze lifting her hair.

"Tell me, how is life in the balloon unit?" he asked.

"Much the same as it always is. We take the balloon out, we put it up, we bring it down, we repair it," she said.

"Why do I suspect there's more to it than that?" he asked with a laugh.

"You're right," she admitted. "We trained for weeks before we were transferred here. I now know more about meteorology than I ever thought I would."

"'We' is all of the girls I met at the dance?" he asked.

"And a woman named Nancy. She was a little . . . preoccupied."

"What's the name of this preoccupation?" he asked.

"Flying Officer Charles Gardner," she said.

"Lucky man," he said with a grin.

"They're both smitten, although Nancy's not one to admit it. She's a bit stuffy, but she's one of us, so we put up with it," she said with affection for her fellow balloon girl.

"And what about you, Isabelle Shelton? Has anyone caught your eye?" he teased.

She slid a look over to him. "Maybe."

He gave her arm a gentle tug. "Maybe? Sounds like that 'maybe' will have to try a lot harder. I hope you don't mind walking a bit."

"Not at all."

They turned off the road and onto a public footpath through the trees. Izzie had never realized how wooded Norfolk could be until she arrived at RAF Horsham St Faith, but she and Molly had taken several walks among the trees not far from base, two London girls marveling at how green and peaceful everything was.

Up ahead, the dirt path opened out into a clearing of trees and ferns, leaves padding the forest floor.

Jack took off his cap, and rubbed the back of his neck. "It isn't much, but I found this spot the other day and thought it would be the perfect place to have a picnic with a pretty girl."

She looked around, charmed by the idea. However, when she didn't respond immediately, he hurried to say, "This was a silly idea. You don't want to sit on the ground and eat. You probably want to go to a restaurant or go dancing or—"

"Jack, it's perfect."

His easy smile slid back onto his face. "All right then."

He spread a blanket she suspected was regulation and began to unpack his bag as she arranged herself on it. Her eyes went wide as he pulled out all manner of things.

When he caught her stare, he said, "My mother doesn't trust that the USAAF will feed me properly, so she sent me a care package stuffed to the brim."

"You can't share this with me," she said, picking up a bit of cheddar cheese. Her mouth was already watering at the abundance of it.

"Sure I can."

"But this is more than my entire week's cheese ration was before I became a WAAF," she protested.

He placed a hand on hers to still her. "Izzie, there is no one else I would rather share Mom's care package with. Trust me. Now sit yourself down there and let me spoil you with a little American hospitality."

She sank down on crossed legs to the spot he indicated on the blanket and watched him unpack the rest of his treasures from his bag before sitting across from her. Then he took out a penknife to slice up the cheese and a couple of apples, she watched his long fingers move with self-assurance, and when he caught her studying him he shot her a grin that made her go warm all over.

As they ate, they talked, and Izzie could feel herself loosen up. She liked this man. She enjoyed his easy company and the way he looked right at her with a little sparkle in his eyes when she spoke. He leaned back on his elbows, giving her a chance to study his face. He had a good, strong jaw and eyes that flashed and sparkled with amusement as he talked. When he listened, he would tilt his head a little, as though not wanting to miss a single thing she said.

When all that was left of their picnic was crumbs, Jack pulled out a candy bar of a brand she didn't recognize. "Here," he said, breaking it in half and handing it to her.

"I can't eat half of your chocolate," she protested.

"I thought we sorted this out already?" he asked.

She laughed and took the treat. When she broke a small square off and took a delicate bite, the richness of it burst in her mouth and she had to stop herself from moaning.

"I had forgotten how good that tastes," she said.

"I thought you could get chocolate on the ration here," he said.

She made a face. "You can, but it's not the same as it used to be. Cadbury's stopped making Dairy Milk last year because the government told the company there would be no more using fresh milk. Now it's skimmed milk powder."

Jack pulled a face of his own. "Sounds about as good as a D-ration bar."

"What's a D-ration bar?" she asked.

"Trust me, you don't want to know," he said, taking another bite of chocolate. "Have a bit more. Come on."

She smiled at his teasing encouragement and took another sinful bite.

"That's more like it. I can almost imagine you as a little girl, saving up your chocolate squares for a rainy day," he said.

"Oh, no. I wasn't like that at all. That was Sylvia. I was always the first to finish my sweets."

"Are all sisters such opposites?" he asked.

She shrugged. "Maybe."

"What did you decide in the end?"

"Hmm?"

"About your sister. Did you write to her?" he asked.

Her thoughts immediately flashed to the letter in her tunic pocket.

"She wrote to me again, actually. Lottie from my unit brought us the post just as I was leaving to meet you. I haven't opened it yet."

"Do you want to?" When she hesitated, he said, "Go ahead. I'm not going anywhere."

"Can . . . can I read it to you?" she asked, unbuttoning the flap on her pocket and pulling the letter out.

His eyes softened. "Of course you can."

She tore open the flap and pulled out the letter, her sister's handwriting sending a fluttering through her stomach.

"'Dear Izzie,'" she started to read out loud. "'I have some news that I hope you will find as exciting as I do. Last week, I suggested that the War Widows' Fund host a fundraiser for the war effort featuring local dressmakers, and I was gratified that our committee chair, Lady Nolan, was delighted by the idea.

"'Obviously, I will include Mrs. Shelton's Fashions in the list, but I wanted to ask your opinion about other dressmakers that you admire. I trust your taste implicitly.'"

"As she should," muttered Jack loyally.

She shot him a little smile and then continued, "'I know that you are probably tired of me saying this, but I wish that you'd let me include one of your designs. You are so talented, and people should know that.'

"Then she sends some news from the neighborhood and that's it."

She stared at the letter for a long moment before Jack gently asked, "What do you think?"

"The fashion show is a good idea. It will be good for business," she said, fumbling to return the letter to its envelope.

Jack reached out to still her hand. "Izzie, that's not what I meant. Your sister seems to think you have a real talent for designing."

"She just feels guilty," she said, explaining what had happened when she'd gone to London on leave. He listened politely, his head slightly tilted as he took it all in, and when she was done he nodded.

"I understand why you were offended by what Sylvia did, but, Izzie, it sounds like she could really use your designs."

She closed her eyes. "She's wrong. Mum always made that clear." And that was the blunt truth of it that she couldn't escape.

"Did your mother say that to you?" he asked.

She sighed. "Not in so many words, but it was obvious. She was always telling me that I was being unreasonable. That what I was sketching was all wrong for our clients."

"You know," Jack started slowly, "when my brother went away to college, I missed him something fierce—we all did—but I think, more than anything else, I was jealous of him. Families tell each other all sorts of stories about one another until it feels like they must be true. In our family, Louis was the smart one. He was the athlete, the scholar, the golden boy. He was *going* places.

"I was the talker of the family—a 'charmer' Mom calls me. Dad never thought much of that. All through school, I would bring home my report card with straight Cs and he would just shake his head and ask why I couldn't be more like my brother. I thought that, since I was never going to have the book smarts to make him proud, I'd turn myself into the best football player in Iowa." He laughed. "That didn't exactly come naturally either. I had to work at it in a way that Louis never did.

"As far I knew, the only thing I was good at was talking to people. They'd tell me things that they swore up and down they'd never told another soul, and I'd try to help them with whatever problems they had."

"That's a rare thing," said Izzie.

"Thank you. I know that now, but I never really thought it was useful until I started working for Dad selling harvesters and tractors. Then, he started to say, 'That boy could sell sawdust to a lumber mill.' It wasn't much, but, finally, Dad thought I was good at something, even if he still didn't trust me to help decide what new equipment we should offer or how we should reinvest into the business.

"Then Dad died and Louis came back. I started to make those decisions that Dad always told me I didn't have the head for without even realizing it. Advertising, marketing, research—it turns out I'm good at all of it.

"I'm rambling on," he said, shooting her a sheepish smile. "I do know that the one thing I learned was that I didn't have to be the man my father thought I was. I could be more than that."

She felt something warm slide down her cheek, and when she lifted her fingers to touch it, she realized it was a tear.

"You think I should let my sister use my sketches," she whispered.

"I think it sounds like your mom loved you very much and wanted what she thought was the best for you, but sometimes you need to decide what that is for yourself," he said.

Something twisted in her gut. She respected Mum and everything she'd done with the shop so much, but she couldn't deny that for years there had been little voices whispering to her, urging her to rebel. As she'd grown older, she'd found it harder to understand why Mum was so resistant to change.

Why weren't her designs right for Mrs. Shelton's Fashions?

Why couldn't they court a newer, younger customer?

Why was change so frightening?

Why continue to say no when Sylvia so clearly wanted to try something—anything—different?

"I've been angry at my sister for so long," she said. "I don't know if I can say yes."

Jack smiled. "Do you get called stubborn much?"

She gave a watery laugh. "Oh, I don't know, Jack. Maybe a little. Sylvia keeps writing to me even though I haven't really written her back properly in weeks."

"Sounds like stubbornness is a family trait," he said. "You know what I realized when Louis came back? I had something that he never would: memories of Mom and Dad and life in Newton that were all mine. I'd resented him for so long, I didn't think I even considered that Louis might have regrets about everything he missed out on."

He grasped her hands in his. "I'm not a perfect man by any means, but I can tell you I became a lot happier when I decided to stop being angry with Louis. I don't pretend to know all of the intricacies of what's happened between you and your sister, but you strike me as the sort of woman who would have the grace to forgive when forgiveness is earned."

For the first time in her life, she wanted to be the woman he described. The one who could leave things in the past, who could give second chances and let go of grudges.

"Izzie," he said softly, his thumbs stroking over the tops of her hands, "you never answered my question about where you had your first kiss."

Her heart skipped. "The back of a cinema in Maida Vale. I was sixteen. It wasn't very good."

"I think we can do better than that, can't we?" he murmured.

He closed the gap between them. His right hand slipped around the back of her neck, his fingers tangling in her hair. He eased her head back a little, and she lifted her lips to him as though it was the most natural thing in the world to be kissed by an American staff sergeant in a forest clearing.

When he lowered his lips to hers, her eyes fluttered shut and she thought for a moment that her body would give way from the heat and spark and swoon of being kissed by Staff Sergeant Jack Perry. She leaned into their kiss, deepening it.

When, finally, he pulled back, he wore a rueful smile, his hair sticking up where her fingers had mussed it.

"I could do that all day, but somehow I suspect you have a very stern commanding officer who would disapprove."

"Corporal Richardson. She's not so bad really, but you're right. She is expecting me back on base as some point," she said with regret, patting down her own hair.

"Here," he said, pulling a comb out of his uniform pocket.

"Thank you," she said.

As she wrestled her curls back into place, he asked, "May I see you again?"

"Yes! Yes, I would like that very much."

She handed him back his comb and watched him tame his sandy hair back into place before starting to pack up their picnic. As they folded the blanket, they agreed that they would write to one another and fix a date when both of them were granted passes off their base. Then he stood up and helped her to her feet.

As Jack tucked the blanket away, Izzie looked around, memorizing every detail of the clearing. It might not be where she had her first kiss, but it was where she'd had her best one.

8 May 1942

Dear Sylvia,

I hesitated to write to you after your last letter. It was not easy to read, in part because it has always been simpler to remain angry and not to think about what growing up must have been like for you. I remember you talking about all of the little jokes you used to have with Dad, but all I have of him are snatches of memories that, like ghosts, I can never really be certain were real. I should have realized what it might have been like to be you, four years older than me, as you lost him and saw our lives change.

I knew something of the story of Mum speaking to the Sheltons, but I don't remember going with her. I don't recall the shame or the embarrassment that you wrote of. Instead, my clearest early memories are happy ones of the shop and our flat with the little bedroom we shared or sitting on the sofa while you read to me and Mum finished off hand sewing in the evenings.

I realize now how that flat must have seemed like such a step down in our circumstances to you. How could you not resent it and the shop along with it? I don't blame you for running toward a life with Hugo, but I wish you'd made room for Mum and me along the way.

I hated it when you left. You were my best friend. I looked up to you in so many ways, but when you met Hugo it was as though Mum and I never existed. Watching you marry him while sitting in the front pew rather than standing with you as a bridesmaid hurt, and when you failed to come by the shop or even telephone, it felt as though you were happy to wash your hands of us.

That is why I hated it so much when I found out that Mum left Mrs. Shelton's Fashions to both of us. You left and I stayed, and she still didn't trust me to take over the shop.

I know you think I worship Mum, but I was <u>angry</u> when I found out what she had done. You were right when you wrote that our mother was many things.

She was brave, as you said, but she was also wrong. She should have advertised. She should have freshened up our designs. She should have continued to do all of the things that had helped her in those early years of the shop.

She should have trusted me.

Thank you for taking care of the shop while I am away, whatever your reasons were for saying yes. Again, there are probably a number of things I haven't even considered you might have had to give up by agreeing to do it—although I am selfishly glad, for Mrs. Shelton's Fashions' sake, of your committee meetings—and it appears I have underestimated your energy when it comes to the business. I thought you would hardly last a month before you threw your hands up and left. For that, at least, I owe you an apology.

Regarding your fashion show, I would consider speaking to Miss Taylor, Mrs. Stevens, Mrs. Moss, Miss Burton, and Mrs. Lewis. If you can convince Mrs. Nickelson to agree to the show, I would specifically ask her to present a coat. However, the chances of Mrs. Becket agreeing are slim, as she's as thorny as they come. You might also wish to speak to Mrs. Davies.

Miss Reid should have all of their addresses.

You wrote that for all of Mum's bravery and determination, she was flawed. Perhaps it is time for me to begin trusting some of my own instincts.

After a great deal of thought, I have enclosed a sketch of a dress that I hope you think might be suitable for the fashion show you are preparing for. Miss Reid should be able to make a pattern from it, but please let her know that she may write if she has any questions.

Your sister,
Izzie

P.S. If you think that Willie is stopping by the shop merely because he is lonely, you are not as clever as I always thought you were.

———————

9 May 1942

Dear Jack,

I hope you won't think me ridiculous writing to you so soon after seeing you, but I couldn't wait. Something will happen and I find myself wanting to tell you straightaway so I can see your smile and hear your laugh. I want to hear all of your stories about your time in Iowa and what your family are like. I hate this war, but I am grateful that we met.

I suspect you will be happy to read that I have written to my sister. After our date, I went straight to my barracks, but Amelia and Alexandra were playing a spirited game of gin rummy and it was far too loud for my tastes, so I took some writing paper and my pencil and went off to the NAAFI to find some quiet.

I started to write to Sylvia, but as I read what she'd written over the last month, the words wouldn't quite form. Out of habit, I picked up my pencil and began sketching. It was a dress with simple and clean lines and very little embellishment save for a gathering at the side and a deep vent in the back of the skirt.

When I finished, I realized that it was the perfect combination of my mother and me: her tailoring and my taste. I could imagine it in a rich claret.

I picked up my pencil again and began to write to Sylvia, the words flowing better this time. At the end of the letter, I told her I was including a sketch for her fashion show. I do not know what she will do with it, but perhaps it will help.

I cannot wait to see you again, and I hope more than anything that I can be . . .

Yours,
Izzie

Chapter Twenty-Eight

*S*ylvia rushed through the door of the flat and tossed her handbag down on the entryway table. Toeing off her shoes as she went, she peeled off her jacket and let it dangle from her right ring finger as she reached up to take off her earrings.

She was late—why was she always late?—but this time it wasn't a committee meeting or a luncheon she was rushing home for. She and Hugo were meeting Claire and Rupert at the club for dinner before going out dancing.

The door to her bedroom was open. She strode through it without thinking, stopping only when she saw her husband standing in front of the long cheval mirror that occupied the corner of the room. His eyes caught hers in the glass.

Once he might have teased her, saying, "We really must keep meeting like this, Mrs. Pearsall." Instead, he glanced at the clock on the bedroom's mantelpiece and frowned.

"You're cutting it rather fine, Sylvia. Dinner is at half past seven," he said.

"I do apologize. My bus became stuck in traffic near Piccadilly," she lied smoothly as she set her jacket on the bed and then moved to her jewelry box to set her earrings safely inside. She hadn't been anywhere near Piccadilly, but she hoped that he might assume she'd been visiting some society matron or another in Belgravia or Kensington. That at least should appeal to her husband's sense of cultivating the right sort of company.

"You have ten minutes," he said.

She bit her tongue to keep from sniping back that it was rather rich of him to order her about their flat when he was so rarely there. However, that was not the way to start what was supposed to be a pleasant evening with their friends.

There had been a time when this sort of dinner would have been de rigueur. Their social diary had once set her head spinning it was so full of Hugo's friends and those he wished to make friends with, either because they might become patients at his discreet Harley Street surgery or simply because he wanted them in his circle. How thrilling it had been when she'd realized that she could help! While he had spoken to the husbands, she'd taken the wives, asking them about themselves and listening because her mother had taught her that most customers want little more than the indulgence of being allowed to speak about themselves.

She recalled how proud she'd felt when he'd begun to tell her a little bit about who he wanted to meet, and when she'd been able to make her first introduction, she'd practically floated to the ceiling. She'd done it all just to earn that satisfied smile from him.

Now, as she turned away from him to unzip her skirt and step out of it, she couldn't help but wonder at the pleasure she'd derived from being Hugo's helpmate. Now that the shop was her primary concern, she could hardly remember what it had been like when her only worry had been whom she would speak to on a given evening.

She dressed quickly in her navy silk satin gown. She'd bought it in 1938 from Molyneux, but it wasn't too out of fashion. Besides, she knew that the wide slash of a boatneck showed her delicate collarbones off beautifully. On went the sapphires that had been a twenty-eighth-birthday gift. Silver shoes and a matching clutch finished the effect.

"Sylvia—"

Hugo stopped, and she glanced up. He was standing in the doorway, watching her.

"What's the matter?" she asked.

"You look lovely," he said.

Despite herself, pride swelled in her chest. She knew that he'd fallen in love with her first for her beauty, and she was grateful that she could still make him stop and admire her fourteen years later.

She popped her lipstick into her handbag, closed it, and said, "I'm ready."

He nodded and she followed him out of the bedroom into the entryway.

"Let me help you with your fur," he said.

She turned, holding her breath as he settled her mink wrap onto her shoulders. His hands lingered for a moment. She closed her eyes, tempted to lean against him for a moment. But then he dropped his hands and straightened.

"We should leave," he said.

She nodded, but as soon as his back was turned, she let a little smile play over her face. Perhaps all was not lost between husband and wife.

———

"It feels as though all of London is here!" Sylvia shouted above the din of band, dancers, and drinkers who filled the nightclub where she had decamped with Hugo, Claire, and Rupert after supper at the men's club.

"They could be a little more discerning about their patronage," said Claire, huffing as someone bumped into her elbow.

"Have another drink, darling. Perhaps it will improve your

mood," said Rupert as he reached for the bottle of champagne chilling next to their table.

Claire stuck out her glass without looking at her husband.

Sylvia raised a brow in Hugh's direction, but he was watching the dancers on the increasingly crowded floor. There was something in the air that evening, and it wasn't just the almost-manic desperation to drink and dance and generally let loose that had characterized all nights out since the Germans had started dropping bombs on London.

Sylvia and Hugo had arrived at supper and found Claire and Rupert sitting at their table in silence. Both husband and wife had nearly finished their cocktails.

"Sylvia, thank goodness you're here," Claire had said, rising half out of her seat to give Sylvia her cheek to kiss. The distinct scents of gin and musky rose twined around the other woman.

"I hope you haven't been waiting long," she said, settling into her seat.

"Five minutes," said Claire, as though five minutes alone with her husband was far too long.

"Claire is eager to see you both," said Rupert, an edge to his voice.

She'd slid a glance at Hugo, but he was busy taking out his cigarette case.

"Claire?" he asked, holding the case out.

"Thank you, Hugo," said Claire, accepting the cigarette and leaning over so he could light it. She caught Hugo's hand to steady the flame and then let go to settle the cigarette between her long fingers. "Now, Sylvia, you must tell me everything you've been up to lately. I feel as though I hardly see you anymore."

"Oh, everyone is so busy these days," she said, again trying to catch Hugo's eye, but her husband was already engaged in conversation with Rupert.

"Is everything all right?" she asked Claire in a low voice.

"Rupert's just being a bit of an ass," said Claire.

"What's happened?" she asked.

"Apparently he's been operating under the assumption that, while he was serving, I was going to sit at home like a nun and think about nothing but him. Ridiculous man. Anyway, we don't need them to have an excellent evening."

The two couples had spent most of the meal speaking husband to husband and wife to wife, but despite Sylvia's gentle suggestion that perhaps they have an early night, everyone insisted on going dancing.

Now Sylvia was beginning to regret not being more forceful in her insistence. She really should find a way to speak to Hugo privately and suggest that carrying on with an arguing couple might not be the best idea as the night rolled on. However, before she could suggest that they dance, he said, "Claire, old thing, finish that and I'll push you around the dance floor a bit."

Claire gave him a look and then tipped her glass back to drain every last drop of champagne. Then she popped the glass down on the table and stuck out her hand. "If you insist."

Sylvia watched Hugo place a hand on the small of Claire's back and guide her friend out to the floor to join the throng. Perhaps she could defuse whatever was going on between the Monroes that evening.

"What do you say, Sylvia?" asked Rupert. "Do you fancy a dance yourself?"

It couldn't be worse than sitting at the table with a fog of discontent hanging over it, so she nodded and rose.

Rupert was a better dancer than most of Hugo's friends, and he led her confidently into a fox-trot, holding her at a respectable distance. They'd never been close the way she was with Claire, but he listened when she spoke, never made any inappropriate suggestion while drunk that he later tried to laugh off, and generally seemed like a good egg.

She was about to ask him about his time in Scotland, but he asked, "Have you seen much of Claire recently?"

"Well," she said carefully, "we sit on the committee together and—"

"Do you see her socially?"

"I haven't felt much like doing this sort of thing in the past few months," she said with a tight smile.

"Yes, I imagine the war does rather put a damper on things," he said.

They continued to quick-quick-slow step for a few bars, and then he said, "It's funny being married."

"Is it?" she asked with surprise.

"Do you think people believe half of the things that the priest asks them to repeat back?"

"Well, yes." She certainly had.

He pursed his lips. "I suppose you would."

She jerked back a little, stung.

"I just mean that you obviously were crazy about Hugo," he said quickly. "As he was about you."

"Thank you."

"How long have you two been married now?" he asked.

"Fourteen years," she said.

"It will be twenty for Claire and me next year. Two decades is a lot of time with the same woman," he mused. "I haven't always been the best husband to Claire, I'll admit that. I don't know if it's in a man's nature to be faithful."

Good lord, was he going to confess to an affair?

"I've never thought it very fair that a man should be held to one standard of behavior and a woman to another," she said rather curtly.

His gaze flashed to hers in surprise, as though just realizing he was saying all of this out loud.

"The band is very good, aren't they?" he asked, pulling the conversation into a sharp left turn and saving them both the embarrassment of whatever was really on Rupert's mind.

Thank goodness, she thought for what felt like the tenth time that day, and let the music take her.

———————

Hugo was remarkably quiet as they took a rare cab home, but Sylvia didn't mind. Her feet were aching from her now-unfamiliar dancing shoes, and she enjoyed the luxury of being ferried to her front door in a way she would have taken for granted before the war.

They rode the lift up to their floor, and Hugo unlocked the door.

"Would you like another drink?" she asked, the way she always had when they were first married. They would stay up with a nightcap and laugh about whatever had happened over the course of the evening, Hugo rubbing the ache out of her feet.

"If it's all the same, I'd rather go to bed," said Hugo.

"Of course," she said. "It's late."

She trailed after him to the bedroom, picking up the shoes she'd abandoned in the corridor at the beginning of the evening. She placed them and her silver shoes in their respective boxes, emptied the contents of her evening bag, and removed her jewels. Then she turned with her back to her husband.

"Would you help me?" she asked.

After a moment, she felt his hands light on her back. She sucked in a little breath as he tugged down the zip of her dress. Her skin tingled with champagne and anticipation, wondering if he would slide his hands into the gap made by her zipper as he used to do.

"There you are," he said, stepping away.

She swallowed her disappointment. "Thank you."

She stripped off her dress and stepped out of her girdle and undergarments without turning around. Then she slipped on her light pink silk negligee and matching dressing gown before sitting down at her vanity to take off her makeup and pin up her hair.

Behind her, she could hear Hugo shedding his uniform and climbing into his pajamas. Then he retreated down the corridor to the loo.

When she finished with her cold cream and pins, Hugo returned, announcing, "It's free."

"Thank you," she said.

In the loo she brushed her teeth. After she rinsed, she straightened and caught sight of herself in the mirror. Even in the harsh overhead light and with the greasy residue of cold cream on her face, she still looked beautiful. After all, thirty-two was not so very old, no matter what the ladies' magazines seemed to imply.

Sylvia straightened as best she could in her tipsy state, admiring her trim figure exaggerated by the tightly cinched belt of her dressing gown. She was beautiful—Hugo had said so just that evening while standing in this very flat—and wasn't that something?

With her chin lifted, she strode back to the bedroom, where Hugo's attention was fixed on a book. He looked up as she stopped at the foot of their bed, untying her dressing gown.

"Is this any good?" he asked, showing her that the book he'd chosen was the copy of *The Beautiful and Damned* she'd just finished.

"Yes," she said, letting her dressing gown slide down her arms. She tilted one hip to emphasize the drape of her silk negligee against the scoop of her waist.

"I never could get on with *The Great Gatsby*. What is this one about?"

"Two people who marry and proceed to destroy each other," she said, sliding into bed. She could feel the comforting warmth of him that had been captured by the sheets.

"Sounds cheerful," he said.

"Hugo," she started, placing a hand on his leg.

"How do you think Claire and Rupert seemed?" he asked abruptly.

"Claire and Rupert?" she asked.

"Did they seem . . . off?"

She removed her hand and leaned back against her pillows. "Yes, they did. Something must have happened before we arrived."

"I can't imagine what," he said.

She frowned. "I think Rupert is worried about how much Claire has been going out while he's been away. He started to ask me about it while we were dancing, but then he started to talk about how he was far from perfect." She paused. "Do you think he's had an affair?"

He laughed. "Rupert? Claire would have his guts for garters if he ever tried."

"Did she say anything to you?" she asked.

"She was drunk. It's hard to get any sense out of a drunk woman," he said, putting her book down on his bedside table.

"Do you know what I think?"

"What is that?" he asked.

She placed a hand on his leg once again and began to slide it upward.

For a moment she thought he would let her, but then he reached down and plucked her hand away and dropped it on top of the duvet.

"Don't make a fool of yourself, Sylvia."

"Is it so foolish to want one's husband?" she asked, more than a little stung by his scorn.

"It's late, and I need to be at the Admiralty early tomorrow."

He reached over and snapped off his bedside light, plunging them into darkness and leaving Sylvia alone with her thoughts.

11 May 1942

Dear Sylvia,

This is just a quick note to apologize if my husband was an absolute bore on Saturday evening. I fear that he was because he heard from someone at the club that I had been out with Patrick Alcott. Well, I don't need to tell you that that simply isn't true! Patrick was seated next to me at dinner a fortnight ago, and he danced with me a couple of times that evening out of pity for a poor old married woman.

I'm afraid Rupert has always had a bit of a jealous streak, and it probably isn't helped by the fact that Patrick is nearly half a head taller than him.

I hope you don't think I'm too wicked for saying that I will be glad when his leave is over. I've become rather used to my little habits while he's been away.

Yours,
Claire

———————

May 11, 1942

Dearest Izzie,

I hope you don't mind me calling you "dearest" because that is what you are. The dearest girl I've ever met.

I have not stopped thinking of you all weekend, and I would have written sooner if I hadn't been running around the countryside. It feels as though I did nothing but push the jeep out of the mud every few miles, but we managed to make good progress on our assignment and my commanding officer is pleased.

I am delighted that you decided to write to your sister. I have no doubt that she will appreciate the sketch, and you can be proud that one of your dresses will be modeled at her fashion show.

I want nothing more than to see you again. I am working hard to figure out when I can come up Norwich way again.

Yours,
Jack

Chapter Twenty-Nine

All of the balloon girls except for Alexandra stood, hands on their hips, as they stared up at their balloon. Despite a forecast that Monday morning that had called for calm weather all day, the wind had picked up around three o'clock, and now the balloon's wires were beginning to creak ominously.

"I think we should take her in," said Grace.

Molly worried her lip. "I don't know . . ."

"We'll see what Alexandra finds out," said Nancy, but the way her brow furrowed told Izzie everything she needed to know. If they didn't take the balloon down soon, there might not be any balloon left.

"Oh!" cried Izzie as she spotted Alexandra's tall frame racing up from where her friend had been using the field telephone. "There she is."

"Take her in!" shouted Alexandra. "Quick!"

Immediately, the girls scattered to their positions to haul in the massive balloon.

"Start winch!" Molly shouted. "Haul in winch!"

A moment later she triggered the mechanism on the back of their vehicle to pull the balloon in.

"Come on, come on," Izzie muttered as the balloon slowly began to descend, tugging on its wires.

"Apparently a unit over in Great Yarmouth lost a balloon about half an hour ago. It ripped clean off of its mountings, and one of the wires almost took a girl out," said Alexandra.

296 • JULIA KELLY

"Oh goodness," said Amelia.

"That is not happening to us," said Nancy with determination as they caught the winch cable. Grace scrambled to anchor it to the tether on the back of the balloon truck. As soon as the balloon was secured, audible sighs of relief ricocheted around the group.

"Let's get out of this wind," said Alexandra.

They secured the tail rope to the lorry and climbed on. Driving slowly, Molly steered them back to base, fighting against the increasing wind as she went.

"At least we're home sooner," said Nancy as the guards opened up the gates and let them in.

"Is there any particular reason you're happy to be home sooner?" asked Amelia with a sly smile.

"Like the fact that the post should be here by now?" said Lottie with a grin.

"Stop it." Nancy blushed.

"I think she's hoping to hear from Flying Officer Charles Gardner," Amelia teased.

"Oh, you two," said Nancy, but rather than scowl she was laughing. "I'm not supposed to know anything, but I think he flew yesterday. The conditions were right for it."

It was true that it had been clear the night before, the perfect conditions for flying. As she lay in bed listening to the sound of planes taking off, Izzie had been incredibly grateful that Jack's assignment kept him firmly on solid ground.

"Well, I think that means that Nancy's going to do the post run today," said Amelia cheerfully.

"Fine," said Nancy.

"I'll go with you," Izzie volunteered.

"Hoping for a letter from the wonderful Jack?" asked Amelia.

"I am actually," she said, catching Alexandra's smile.

As soon as Molly pulled into the hangar, the girls jumped off the lorry and set about putting their balloon to bed. Given the conditions they'd just come in from, they took extra time to check over all the ropes and wires, much to their NCO's approval.

Finally, Izzie and Nancy set off for the base's post office.

"Are you seeing Charles soon?" Izzie asked.

"He's supposed to write to me with news of his leave. We're hoping to coordinate so we can be together," said Nancy.

"So soon? It's only been—what?—a month?" she asked.

"About three weeks," said Nancy. "I know it sounds mad, and I would never have believed it if you'd told me that I would fall in love with a man in three weeks, but that's exactly what happened."

"Goodness," Izzie breathed.

"Don't you feel that way about Jack?" Nancy demanded, as though wanting to cling to someone else in the whirlwind she was in.

"I don't suppose I've really thought about love. I like him. I really do," she said.

Nancy tossed her hair behind her shoulders. "With Charles I just knew. He wants to meet my family, and I know he's written to his mother about me. This is real, Izzie. I know it is."

"I'm very happy for you," she said sincerely. Nancy certainly seemed happy. She'd been less snippy, less concerned about being right all the time. If anything, Flying Officer Charles Gardner had made all of the balloon girls' lives that little bit easier.

The wind tried to tear their hats from their heads as they leaned heavily on the post office door to push it open. They stumbled in, laughing.

"Close that door!" shouted one of the WAAFs behind the

counter who had her arms spread as she tried to hold down stacks of paper. "It creates a vacuum every time it opens."

"Sorry!" Izzie called as she struggled with the door.

When she managed to wrestle it closed, she joined Nancy at the counter, where she had already given the harried post office WAAFs their unit's names.

"I wonder what will happen to the unit that lost their balloon?" Nancy asked.

"It wasn't their fault," Izzie said. "We all got the same meteorology report this morning."

"I suppose so," said Nancy, although she didn't sound convinced.

"Here you are," said the WAAF who'd yelled about the door, handing a bundle of letters across the counter.

"Thank you," said Izzie.

"Wait! This just came in," said the WAAF's counterpart, holding up a slip of paper in a telegraph envelope.

Nancy froze, her eyes fixed on the envelope. "Who is that for?"

"It says—" The WAAF squinted at the small text. "—Aircraft Woman Second Class Nancy Dixon."

All the color drained from Nancy's face. "Charles."

"You don't think it's a—" Izzie stared at the telegram in horror. "But surely if something happened they would send a casualty telegram to his mother. That's a civilian telegram."

Nancy buckled over, gasping for air as panic clearly began to take over. "I know—he asked his friends—if anything happened—"

The WAAF holding the telegram dropped the message on the counter and backed a step away.

Izzie gripped her friend's shoulders. "Nancy. Nancy, listen to me. We haven't read it yet. We don't know."

"I know," Nancy gasped out. "I know."

"Give me that," Izzie ordered. The WAAF behind the counter quickly scooped the telegram up and handed it to her, and she ripped it open.

CHARLES KILLED IN ACTION YESTERDAY
DEEPEST REGRETS

"What does it say?" Nancy asked, trembling.

Instead of speaking, Izzie gathered Nancy up in her arms and hugged her tight as her friend let out the long, low cry of a dying animal.

12 May 1942

Dearest Jack,

I know this is not the response to your wonderful letter that you will have hoped for, but I'm afraid that I can't be joyful today.

Nancy Dixon, one of the girls in my unit, lost her boyfriend Charles yesterday. All we know at this point is that he was killed in action, presumably on a mission. He was a flying officer at a nearby base, and Alexandra managed to convince our NCO to allow us to telephone there to speak to Charles's friend. He couldn't tell Alexandra much because missions are classified, but he said that Charles's plane was hit somewhere over open water. He saw Charles eject and pull his parachute, but he was hit by machine-gun spray before it could fully open.

Nancy is inconsolable. She told me just this afternoon that they were in love. They were making plans to meet each other's families. We believe she will be sent on bereavement leave for a period.

The rest of us do not know what to say. All of us are thinking of the people we love and care for.

I will be honest with you, Jack, I cannot stop thinking of you. I would not be able to stand it if anything happened to you. I know I can't ask you to run away from danger in this war. We're all vulnerable. But promise me that you will do everything you can to come back to me.

Yours,
Izzie

Chapter Thirty

Sylvia looked up when, through the open doors of her flat's dining room, she heard the grandfather clock by the sitting room chime ten. She put down her pencil and stretched her arms overhead, her cramped muscles relaxing with relief.

The table was a mess of newspapers, notebooks, and the afternoon post that she hadn't yet had the chance to open. She'd come home early to work on her fashion show plans, and somewhere along the way she'd lost track of the time. If Mrs. Atkinson hadn't placed supper in front of her with a tut before leaving for the day, Sylvia probably wouldn't have even eaten.

She would clean it all up before she went to bed, but she still had work to do.

She looked down at her list of dressmakers with satisfaction. Half of them had ticks next to their names with notes regarding their commitment to the fashion show. Entrusted with shaping the fundraiser, she'd gone above and beyond, making notes as she assessed what each dressmaker's skills and strengths were so that the committee could recommend what sort of garment was needed for the show and help dressmakers present their businesses in the best light. Likewise, she'd created lists of members of the press, trade publications, and ladies' magazines she wanted to target to drum up attention and support for the charity.

At tomorrow's committee meeting, she expected Lady Nolan to announce that the fashion show would be their next fundraiser.

She would continue to work securing the agreements of her fellow dressmakers, but then she would refocus her attention on the shop once again.

"Right," Sylvia said, placing her palms firmly on the dining table and pushing away. She needed to be sharp, so she would forgo a nightcap and make a cup of tea instead.

She started to turn, but then the post caught her eye. She swept it up and carried it with her to the kitchen, flipping through the envelopes as she went. However, she stopped when she saw the fourth letter. It was addressed to her in her sister's hand.

Sylvia pushed open the kitchen door and set the letters on the counter, leaving Izzie's on top. Moving deliberately, she filled the kettle and put it on to boil. Then she opened the cabinet and rummaged around for the tea tin Mrs. Atkinson did her best to keep as full as the ration would allow. She'd recently switched to Darjeeling so she wouldn't miss the lack of real milk as much. Carefully, she spooned out a scant measure of leaves into the Royal Doulton pot that had been a wedding gift from Hugo's parents. When she reached for a matching teacup, however, she accidentally nudged the one next to it and sent it clattering to the floor.

Cursing softly, she took the broom and dustpan from the small cabinet on the far end of the kitchen and set about sweeping up the broken china. With this done, she glanced at the letter again.

It wasn't that she was afraid of what might be inside, exactly. It was just that Izzie's last letter had been so brief and so abrupt.

Do not pretend that you know the first thing about what Mum was like.

Chastising herself for being afraid of a piece of paper, Sylvia tore the letter open, drawing out an unusually thick sheaf of sheets.

When she unfolded it, her breath hitched. Sitting in the center of the handwritten pages was a sketch.

She touched her finger to the drawing, following the lines of the dress with modest gathers on the right side. It fell just below the knee, with long, tight sleeves that would emphasize the slimness of the wearer's wrist. To the side, Izzie had written, "I would suggest a fine claret wool or, if that is not available, navy for autumn."

The dress was beautiful, and Sylvia could imagine a model walking out into the middle of the crowd of onlookers at the charity fashion show, gloriously dressed in a way that showed off her sister's talent perfectly.

Carefully, Sylvia set the sketch aside and began to read. She wasn't even to the end of the first paragraph when she began to tear up. By the bottom of the first page, she was crying. When she finished reading, she felt completely drained.

The letter was part apology, part acknowledgment, and it was exactly what she'd wanted the moment Izzie had come back into her life.

She'd wasted too much time pushing her sister away, and she was done with that misguided part of her life. She would be glad however Izzie would take her back, and she would prove that she wasn't the neglectful, profligate sister Izzie seemed to have thought she was for years.

Sylvia wouldn't fail her sister.

The kettle began to scream, and she composed herself enough to lift it off the hob and pour boiling water over the tea leaves. Then she loaded up a wooden tray with the pot, a fresh cup and saucer, a teaspoon, and the post. Already she was writing a letter in her head, wanting to pour so many things out onto the page.

Perhaps that is why, as she made her way out of the kitchen and back to the dining room, she didn't notice that anything was awry until she saw Hugo, standing next to the dining room table, peering down at her papers.

He turned to face her, his lips so thin they'd nearly disappeared. "What is this?" he demanded, pointing at her list.

Her hackles immediately went up. How dare he go through her things?

"Good evening to you too, darling," she said, her tone rather arch as she set the tray down next to her work and carefully moved Izzie's sketch and letter out of the way of her tea.

"What is this?" he repeated.

"Something I'm working on for Lady Nolan on behalf of the War Widows' Fund," she said as she poured herself a cup.

"Why is your mother's dress shop at the top of this list?" he asked, holding up the notebook. "We agreed that it would be best if you didn't mention your association with the shop socially."

She stiffened, cheeks ablaze. It was true she had once agreed to that. It had seemed more important to be accepted by the Pearsalls, the members of Hugo's club, his friends and patients, and to do that, she knew she couldn't be Sylvia Shelton, whose mother was a dressmaker. She had whittled away her rough edges until only a perfectly smooth acceptability was left behind, but in doing so she'd taken away all of her supposed imperfection—all of the things that made her who she was—and more and more, she found herself missing that woman.

She cleared her throat. "The fashion show is for charity. I suggested at a committee meeting that it might be a good way to raise money for the war widows given all of the recent attention on the utility scheme."

He sighed. "Sometimes, Sylvia, I really wonder whether you have a clear thought in your head."

She jerked back. "I beg your pardon?"

"What would happen if someone connected the shop and your sister back to you?" he asked, as though speaking to a child.

"Then they would know that my sister is a very talented dress-maker." They would see the beautiful work Miss Reid had produced of late, as Lady Winman had. They would discover a place that was a beacon of style in a time when women desperately needed some-thing chic in their lives.

"Shouldn't Isabelle have been conscripted anyway?" he asked, tossing the notebook down on the table. "She's about the same age as the Wrens they keep sending us."

She stared at him. She'd written to him and told him that Izzie was being sent away to train in the WAAFs. When he'd rolled in one night, half-tight after being at his club, she'd mentioned to him that her sister had been dispatched to East Anglia. He'd made a noise in the back of his throat—an acknowledgment that he'd heard her—but nothing more.

"Izzie is with her barrage balloon unit in Norfolk," she said, trying to keep a measure of calm in her voice.

He screwed up his face in confusion. "Then who is running the shop?"

"I am. I own half of it, after all."

Hugo stilled. "You told me that you were selling to her."

She lifted her chin. "The sale didn't come through in time for Izzie's deployment, so she asked me to take over."

"But you don't speak to your sister."

That stung, but she held her husband's gaze.

"Sylvia, what do you really know about running a business?" he tried again.

"I know a great deal more than you think, Hugo. I was doing the accounts and running orders for my mother long before I met you. It isn't something a woman readily forgets."

"Be reasonable."

She planted her hands on her hips. "I am being perfectly reasonable."

"No." He bit out the word so hard she almost flinched. "I will not have any wife of mine playing at running a shop."

"I'm not playing at anything. If you ever came home for supper, you'd realize that I was spending more time at the shop than I am here. I'm working harder than I've ever worked before—"

"You are my wife, and you will not work!" he exploded.

She stared at the red-faced man in front of her and realized for the first time in her marriage that she had no idea who he was—not really—because the brilliant young doctor who had swept her off her feet with promises of love and comfort was gone.

"You have no idea what it took to convince my mother and father that you were worth marrying," he gritted out, clearly trying to pull his temper back under control. "They agreed that you were beautiful, but they didn't think I could mold you into an acceptable wife. *I* did that. I brought you into this world, and I taught you everything."

"They didn't?" she whispered, feeling almost sick as she remembered how kind Mrs. Pearsall had been to her. How much she'd looked to the older woman for guidance before the wedding.

"No one did. I took you away from that miserable shop and your miserable little life with those miserable people."

"Those people were my family."

He scoffed. "Don't pretend that you ever gave them a single thought. You *wanted* to leave, Sylvia. You practically begged me to take you away from that place."

He was right. He was right, and she'd never felt so ashamed of that fact. She'd thought that he would be her knight in shining armor, taking her away from all of the unhappiness that tainted her life at Glengall Road. But over the years something had shifted. It had been slow at first, almost imperceptible, but ever since she'd found the letters in his desk it had been clear. At first, she'd been convinced that the change had been in him, but he was the same man she'd married—charismatic, charming, obstinate, and imperious. She'd been wrong.

She was the one who was different now.

"I have spent years trying to be the perfect wife for you," she said slowly. "I've entertained your friends. I've joined the committees that you thought would be advantageous for your practice. I've kept your home. I changed everything about myself, from how I wear my hair to where I shop, to suit you, and I didn't complain. Not once. But it isn't enough any longer.

"I love my mother's shop. It wasn't always like that, but it is now. I love helping customers and chasing down missed deliveries. I find an immense amount of satisfaction in sitting down at my mother's desk and sorting through the accounts. I even like Miss Reid.

"I'm good at all of it too, and what's more, I think I need it. The dinner parties and committees and even the war work—it isn't enough anymore, Hugo. You must understand," she said.

He looked down and for a moment she thought that maybe he understood, but when he lifted his head his gaze was like ice. "Sell the shop. Give it away. I don't care, but your association with it ends tonight."

"If you will just listen to me—"

"No wife of mine will serve other women! You are demeaning yourself."

She laughed in disbelief. "Demeaning? You call what I do at the shop demeaning? That's rich coming from you, Hugo."

"Sylvia—"

"Perhaps before you begin slinging accusations at me, you should take a long, hard look at yourself. You have been assigned to London for weeks, yet I've hardly seen you except when we had supper with Claire and Rupert, and what an evening *that* was. You won't come home, and when you are here—on those very rare occasions—you cannot wait for the moment when you can leave again."

He stretched his neck, as though the collar of his uniform was suddenly too tight. "That isn't true."

"You're able to sleep in your own bed and kiss your wife good night every evening if you wish. Do you know how many men would trade the world for that privilege if only they could?" she asked.

"I have certain obligations," he said, looking away.

"What is more important than your wife and marriage?"

As the silence stretched between them, Sylvia's last illusions shattered. If he wasn't going to fight for their marriage, she wasn't going to pretend any longer.

She broke into a stride, making for the dining room door.

"Sylvia? Where are you going?" he called after her.

She went straight to his study and wrenched open the drawer that held his love letters. She began pulling them out, tossing them onto the desktop one by one.

"What is the meaning of this? Why are you in my study?" he demanded from the doorway.

She stopped, chest heaving, and braced one hand on either side of his green leather blotter.

"Who is she?" she demanded.

Hugo's eyes fixed on the letters, but he said nothing. She picked up an envelope and flung it at him. It sliced through the air and bounced off his thigh before falling to the carpet.

"Who is she?" she repeated, louder now.

Hugo stepped into the study and closed the door behind him, even though they were the only ones in the flat.

"You are making a spectacle of yourself," he said.

"So I'm a spectacle? I'm absurd? Is that what you really think of me, Hugo?" she raged.

"The neighbors will hear."

"I am standing here telling you that I know of your affair and all you can say is the neighbors might hear?"

Hugo sighed. "If you will just take a moment to compose yourself, I can explain."

She picked up one of the letters and ripped it out of its envelope, the paper tearing. She didn't miss his wince.

"'My darling,'" she read out. "'I cannot tell you how horrible it is waiting for you. I lie in bed and think about your touch. Your clever hands sliding—'"

"Sylvia, that is enough," he barked, his composure breaking.

"Who is she?"

"A gentleman never speaks of matters of the heart."

She gasped, hinging at the waist as his words stole the breath from her. "Matters of the heart? You are my *husband*. No one else is supposed to hold that place in your heart."

"You're being ridiculous," he muttered.

"Do you love her?"

There was that condescending sigh again as he rubbed a hand over his forehead. "I should have expected you wouldn't understand."

"Why? Because I'm common? Because I grew up above a shop and you went to bloody Eton with Rupert and all your other wretched friends who seem to treat their wedding vows as they would the morning's paper—useful for a time but then disposable?"

"That is enough."

"You took a vow, Hugo!" she continued, rage pulsing hot in her veins. "You stood at an altar and promised that you would love me and only me. You're my husband. That is supposed to mean something!"

Revulsion, clear and forceful, flashed across his face, and Sylvia stepped back in shock. He hated her. Her husband, whom she had given so much up for, hated her.

"Do you love her?" she repeated in a whisper.

"I—" His voice broke and his features fell, leaving behind nothing but exhaustion. He looked a good twenty years older than he really was, and for the first time she could see the deep grooves etched into his forehead as he frowned.

"Whether I love her or not is a private matter."

"Is" a private matter. Not "was."

The affair was still happening.

"Do you regret marrying me?" she asked, unable to stop herself.

"You should not insist on embarrassing yourself, Sylvia. Besides, this matter is not up for discussion. I don't care whether your sister buys half of it or someone else does, you will sell your stake in your mother's shop. You will return to whatever it is that you do when I am not at home."

Then he turned and left her standing behind his desk, the evidence of his love affair scattered in front of her. A few seconds later, the front door to the flat opened and shut with a firm click.

She wrapped her arms across her stomach and waited for the tears to come.

Nothing.

After years of pushing down every one of her own desires in service of her husband, she was hollow.

She let her arms fall to her sides.

Enough.

She didn't know what she would do, but she couldn't stay there in the home they had shared, waiting for him.

She went to the bedroom, slipped off her shoes, and dragged the small upholstered stool that usually sat in front of her vanity over the carpet to her wardrobe. Climbing on it, she balanced on her tiptoes and managed to grasp the handle of first one and then another of her largest suitcases.

She placed both on the bed, opened them, and went to her wardrobe. She began to pull out skirts, dresses, blouses, and even the pair of trousers she only wore around the flat because Hugo hated how unladylike he thought they were. Into the cases went jumpers and cardigans, slips, underthings, and the precious silk stockings she had been hoarding for months. She chose the best of her shoes and added gloves and her second-best handbag.

From inside her wardrobe, she drew out her train case. She put her makeup and cold cream inside. She glanced at her jewelry box, hesitating before opening it and adding the pieces that Hugo had given her. She left behind anything she knew had once belonged to his mother or grandmother.

In the dining room, she swept up her paperwork along with Izzie's letter and sketch. Then she went to the sitting room desk where she kept her correspondence. Looping back, she placed everything on top of her clothes, slipped in her library books from her bedside table, and closed the last case.

The suitcases were heavy, but she managed to make it out of the bedroom without knocking into any of the walls. When she reached the hall closet, she put them down to retrieve her coat, put her hat on, pull on her gloves, and loop her best handbag around her right wrist.

She thought for a moment about ringing down to the night porter, but she shook off the idea. Instead, she eased open the front door, lifted her cases once again, and left the flat.

Part IV

13 May 1942

Dear Lady Nolan,

Please accept my sincere apologies that I will be unable to attend this afternoon's committee meeting. I am indisposed.

If you will please defer the announcement of the fashion show until our next meeting, I will be able to bring a full accounting of the dressmakers who have agreed to show garments, as well as other press lists and other materials.

Yours faithfully,
Mrs. Hugo Pearsall

———————

13 May 1942

Dear Mrs. Pearsall,

It was more than inconvenient to have to change the agenda of the War Widows' Fund committee meeting at the last minute. However, when I received your message sent by courier I was left with no choice. I expect a full accounting of the work you have completed on 27th May. I sincerely hope that your unexpected absence will not set back the committee's fundraising efforts.

Yours faithfully,
Lady Nolan

———————

May 14, 1942

My darling Izzie,

I am very sorry for your friend Nancy. I cannot imagine what it must be like to lose the person you love like that.

This war is too cruel for words.

I only have a few minutes before I'm due on the road, but I wanted to write and tell you I promise I will do everything I can to stay safe. I would never want to jeopardize the chance to see you again.

Ever yours,
Jack

———————

May 16, 1942

My dearest Izzie,

We have finally stopped moving for more than what feels like a half an hour, and I wanted to apologize for not writing and let you know that I'm thinking of you. In fact, I have not stopped thinking about you since I received your last letter, which is no change from the usual, but now it feels weightier. None of us know how much time we might have during this war. Let's not waste it.

I have a special favor to ask you. Do you remember my friend Sergeant Ben Martin from the dance at the Assembly Hall? Well, we ended up on this assignment together, and when he found out that you and I had gone out he wouldn't stop talking about your friend Alexandra. He thinks she's a knockout.

What do you think about a double date? You and me and your friend Alexandra and Benny? We could go out this Friday if you ladies can get permission to leave base.

Let us Yanks lift your spirits a bit.

Ever yours,
Jack

———————

18 May 1942

Dearest Jack,

If anyone should apologize for not writing, it is me. The truth is that we've been rushed off our feet recently. One of the mobile balloon units temporarily assigned to our area (I'm being careful, censors!) has been redeployed, so now there is twice as much work for us to do as we manage our balloon and theirs. We're all exhausted, especially with Nancy gone on bereavement.

Nancy is never far from my thoughts, but neither is Sylvia. I keep turning over in my mind all the memories I have of her, examining them in a new light.

I don't know why I'm telling you this except that the thought of seeing you again is the one thing sustaining me through this week. I'm delighted that Sergeant Martin wants to see Alexandra again and, although she is slightly skeptical that he is just being kind, she's agreed to come on Friday.

I cannot wait until I can kiss you again.

Yours,
Izzie

Chapter Thirty-One

S ylvia eased her soft cream cardigan from off her shoulders and slipped her arms into it, wrapping the two fronts tight across her stomach. Despite the fact that it was the nineteenth of May, three days of soaking rain had left her unable to shake the deep chill of damp air that settled into her bones.

She glanced out of the door of the shop's office and across the empty workroom. It would be warmer in the flat, she knew, but she couldn't quite bring herself to mount the flight of stairs yet. Not until her eyes burned from the effort of staying open. Only then would she go upstairs and try to sleep.

When she'd left Nottingham Court the previous week, she hadn't had a plan. She'd thought she might avoid the night porter, but he had been in the lobby when she'd appeared with her cases under her arms, so she'd asked him to hail her a cab. A middle-aged woman, who'd no doubt taken up driving to free up a man to fight, had pulled up the building's sweeping drive and rolled down the window of the cab.

"Where would you like to go, dear?" the cabbie had asked.

Without even thinking, Sylvia had said, "Number four Glengall Road in Maida Vale, please."

Because, really, where else could she go?

Yet when the cabbie had pulled up to the flat's door, she'd hesitated in the back seat. She had never imagined she would be back here again. The shop had been one thing, but the flat?

She'd met Hugo and that was supposed to be it. He was her husband. He was her life.

Until she realized that he'd never really felt that way about her.

With a sigh, she'd hauled her suitcases out of the cab and up the flat's stairs, and collapsed into a deep sleep on the bed in the room she'd once shared with Izzie.

Over the past few days, she'd pulled up the drawbridge on her life, ignoring everything happening outside of the shop. She'd written to Lady Nolan, making her excuses for missing the committee meeting. She'd put off a dinner she'd been invited to by the wife of a literary critic she'd met at the London Library. When Miss Reid raised a brow after spotting her coming through the door joining the flat's staircase and the shop, she'd simply put her head down and carried on with her day.

However, despite plunging herself into her work, Sylvia couldn't resist the compulsion to replay every aspect of her marriage, looking for where it had gone wrong. She'd thought of all the nights she'd gone out with Hugo and his friends, but instead of the happy memories she'd once had she remembered the little barbs of criticism he'd laid on her that she'd brushed off as her own sensitivity. She remembered how he'd pushed her to outfit herself with a new wardrobe after their marriage and how he'd come with her to nod or shake his head at her selections. She thought of his objections to signing the annual Christmas card she sent to her mother and sister. But mostly she remembered every smile he'd bestowed upon other women, now suspicious of what might have been behind them.

She blamed him for his affair and all of the horrible ways he'd treated her, but she also wondered what portion of blame belonged to her.

She had said yes to the wrong man. Perhaps he had been right at some point, when she had been the young, wide-eyed girl eager to please, but she hadn't stayed naive. She'd become a woman—a complicated person with ambitions all her own. And he hadn't wanted that.

She could see all of the facts laid out so plainly before her now, but that didn't make it any easier to admit that the life she'd built for herself had turned into a disappointment.

She told no one about her slow realization that the inevitable had happened. Not Miss Reid. Not Izzie. Not Claire or Lady Nolan or any of the other ladies on the committee. Neither had she spoken to Hugo since she left. He hadn't telephoned the shop or come around. She didn't even know if he was aware that she was no longer living at the flat, although she supposed that Mrs. Atkinson had likely raised the alarm. She'd seen the housekeeper once two afternoons ago when she'd returned to retrieve a few more things and pick up her post. Mrs. Atkinson, teary-eyed, hadn't asked any questions but instead had left a cup of tea for her on her writing desk in the sitting room. It was, Sylvia supposed, a tacit sign of understanding.

She sighed. Hugo and their marriage were a mess that she would have to confront at some point, but for now she had the lifeline that was the shop.

I hope that, as it has for me, the shop will take care of them when they need it most.

She had to admit, her mother's words had certainly come true.

A knock on the front door set her heart leaping in her throat. She glanced at her watch. It was past eight o'clock. Who could be—?

THE DRESSMAKERS OF LONDON · 321

She hurried through the shop to open the front door and let him in.

"Hello," he said, rain dripping off the brim of his hat as he lifted it off his head.

"Hello. No sandwiches tonight?"

He played with the brim, scooting the felt between his index fingers and thumbs. "I know it probably isn't exactly what you're used to, but I don't suppose you would fancy a drink at the pub, would you?"

She couldn't remember the last time she'd been in a pub. It had to be before she'd met Hugo, probably with some long-forgotten local boy who had taken her after going to the cinema, because her husband didn't frequent them himself. His world was private clubs, restaurants, and dining rooms in the homes of friends and acquaintances large enough to have a table that seated at least eight.

"Do you know what? I think a drink sounds like just the thing," she said.

William's expression brightened instantly. "Really? I mean, I'm glad to hear it."

The delight in his voice warmed her, the first bright spot in a long day. "I'll just fetch my things."

———

When they arrived, the pub's lounge was only half-full. William found them a cozy corner where Sylvia sat while he went to the hatch in the wall to order their drinks from the publican on the other side. She watched him carefully carry back a pint of bitter for him and a gin for her before settling down across the table from her.

To her left, a table of young women with their hair rolled away from their faces watched William pass by before breaking into giggles.

Sylvia dipped her chin to hide her smile at their open interest.

"Is something funny?" he asked, peering around.

"It's nothing. To your health," she said, raising her glass.

He tapped it lightly on the rim and took a sip of his beer, a little mustache of foam clinging to his upper lip before he licked it off.

He looked so much like the boy she'd known years ago, but she could see why the girls at the next table had looked him over with such complimentary gazes. His face had hollowed out to sharpen his cheekbones, and the way he wore his hair in a deep part gave him a dashing look she was certain he hadn't realized.

"How are things at the shop?" he asked.

She smiled. "Better. Izzie finally wrote to me."

"Did she?" he asked.

She nodded. "I don't know whether it really helped or not, but I'm trying to be more honest with her and explain some of the decisions I made. Why I left the way I did."

"Why did you leave?"

There was something about the sharpness of his tone that made her look up.

"I'm sorry," he said, immediately backtracking. "It's not my place."

"No, you clearly have something to say, William. I would appreciate it if you would say it," she pushed.

He toyed with his beer, spinning the glass so that it jittered against the rough wood of the pub's table. Finally, he said, "One day you were there and the next it was as though you had never lived on Glengall Road at all."

"I married. I moved away."

"Yes, but people who marry go home to see their friends and family, Sylvia. Everyone on the road wondered about you. Before my mother died, she used to ask me about you from time to time. And I know that Mr. and Mrs. Meed from the tea shop always asked your mother what you were up to. Even Mrs. Reynolds wanted news."

She remembered the grocer telling her about taking tea with Mrs. Meed and her mother. Asking after her.

"Did you know that when you became engaged, Mrs. Weatherstone who lived at number ten took out a subscription to one of the society magazines so she could scour the columns to see if there was any mention of you? She showed my mother your wedding announcement in *The Times*, she was so proud," he continued.

"William . . ." She wanted him to stop. She didn't want to think about all of these people she'd once known thinking about her like that, wishing her well when she hadn't had a single thought for them.

"And then there's your mother," he said. "When she came to have me write her will, I asked her why she wanted to leave the shop to both of you. I never question clients' decisions, but I had to know, because as far as I knew, you hadn't been back in years. Do you know what she told me?"

"No," she whispered.

"She said that one day you might need it. That was why she put that line in. To explain a little."

She wrapped her hands around her drink, holding on to it as though it were a talisman.

"William," she said slowly, "I need your advice."

He shot her a look over the top of his pint. "As a solicitor or as a friend?"

"Both? I'm not certain."

He put his drink down. "Tell me."

"Last Tuesday, I left my husband. Or at least I left the flat. I'm not entirely certain yet."

His jaw dropped, but then he seemed to remember himself and schooled his expression into one of calm neutrality.

"I'm very sorry to hear that. Would you like to talk about it?" he asked.

She bit her lip and nodded.

"Go ahead," he said.

"Just before my mother died, I found out Hugo has been having an affair. I don't know how long it's been going on, but I do know that he is still . . . involved with this woman."

He let out a heavy exhale. "I'm sorry, Sylvia."

"Thank you," she said softly. "I confronted him about it the night I left."

"What did he say?" he asked.

"He told me that I was being dramatic, and that a gentleman never speaks of matters of the heart. He implied that if I had come from his world, I would understand," she said with a hollow laugh.

"Bastard," William cursed. "Excuse my language."

She gave a surprised laugh. "He *is* a bastard."

William shook his head. "As though being born into certain circles makes it acceptable to be unfaithful to one's wife."

"But that's just it, William. Hugo seems to think that nothing is the matter at all. It's simply what is done discreetly among his set." It was what was done in the set *she'd* once belonged to.

"Are you telling me that having affairs is just par for the course?" he asked skeptically.

"It sounds silly when you say it like that," she admitted.

"You deserve more than that, Sylvia."

"Well, yes. It's taken me longer to come to that conclusion than I would like to admit, but that's why I packed my bags. I simply couldn't believe that after all those years of marriage my husband hardly flinched when I told him I'd found the letters."

William looked up sharply. "There are letters?"

"Yes. At least half a dozen of them."

"Do they describe the love affair in any detail? Are there declarations?" he asked.

She shifted in her seat. "They aren't signed, but she tells him she loves him. She writes about some of the . . . things they have done together."

"Sylvia, if you wish to, you could sue Hugo for divorce on the grounds of adultery. Those letters you found would be evidence used in court to help your case," he said.

"Divorce?"

"If that's what you want."

She didn't know what she wanted. She'd left the flat with no plan except to retreat to the shop and lick her wounds. Divorce . . . well, that would be an admission that everything she'd built with Hugo was now ash. The flat, her friends, her life. All of it would be gone.

She didn't know any divorcées socially, not only because there were so few of them in Hugo's circle but because those who did leave their husbands—or were left—were pushed out to the edges of polite society. Did she really want to join the ranks of those unfortunate women?

"Do you really think I would have a case for divorce?" she asked.

"With those letters, yes. It wouldn't be immediate. These things take time, but I've handled several divorce cases. I would gladly help guide you," he said.

She opened her mouth but then closed it again. A part of her yearned to say yes, but it was impossible to override more than a decade of careful choices so quickly.

"I don't know if I can do it," she said, her voice cracking a little.

He reached out a hand, but he stopped just short of touching her.

"Sylvia," he said quietly, "don't you deserve to be happy?"

She stared at their hands. To be a divorced woman ... It wouldn't just mean the end of her married life. It would mean being alone, and that frightened her more than she could say.

"I can't become my mother," she whispered.

"You wouldn't be—"

She shook her head emphatically. "William, you didn't know my mother before coming to Glengall Road. She was a sweet, loving woman, quick to laugh and easy with a joke. Then my father died and everything changed. She was alone in the world with two children and no money. The shop saved her, but it killed her too."

"You don't know that," he said softly.

"I do," she said firmly. "How could it have not? Every night she would drag herself up the stairs from the workroom to the flat, overworked and defeated. She always had some complaint or another—an aching back, tired eyes, fingers that had been pricked over and over again by pins. Even when the business began to do well enough, there was never enough money to save her from the fear that one day it would all disappear again.

"She used to try to hide it from Izzie, but she was honest with me about how much she resented needing to work again. She blamed the Sheltons, who refused to help her. She blamed my father. She blamed me."

"Why would she blame you? You were just a child when your father died."

She squeezed her eyes closed. "Because I'm the reason Papa died."

"Sylvia, you can't be serious."

"I am."

"But your father died in a traffic accident," he said. "How could that be your fault?"

"He was only on that road that evening because of me," she said, the truth she'd kept locked away in her heart for so many years pouring out of her. "It was my birthday and he was buying me flowers. Sunflowers. They were always my favorite, and he would bring them home for my birthday every year even though they were out of season. I insisted on it even though it meant that he had to go to an entirely different neighborhood to a florist that sold hothouse flowers.

"If it hadn't been for me, he never would have been taking that route home. The lorry driver never would have hit him."

"Sylvia, you weren't to know. No one could have known."

The tenderness in his voice sliced into her. She didn't deserve his pity.

"Oh, I knew that if I demanded something, Papa would go and fetch it for me. He used to call me his little princess, which my mother hated. She told him he should stop spoiling me.

"Have you ever noticed that I call him Papa and Izzie calls him Dad?" she asked.

"I don't suppose I ever really thought about it, but now that you mention it," said William.

"That was my mother's doing. She thought 'Papa' sounded like I was putting on airs, but that was how he referred to himself

328 • JULIA KELLY

so she let it go. However, Izzie was so young when he died that, when my mother began to call him 'Dad,' Izzie followed suit. I think it was her way of proving I thought I was above her way of doing things. She was always a bit spiky about the fact that she'd married up.

"After Papa's death, my mother was furious at me. She told me it was all my fault. It only became worse after she found out about Papa's debts. The house was mortgaged and mortgaged again, and it seems that he hadn't been making the payments. Papa's family turned their backs on her, and she was left scrambling. All because of me."

"You were only eleven," said William, still trying to soothe her. She didn't want his kind words. She didn't deserve them.

"When we moved into the flat, I threw a tantrum because I didn't want to share a bedroom with my sister. I'd never had to before, and I didn't understand why I should start at eleven. My mother grabbed me by the shoulders and slapped me. She told me that this was all my fault and that if I hadn't been so demanding my father would still be alive and we'd still be living in our old house with our old life."

William pulled out his handkerchief and handed it to her.

"Thank you," she sniffed, dabbing at her tears. "It's silly crying really. It was so many years ago."

"I had no idea," he said.

"Of course you didn't. No one knows about that part. Not even Izzie." She'd only dared go so far in her letter because she didn't want to taint her sister's memories of their mother. Not like that.

"After that, the guilt set in and I tried my hardest to show my mother how sorry I was. I kept the shop neat and tidy. I delivered orders. I managed the paperwork and did all the accounting. I kept thinking that one day she might notice how hard I was working and she'd forgive me at least a little bit.

"Instead, she poured all of her love into Izzie. How could she not? Izzie was so like her. Izzie could sew, and she seemed to know inherently how clothes should fit. When I was living at home, they never argued because Izzie never pushed back. She was so good.

"By the time Hugo came along, I felt like a stranger in my own family. For the first time since my father died, there was someone telling me I was worth loving." She smiled sadly. "When he asked me to marry him, the choice seemed obvious. I could stay at the shop and know that every day I reminded my mother of everything she'd lost, or I could become Hugo's wife and live my own life."

"And so you said yes," said William.

She nodded. "I suppose I should have expected it, but when I told my mother about the engagement, all she said to me was 'I suppose you'll be happy to see the backs of us.' I said I would never think that, but then at the wedding everything went wrong. I remember looking up at the wedding breakfast and watching them walk out early. That made me angry. I thought that if they couldn't even stay for the entirety of my wedding, I didn't need them anymore. They could telephone or write to me when they decided they wanted me around. Then, before I knew it, months had gone by and I didn't know how to even begin to repair things."

She twisted her empty glass in her hands, wishing that it was full again. Wishing that she hadn't said any of that to William, yet it had broken her heart a little to think that he or any of the other people who had watched her grow up thought she hadn't cared.

"Have you told your sister any of this?" he asked.

"Not really. I told her a little bit about the Sheltons."

"You should tell her about your mother and what it was like living under the same roof with her," he said.

"I can't do that to her. Izzie idolized our mother," she said.

He sat back and studied her. "Do you know, I think that neither you nor Mrs. Shelton had any idea just how strong a person your sister is. Whether your mother gave her credit or not, Izzie had been all but running that shop day to day before being conscripted. Now she's off serving—something neither you nor I are doing."

"You're right," she whispered. "I don't know how to be a sister to her anymore. She doesn't trust me."

"You have to earn her trust, Sylvia. There's no quick way about it, but it will happen over time," he said.

She opened her mouth to protest that it was no use, but then she thought of the letter that remained unanswered on the bedside table in the room she used to share with her sister. Izzie had sent her a sketch, and wasn't that a start?

"There are so many things I need to say, but I'm afraid she won't want to hear them," she said.

This time, when William reached for her, he closed the gap and touched her. She sucked in a breath as his fingers wrapped lightly around her hand, enveloping her in comfort even as she felt as though she was dancing on a knife point.

"Start with what happened after your father died," he said.

"I don't know if I'm brave enough to do that," she admitted.

"The Sylvia Shelton I once knew was fearless."

"Too much has changed. I'm not that girl any longer," she said.

"No, you're not," he agreed. "You're something more. I've always thought that."

There was another meaning behind his words—a meaning she

couldn't begin to examine. Not while she was desperately trying to grasp at the unwinding threads of her life.

"I think that what I want right now is a friend," she said softly.

He nodded, gave her hand a light squeeze, and then let go.

"I've always been your friend, Sylvia. Nothing will ever change that."

―――――――

That night, after William had gone, Sylvia lay on her sister's bed staring at the ceiling. She supposed that she should be grateful that, sometime after she'd left, Izzie had changed from the single bed that had once matched her own to a double. Still, her mind was fixed on her conversation with William.

She hadn't meant to tell him about Papa. It had just slipped out, the confessional mood of the evening loosening her tongue. She'd regretted it as they walked back to the shop—perhaps she should regret it now—but after the initial shock of sharing something she had kept bottled up for so long had worn off, she'd found herself glad. She trusted William, and it wasn't just because her mother and Izzie trusted him. It was because he was solid, steady, dependable.

Only that wasn't all he was.

She flexed her fingers, remembering the way he'd touched her hand. It hadn't made her feel the way a childhood friend or a trusted confidant should.

Sylvia sat up abruptly, throwing off the covers in the darkened room. If she was going to lie awake, thinking ridiculous things, at least she could do something useful.

She swung her feet to the ground and quickly crossed the room to the chair where she'd left the day's clothes neatly folded. She dressed swiftly and pulled on her coat, hat, and gloves. Then she retrieved her handbag from the side table by the flat's front door and let herself out.

It was fortunate that there was only a quarter moon that night, reducing the chance that the Germans might decide that that evening was the right time to come back and bomb London to bits once again. Still, she hurried to the bus stop, grateful when one of the last buses of the evening came quickly.

She sat, staring out the window at the unlit streets of London, until they neared her stop. She pulled the cord and the bus slowed to a stop.

Sylvia stepped off onto the pavement and looked up. Overhead she could see the faint outline of a distant barrage balloon. She wondered where Izzie was at that moment, and the low ache for her sister's company rose up in her. She wanted to pull Izzie into a big hug like she used to do when they were children. She wanted her sister to tell her that everything would be all right. That what she was about to do was the right thing.

She dipped her head and forced herself to walk in the direction of her building.

The lobby, she was grateful to see, was empty, and the lift opened immediately when she pressed the button.

She let herself into the flat, pausing on the threshold to listen out for any signs that Hugo was home. The lights were all off and the air still. She flipped the switch by the door, flooding the entryway with light, and closed the door behind her.

Without stopping to remove her coat or hat, she walked straight down the corridor to Hugo's study, pushed open the door, and made for his desk. The love letters were in the top right drawer, neatly stacked as they had been the first time she saw them.

"He put them back," she scoffed, amazed at the arrogance of the man.

With renewed determination, Sylvia picked up the first letter and set it aside. She scooped up the others and tucked them into her handbag. Then she opened the drawer on the left side of Hugo's desk and pulled out a stack of envelopes and some writing paper. Working methodically, she folded each sheet of paper and slid it into an envelope. When she'd stuffed enough envelopes to satisfy herself, she stacked them neatly where the love letters had been and placed the one she'd set aside on top. Then she closed the drawer, shut the study door, turned off the lights, and left the flat to write a letter of her own.

20 May 1942

Dear Izzie,

A great deal has happened in the past few days, and I've hesitated to tell you because I haven't been certain that you would want to know. Even now my instinct is to try to protect you from difficult things, much as I did when we were younger. However, William reminded me that you are no longer a child and that you deserve to know the truth about many things.

The first thing is this: I am no longer living with Hugo at the flat in Marylebone. Last autumn, I discovered that he has been conducting an affair, which I have no reason to believe has ceased. Although I do not know who the other woman is, I have read letters that lead me to believe that the affair is not merely physical. He loves her, and that makes it so much worse.

When I confronted Hugo about the affair, he didn't deny it. Instead, he seemed to think that I should accept it as inevitable, and so I left. I am not entirely certain of the state of my marriage, but I plan to speak to William about my options from a legal standpoint.

I did not have anywhere else to go, so I have moved back into our old bedroom in the flat. It feels strange returning when I was so determined that I would never live there again. However, it has also forced me to confront some truths that I have long set aside.

Leaving the shop was never about leaving you, Izzie, but I thought that you would be better off without me. You and Mum had formed your own little unit that was so tight, I could hardly see daylight between you two. You were so alike, and you seemed to understand one another in a way I never could. You didn't need me.

You wrote that you thought that I met Hugo and decided that I was too good for Mrs. Shelton's Fashions and this family. Perhaps in some way

I did. I was so wrapped up in being enough for him, I was terrified that if I misstepped I would lose him. He seemed so confident and erudite, his parents so intimidatingly proper, his friends so glamorous, that I was desperate to become a part of that world. I thought that if I did I would be happy, and leaving the girl I had been in Maida Vale behind was just a part of that.

I believe that, for a time, Hugo found my background amusing. He used to laugh at my little faux pas and patiently teach me how to be better. I was a project to him, and I was glad of it. For the first time in a long time, I felt as though someone wanted me around.

This is the second difficult thing that I must tell you: our mother blamed me for Papa's death. You might protest and tell me I'm being too hard on myself, as William tried to. However, I remember what she said to me after his death all too clearly, and I recall all of the times that she would kiss you good night and then turn away from me. I tried my best to be a daughter she could love even a little, but I truly believe that she never forgave me.

There it is. The other reason I left Mrs. Shelton's Fashions. Our mother was clearly happiest when she was in the workroom with you, teaching you some new stitch or debating the best way to construct a garment. I was only a burden and a reminder.

Our mother might have resented her reduction in circumstances, but she had a natural talent for dressmaking. She passed some of that talent on to you, but you have more than that, Izzie. You have an eye and a boldness in your designs that she never did.

You are brave.

I know that you will protest against what I am writing, but I can see it in your sketches. The one you sent me in your last letter is exquisite and exactly what we need for the fashion show. I have no doubt that it will attract exactly the right kind of attention, and hopefully bring in scores of women wanting to wear an Isabelle Shelton original.

I hope that you will believe me when I tell you how much I want to one day see your designs worn by the most fashionable women in London and across the world.

I hope you will believe me when I tell you how many regrets I have. I hope that you will forgive me.

Your loving sister,
Sylvia

Chapter Thirty-Two

Izzie beamed up at Jack through the fug of smoke that hung in the pub. They were crammed into two chairs in the corner, Alexandra and Ben across from them.

"How do you think it's going?" Jack asked, jerking his head toward the other couple.

"He looks smitten," she said, watching Ben, who was resting his chin in his hand as he watched Alexandra explain in great detail the art of the English steeplechase.

"He's a good Kentucky horseman."

"And Alexandra is a horsewoman," she said with a laugh.

"I don't know how those people manage to find each other in a crowd, but they always do," said Jack before leaning over the table. "Hey! Are you two going to stay here for a while?"

"Sure," said Ben, not taking his eyes off Alexandra.

"Let's go for a walk, Izzie," said Jack.

"It's raining," Alexandra protested. "You'll both be soaked through."

"It's always raining in this country," said Jack with a laugh before turning to Izzie. "Are you coming?"

She nodded and shimmied her way out around the table. She let Jack pull her by the hand to the door. When he opened it, she saw that the rain had stopped, and she could smell the fresh scent of damp leaves that surrounded the country pub.

"I love that smell," she said, breathing deep.

"Can't imagine that you have much of that in London," he said, offering her the crook of his arm.

She slipped a hand onto it, tucking in next to him. "No. Our most common weather seems to be the London fog."

"I've never seen a London fog, but I've read about it in Sherlock Holmes stories. I'd like to see it one day."

She smiled a little at the thought of Jack in London, his American enthusiasm brimming over as he took in every bit of her city. She wanted to walk all over the roads, seeing whatever monuments and sights would satisfy his curiosity. She wanted to do completely normal things that she heard other women talk about doing with their admirers, like going to the cinema or dancing.

But it was more than that. She wanted to show him the shop and the flat, to introduce him to Miss Reid and the neighbors. She wanted to show him off to Sylvia.

And then . . .

She stole a glance at him. She could see a future with this man, and it terrified her as much as it thrilled her.

It was mad, but who wasn't doing mad things these days? Everyone seemed to have a story about men and women meeting and marrying mere weeks later. No one wanted to be alone during this war.

"I want to show you Iowa," he said, as though reading her thoughts. "Beautiful prairie as far as the eye can see."

"Before joining the WAAF, I'd hardly left London except to go to the seaside," she said with a laugh.

"You'd love it. There's nowhere more beautiful in the winter when the snow covers the hills around Newton, and when Rock Creek Lake freezes over we go ice-skating."

"I've never ice-skated before," she said with a laugh.

"I'll teach you," he said.

"What if I fall?" she asked.

"You won't fall. I won't let you."

She smiled at that. "What do you do during the summer?"

"The summer is the best. We could go dancing, or we could just sit out on the back porch, watching the fireflies light up the night. Sometimes, if you're lucky, you can watch a storm roll in in the distance and run into the house just before the rain starts."

He stopped, his hand finding hers to twine their fingers together.

"I want to take you up to Iowa City to watch a football game and show you off to all my brother's college friends," he continued. "He'll love you, by the way. And his wife, Muriel, won't be able to get enough of you."

"What's she like?" she asked, warming at his confidence that these people who clearly meant so much to him would adore her.

"Sweet as pie but with a backbone of steel," he said with a laugh. "They have three boys who run wild around the house, but they all fall into line when Muriel raises so much as an eyebrow. Come to think of it, my brother does too."

"It sounds like you miss them," she said.

He squeezed her hand. "Maybe a bit, but I've found some things here in England that sure are worth sticking around for."

Warmth bloomed in her heart, and she went up on her tiptoes to kiss him on the cheek.

With a laugh, he caught her around her waist and pulled her into him, kissing her properly. When he finally pulled away, he leaned his forehead against hers and said, "You sure do make a man think, Izzie Shelton."

"About what?" she asked, every nerve in her body alight.

He kissed her quickly again. "All sorts of things."

———

Izzie didn't want the night to end, but as time slipped away, it was Jack who reminded everyone that they had to make it back to base before Izzie and Alexandra's curfew.

"Here we are," said Jack, slowing the car he'd managed to borrow for the evening just before the gates to their base.

"With two minutes to spare," said Alexandra, sticking her arm through to the front seat where Izzie was tucked up against Jack's side to show Izzie her watch. "We'd better hurry."

"She's right," said Jack with a rueful smile.

"I know," said Izzie with a sigh.

"Come here," said Jack, dipping his head to kiss her. She leaned into him, drinking him in because she knew it would be far too long until she saw him next.

"When will I see you again?" she could hear Ben ask Alexandra behind them.

"When will *I* see *you*?" Jack murmured against her lips.

"Next Friday, I think." She hesitated. "Unless you're going to be near Great Yarmouth. That's where we've been flying our balloon recently."

"Are you suggesting I come see my favorite balloon girl in action?" he asked.

She blushed. "Only if you can."

"I can't make any promises because I never know where they'll want me, but I'll do my best to try to make it out to Great Yarmouth," he said.

"Izzie, we need to go now," Alexandra interrupted.

Izzie gave Jack one last, swift kiss, and then flung open the car door to sprint to the gate.

She and Alexandra skidded to a stop in front of the gatehouse, pulling out their passes for the bored-looking guard on duty. He glanced at them and then waved them through. Safely on the right side of the gate, they turned to wave goodbye to Jack and Ben, who were both hanging out of the car windows to watch them.

"Move on, you two," the guard droned.

They glanced at each other and burst into giggles as they scampered away.

"I thought Jack would never let you go," said Alexandra.

"Oh, stop it," said Izzie.

"I'm serious. The man is utterly head over heels in love with you," said Alexandra.

"We hardly know each other," Izzie protested.

"That doesn't seem to matter much these days," said Alexandra, a little more sober now.

Izzie knew that her friend must be thinking about Nancy and her flying officer.

"What about you and Ben?" she asked, trying not to let melancholy creep into the evening.

"He's nice enough," said Alexandra with a shrug.

"I think he thinks you walk on water."

"That's just because I can speak horse," said Alexandra.

It's because you're five foot ten inches of beautiful, sunny, intelligent aristocrat, and he's never seen anything like you before, she wanted to say, but she had a sneaking suspicion that would only make Alexandra clam up.

"He's sweet," Alexandra continued, "but I'm not interested in attaching myself to a man who's only going to be sent away and forget me as soon as his assignment here is done."

Some of the wind went out of Izzie's sails. "That's very practical of you."

Alexandra clapped her hands over her mouth. "Oh, dear, I'm very sorry, Izzie. Jack's not like that, I'm certain of it."

Izzie laid a hand on Alexandra's forearm. "It's all right, really it is. I like Jack, but I know that it's early days and none of us know what's going to happen in this war."

Alexandra covered Izzie's hand with her own and gave it a little squeeze. "Forgive me?"

"There's nothing to forgive," said Izzie firmly.

They walked back to their hut, perhaps a little more subdued than before, but happy nonetheless. When they pushed open the door they found the usual cheerful chaos of their unit.

"Izzie, thank goodness!" Amelia cried out, brandishing a uniform skirt. "It's a disaster. I've torn a hole in my skirt."

"Izzie and Alexandra have just come back from a date," admonished Grace. "Izzie doesn't want to fix your skirt, she wants to swoon about Jack."

Izzie laughed and stuck out her hand. "Give it here, Amelia. I'll see what I can do."

Alexandra flopped down on her bunk. "I'm exhausted."

"Tell us everything," said Lottie, who had already wrapped her hair in rags. "Did you dance?"

"Izzie," said Grace, looking up from the magazine she was reading, "there's a letter that came for you while you were out. I left it on your bed."

"Thank you," she said. "Amelia, give me one moment while I read it and then I'll take a look at your skirt."

She picked up the letter and immediately recognized her sister's handwriting. She set the skirt aside, sat down on her bunk, and tore open the envelope.

The letter was long, and as she read her eyes widened as sentences jumped out at her.

I am no longer living with Hugo at the flat in Marylebone . . .

Last autumn, I discovered that he has been conducting an affair . . .
I have moved back into our old bedroom . . .
Our mother blamed me for Papa's death . . .
I thought that you would be better off without me . . .

When she finished the letter, she sifted back through the pages and read it all over again. Then she lifted her head and said, "I'm sorry, Amelia. I must answer this."

22 May 1942

Dear Sylvia,

I am at a loss for words. I won't pretend that I have ever liked Hugo, but I never imagined that he would betray you. I hope you know that, no matter what he told you, you deserve better.

I cannot pretend to be surprised at his scorn for your background, but I hope you no longer feel it is shameful. Mum did what she had to do in order to feed us and house us, all while paying down Dad's debts. She was skilled and talented, and although she might not have had the ambitions of some, she turned Mrs. Shelton's Fashions into something special. There is nothing dishonorable or common about that, and I'm sorry Hugo ever made you feel ashamed of any of it.

With regard to the rest of your letter, I'm left with more questions than answers. Why did you never tell me about what happened between you and Mum after Dad's death? I knew that things were strained between you two while we were growing up, but I thought that was due to a clash of personality more than anything else. A part of me cannot believe that she would have been so cruel as to blame you for our father's death. Yet another part knows that Mum was . . . Mum.

I know you think I believe she could do no wrong, and perhaps I did for a time. However, I saw more than you know. I remember the way she could snap when she was tired, and she was always tired. I recall the long nights poring over paperwork in the office. I know she worried about everything from taxes to the price of fabric.

I think that all of those worries culminated when the war started, and it became too much. She refused to let go of the shop when she should have. I should have pushed harder. I should have been more insistent that she listen to me and allow me to try some of the things that you've had such success with.

I have not always been gracious or told you how much I appreciate everything you have done these months. I understand now that you are trying your best to save a dying business and, although we haven't always agreed, that your heart is in the right place.

Yours,
Izzie

P.S. It seems as though, after sending you the sketch of the claret dress, I cannot stop sketching while sitting in bed in our hut while the other girls read or play games. I have enclosed several new designs that I thought might be useful for you and Miss Reid. You should, after all, have some things to sell after your fashion show is a roaring success.

Chapter Thirty-Three

Izzie tilted her head back, watching from her spot along the south edge of the beach parade as her unit's balloon reached its peak.

"Balloon flying thirty feet!" Molly shouted.

"Stop winch!" Nancy called back.

"Stop winch," Molly replied.

The engine shuddered to a stop and the balloon pulled lightly on its cables in the direction of the light wind along the Norfolk coast.

The day was hot, and Izzie could feel the sweat rolling down her back as the sun beat down on her.

"How much trouble do you think we would find ourselves in if we took off all our clothes and jumped into the water?" asked Alexandra as she stopped next to Izzie.

"A fair bit, I would think," said Izzie with a laugh.

"What if we left all of our clothes on?" asked her friend.

Izzie pretended to consider this and then shook her head. "Probably still a fair amount. Besides, how would we keep the fabric from snagging on the barbed wire?"

"I suppose we'll just have to stay hot and sticky then. Shame," said Alexandra, gazing out over what once must have been a beautiful strip of white sand but was now dotted with beach scaffolding, barbed wire, and other invasion defenses. An anti-aircraft tower loomed in the near distance, punctuating the entire scene. It was impossible not to remember that they were at war.

"Can you imagine it before all of this? It must have been filled with families holidaying," said Izzie.

"I've never been on a holiday to the English seaside," said Alexandra.

"Never?" Izzie asked with incredulity.

"Mummy always liked going to the Continent. We did spend some time in Biarritz. I wonder if the hotel we used to stay at will still be standing by the end of the war," Alexandra mused.

The longer she knew Alexandra the more comfortable Izzie became with the difference between their backgrounds. Her friend was not, as she once might have feared, a snob. Alexandra was unfailingly kind, curious, and open with everyone she met, and when she thought about it, Izzie found herself more than a little ashamed that she'd ever thought the earl's daughter might be anything but.

"Once a summer, I would go to the seaside with my sister. It was usually Brighton, although once we went to Margate," she said, recalling the trips with a smile. The sisters would wait all summer for the perfect combination of hot weather and Mum's willingness to release them from their duties at the shop with an exasperated yet indulgent "You keep talking about it so much, you might as well go."

There would be a scramble to pack a picnic lunch, gather up swimming costumes and blankets, and find sunglasses and straw bags. Then, with all of their kit assembled, the Shelton sisters would troop off to Victoria Station and board the train for Brighton that was brimming with fellow holidaymakers.

After alighting at Brighton Station, they would make their way straight for the sea, stopping only for Sylvia to buy them two ice cream cones. The sisters would hurry along, licking up sweetly sticky drips of ice cream until they reached the edge of the shingle beach. Slipping and sliding, they would stake out the best spot and set up for the day, only packing up reluctantly when they were crisp and exhausted from a day in the sun.

All her childhood, it had been Izzie's idea of bliss.

"How is your sister?" asked Alexandra in a low tone.

Izzie sighed, reality pulling her out of the rose-tinted memories of past summers. She'd told Alexandra about Sylvia's letter and what she'd written back.

"I don't know yet. I hope there will be a letter waiting for me when we return to base," she said.

"You're worried about her," said Alexandra.

"Yes. No? I don't know." She peered out over the ocean, watching the whitecaps on the waves. "Hugo was her entire life."

"I don't know about that," said Alexandra.

Izzie tilted her head. "What do you mean?"

Her friend shrugged. "Just that it sounds to me like your sister had an entire life that had only bits and pieces to do with her husband. Didn't you say that she has all of her committee work?"

"That's true," said Izzie slowly.

"And it sounds like she has all sorts of friends. Surely they're helping her through this."

"I hope so," she said, but she doubted it very much. She suspected that Sylvia had been able to navigate years in Hugo's social circle because she wasn't the sort of woman who let people in. Close friendships could leave one vulnerable in a way Sylvia would never have wanted.

"Well, isn't this a sight?"

A smile spread across Izzie's face.

Jack.

She turned and sure enough there he was, watching from a distance with his arms crossed over his chest and his usual grin fixed on his face. Her friends started to giggle, but Jack hardly seemed to notice, his gaze fixed firmly on her.

She touched her hair as she approached, certain she was red-faced and glistening with sweat, but when she stopped in front of him, she found she didn't really care.

"What are you doing here?" she asked.

"You told me you'd be here, so I came," he said.

"I didn't think you'd actually do it."

"Can't a man drop by to see his best girl on a whim?" he asked.

She smiled. "Certainly, but when that man's life is run by the USAAF, it usually becomes a little bit harder to be spontaneous."

He shook his head. "I'll have to file a complaint with Brigadier General Eaker about the lack of romance in the Eighth Air Force."

She was about to tease him back when a gloom fell over his face. She'd seen him playful, joyous, thoughtful, and even concerned for her, but she'd never seen him sad, and it sent her nerves pickling.

"What's the matter?" she asked.

"Jack!" called out Amelia from the balloon vehicle. "Are you going to bring your friends to the next Assembly Hall dance?"

He looked up, startled by the interruption, but then recovered his easy way. "Sure thing! Anything for the WAAF!" Then he lowered his voice. "Can you step away for a moment to talk?"

She really shouldn't—she was supposed to be on duty and alert at all times while the balloon was flying—but something told her this conversation would be too important to rush.

"Over there," she said, nodding to a row of brightly painted beach huts along the promenade.

Jack took her by the elbow, and once they ducked behind a hut and out of sight of her unit, he swooped in for a kiss. Izzie grasped at the lapels of his uniform, pouring herself into the kiss in hopes that it would never end, but she couldn't help feeling that she was trying to drive back an incoming tide.

When they broke apart, he let out a long breath. "I needed that. I'm sorry I can't stay."

"I'm happy to see you at all," she said with a laugh.

"Izzie . . ." he started, but then he stopped.

"What's the matter?" she asked.

He gave her a little smile. Against the brilliant force of his usually sunny smiles, it felt dim. "Nothing's the matter. I was driving by Great Yarmouth, and I remembered you telling me that you'd be here. And . . . and I wanted to ask you something."

She sensed that he was holding something back, but she didn't know him well enough to figure it out on her own and she still felt a little too shy to ask.

"You can ask me anything, Jack," she said.

"I . . ." He hesitated, threading the brim of his cap through his thumbs and forefingers. "I have twenty-four hours' leave coming to me."

"I do too," she said. "I had been planning to keep my leave back to go up to London and check on the shop, but unfortunately twenty-four hours won't be enough with the trains being what they are."

Now his smile returned with its full wattage. "In that case, we could try to arrange our leave together. We could go away somewhere nearby. Just the two of us."

Go away somewhere? Together?

"Unless you don't want to," he said, seeming to take her hesitation as reluctance.

"No," she hastened to reassure him. "No, it's just that I don't really know what to say."

"What is there to say other than yes?" he asked.

"Well," she started, "where would we stay?"

"There are plenty of pubs with rooms or little inns dotted around. I could find one that wouldn't ask too many questions. Or we could say we were man and wife?"

"Newlyweds?" she asked with a laugh, hoping it covered up how racy and intriguing she found the idea.

He caught up her hand in his. "Something like that."

"Would we share a bed?" she asked, forcing herself to be bolder than usual because she wanted as many answers as possible before she agreed to anything.

His neck went red under his tan. "If you like. Or I could sleep on the floor, if that would make you more comfortable. I don't want you to do anything you don't want to do."

She thought about it for a moment. She didn't know what she wanted. A part of her was so drawn to him and the way he made her feel when he kissed her. A part of her knew that well-behaved women weren't supposed to go away with any man who wasn't their husband, but she was fairly certain well-behaved women weren't supposed to spend their days repairing balloons and wearing work boots.

"Think about it," he said. "You don't have to tell me now, and besides, we don't know if we could make it work at all."

Seeing the possibility of a trip with Jack slip away from her made something lurch in her stomach.

"I'll see if I can manage the time, and I'll write to you," she promised.

He kissed her swiftly. "Just tell me the date—if that's what you decide. I'll make the arrangements."

She couldn't help herself from returning his giddy grin.

"Can I walk you back?" he asked, offering her his arm.

She took it and, when they emerged from around the beach hut, she could see Lottie yell something to the rest of the unit. A cheer went up, and Izzie started to laugh.

"Do I want to know how badly I've ruined your reputation?" he asked.

"Probably not," she said cheerfully.

"You know, it's really not fair keeping all of the Americans to yourself," called Amelia.

"Not all of the Americans, just one!" Jack shouted back, sending the unit into fits of laughter.

When Jack stopped in front of their vehicle, Alexandra said, "I'm going to have to ask what your intentions are toward our friend, Staff Sergeant Perry."

"Only honorable, I promise," said Jack, placing a hand on his heart.

"That's a shame," called Lottie.

"There's a certain man who keeps asking after you," he said to Alexandra.

"Does he? Isn't that sweet?" asked Alexandra with a smile that Izzie could tell meant that her friend wasn't entirely convinced.

Jack seemed to take this as his cue, because he tipped the edge of his hat to the balloon unit and said, "Ladies," before ambling off in the direction of a car parked a few hundred feet down the promenade.

"How do I find one of those?" breathed Molly.

"She walked into him," said Alexandra with a laugh. "And he looked as though an angel had just fallen from the heavens."

"Stop it," said Izzie.

"If that man doesn't tell you he's in love with you by the end of the month, I'll be shocked," said Alexandra.

"The end of the month is only days away," said Grace dreamily.

Alexandra shrugged. "Like I said . . ."

"Really, Alexandra. Don't be ridiculous," Izzie said, nudging her friend.

"Fine," said Alexandra with a laugh.

But when Izzie looked back at her friend, she found Alexandra watching her with a knowing look.

25 May 1942

Dear Izzie,

   I am not ashamed to say that I cried when I received your letter. I am sorry for so many things in my life, but the one I will always regret the most is that I ever left you in any doubt that I love you.

   I don't know what I will do about my marriage. I feel as though I am at an impasse. The only good thing is that it seems as though the only person other than Hugo who knows I am no longer living at the flat is my housekeeper, Mrs. Atkinson. This buys me some time to think about what it is that I really want, and what I'm willing to give up.

Yours,
Sylvia

P.S. The sketches that you sent are beautiful, and Miss Reid and I have already identified two women we think might be perfect for the trousers and blouse and the summer jacket and skirt, respectively. Please send more, and if you feel inclined to design for the cooler weather, we have already had inquiries from customers looking for autumn. Our new ration books come out in a matter of days, and already there is an excitement about new, fresh things—especially since people are worried that the government might again decide that we should receive less for our coupons.

Chapter Thirty-Four

Sylvia rang the bell of Lady Nolan's home with a sense of profound relief. Not only was she early, but she had her proposal for the fashion show all bundled up in an old attaché case of her father's she'd found tucked away in a cupboard in the flat.

She probably should have sent Lady Nolan the papers before that afternoon, but just as her personal life had begun to spiral out of control, the shop had also descended into controlled chaos. The happy result of the new ration books that would be issued in June was that everyone was rushing to use up the last of their current coupons before they were declared invalid. The telephone never seemed to stop ringing, and Miss Reid had stayed late the past two nights in order to finish up garments that were due for collection the following day.

A flutter of nerves stirred in her stomach at the idea of Lady Nolan briefing the committee on the fashion show, revealing all of the work Sylvia had already done to ensure it was a success. Over the past weeks, she'd come to know some of her fellow proprietors a little bit, and she was more determined than ever to serve as their champion. They deserved to share the spotlight, and so did Mrs. Shelton's Fashions.

However, it wasn't just nerves or a sense of responsibility to the project that had driven Sylvia to take a bus from the shop so early that she'd had to spend three quarters of an hour in a nearby tearoom to pass the time. She also wanted to select a seat before Claire arrived and suggested they sit together.

She didn't know how much Claire might know about the rift between Sylvia and Hugo, but Rupert was Hugo's best friend, and at some point the two men would surely speak. It would be the most natural thing in the world for Rupert to confide in his wife, and then Claire might—

The door opened, abruptly stopping Sylvia's spiraling thoughts.

"Good afternoon," she greeted Lady Nolan's housekeeper. "I had hoped that Lady Nolan might be able to spare me a few minutes before the meeting."

"Lady Nolan asked that you join her in the morning room as soon as you arrive, Mrs. Pearsall," said the housekeeper.

"Excellent," she said, pleased that her instinct to arrive early to discuss the plans ahead of the committee meeting seemed to have been anticipated.

She followed the housekeeper in the opposite direction of the drawing room where the committee normally met and into a part of the Nolan home that she'd never entered before. The hall was all done in light wood with oil paintings of landscapes mounted on the picture rail. Her heels sank into soft pale-blue-and-cream carpet as they passed several doors before stopping in front of one of polished oak. The housekeeper knocked and then opened it.

"Mrs. Pearsall, madam," said the housekeeper, stepping back to let Sylvia in.

"Mrs. Pearsall," said Lady Nolan, not rising from her seat.

"Good afternoon. I think you will be pleased to hear that I have all of the plans here," Sylvia said, touching the attaché case lightly with her free hand.

"Thank you, Mrs. Goodson. That will be all," said Lady Nolan.

As soon as the door was closed and they were alone, Lady Nolan said, "Mrs. Pearsall, I wish to speak to you about a rather distressing matter."

"Distressing?" she asked, moving to a chair.

"I must ask you not to sit."

Sylvia froze at the incredible breach of etiquette and good manners.

"It has come to my attention that you have been misrepresenting yourself to this committee," said Lady Nolan.

"Misrepresenting myself?"

"Is it not true that you are the proprietress of a dress shop in Maida Vale?" asked the committee chair.

"I beg your pardon?" she asked, a flush of heat sweeping over her.

"Do you own a shop called Mrs. Shelton's Fashions?" asked Lady Nolan.

For a moment, Sylvia thought about denying it, but the thought of pretending made her tired deep down in her bones. She had spent so many years cloaking, hiding, and denying where she was from, and for what? So that in the middle of a morning room on South Audley Street, she could find herself having to account for a fact that her accuser clearly already knew to be true?

"I do not solely own it. My sister has an equal share," said Sylvia.

"I was not aware that you had a sister."

The simple sentence stole her breath. No wonder Izzie had hated her for so long. No wonder her mother thought so little of her. She'd erased them so thoroughly from her life that even the people she saw regularly didn't know about them.

"My sister and I recently inherited the shop from my mother," she said.

"I see. And is your Mrs. Shelton's Fashions on your list of recommended dressmakers to feature in the committee's fashion show?"

"Yes," she said.

"Why?"

"Because the work we do at Mrs. Shelton's Fashions merits our being included on that list."

Lady Nolan gave her a condescending smile. "Mrs. Pearsall, I must ask for your resignation from this committee. Effective immediately."

She stared at the committee chair. "Why?"

"I am sure you can understand that, given the circumstances—"

"Why?" she demanded.

"Mrs. Pearsall, it will do no one any good for you to make a scene."

"I am not making a scene, I am asking a perfectly reasonable question in response to a very unreasonable request."

Lady Nolan smoothed a hand over the fussy pin tucks of her blouse, which certainly would not have passed muster with the Board of Trade's new regulations. "You have misrepresented yourself to the ladies of this committee and to myself."

"I have done nothing of the sort," she said. "I am Mrs. Hugo Pearsall, the very same woman who helped you organize a number of events in the past. I have raised money just like the rest of the ladies. I have done my bit—more than my bit, if you compare my work to some of the other committee members."

"Nevertheless," said Lady Nolan.

"I have been a member of this committee in good standing for years," she began, unable to countenance the snobbery of the other woman.

"You have been late twice this year alone, and you missed the last meeting."

"Lady Nolan, there is a war on. Certainly that is reason enough for a little compassion."

"I am not certain that you can be relied upon any longer to focus the attention that is needed for this committee," said Lady Nolan.

"And you don't like that I own a dress shop," she said.

Lady Nolan sniffed. "If you simply owned it, that might be one thing."

Sylvia straightened. "I work there too. Is that the real heart of the matter? You can't countenance a woman who works mixing with the good and proper ladies of your precious committee."

"Mrs. Pearsall, I am certain that neither of us would like to say anything unbecoming that we might regret as part of this conversation," warned the other woman.

"And what happens to the fashion show?" she asked.

"I believe that, given the current circumstances, it would be best for all involved if we set the idea of the fashion show aside for the time being. However, if you will leave your notes with me, we may revisit it at a better time."

Lady Nolan held out her hand for the attaché case.

"No."

"I beg your pardon?" asked Lady Nolan.

"No. Each and every dressmaker on that list has been contacted by me. I will need my notes so that I may telephone them and explain that the War Widows' Fund is no longer interested in supporting them because, while the ladies of the committee are perfectly happy to have dressmakers make up their clothes when they cannot afford to buy more than the occasional dress from one of the more prestigious designers, they are not willing to include one in their ranks."

"Mrs. Pearsall, you are being rather unfair . . ."

"I think you will find that I am not the one who is being unfair. I will take my case and go," she said.

Lady Nolan lifted her nose. "I think that would be for the best."

"At least in that we are in agreement. I suppose I will be allowed to exit via the front door, or would you prefer that I use the tradesmen's entrance?"

"Really, there is no need to become spiteful, Mrs. Pearsall."

"Isn't there?" Sylvia gave her a tight smile. "Why don't I see myself out?"

She strode out of the room, not bothering to close the door behind her. Her heels clicked on the polished wood floor, drawing the attention of Lady Winman and Mrs. Hunt, who were shedding their summer coats. As she caught Lady Winman's eye, she could see the confusion in the other woman's expression, but she didn't stop. Instead, she wrenched open the Nolan front door and stepped out into the road.

"Mrs. Pearsall!" she heard Lady Winman call out after her. "Mrs. Pearsall, wait!"

It was the concern in the other woman's voice that stopped Sylvia, despite her desire to flee. When she turned, she saw Lady Winman trot down the steps, her coat still in her hand and her handbag swinging from her wrist.

"You aren't leaving, are you?" asked Lady Winman. "I had hoped that I wouldn't have to face them all alone this time."

She gave the countess a grim smile. "I'm afraid I won't be attending meetings any longer."

"Why not?"

"I've been invited to step down from the committee because apparently I've 'misrepresented' myself or some such tosh."

"I don't understand," said Lady Winman, but the countess's eyes flickered over Sylvia's shoulder. "Mrs. Monroe."

Sylvia's hands clenched as she turned to face Claire, who stopped abruptly in the middle of the pavement.

"Mrs. Monroe, listen to this absurdity. Lady Nolan has asked Mrs. Pearsall to resign from the committee," said Lady Winman with disbelief.

Instead of the surprise and indignation Sylvia had expected to see in Claire's eyes, she saw something else. Relief.

"That is a shame, but I'm sure our chairwoman has her reasons. Now, I really must go in or risk being late," said Claire, dipping her shoulder to round them.

"But Mrs. Pearsall—"

"What reasons would Lady Nolan have to ask me to resign, Claire?" Sylvia cut across the countess.

"I don't know," said Claire, a few shades paler than she had been the moment before.

"How did you find out about the shop?" she pushed. "Did you follow me one day because I wouldn't take tea with you? Or was it just the fact that you had to know? You are, after all, one of the most shameless gossips I know."

Lady Winman began to edge away. "I think perhaps I should leave you both to speak."

Claire squared off with Sylvia. "I don't think I like what you're accusing me of."

"I've always been so very careful," Sylvia said.

Claire scoffed. "Careful? You forget that when I met you your accent would still slip after two glasses of wine. You should know best, Sylvia, that a well-made dress does not make a shopgirl any less of a shopgirl."

There it was, the crack in Claire's resistance.

"Why did you do it?"

Claire lifted her chin. "I simply did what I thought was best."

"What is best?" She laughed bitterly. "Best for whom? You?"

362 · JULIA KELLY

"Hugo."

When Claire said Sylvia's husband's name with such tenderness and pain, the final missing piece fell into place and at last Sylvia knew.

It was Claire.

Claire was the woman who had written those letters. Claire was the woman Hugo loved.

How stupid Sylvia had been. What an absolute and utter fool.

"But you've been my friend for years," she whispered.

"I wasn't your *friend*," spat Claire. "Why would I ever be friends with you?"

"But all of the luncheons, the teas, the dinners," she said, scrambling for words as her entire world shifted. "You were so kind to me when Hugo and I first met. You were the bridesmaid at my wedding."

"I loved him from the moment I met him. Can you imagine the irony of it?" Claire laughed. "Newly married and I fall in love with Rupert's best friend because Hugo happened to be abroad during our engagement. But what could I do? I couldn't leave Rupert without creating a scandal, so I pretended that everything was wonderful. That nothing could be better than sitting next to Rupert at every dinner and concert while Hugo was just out of reach.

"I watched women flit around Hugo, but none of them really caught his eye. Until you. Then I had to watch him fall in love with you. What a ghastly time that was! Rupert and I tried to warn him away, but like an idiot, Hugo went after you." Claire narrowed her eyes. "He knew he was marrying beneath him, but you were the one he wanted so I made a choice. I would help you because it would mean I could be close to him. I knew it wouldn't be too long before he realized the mistake he'd made."

"How long has the affair been going on?" Sylvia asked, horrified but unable to stop herself.

"Years," hissed Claire with obvious satisfaction. "Since the summer before the war. Every time Rupert went away for a sailing trip or some other such nonsense, Hugo would find a way for us to be together. Then the war broke out and it became easier. Then he could use his leave."

Everything Sylvia had known to be true rearranged itself into a new reality. She'd thought it strange at first that Hugo seemed to have far less leave than some of the other men she knew who were serving, but he'd told her how important his role was and that he couldn't be spared. She'd believed him because . . . because she supposed it had been easier than to wonder why her husband hadn't wanted to come home to her.

"Does Rupert know?" she asked.

"No," said Claire.

"Are you certain of that?" she asked, remembering the strange conversation she'd shared with Rupert while dancing.

Her former friend's hand shot out to grip Sylvia by the wrist. "You cannot tell him."

Sylvia shook her off. "It's a bit late for you to begin making demands of me, Claire."

"If he knew . . ."

"He would divorce you? Is that what you're frightened of? Claire, you really should have thought about that before committing adultery with my husband," she said, making her disgust obvious.

Claire lifted her chin. "He said you would be small-minded about this. You would not believe how we laughed at you and your prim little ways, trying so hard to pretend as though you belonged."

How deeply those words would have cut Sylvia once. They

hurt, but now they were only flesh wounds, just scratching the surface of who she was.

"Do you know, Claire? More than anything else, I pity you and your sad, sorry little life spent judging everyone but yourself. Good afternoon."

She brushed past Claire, knocking the other woman's shoulder as she went. She was furious—not only because of Claire and Hugo's betrayal, but at herself and her willful blindness.

No more. Claire, Rupert, Hugo—she owed these people nothing.

Ahead of her on the road, the door to a black cab opened and Lady Winman stuck her head out.

"Mrs. Pearsall, can I offer you a lift?" the countess called out.

Sylvia supposed that she should have felt humiliated that Lady Winman had witnessed so much of her social undoing and the crumbling of her marriage, but in that moment, she found that she didn't really care.

"Thank you, I would appreciate that very much," she said, and slid into the car next to the Countess of Winman.

———

After Lady Winman gave the cabdriver an Eton Square address, silence fell over the cab. It was just long enough for uncertainty to take hold of Sylvia. First she lost her husband. Then her closest friend. She could see her world shrinking before her.

As though sensing Sylvia's weakening resolve, the countess leaned over and said, "I'm very sorry."

Heat crept up the back of Sylvia's neck. "I take it you heard all of that."

"Enough to understand the gist of it," said Lady Winman.

"Am I to understand that you knew something of your husband's infidelity?"

"Yes. And a little over two weeks ago, I walked out of my home and haven't seen Hugo since."

"How did that feel?" asked Lady Winman.

"Liberating and embarrassing in equal measure."

Lady Winman nodded. "Well, I've never met your husband, but I have met Mrs. Monroe and I can honestly say that I've never liked the woman."

Startled, Sylvia twisted in her seat to look at Lady Winman, who watched her with a quirked brow. Suddenly a bubble erupted in Sylvia's chest, and she fell back laughing.

She laughed so hard that her eyes began to leak tears. "Oh, Claire is wretched. She's mean-spirited with hardly a good word for anyone. Even being her friend was like tiptoeing around a sleeping lion. One false move and she might swipe at you."

"Mrs. Monroe reminds me of the dowager countess and all of her friends who turned their noses up at me when I first married Alistair," said Lady Winman.

Sylvia started laughing again, shaking her head as she did. "I'm very sorry, it's just that Claire would be *devastated* to hear that a countess disapproves of her."

"I'm not much of a countess," said Lady Winman.

"Oh, I'm not sure I'd say that."

The countess gave her a little smile as the cab pulled up to the curb and the driver hopped out to open their doors. "Anyway, we're here."

Sylvia looked out of the window and up at the imposing white facade of the huge Eton Square mansion they'd pulled in front of.

"I thought you might like a cup of tea on neutral ground before you have to face the world again," Lady Winman added.

"That would be lovely."

"Good," said Lady Winman, "because I have a proposition for you. But first, tea."

Sylvia followed the countess out of the cab and up the steps to the mansion's front door, where they were met by a tall, slender woman in housekeeper's black.

"Good afternoon, Mrs. Teaks. I'm afraid I'm back rather sooner than I expected, and Mrs. Pearsall and I are both in need of refreshment," said the countess, handing the housekeeper her things.

"Very good, madam. Would tea in the drawing room suffice?" asked Mrs. Teaks with a small but warm smile for Sylvia.

"I think we'll be more comfortable in my study, actually, if you don't mind, Mrs. Pearsall?" asked Lady Winman.

"Not at all," she said.

"Good," said Lady Winman as Mrs. Teaks disappeared to arrange for tea. "Right, then. I'll show you the way."

However, before they could move off, a door opened behind them and a tall man with wildly curling dark hair and a pair of dark-framed glasses perched on his nose strode in. Immediately, everything about the countess seemed to soften as the man's face lit up at the sight of her.

"Darling, I thought you were at the ministry for the rest of the day," said Lady Winman.

"Goodness, you look beautiful today." The earl stooped to kiss his wife. "I'm afraid this is just a quick stop for me. I left some papers behind and I need them for my next meeting. I could have sent a courier, but I decided I could do with the walk.

"Hello," said the earl, letting go of his wife's waist as he seemed to realize for the first time that Sylvia was there. "I hope you don't mind a horrible display of affection between two married people."

Sylvia laughed. "Not at all. It's rather refreshing actually."

"I'm Winman," said the earl, sticking out his hand for her to shake before his wife could make an introduction. "How do you do?"

"Darling, this is Mrs. Pearsall," said Lady Winman. "I'm about to try to convince her to defect from Lady Nolan's committee with me."

Sylvia shot a glance at Lady Winman, who grinned at her.

"That won't take any convincing. I've been given the boot," said Sylvia.

"Better and better," said Lord Winman. "You two can be rebels from stodgy old Mayfair and set the world on fire."

"That is the plan," said Lady Winman.

"Well, I'll leave you to your scheming," said the earl.

"I'll see you for supper, darling," said Lady Winman.

The earl kissed her again and sprang up the stairs, taking them two at a time.

Lady Winman turned back to Sylvia with an indulgent shake of her head. "That man is a boundless ball of energy. I sometimes wonder if he leaves papers at home simply so he can have an excuse to race out of the endless ministry meetings."

Sylvia suspected that it had far more to do with the earl wanting an excuse to see his wife during the day, but she kept that to herself.

Lady Winman led her to her study, a restrained room painted pale blue, with bookshelves lining one wall. There was a large light-wood desk facing a window trimmed in cream curtains and a pair of armchairs set up in front of an unlit coal fireplace.

"Welcome to my favorite room," said Lady Winman as Mrs. Teaks followed them in with the tea tray. "I claimed it when I came to live at Winman House. I wanted a place to work."

368 • JULIA KELLY

"Work?" asked Sylvia as the housekeeper closed the door.

"I gave up editing and magazine work when I married Alistair, but I still write. I'm always working on something. It's been a novel for about two years now, for my sins," said Lady Winman as she set about pouring the tea.

"And Lord Winman is supportive of your working?" she asked, taking a cup.

"Yes. Both of us are always happiest when we're occupied. Now," said Lady Winman, settling back in her chair, "how are you *really* feeling?"

"Well," she said slowly as she stirred her cup of tea, "I've just found out that the woman I thought was my closest friend has been having an affair with my husband since at least 1938. I've been unceremoniously invited to leave a committee I've given more than five years of work to. I believe my entire social circle is about to vanish, and I am currently living above a shop that I own half of, sleeping in my sister's bed in the room we shared when I was eleven."

The countess tilted her head to one side. "Then you've had better days."

"Days? Weeks? Months?" Sylvia sighed. "Do you know what the worst part is? I'm upset about Claire and Hugo, but in some ways I'm most disappointed I'm going to have to let down all of the dressmakers."

"The dressmakers?" asked Lady Winman.

Sylvia quickly explained about Lady Nolan's unilateral decision to select the fashion show as their next fundraiser and the work that she'd already done to make the arrangements.

"Without the committee, there's no fashion show," she finished. "I promised these women the chance to showcase their clothes and hopefully bring everyone more business. But now . . ."

"I suppose this is the time for me to present my proposal," said Lady Winman.

"Please do," she said.

"It's an evolving plan as I keep learning new things, but the latest iteration is this. How would you feel about putting on the fashion show as a fundraiser without the involvement of the committee?"

She frowned. "I don't really know how I could."

"You have the dressmakers," said Lady Winman. "What else would you need?"

"So many things," she said.

"Tell me," said Lady Winman.

"I suppose I would need space," she started. "Then there are the models—the committee members were supposed to serve that role, if you recall—and refreshments. And, of course, there would be the press invitations. I was also hoping that the committee members might lean on their connections and invite whichever well-dressed friends they had to use their coupons on the designs in the show.

"But how can I possibly do all of that without the committee? It gives the event more weight having a name like the War Widows' Fund behind you, especially when you're asking for a hotel to donate the space, a restaurant to give refreshments gratis. That sort of thing."

"What if I act as sponsor?" asked Lady Winman.

"You?" she asked with surprise.

"You said you needed a name," said Lady Winman. "The proceeds could still go to the war widows—or you could focus on another charity if you wish—but I imagine it would be helpful to approach a charity with the Countess of Winman behind you."

Having the backing of a countess with an influential husband . . . Well, it certainly wouldn't hurt their efforts.

"But where will we have it?" she asked, doubtful even as she warmed to the idea. "I'd hoped to tie the fashion show into the new coupon books coming out, but that was assuming the same hotel the committee always uses would agree to it. The owner is a friend of Lady Nolan's, so there is a possibility that they will be reluctant to help on such short notice."

"Have it here," said Lady Winman.

"Here?" Sylvia asked, looking around.

"Well, not this room, but in Winman House. We have a ballroom that isn't being used for anything at the moment. It's a wretched waste of space and, quite frankly, I'm shocked the government hasn't requisitioned the house yet. It might as well be put to good use."

"Won't the earl object?" she asked.

Lady Winman smiled. "The earl would be more offended if I didn't offer up the house for the good of war widows or whichever worthy cause we think suits. You and I can split the responsibility of running the show. I'll take on the press, promotion, and sale of tickets. You can take care of all the dressmakers and models. We'll be co-chairwomen. What do you say?"

Sylvia blinked a couple of times. "Are you certain? I wouldn't want you to lose your friendship with Lady Nolan."

Lady Winman laughed. "Friendship? The only reason Lady Nolan invited me onto the committee is because her husband was trying to place himself in Alistair's good graces for a business deal that never went anywhere. Then Lady Nolan found herself stuck with me, much to her chagrin. Trust me, Mrs. Pearsall, I would much rather be in business with someone whose company I enjoy than with Lady Nolan."

Sylvia flushed a little and said, "Well, if you're certain."

"If you still have your notes, we can take a look at them this afternoon," said the countess.

She had to suppress a smile. "Oh, I still have them. I refused to hand them over to Lady Nolan even after she asked for them. Why should she benefit from my hard work?"

That earned her another grin. "Mrs. Pearsall, I suspect that you and I are going to be great friends."

27 May 1942

Dear Sylvia,

I need your advice on a matter that requires a level head, and as much as I value the friendships of my balloon girls, I don't trust them not to become so excited for me that they fail to think clearly about my question.

There is a man here in Norfolk who I suppose you might say has begun courting me. (How old-fashioned that sounds!) His name is Staff Sergeant Jack Perry, and he is one of a small number of American GIs stationed at one of the RAF bases near Norwich. He is kind and sweet, and I think that there is a real affection developing between the two of us.

He has asked me to go away with him. You might be shocked by this, but it is far more common during this war than you might think, especially for those of us in the services. He has promised me that he will be a perfect gentleman.

Should I go?

If I do, it will be on only twenty-four hours' leave. I had thought to use anything longer to go up to London. I know that, given my last trip home, you might bristle at this idea, but I promise it is only because I miss the shop and not because I don't trust that you are doing your very best to run it.

I know that I had my hesitations in the beginning, but since meeting Jack I've come to understand that there are things that you can bring to the shop that I never could. (He found himself in a similar situation with his brother back in Iowa after his father died.) You have the head for business that both Mum and I never did, and I appreciate everything that you are trying to do to bring in business. I really do.

I also want to come to London so that I may see you. I realize now that I risked angering you in my last letter by saying that I never liked Hugo because you were undecided on what to do about your marriage. Know that whether you decide to stay married to him or divorce him, you are my sister.

Yours,
Izzie

P.S. I've included another batch of sketches for you in this packet. I will turn my mind to autumn, but you might look to my old sketchbook I left behind. I seem to recall that I had an idea for a collection of woolen dresses last year that might suit.

---

29 May 1942

Dear Izzie,

Will you be shocked if I say that I am delighted you've asked me for advice? I wish you were here, sharing a cup of tea or a glass of wine so that I could ask you all manner of questions about this Staff Sergeant Jack Perry from Iowa. However, I will suppress all my nosy questions until the next time that I see you in London.

Instead, I will ask you two things: do you trust him, and will going away with him make you happy?

If you can say yes to both of these questions, I think you have your answer already. Your own happiness is worth taking risks for.

I suppose I owe you my own bit of news, because a great deal has happened since I last wrote. (Will there ever be a time again when a great deal is not happening? I remain unconvinced.)

I have learned more of the painful details of Hugo's affair. The woman is Claire Monroe, someone whom I considered one of my closest friends in London. (You might recall her because she played bridesmaid in my wedding.)

Her betrayal is almost as painful to me as his, and I cannot forgive her.

The other bit of news is that I have left the committee that planned to host the fashion show—or been forced to leave, depending on whom you ask. I doubt this will surprise you, but the committee chair, Lady Nolan, has revealed herself to be a horrible snob. After Claire told her about my connection with the shop (which I suspect she learned about from Hugo),

Lady Nolan told me in no uncertain terms that my services were no longer needed.

However, there is a happy ending to this story! The fashion show will go on thanks to the intrepid work of the Countess of Winman, a fellow former committee member who defected in solidarity. (And because she too found Lady Nolan to be a horrible snob, which I think shows Lady Winman is a good judge of character.)

The countess is sponsoring the show and, with the help of her connections and her husband's newspaper, we have already begun to stir up interest in the press and with potential benefactors. I had the idea to ask women from the various auxiliary services to be our models. I was worried for a spell, but I'm beginning to believe it might be a success.

I think you would like Lady Winman. She is unconventional and knows her own mind. She is also a great fan of your designs, and every time she comes by the shop I catch her eyeing up the dress Miss Reid is working on. I hope you don't mind, but I have sold her a green-and-white-striped summer dress from one of your earlier sketches.

Yours,
Sylvia

P.S. We never stopped being sisters, but I promise you that I will do a better job at it.

———

2 June 1942

Dear Sylvia,

I have only a few minutes because our unit is due to report, but I could not leave your letter unanswered and so I am dashing this off in hopes of making the day's final collection.

I hope you will follow the advice that you gave me in your last letter and take risks to find your happiness as well. You deserve more than what Horrible Hugo and that woman did to you, just as you deserve to surround yourself with people who embrace you rather than look down their noses at you.

I will let you know how my evening away with Jack goes.

Your sister,
Izzie

P.S. I know the dress you're speaking of, and I can think of no greater honor than having a countess wear it.

—————

2 June 1942

Dearest Jack,

I have been approved for leave for twenty-four hours starting at five o'clock in the evening on 9th June.

I cannot wait to see you.

Yours always,
Izzie

Chapter Thirty-Five

Sylvia quickly checked her hat and hair in her gold compact before snapping it closed and knocking on William's office door. She waited, her ears straining, until she heard the heavy tread of his shoes stop. The door swung open, and immediately her shoulders relaxed.

"Sylvia, what are you doing here? Is everything all right?" William asked, concern etching his brow.

The sight of him bolstered her, and she smiled. "Everything is just fine. I've come to speak to you about that legal matter we discussed."

He hesitated, and for a moment she wondered if he wasn't going to let her in. But then he stepped back and said, "Why don't you join me in my office?"

She brushed past him and into the space where nearly seven months ago William—and her mother—had changed her life. Without her mother's bequest, she never would have reconnected with her sister, rediscovered her talent for business, or seen her married life for what it is. She certainly wouldn't have had the courage to ask William for help with what she was about to do.

Sylvia took the same seat she'd sat in for the will reading and watched as William rounded his desk. He sank down into his leather chair, steepling his fingers and taking a breath like a battle-weary knight pulling on his armor for one last fight.

"What can I help you with?" he finally asked.

Rather than replying, she opened her handbag and pulled out

a package wrapped in brown paper. She opened it and placed the precious squares of chocolate on the desk between them.

"You're always bringing me sandwiches, so I thought it was only fair to return the favor. I seem to remember that you always did love chocolate as a child," she said.

"I never did grow out of my sweet tooth. Thank you."

She watched him reach for a piece of chocolate and pop it into his mouth. She could see the slight bulge in the side of his cheek as he tucked it there to melt away more slowly—exactly the thing she did in this age when the sweetness of rationed chocolate felt like almost an illicit indulgence.

"Please have some," he said, gesturing to the chocolate.

"It's supposed to be for you," she said.

He shook his head. "Chocolate is always best when shared with a good friend."

There was something about being called a good friend that lifted her spirits. She took a piece and popped it into her mouth, imitating him and almost laughing at the thought that they must look like a pair of chipmunks.

"Now, will you tell me what brings you to my office?" he asked.

She took a deep breath. "I've thought a great deal since our conversation in the pub."

"Sylvia, about that." He shoved a hand through his hair, looking more than a little abashed. "I said something—"

"You said all of the right things," she said firmly. "I simply wasn't ready to hear them yet. William, I've decided that I want a divorce."

She'd come to the decision on her own over the past two weeks. The fashion show and their ambitions to catch the excitement of the new ration books had necessitated her splitting her time between Mrs. Shelton's Fashions and Winman House. In that time,

378 • JULIA KELLY

she'd had the chance to watch a happy couple in the earl and countess. They clearly adored one another but were happy to let the other have their own interests.

"He understood that I almost said no when he proposed because of what it would mean for my career," said the countess one night after a particularly long day of organizing led to a light supper and a generous glass of wine. "He promised me that there would always be time and space for my pursuits, and I promised him that I would support him and his business however he needed me to."

The countess had smiled then and taken a sip of wine. "Of course, that doesn't mean we aren't without our arguments—he is impulsive and gregarious, and I am considered and shy—but in the end we find a compromise."

Sylvia wanted that. Or a version of that that suited her. Through the shop, she'd found something that was her own. She had ambitions and desires, and she knew that Hugo would never countenance that.

But it had been her sister's last letter that had made up her mind. When Izzie had repeated back to Sylvia her own advice about taking risks for happiness, Sylvia had known that she could not stay married to Hugo any longer.

Now, sitting across his desk from her, William blinked twice before asking, "Are you certain?"

"I'm more certain about this than I have been about anything for a long time."

He nodded. "What changed?"

"I did," she said.

"Well then . . ." William trailed off.

"I have these," she said, producing from her handbag the

letters she'd taken from Hugo's desk and placing them next to the chocolate.

"What are they?" William asked, lifting the top letter.

"Some of the love letters that Claire Monroe sent to my husband over the course of their affair. I took your advice and went back for them."

He looked up at her sharply. "Are they—?"

"Salacious? Yes."

He cleared his throat. "So you want to pursue a divorce on the grounds of adultery."

"Yes," she said.

"You know that means that both Mr. Pearsall and Mrs.—Monroe, was it?—will have to appear in court to answer the charge?" he asked.

"Yes." Let them stand up before a judge and answer for the choices they'd made.

"Right," said William, placing the letter carefully back down on top of the pile. "Well, then I wish you the best of luck."

She frowned. "What do you mean, 'the best of luck'? I want to retain your services as my solicitor, William."

William nodded. "I understand, but I'm afraid that will be impossible."

"Impossible? But why?"

"I have a conflict of interest," he said. "I promised to guide you, and to that end I can recommend several other very good solicitors who each work with excellent barristers who I am sure would be happy to represent you, but I'm afraid that I cannot."

"But that doesn't make any sense. You've known my mother for years, but you were perfectly willing to be her solicitor," she argued.

"Yes, but the circumstances were very different," he said with a rueful smile.

"William, I don't understand why—"

"I wasn't in love with your mother."

Her protest died in her throat. "Oh."

After a moment of silence, he said, "I thought that might shock you, but I didn't realize I would render you speechless."

"William . . ."

"My conflict of interest is you, Sylvia. It's always been you. I know that this is probably all wrong. I should wait a year—maybe two—until you've had some time, but I can't stand the thought that while I'm sitting back and waiting, another man could sweep you off your feet. You are too wonderful for me to risk that, so I'm telling you now. So that you know."

"William . . ." she repeated, his name a whisper now.

"I can't compare to a Harley Street doctor who went to Eton and whose family can probably trace their line back centuries. I'm proud of what I've built here, but I'm probably never going to be the member of a club or be able to bring my daughter out as a debutante. However, if one day you think you might feel any sort of tenderness toward me, I'll be right here. Waiting. If not, I would count it one of the great privileges of my life to call you my friend."

His confession was more intimate, more loving than anything Hugo had ever said to her, and what's more, she believed William. In this moment, she saw a lifetime of memories in a new light. William trailing around after Izzie and her when they were children because they happened to be around the same age became William wanting any chance to be around Sylvia. His subdued response to finding out that Hugo had asked her to marry him hadn't been because he thought she was putting on airs but because another man had captured her heart. William bringing sandwiches to the shop over the past few months hadn't just been a gesture of friendship but a chance to spend time with the woman he loved.

"I don't know what to say," she whispered.

"Then don't say anything."

"I just—I've only just decided to divorce Hugo and—"

"Sylvia, you don't need to explain anything to me."

"But I do, because I don't want you thinking that you've frightened me off." She smiled when he looked at her, unabashed hope in his eyes. "You're right that it is too soon, but that doesn't mean that it was a bad idea to tell me. It is the very opposite of bad.

"I can't make any promises, because I need to make sense of my life and think about the woman I want to be now that I'm not pretending to be the woman Hugo wants me to be. I need time."

"You can have all of the time in the world," he said.

"Have patience with me, William, because my answer is not no."

A grin split his features. "I can live with 'not no.' 'Not no' is wonderful!"

She laughed. "I'm very glad to hear that you think so. I should say, there is one thing that I can emphatically say yes to."

"What is that?" he asked.

"I would love nothing more than to continue to call you my friend."

He dipped his chin. "Thank you, Sylvia."

"I must apologize if, for a number of years, it felt as though I didn't appreciate that," she said.

"All that matters is that you found your way back to Glengall Road."

She smiled. "I think you may be right about that."

You are cordially invited to
a showcase of original designs by
fourteen London dressmakers
in aid of the War Widows' Fund
16th June 1942
Two o'clock
Winman House
Eaton Square, Belgravia
RSVP

Izzie,

    I thought you'd like an official invitation to the proceedings. I wish you could attend and see what a wonderful thing we have created.

Your loving sister,
Sylvia

Chapter Thirty-Six

Jack picked Izzie up in a civilian car at five o'clock sharp on the ninth of June.

"How did you manage to borrow a civilian car and find enough petrol to run it?" she asked in wonder as he held the passenger door open for her.

"I have my ways," he said with a grin.

She climbed in and, once she was settled, held her hands on her lap to keep them from shaking.

The rest of the unit thought that Jack was taking her to the train station to visit an aged aunt just over the border in Essex, but when Alexandra had shot her a look as though to say *And what aged aunt would this be exactly?*, Izzie pulled her away and confessed.

"Going away with a man?" Alexandra asked, sounding impressed.

"You don't think it's a bad idea, do you?" she asked.

"Izzie, all I've ever had are a few chaste kisses. What do I know?"

"There's always Ben," she teased.

Alexandra made a face. "Ben Martin is the kind of man who doesn't think he's looking for a wife but most certainly is, and I'm not looking for a husband quite yet. I still have some adventures I want to live. Anyway, this is about you and your night with Jack. Just remember, don't do anything you don't wish to and make sure that Jack takes precautions if it comes to that."

"Alexandra," she hissed, blushing fiercely.

Her friend shrugged. "I'm simply saying, it makes sense to be sensible if you don't want to be bounced out of the WAAF for falling pregnant. Otherwise, go enjoy yourself. It's boring being too good."

Now, bolstered by both her sister's advice and Alexandra's endorsement, Izzie sat nervously but happily while Jack rounded the bonnet and climbed behind the wheel.

"Nervous?" he asked as he turned over the ignition.

"A little," she admitted.

"Don't be," he said. "I'll be a perfect gentleman."

She smiled. "I've missed you."

He sighed as he pulled into the road. "They've had me on the move. I've covered so much of East Anglia, I'm surprised I'm not dreaming of maps at this point. What about you?"

"The replacement units still haven't come, and the other day one of the units stationed here lost another balloon."

"How did they manage that? The things are bigger than a football field," he said with a chuckle.

"It wasn't secured properly and it broke away. It's the second we've lost in a few weeks. They're both probably somewhere over the North Sea," she said.

"If the Luftwaffe hasn't shot them down," he said.

They drove on, chatting away about the men from his unit she'd met and the girls in the balloon unit. When she told him about Sylvia's letters, he called Hugo a son of a bitch and then apologized for his language. When she told him about her sister's plans to save the fashion show, he asked questions about her designs.

Finally, he turned off the road and parked next to an old coaching inn. He twisted in his seat and took her hand. "Are you sure this is okay?"

She nodded, liking the pressure of his hand on hers.

"In that case, let's go."

At the front desk, Jack signed the book as Sergeant and Mrs.

Jack Perry and collected their key from a rosy-cheeked woman who gave Izzie an indulgent smile. Then, lifting her small bag for her, Jack led her to room twelve.

He unlocked the door and let her inside. She stepped in, taking the room in. It was large enough for a dressing table and mirror, a chest of drawers, and an old-fashioned ceramic basin and jug that she suspected would have water for washing already in it. In the middle of all of it was a double bed with a wooden headboard and a pale blue duvet spread over it.

Her eyes were fixed on the bed when she felt Jack come up behind her, slipping his arms around her waist. He kissed her on her neck, and she closed her eyes as she let her head fall back to rest against his chest.

"I've missed you," he said.

She turned in his arms, tilting her face up. "I've missed you too."

She expected him to kiss her then, but instead he set her back with a determined look.

"There's something I need to tell you," he said.

Her heart began to beat faster, every possible scenario racing through her head. He thought this all was a mistake. He'd just been being kind when he asked her to go away with him because he'd never thought she would say yes. He was engaged to be married. He already *was* married.

"What's the matter?" she asked, her throat dry.

"The thing is, it's really out of my hands," he began, pacing back and forth before the foot of the bed. "I tried to say no and stop it, but there's nothing I can do. That's the military for you."

"To stop what?" she asked. "Jack, you haven't told me what's wrong."

He looked up and shot her a sheepish smile. "They're sending me away."

"What?" she asked.

"The reports I've been working on are done. It's now up to the top brass in the air force and the RAF to work out which bases will be used for what and by which country. I'm being sent away to do this all over again somewhere else," he said.

"How long have you known?" she asked.

He rubbed the back of his neck. "I found out I was moving on the morning of the day I drove out to Great Yarmouth to see you. They told me yesterday it's going to be down south. A place called Portsmouth."

Emotion began to rise in her throat. She hadn't known him long, but she saw such promise in him and he'd understood her enough to help her repair things with Sylvia. Surely that meant something.

"Is this supposed to be goodbye?" she asked.

"No! No." He crossed to her, catching her hands up in his. "Izzie, listen. I've been going over this in my head ever since I found out I was leaving. I don't think this should be goodbye. I don't *want* it to be."

"But what do we do?" she asked softly.

"We write to each other. We're good at that already, aren't we?"

"We are," she said cautiously.

"Any leave we have, we use to try to see one another," he continued.

"I don't know if I can do that," she said.

"Why not? It would be a chance to see one another."

"I told you I'm planning to use most of my leave to go back home to London."

"Maybe I could figure out a way to meet you in London then," he said. "We could kill two birds with one stone."

She let out a breath and nodded.

His hands slid up her arms until they rested on her shoulders. "And then, at some point, maybe we can talk about what's next for the two of us."

"After the war," she agreed.

He brushed back a bit of hair that the wind had stolen from its neat, regulation roll. "Unless you didn't want to wait."

She searched his face. "What are you asking me?"

"I don't want to scare you off, Izzie," he said.

"I'm here, aren't I?" she asked.

"You are." He dipped his head close to hers, their lips almost touching. "I've thought about you so much. I've thought about what life would be like with you if we were together, married."

Married. Goodness. She'd never really thought that she would marry—that had been her sister's prerogative. After all, she'd expected to run the shop as her mother had. However, during this past six months in the WAAF, a part of her had woken up. She had friends who, as far as she could tell, couldn't execute anything more complicated than a running stitch, and one of whom was an earl's daughter. She'd danced until the wee hours of the morning, drunk beer, and kissed a handsome American. She'd lived more of life than she had in her first twenty-eight years, and she'd surprised herself by loving every moment of it.

"I can't wait to show you Iowa. Louis and Muriel will love you. My mother will think you're heaven-sent," he said.

"If I said yes," she said with a smile, "when would we go?"

"As soon as the war is over."

"If it ever ends," she said with a sigh.

"Everything ends eventually, Izzie." He grinned. "You'll love it in Newton. I have a bit of land picked out on the edge of town where we can build a house, exactly the way you want it."

She pulled back with a frown. "A house?"

"Or if you want to live somewhere in town, we could do that too. That might be a bit more sociable for you," he said.

"Jack, I'm confused," she said.

He laughed. "About what?"

"I can't move to America."

He smiled. "Of course you can't. Not yet. You're a WAAF. Can't have you earning a reputation as a deserter. We'll have to wait until you're demobbed."

She shook her head. "No, Jack, you don't understand. I can't move to America at all."

"Why not?"

She eased a step back from him. "Because I have a life here."

"In Norfolk?"

"In England," she said, beginning to grow exasperated because really, was he trying to be difficult? "I own a business—or at least half of one."

"Exactly," he said. "You own half of one. It sounds like your sister is managing just fine. You could sell the business to her."

Izzie laughed in disbelief. "I can't do that, but, more importantly, I won't do that."

Jack frowned, what she was saying seeming to finally make its way through to him. "But I thought that we—"

"We like each other, but we hardly know each other really," she said, good sense finally penetrating her romance-addled brain.

His brow furrowed deeper. "I already said we would write to each other. We would see each other whenever we could. People have married after less. Didn't you say your friend Nancy was ready to get married to that RAF pilot who died?"

"But you don't love me," she said.

"Sure I do," he said. "You're beautiful. You're caring. You're intelligent. I think you're just about the best girl I've ever met."

They were all compliments, so why, when he strung them together like that, did it all feel so . . . impersonal?

"Izzie, I know this is all very new to you, and maybe it was a bad idea to spring it on you. Why don't you take some time while I'm gone and think about it?" He caught her hand and shot her that smile that had made her so weak when she first met him. "Miss me a bit."

She freed her hand again and crossed her arms over her chest. How was it that all his flirtatious, chipper confidence now felt as ill-fitting as a badly cut jacket?

"If I did decide that I loved you and I wanted to marry you, would you move to London after the war?" she asked.

He hesitated but then shook his head. "I have a business back home, Izzie."

"*I* have a business back home, Jack."

"Come on, now. There's no need to take that tone." He closed his eyes and took a deep breath. "I thought that you might like the idea of starting again. Getting away from it all."

"Whatever gave you that impression?" she asked.

"I don't know," he said, a little sheepishly. "I just thought most women don't want to work if they don't have to. I'm telling you that you don't have to work."

"Make no mistake, Jack, I want to work," she said firmly.

"That's fine. You could start a shop in Newton or Des Moines. Bring a little bit of British tailoring to the Midwest," he said.

"Why should I be the one to leave my business behind?" she asked.

"You have Sylvia," he said.

She had Sylvia, and for the first time in a long time that felt like it meant something.

"And you have Louis."

Jack stared at her and then stepped back. He scrubbed a hand over his mouth.

"Maybe this all was too fast," he finally said.

"I think it probably was." She'd become swept up in the romance of him, the good looks and the charming ease with which he moved through the world. He'd given her all the attention she'd never experienced from a man before and it had been intoxicating, but she was not a naive ingenue. Far from it. She was a woman with her own life and her own dreams, and she was not willing to throw them away on a man who didn't understand the most fundamental thing about her.

"There's something here, Izzie. I know there is."

"I think you're right, Jack, but I also don't know that either of us will ever be willing to budge." One of them would have to accept that unhappiness would be a part of their life.

"I think I could love you," he tried again.

She shook her head slowly. "I'd like to go home now."

His shoulders slumped, but he picked up her case without protest and retraced their steps back to the car.

———

Jack pulled up to the gate of her base and killed the engine. The silence stretched between them until he finally asked, "Will you still write to me?"

She stole a look at him staring clench-jawed out of the windshield. It would be so easy to say yes, but she couldn't risk falling any further.

"I don't know."

He let out a long sigh, his head falling back against the headrest.

She leaned across the gap between them and kissed him on the cheek. Then she collected her things. When Jack reached for his door handle, she stopped him, saying, "Stay. Please."

She climbed out of the car and walked up to the gates, refusing to allow herself to look back as the guard examined her pass.

"You still have a lot of leave left," he said with a nod at her pass.

"Things didn't turn out as I thought they might," she said.

He gave a grunt and handed it back to her.

She made her way across camp and back to her hut, her head and her heart warring with every step she took.

What if she was wrong?

What if Sylvia didn't need her after all?

What if she came to regret choosing the shop over Jack?

She opened the door to the hut and was relieved to find all the bunks empty except for Alexandra's. Her friend looked up from a magazine and immediately jumped out of bed.

"What's the matter?" asked Alexandra, rushing up to her.

"Jack's going away," she said.

"Away?"

"He's being sent to Portsmouth."

Alexandra pursed her lips and then gave her a nod. "It's not ideal, but it's perfectly possible for you two to—"

"That isn't it at all. He wanted . . . He talked about marrying. One day."

Alexandra stooped a little to examine Izzie's downturned face. "You're not jumping for joy."

"He had it all planned out. We would marry, and we would build a house in Iowa. I would love his family. They would love me."

"And you would love none of it because it isn't what you want," said Alexandra, understanding her completely.

She burst into tears.

"Oh, Izzie." Alexandra pulled her into a hug. "I'm sorry."

Izzie sagged against her friend until, finally, her sobs began to subside. Then Alexandra held her at arm's length and peered at her tearstained face.

"What will make this better?" asked Alexandra.

"I don't know." She wanted to be in her bed in the flat above the shop. She wanted to be surrounded by the familiar. To feel the weight of tailor's shears in her hand. To sketch and sew and be.

"I wish I could go home," she said miserably. "Just for a visit. I miss it."

"Of course you do," said Alexandra.

"It's silly, but I wish I could see the fashion show my sister is putting on."

Alexandra's lips fell into a thin line. "When is that?"

"Next Tuesday," she said.

Alexandra nodded, and then announced, "We need tea. If you'll be all right for just a moment, I'll go to the NAAFI and find us some and something sweet to go with it."

She gave a watery laugh. "That would be lovely."

"Unpack your things and then put on your most comfortable clothes and climb into bed. The other girls are all watching the film tonight, so no one should disturb you. I'll be back as soon as I can," said Alexandra.

Izzie did as she was told, pulling on a jumper and a pair of socks even though it was practically the middle of June because she needed the comfort of warmth. In her bunk, she pulled her sketchbook to her and began to draw, losing herself in the soothing rasp of pencil on paper.

She didn't know how long Alexandra had been gone when there was a noise at the door and she looked up to see her friend walk through, bearing two cups of tea, two chocolate bars sticking out of her tunic's breast pocket.

"Here you are," said Alexandra.

Izzie accepted her cup and sweet gratefully.

"I'm sorry I took a little longer than I expected, but I had to send some telegrams and then there was a telephone call," said Alexandra as she sat on the edge of Izzie's bunk.

"Telegrams? Telephone call?"

Alexandra grinned. "Do you trust me?"

"Of course I do."

"Good," said Alexandra. "Then here's what we're going to do ..."

Chapter Thirty-Seven

The room might have looked like pandemonium, but there was order if only one knew where to look. Sylvia, clipboard in one hand and pencil firmly gripped in the other, was ticking things off, making sure everything was in its rightful place, because in ten short minutes her fashion show would start.

"Lance Corporal White," she called out to a girl who was struggling to reach around her back and zip up the chocolate-brown wool dress Mrs. Moss had made. "You'd better let me help you with that."

The young woman gave her a grateful smile and turned to show Sylvia her back. Setting down her things, she zipped the young woman up and said, "There you are. Now, do you know who you're meant to walk after?"

The young woman, who Sylvia had learned that morning was usually in the mechanic shop working on transport vehicles in her capacity in the Auxiliary Territorial Service, nodded.

"Good. Then good luck and enjoy the show."

Out of the corner of her eye, Sylvia saw Lady Winman approach. The countess, who was wearing the dress she'd ordered from Mrs. Shelton's Fashions, was sporting the little satisfied smile that Sylvia had learned over the past weeks was the equivalent of a whoop of joy.

"How is it looking out front?" she asked.

"Standing room only," said Lady Winman triumphantly. "And it isn't just Alistair's connections either. I don't recognize half the members of the press who are all packed in."

"But the *Vogue* people are in the best seats?" she asked anxiously.

"Right next to Edward Molyneux."

"Edward Molyneux?" she gasped. Molyneux had made the navy silk gown she'd worn on her last evening out with Hugo, Claire, and Rupert. It would forever have memories of her husband, and she wasn't certain she would be able to bring herself to wear it again, but she couldn't deny that it was utterly gorgeous.

"Apparently he has a keen interest in promoting British fashion," said Lady Winman, pulling Sylvia's attention back to matters at hand. "I think Audrey Withers invited him."

"Well, that's all rather exciting isn't it?"

"It is. How are the dressmakers?" Lady Winman asked, nodding to several women who were calmly making final tweaks and alterations while helping models into their dresses.

"They're ready," she said.

"Excellent. Oh, there's one more thing," said the countess with a wicked smile. "Don't be surprised when you see the film cameras."

"Film cameras!" Sylvia couldn't keep the shock out of her voice.

"Yes. I didn't want to raise our hopes too much because film people can be so finicky, but Alistair spoke to a fellow at the Ministry of Information who spoke to someone else, and the news of our little fashion show landed with the department that produces newsreels. There's no guarantee that they'll use it, but if they do . . ."

"Our fashion show could be in every cinema across the country," she breathed.

Lady Winman's eyes sparkled as she nodded.

"Right." She cleared her throat. "I suppose we should start."

Sylvia poked her head around the wide double doors of the Winman House ballroom. Lady Winman had instructed that chairs be set up in a semicircle, creating a stagelike area where the models would walk out, pause, and then retreat, showing off all angles of the creators' craftsmanship. Now all of those seats were filled with people, some with notebooks out on their knees, all murmuring among themselves, the buzz of their voices filling the room.

Goodness, she wished Izzie could see this.

"Nervous?"

Sylvia pulled back to give Miss Reid a smile. "I would be lying if I said I wasn't eager to see things underway."

Miss Reid placed a hand on her arm. "You've done a fine job. Mrs. Shelton would be proud."

A lump rose in Sylvia's throat. "I'm not certain about that."

"She loved you," said Miss Reid firmly. "She could be a hard-headed woman sometimes, but even she admitted that she could have been kinder to you after your father's death."

"She did?" she asked.

"From time to time when it was late at night and there were orders to fill, she would open up a little bit. She knew that she pushed you away. She said it had something to do with what happened to your father, but that never sat well with me. You were just a child."

"Thank you, Miss Reid." Sylvia gave a weak smile. "You know, for a long time I was convinced you disliked me."

Miss Reid looked shocked. "Disliked you?"

"When I was a child." And maybe as recently as that spring.

"I never—" Miss Reid stopped herself and swallowed. "I suppose I found it easier to speak to your sister because at least she could sew."

"I can sew!" she began to protest until she caught Miss Reid's skeptical look. "I can sew enough to mend things."

"Yes, well. I don't find small talk exactly easy," said Miss Reid.

Sylvia pressed a hand to the other woman's forearm. "I understand."

"I know that you wouldn't have chosen to return to the shop if you hadn't needed to, but I'm glad you did." Miss Reid nodded toward the models lining up in the corridor. "Look at what you've done."

Sylvia cast an eye over all the models in their beautiful clothing. "Look at what *we've* done, Miss Reid."

It was very slow, and at first Sylvia didn't recognize it for what it was, but eventually a smile bloomed on Miss Reid's face. "I wish Miss Shelton could be here to see it."

"I was just thinking the same. Izzie would love this."

"But perhaps Mr. Gray will be able to tell her all about it."

"Mr. Gray?" Sylvia asked sharply, twisting to look over her shoulder. Her eyes scanned the crowd before landing on William. He was standing at the very back of the room, hands folded in front of him. Immediately, her heart softened.

"He came into the shop to ask when and where the show would be held," said Miss Reid from her spot at her shoulder.

"Did he?" Sylvia asked.

"Mm-hmm."

William glanced their way, eyes locking with Sylvia's. He lifted a hand. She mirrored the gesture. He mouthed, "Good luck," and she dipped her head to hide her smile. He was a good man—probably far better than she'd once deserved—and when she was ready, she planned to work her hardest to be worthy of his love.

She would find him afterward and perhaps suggest a place where they could find a cup of tea and chat. They did have so many years to make up for.

"Sylvia," said Lady Winman, hurrying up, "I think we should begin."

Miss Reid pressed a hand against Sylvia's forearm and melted away in the direction of Mrs. Shelton's assigned model, a tall girl with a perfect Cupid's bow mouth and beautifully curling dark hair who fitted into Izzie's claret dress like a dream.

Sylvia drew back her shoulders. "Ready when you are, Felicity."

Lady Winman nodded. "Then away we go."

A triumph.

That's what it was.

An honest-to-goodness proper triumph.

Sylvia could hear the applause before the final model finished her last twirl and exited the floor. She and Lady Winman caught each other's gaze and smiled.

"Are you ready to say a few words?" she asked the countess.

They'd debated long and hard about who should address the patrons and press once the show was done. Lady Winman had argued that there would be no event without Sylvia, but Sylvia had turned the argument right back around on her and pointed out that the countess had saved the day.

Since Lady Winman was the sponsor and technically the hostess of the day's proceedings, they'd finally agreed that she would thank everyone for coming and remind those who were in a mood to buy that designs could be commissioned from each of the participating shops.

"Ready as I'll ever be," muttered the countess.

She watched as Lady Winman, whom she was beginning to think of as a friend, rolled her shoulders back, set her chin, and glided out from around the ballroom's double doors to a wave of applause.

THE DRESSMAKERS OF LONDON • 399

She was so proud of what they'd done that day, but even more so of everything that Mrs. Shelton's Fashions had achieved that year. There was hope and light about the place, and it looked as though, if they kept ahead of the Board of Trade and continued to promote, they might just survive the war.

She was proud of Miss Reid, who had thrown herself into every order, creating beautiful things in a time when beauty could feel so rare.

She was proud of Izzie and her designs that kept coming in the post, gorgeous dress after gorgeous dress.

She was proud of herself for finding her way back here, where she belonged.

A light touch on her shoulder made her glance over to find William next to her.

"It was wonderful," he said, before she could even ask him what he thought.

Something in her warmed the way that it had started to whenever she saw him. "Thank you."

"I overheard some of the journalists talking about it, and I saw a few women flipping through their ration books to count coupons," he said as Lady Winman's speech drifted back to them.

"That is exactly what we need," she said.

"A few were opening their checkbooks too," he said.

"All the better for the war widows," she said with a smile. "It was good of you to come."

"I wouldn't have missed it for the world," he said.

There was another round of applause, and William stepped back, looking at her expectantly. She frowned. "What?"

Lady Winman stuck her head around the door. "They're waiting for you."

"For me?" she asked.

"I couldn't stand up there and pretend this was all my doing," said the countess. "You should have your moment too."

She glanced at William, and he nodded.

"But I haven't prepared anything," she protested.

"As though a little thing like preparation would ever frighten the likes of Sylvia Shelton," said William.

With a laugh that was half-exasperated and half-indulgent, Sylvia eased her way around the door and out in front of all of the people. The models stood to the left of her, all lined up in their ensembles. At the back of the room were the film cameras.

She spread her hands out. "I haven't prepared anything because I thought I had convinced Lady Winman that she should take on the responsibility of speaking today, but I can see that it is impossible to tell a countess what to do."

Lord Winman gave a hearty guffaw from his seat in the front row.

"I am the daughter of a talented dressmaker, although few outside of our neighborhood would know the extent of her skill," she continued. "That is a great shame, but it is not unique to my mother. Few of the hardworking dressmakers in our neighborhoods who make clothing that is both beautiful and practical are celebrated in the way that we celebrate the great design houses of London and Paris."

She scanned the audience, intending to address Mr. Molyneux, but instead her eyes lit on two women in WAAF uniforms standing in the back of the crowd: Izzie and the unmistakable Lady Alexandra.

Sylvia swallowed as Izzie gave her a little wave and a cheeky grin. She pressed a hand to her chest, checking her emotions, and then smiled at the crowd.

"I hope that this display of unsung talent has inspired you to open your minds—and your checkbooks," she said as people tittered, "to support not only these designers but also the great cause for which we are gathered here today. Thank you very much."

There was another round of applause, but she could hardly hear it. Instead, she crossed the ballroom floor that had served as their showcase space and threaded her way through the crowd to Izzie.

"Hello, Sylvia," said Izzie.

"What are you doing here?" Sylvia asked in disbelief.

Izzie tilted her head. "Well, I couldn't miss your big day, could I?"

Sylvia gave a sob and then fell into her sister's open arms.

Chapter Thirty-Eight

*I*zzie hugged her sister close.

"I'm sorry. I should have written to tell you I was coming, but it was all very last-minute," she said into Sylvia's
brushed-out curls. "I didn't mean to make you cry!"

"No, it isn't that," said Sylvia, laughing and crying at the same
time. "I'm just so glad to see you. How is it that you're here?"

"Alexandra arranged it," she said, shooting her friend a smile.

"I don't like to trot out the aristocratic father too often, but I
thought that in this case I would make an exception," said Alexandra
cheerfully. "Besides, Izzie had leave due back to her, but our commanding officer was being a beast about claiming she had forfeited it."

"There haven't been enough balloon units and— Oh, why am I
explaining this all? The important thing is that I'm here," Izzie said
with a laugh.

"Did you see the show?" asked Sylvia, accepting a handkerchief
from Alexandra.

"I did, and I thought it was exquisite." Izzie leaned in. "Very
clever of you to leave Mrs. Shelton's design for last."

"Organizer's privilege," said Sylvia as she dabbed at her tears.

"Oh, Sylvia, there are so many things I want and need to tell you
about," Izzie started.

"Like Jack?" her sister asked.

"Like Jack," she said with a firm nod. "But this isn't the place.
Shall we go back to the shop?"

"Let's."

———————

They didn't leave straightaway, because Sylvia insisted on introducing Izzie to Lord and Lady Winman, who greeted Izzie like an old friend.

"I hear that I have you to thank for my wife's dress," said Lord Winman with a laugh.

Startled, Izzie glanced at the countess and realized that the light-green-and-white-striped summer dress with the square neck was, in fact, one of her designs.

"I suppose you do," she said cheerfully.

Sylvia, Willie, Alexandra, Miss Reid, and Izzie finally trooped out of Winman House and onto a bus, with Willie offering to take Alexandra and Miss Reid for a cup of tea at a local tearoom so the sisters could chat.

Izzie kept sneaking glances at Sylvia when her sister wasn't looking, taking her in. Sylvia seemed happier somehow, laughing more freely and listening to the conversation intently. However, it was the way that Sylvia and Willie always seemed to be searching for the other in the room that really warmed Izzie's heart.

At the shop door, the rest of the group broke off and Sylvia pulled the key out of her handbag. She held it out. "I thought you might like to open it up yourself."

"Thank you," said Izzie. She took the key, the lock tumblers turning over with their familiar, satisfying click. When she pushed the door open, the bell jingled, and she breathed deep.

"It hasn't changed a bit," she said.

"Oh, you'll change your tune soon enough. Shall we go back to the office?" asked Sylvia.

"Let's," said Izzie.

She followed her sister through the shop, down the corridor, and to the workroom. On the dress forms, she saw her designs, partially constructed and waiting for Miss Reid to return to work. On the cutting table were her most recent sketches, laid out in neat piles.

Sylvia opened the door to the office and let her inside. Immediately, Izzie's eyes widened. "It looks like you never left all those years ago."

Sylvia laughed. "I hope that means you think it's an improvement."

"It is," she said firmly. "You've done a wonderful job."

"I don't know if I'd call it wonderful," said Sylvia, dropping into what had been Mum's chair.

Izzie stared at her sister.

"Oh!" Sylvia said, half rising. "Do you want me to move?"

She shook her head. "I was just thinking how right you look there in her spot."

"I might look right in the office, but not on the workroom floor. That's your domain," said Sylvia, retaking the chair.

Izzie sat down opposite the desk. "Not so long as the WAAF have me."

"It is as long as you want it," said her sister firmly. "You are the heart and soul of this shop."

"Thank you." She looked down at her hands. "You asked about Jack. Things didn't work out between us."

"He didn't try something, did he?" asked Sylvia with a fierceness that took Izzie by surprise.

"No! Nothing like that. He actually wanted to continue courting me. To see if we wanted to marry."

"But—"

"He had it in his head that I would move to America. He thought I would just give up the shop and follow him," she said.

"Well, that goes to show he doesn't know the first thing about you. Stupid man," Sylvia muttered.

"Maybe. In the end, neither of us was willing to budge."

"I'm sorry, Izzie."

She gave a little smile. "Thank you."

"Do you love him?"

It was the question that had been her companion morning, noon, and night since she and Jack had parted. No matter how she looked at it, she came back to the same conclusion every time.

"I was infatuated with him," she said slowly. "And I think I could have loved him, eventually."

"But you love working and this shop more," said Sylvia, finishing her thought.

In that moment Izzie knew her sister understood her more than Jack ever could. They were cut from the same cloth and, although their lives had gone down vastly different paths, that bond could not be broken so long as they both tried to keep it alive.

"Sylvia, I must apologize," she started. "I've spent far too much time angry at you for choosing a different life and feeling left behind. However, I could have done more. I could have picked up the telephone. I could have written to you or marched up to your flat and insisted that you see me. Instead, I resented you, and I let that resentment fester.

"I'd like to try to be sisters again," she finished.

"Oh, Izzie," said Sylvia. "I thought I was doing the right thing for everyone when I distanced myself, but I can see now that it was cruel. I shouldn't have kept things from you. You didn't do anything wrong."

"No, you shouldn't have," said Izzie.

"That changes now." Sylvia drew in a breath. "Starting with the news that I've decided to divorce Hugo."

"You have?" Izzie asked. "Oh, Sylvia, that's wonderful news!"

Her sister laughed. "Well, I'm glad my instincts were correct in thinking that you wouldn't be unhappy to see the back of him."

"I'm sorry that he hurt you, but I'm glad he won't be able to any longer," she said. "Is Willie going to help you?"

"No. He can't."

"Why not?" she asked.

Sylvia looked down at her beautifully manicured nails. "William told me that he—"

"Has been in love with you ever since he first laid eyes on you?"

"Izzie!"

She fell back in her chair laughing. "Believe me when I say that you are the only person that this is news to. The entire road knew, Sylvia. Mrs. Reynolds practically had your wedding date set, but then you met Hugo."

"Goodness," Sylvia breathed.

"And how do you feel about him?"

Sylvia smiled sweetly. "I like him. Very much. It's too soon to say anything more."

That was the Sylvia she remembered, practical to a T.

"That seems very sensible to me," said Izzie.

They settled back in their chairs, a calm passing between them that hadn't been there in many years. It felt good to be together, in the shop their mother had built. There was a legacy in those walls that was undeniable. One she was deeply proud of.

As though reading her thoughts, Sylvia broke the silence to ask, "Do you still want to buy my half of the shop?"

No.

The word almost slipped out, but instinct held Izzie back. It wasn't that she didn't appreciate everything her sister had done, but what had happened between them had wounded her deeply. It would take time to heal the trust between them.

When Izzie didn't answer, Sylvia continued, "Because I have an idea."

"An idea?" she asked.

Sylvia placed her hands on the desk, as though preparing to deliver a speech she'd rehearsed many times.

"What if I stay on and help you run the business—not just during the war but for as long as we have the shop?" Sylvia asked. "I don't have your talent for design and sewing, but I'm good at the business side of things. I've been thinking about how we could grow and change. What our mother built from nothing was incredible, but it could be so much more. With your eye . . . Izzie, I don't see any reason that Mrs. Shelton's Fashions couldn't become a Hartnell or a Molyneux."

Izzie let out a long breath. "That's ambitious."

"It is," said Sylvia, her eyes sparkling. "It might even be mad, but I don't think it's *completely* mad."

It was, Izzie realized, what she wanted but had never had the courage to dream of. A fashion house that was built on her mother's legacy, her talent, and Sylvia's acumen? That would be something to see, wouldn't it?

"We'll have to make it through the war first," she said slowly.

"I agree," said Sylvia. "Grand ambitions aren't any good if we can't make it out of rationing. I propose that we continue to operate as a dressmaker, but I could begin to pursue the type of client who is used to spending her money on Chanel and Schiaparelli and see if she will instead try bespoke British design while Paris is under occupation. Felicity's—that is, Lady Winman's—patronage will help."

"And hopefully you can tempt some of the women who were at the fundraiser today," said Izzie with a wry smile.

"Precisely," said Sylvia. "I think that, with the press coverage that we received and the helpful fact that Lady Winman has the ear of the editor of *Vogue*, we could begin to build a truly bespoke side to the business slowly. No more of Maggie Shelton's sketchbooks, but one-off designs that are exactly to the specifications of the client."

She frowned. "How would that work? I'm stationed in Norfolk now, but I could be sent anywhere."

"I would interview clients and take extensive notes that I could then send you via the post. You'd send back sketches until the client was satisfied. It might take a little longer, but these are women who are used to multiple fittings to perfect a dress. They will wait if it means having a one-of-a-kind Isabelle Shelton design."

Izzie flushed at the thought of that. "An Isabelle Shelton . . ."

"It rolls off the tongue nicely, doesn't it?" Sylvia asked.

It did indeed.

It felt almost too good to be true, but if Izzie knew one thing about her older sister, it was that Sylvia would will a promise into reality rather than let it fail.

Izzie leaned over the desk and stuck out her hand. "Shall we shake on it like in the films?"

Sylvia grasped her hand. "It's a deal."

Epilogue

*S*ylvia stood on the corner of Davies and Bourdon Streets in Mayfair, surveying the shop front with her hands planted firmly on her hips.

It had taken Izzie and her months to find the right spot for their new home. She'd been surprised at how amenable her sister had been when she'd brought up the idea of moving from Glengall Road six months ago, but Izzie had simply put down her newly acquired reading glasses and said, "If you say it's time, it's time."

They'd run the business via the post while Izzie served first in Norfolk and then in Dover. When the RAF had begun winding down the use of balloon units and Izzie had retrained as a telephone operator in Scotland, their letters had continued in just the same manner.

Then Izzie had been demobbed in August of 1945, and the sisters had had to learn once again how to work together in person. There had been growing pains, but everything had been helped by the soothing presence of William, whom Sylvia had married in 1944, a year after her divorce from Hugo had become official.

She smiled up at the shop front, remembering the lean times as the Board of Trade cut the value of coupons again and again. She and Miss Reid had despaired then, wondering how any women would be able to buy anything at all, but their customers, old and new, had continued to come to them with curtains, tablecloths, bedsheets—anything that could be made into clothes.

Steadily, through all of it, their bespoke clients had grown in number thanks to the help of Lady Winman and the women who had attended the first War Widows' Fund fashion show. It was, Sylvia had to admit, more than a little satisfying to note that the charity's heads were perfectly content to accept Sylvia and Felicity's fashion show as a staple on its calendar on the understanding that it be kept at an arm's length from the usual committee.

The Shelton sisters had both rejoiced after VE and VJ Days, assuming that the end of the war would spell the end of clothing rationing, but austerity measures had crushed that hope. However, on the fifteenth of March of that year, it had finally happened. Clothing was no longer on the ration. William had produced a bottle of champagne out of nowhere to celebrate, and even Miss Reid had taken a glass, a sleepy look settling over her expression by the bottom of it.

The end of rationing had been the push the sisters had needed to finally embark on the second stage of their plan: expansion. Together they'd searched high and low for a shop with the right sort of address for the clients who were now coming through their doors more and more often asking for Izzie's bespoke designs. Finally, they'd settled on the shop on Davies Street.

Sylvia had taken charge of the lease and fitting out the shop, leaving Izzie to the design and production side of things. They'd discussed everything together, sharing all the decisions—well, all except one.

Sylvia glanced at her watch. William had promised that he would deliver her sister at precisely eleven o'clock, which meant that, in one minute, Izzie would see what she'd done.

While she waited, she touched the collar of her navy-blue jacket and made sure the hem was sitting straight. It was silly to be nervous, but the sisters had promised each other that they would share every decision related to the business, and Sylvia had deliberately violated that agreement. She just hoped Izzie would agree with her that it had been worth it.

Sure enough, one agonizing minute later, she spotted the top of William's gray felt hat round the corner, Izzie on his arm, blindfolded and looking less than delighted with the situation.

"We're here!" called William with a wave, as though he didn't have an irritated Shelton sister hanging on his arm.

"Sylvia, is this really necessary?" asked Izzie. "I've seen the shop before."

Sylvia held back a laugh as William grinned at her.

"You did say she would be angry," she told him.

"I did," he agreed.

"I'm not angry, I'm annoyed," Izzie insisted. "There is a difference."

"This isn't a time to argue semantics, Izzie," said Sylvia.

"Sylvia!"

"Shall we put her out of her misery?" Sylvia playfully asked her husband.

"Yes!" Izzie shouted.

"Fine, you can take your blindfold off," she said.

William stepped back as Izzie tore at the fabric. "What is the meaning of—"

Sylvia pointed past her sister's shoulder to the shop front, and she saw the moment that Izzie realized what she'd done.

Painted across the top of the shop wasn't "Mrs. Shelton's Fashions" but "Isabelle Shelton."

"What . . . ?"

"I thought it was time to consider a new name," she said.

"Consider? It's already painted up there," said Izzie, but her annoyance had been replaced by delight.

"Paint can be changed, but I hope you like it. A new name for a new era," she said.

Izzie stared at the sign, a grin growing across her face. "We'll have to change all of the labels."

"I asked the manufacturer to wait to sew anything in until they received word from us. It's costing us more, but it will be worth it to see labels that say 'Isabelle Shelton' on them from the very moment the shop opens. If that's what you want," she said.

The ready-to-wear line and shop had been a joint idea, one they'd hashed out over many evenings in their mother's office. The bespoke business, which had ambitions that reached the level of the still-recovering French couturiers, would continue as it had, but with a ready-to-wear offering, they would be able to dress more women than ever before. It had taken years of saving and research to make it a reality, but they were all ready to take delivery of garments at the end of the month and launch in October.

"Are you certain?" asked Izzie, glancing at Sylvia. "It doesn't seem very fair that only my name is up there."

"In this one area, I'm very happy to remain in the background," she said. "Besides, 'Mrs. Gray and Isabelle Shelton' doesn't have the same ring to it."

"'Isabelle Shelton and Mrs. Gray,' surely," said Izzie. "Don't you think, Willie?"

He held up his hands. "I stay out of all business decisions unless you require legal advice, remember?"

"Well, then, I think that settles it," said Izzie.

Sylvia held up a key. "Would you like to walk through and see how it's looking?"

Izzie nodded. "Let's."

They crossed the road, and Sylvia unlocked the front door,

letting her sister in first. She lingered a moment, watching Izzie take in all the details of the shop. When William's arms slipped around her and he rested his head on her shoulder, she leaned back against him.

"Thank you for bringing her," she said.

"Of course. I'm proud of you, Sylvia. Both of you," he said.

She smiled. "Me too."

"I think your mother would be too," he said.

She watched her sister examine the counter where the register would go. "I don't think she ever would have imagined this when she left us the shop together, but I am grateful she did."

Author's Note

Clothing is a vital part of our everyday lives. It can at once be functional and a tool of self-expression and taste. It can reveal the personality of the wearer and how they wish to be perceived. It can also hold incredible power, with world figures including the late Queen Elizabeth II using their outfits to convey subtle messages and opinions to the wider public.

However, despite its far-reaching uses and meanings, clothing is also often denigrated as a frivolity. Unless we are speaking about the very highest echelons of fashion—which have at times been dominated by male designers—it is often seen as a woman's pursuit and therefore somehow less serious than other forms of art. Perhaps this is why, while writing *The Dressmakers of London*, I found clothing rationing during World War II and its effect on women so fascinating.

When I started this book, I had a basic working knowledge of the subject. I knew that clothing rationing began on June 1, 1941, and stretched until four years after the war ended. I also was aware that rationing became more and more restrictive as Britain entered its postwar austerity years. However, I wasn't aware of just how dramatic the challenge of dressing and maintaining a wardrobe for an individual or a family would have been for the women of Britain's home front.

The first thing I needed to get to grips with was how different a wardrobe would have been in the prewar years. In Julie Summers's excellent *Fashion on the Ration: Style in the Second World War*, she addresses the amount of clothing that the average middle-class woman would have had in her wardrobe. According to the results of a Mass Observation survey conducted in 1941, it wouldn't have been uncommon for a woman to have a combined summer and winter wardrobe of seven dresses, two two-piece suits, two skirts, three overcoats, one mackintosh, and five or six pairs of shoes, as well as stockings, hats, and gloves. (Men had similarly limited wardrobes compared to today's closets.) Women who could afford to might prefer to have their clothing made for them at a dressmaker's, or they might have supplemented with some items purchased from a department store. Women who had less means would have made do with less.

Rationing was introduced with the immediate order to ration petrol at the declaration of war in 1939, with more everyday items including food coming under the ration as the war stretched on. Clothing escaped for less than two years.

The man at the helm of the government's clothing ration efforts was Oliver Lyttelton, who headed up the Board of Trade. He believed, in direct opposition to Prime Minister Winston Churchill, that rationing was necessary not only as a way to save cloth and preserve resources for the war effort, but to prevent shortages for the British consumer. He feared that, as the stock of clothing held by garment businesses countrywide dwindled in the early months of 1941, panic buying and price rises could see poorer Britons left without in the coming autumn and winter months.

Lyttelton and his supporters wanted to ask people to pull together for the greater war effort by buying fewer items less often. There was a push to "Make do and mend" existing items of clothing and only purchase what was a real necessity. As Summers writes, "The government hoped that clothes rationing would encourage people to take stock of their wardrobes and see what could be made to last." It was a worthy and even understandable sentiment, but it isn't difficult to imagine that wealthier people with substantial pre-war wardrobes might find it easier to buy less when they had already started the war with so much more.

The Clothes Rationing Order caught most people out because the decision had been kept tightly under wraps to prevent the panic buying and hoarding that Lyttelton feared. That morning, he gave a radio address and said, "We must learn as civilians to be seen in clothes that are not so smart . . . When you feel tired of your old clothes, remember that by making them do you are contributing to some part of an aeroplane, a gun, or a tank."

Immediately, what someone could buy was restricted not only by what they could afford but by their coupon book. The first flush of clothing rationing came in the form of sixty-six coupons that had to last a year, and women and men alike were forced to become savvy with predicting what they really would need during those twelve months. If a woman needed a coat that winter, she would have to hold back fourteen coupons toward it. Undergarments, which were likely to wear out faster than other items, cost three coupons, while a dress or a skirt was seven. Every garment had to be carefully considered, and many women were faced with the decision about whether a new dress was really worth the coupons.

In 1942, the rules changed again with the introduction of the Board of Trade's Civilian Clothing Order, or CC41. This utility scheme, which presents Sylvia and Miss Reid with so many challenges in *The Dressmakers of London*, was a further restriction on clothing design. These were the very unpopular measures that dictated how many buttons, pleats, and other design elements could go into a garment. (You might be happy to hear that women were not the only ones affected, as there was outcry about the banning of turned-up cuffs on men's trousers and the regulation of the height of men's socks.) CC41 also standardized which fabrics would be available for garments, which had the unexpected benefit of increasing the quality of some people's clothing because the quality of available cloth also rose.

The idea for the War Widows' Fund fashion show was inspired by the real-life presentation of utility designs by seventeen clothing companies to trade publications in April 1942 to promote the utility scheme. This was followed by the utility collections of ten top London designers, such as Digby Morton, Norman Hartnell, and Edward Molyneux, who formed the Incorporated Society of London Fashion Designers (IncSoc). The IncSoc designers were tasked with creating a coat, dress, blouse, and skirt for the autumn season. These designs were then mass produced for sale to the general public. The happy outcome of the IncSoc scheme was that the average woman could now own a Hardy Amies or a Jacqmar frock.

As the war stretched on, the number of coupons issued by the Board of Trade dropped—in some cases dramatically. In 1942, people received forty-eight coupons, down from the original sixty-six. In 1943, it was thirty-six, and in 1945 only twenty-four coupons were issued. However, the end of the war in 1945 did not spell the end of rationing, and the British people continued with the clothing ration until it was abolished in 1949.

I am a self-professed lover of clothes, and writing *The Dressmakers of London* while researching contemporary fashion, dressmaking, and the ration has given me great cause for reflection. Over the past few years, I have been trying to think more mindfully about my wardrobe while also exploring changes to my own personal style after the pandemic and during the era of seemingly unending microtrends. I have become interested in the slow fashion movement and the discussions around sustainability in fashion that it has brought to the forefront.

Having never had to face the restrictions of a clothing ration, my closet is only really constrained by my budget and storage space. However, I am actively trying to change some of my habits by buying fewer clothes but of higher quality, often turning to secondhand before shopping new. Likewise, I have been creating a handmade wardrobe of jumpers and shirts as I come up to nearly three decades of knitting. (I am a beginner sewer at best and can only aspire to do what Izzie and Miss Reid do in the workshop of Mrs. Shelton's Fashions.) I am a frequent visitor to my local tailor and cobbler, and I mend everything I can to extend the life of the clothes I love.

While writing *The Dressmakers of London*, I thought a great deal about the difference in the size of my current wardrobe and that of even Sylvia, who really does have my fantasy closet. I thought about the craftsmanship that went into a dressmaker's work, and the way that clothes were meant to last the wearer for years and years. I also thought about the joy of a truly well-fitting dress and how transformative a beautiful garment can be.

Acknowledgments

My first and heartiest thanks must go to my incredible agent, Emily Sylvan Kim. The idea for *The Dressmakers of London* came during a phone call to her as I walked circles around St. James's Square on a cold December day, desperately trying to figure out what my next book would be. Out of the blue, I said a combination of "London," "dressmakers," "sisters," and "letters," and Emily ran with it. It is always an adventure, Emily, and I wouldn't have it any other way!

Thank you also to the incomparable Ellen Brescia for all of her help.

My fellow writers Alexis Anne, Lindsay Emory, Mary Chris Escobar, Alexandra Haughton, Laura von Holt, Madeline Martin, Gill Paul, and Dr. Mary Shannon are a font of great inspiration and support during difficult first drafts.

My editor, Hannah Braaten, is a constant source of wisdom, guidance, and reassurance during the long and sometimes bumpy process of writing a book, and Sarah Schlick always keeps the show on the road. Thank you also to the incredible publishing team at Gallery Books, including Jennifer Bergstrom, Jennifer Long, Eliza Hanson, Erika Genova, Christine Masters, Alexis Leira, Caroline Pallotta, Emily Arzeno, Angel Musyimi, Paul O'Halloran, Heather Waters, and Jessica Roth. *The Dressmakers* would not be possible without all of you.

Thank you to my wonderful family, who love me very loudly and never let me take myself too seriously. Mum, Dad, Mark, and Diana, you are all very dear to me.

I could not have written this book without my darling sister, Justine. From pink plastic saxophones to laundry basket boats, burgers in Manhattan to late-night diner trips, driving adventures to virtual knitting circles, bad movies to drag shows, you are the person who showed me how unique the bond between sisters can be. I could not ask for a better one. (You made me cry during your maid of honor speech, so I'm hoping I get at least a little tear out of you for this.)

And, finally, thank you to the love of my life and new husband, Arthur. You have lived the raw, unedited reality of being with a writer, and you never flinch but instead patiently put a cup of tea next to my hand, give me a hug, and trust me to get on with things. I met my match that sunny April day, and I couldn't be happier. I love you.